Bayard Tuckerman, Philip Hone

The Diary of Philip Hone - 1828-1851

Volume II

Bayard Tuckerman, Philip Hone

The Diary of Philip Hone - 1828-1851
Volume II

ISBN/EAN: 9783337017163

Printed in Europe, USA, Canada, Australia, Japan

Cover: Foto ©Raphael Reischuk / pixelio.de

More available books at **www.hansebooks.com**

OF

PHILIP HONE

1828–1851

EDITED, WITH AN INTRODUCTION

BY

BAYARD TUCKERMAN

IN TWO VOLUMES

VOLUME II

NEW YORK
DODD, MEAD AND COMPANY
1889

PRESS OF
Rockwell and Churchill
BOSTON

THE DIARY

OF

PHILIP HONE.

1840.

JANUARY 1.—Another year has passed, and it would be well if the black lines of Benton, the great expunger, could be drawn around 1839 in the calendar. It has been marked by individual and national distress in an unprecedented degree, the effect of improvidence and a want of sound moral and political principles on the part of the mass of the people, and bad government and a crushing down of everything good and great to subserve party objects on the part of the rulers.

The New Year comes in bright and clear. It is by far the coldest day this winter; the ground is partially covered with snow; the ice which covers the walks in some places is hard as adamant, and the north-west wind blows up the cross-streets keen and sharp, as if it had been whetted upon the everlasting ice of the north pole. Notwithstanding all this, the gayety of the season has not been diminished. There has been as much visiting as usual. Broadway was lively as ever, bright eyes and warm receptions indoors, and blue noses and cold fingers without. I took my " auld cloak about me," and trudged about for nearly five hours, paying a large number of pleasant visits, and leaving many more equally pleasant unpaid. The extent of the visiting circle in New York has become too great for the operations of one day.

JANUARY 7. — The Cuttings, who were passengers in the unfortunate packet "Ville de Lyon," from Havre, which put into Bermuda disabled, after a long and disastrous voyage, have had additional troubles by another long and uncomfortable voyage of twenty-six days from the latter place to Savannah, in the British ship "Alexander Grant," which vessel they chartered to bring them out, at an expense of five hundred pounds sterling, and found themselves. By the last accounts they were all safe upon a plantation in South Carolina, where they will remain for the winter. They will not be tempted to tempt the sea again very soon, I am inclined to think. We have had some pretty severe gales and cold weather, but there have been no shipwrecks near to New York.

The "Ville de Lyon."

JANUARY 8. — I was reminded this morning, by seeing the flags displayed upon the City Hall and Tammany Hall, that it is the anniversary of the battle of New Orleans, an event glorious in the history of our country, and consolatory to the pride of every true American, but one which in its effects has proved most injurious to the present prosperity and future prospects of the land, "and all which it inherit." For the laurels gained by General Jackson on that occasion and the popularity which is certain to follow a successful military chieftain, paved the way for his elevation to the Presidency, made him the idol of the people, turned his head, and gave him the power to indulge his personal prejudices and antipathies at the expense of the Constitution and the laws, trample upon the rights of the people who were huzzaing for him, and sacrifice every interest to promote his own objects and those of his party. With a full share of the exultation which all should feel in the event of a battle gained, and with no desire to detract from the well-earned fame of the commanding generals, I do not hesitate to say that, in my opin-

Battle of New Orleans.

ion, the evils resulting from that event, in its consequences as described above, outweigh the benefits of fifty such battles; and so posterity will say, to the third and fourth generation.

BALTIMORE, JAN. 21. — I left Philadelphia at eight o'clock, by the railroad, and got here at three o'clock P.M. On my arrival I found an affectionate note from Mr. Gilmor, who in a few minutes came in person to tell me that he had a party engaged to meet me at dinner, soon after which Mr. Meredith came and invited me for to-morrow; and Mr. McLane, Mr. Birkhead, and Dr. Alexander all called, and there is a seat for me at every man's table, and apparently a place in his heart, and I am received, as I always have been in Baltimore, with the most hearty welcome and overflowing hospitality. We had at dinner at Mr. Gilmor's, besides the host and hostess, Meredith, Dr. Alexander, Mr. Birkhead, John P. Kennedy, David Hoffman, Mr. Pennington, and myself. A most capital dinner, and such wine as scarcely another man can show at present in the United States. There was one bottle which I was told had been kept exclusively for me. I wish I could think myself worthy of the compliment as the wine was of the generosity of the donor. I certainly never drank any better in my life. The pleasure of our party was enhanced by the addition of that excellent townsman of mine, David B. Ogden, who arrived from Washington during the evening on his way to New York. He is a great favourite here, as he is amongst all who know how to appreciate superior talents and honesty.

JANUARY 23. — In the evening I went to a musical party at General Harper's, where I found a great number of very agreeable people. I certainly think there are more handsome young married women and girls in Baltimore than in any circle of society of the same size I have ever known; but you never see them except at a party of this kind; for they are not seen much in the streets, nor have they a Broadway to walk in. I had the pleasure to meet Mrs. Caton and her sister, Mrs. Harper, from whom I received a most friendly recognition. I called upon her yesterday, and received a very particular message, that she was lying down, but that I must certainly call again. She is old, not ugly; infirm, but exceedingly gracious in her manners; and nearly blind, but lively and quick of apprehension. She was unquestionably (as I told her) the belle of the evening. Every gentleman, on entering, made her a bow, which she returned with much grace, after inquiring his name (for she finds it difficult to recognize her most intimate friends except by the voice), and every lady took her hand in parting. How much of this arises from the circumstance of her being the mother of a duchess, a marchioness, and a countess, it might be somewhat difficult to ascertain; but I am quite sure, that if she were haughty and disagreeable as she is affable and ladylike, this homage would not be paid with that willing cheerfulness which I witnessed and admired this evening. "You ought to be happy, madam," said I, "to find yourself so much beloved." — "Indeed, I am, sir," she replied; "you can have no idea how happy it makes me." We had fine music; several of the ladies sang. If we had such parties in New York I would attend more frequently.

WASHINGTON, JAN. 24. — I left Baltimore in the four-o'clock cars. On my arrival here, about seven o'clock, I found everything handsomely provided for me at Gadsby's, by my good friend Mr. Granger, with whom, and his daughter Miss Adèle, I am to mess. After tea I had retired to my room, and in night-gown and slippers was prepared for an hour's reading and an early bedding, when in "came one in hot haste with missives from the king," informing me that a party was assembled to sup at Boulanger's, nearly opposite my lodgings, and that I must report myself forthwith. I went and found Mr. Clay, Mr. Crittenden, General Scott, Colonel Dawson of Virginia, Lee of Maryland, Gen. Waddy Thompson, Mr. Botts of Virginia, and one or two more. We supped in Boulanger's best style, played whist, and talked politics. Mr. Clay looks remarkably well. He is almost worshipped by the Whigs since his late magnanimous conduct in regard to the nomination of General Harrison, and yet occasionally " this eagle towering in his pride of place " is " by an owl hawked at and pecked."   A man from Mississippi, who is known in common parlance and recognized by the laws as a senator of the United States, by the name of Walker, abused him yesterday grossly in debate, the cause of which was that Mr. Clay refused to reply to some of his remarks, but *would* reply to Mr. Buchanan, or some other gentleman of that party. But in truth an attack upon Mr. Clay from such a quarter is about as ridiculous as Noah Brown firing a musket-ball at the British frigate cruising off Rockaway Beach.

I intended to visit, and succeeded only in going to inquire about, Commodore Chauncey.   My excellent old friend is past hope.   I saw his son, who gave me the melancholy intelligence that this will in all probability be the last day of the earthly cruise of the noble old sailor.   I fervently pray that he may find a safe harbour in a better world.   Here is another of my ties of early friendship about to be sundered.   There are few men to whom I have been longer or more tenderly attached.   His son told me that within a day or two he has spoken of me affectionately as one of his oldest and best friends.

Whilst in that part of the city I called upon Baron Marechal, the Austrian Minister.   I am in the mess of Mr. Granger and Abbott Lawrence.   They invited three or four members to meet me at dinner.   I could not have better quarters.

JANUARY 28.—Celeste commenced an engagement at the theatre last evening, and I am told had not fifty people in the house.   I wonder why they come here.   Everybody has some better engagement, and you seldom hear the theatre mentioned.   I dined with Mr. Monroe; an exceedingly nice dinner and a gay party, consisting of Mr. and Mrs. Grinnell, Mr. and Mrs. Curtis, Mr. Hoffman, Mr. and Miss Granger, Mr. and Mrs. Stoughton from New York, Mr. Saltonstall, Mr. Bard from New York, and myself. After which I went to sup at Boulanger's, with Mr. Clay, Mr. Crittenden, Governor Barbour, Mr. Fox, the British Minister, General Scott, General Thompson, and Mr. Lee.   This high living, or the climate, has given me the last two nights the most excruciating cramps, and I have a very interesting touch of lumbago.

William Cost Johnson, of Maryland, has been speaking two days on the never-ending, still-enduring, and ever-exciting subject of abolition petitions. He is a fine fellow and a true Whig, but an out-and-out anti-abolitionist from principle, — not as Bynum and other such fellows are, to turn it to party purposes and make it a vehicle of personal abuse against their political opponents ; and so he told them in the plainest, straightforward manner, and rebutted in his person, and by flat contradiction, that the Whigs, as a body, are inimical to the interests of the South. A resolution offered by Mr. Johnson as a standing rule was adopted after an animated contest by a majority of six in a full house. It goes farther than any former action upon this vexatious subject. It forbids the reception of any petition against slavery in the District of Columbia or elsewhere, or the entertaining of anything by the House which relates to slavery. It strikes me as an unfortunate measure. It is the very thing to please the abolitionists ; the cry of persecution strengthens their cause. It is unjust, and I am inclined to think unconstitutional, and this apparent triumph of obstinacy over fanaticism will redound, I fear, to the benefit of the latter.

I spent a few minutes this morning in the Supreme Court. What a contrast between the gravity and decorum of that hallowed sanctuary of the laws, and the levity and disorder of the House of Representatives ! — the quiet, subdued tone of the former, and the noisy declamation of the latter ; and the reverend black-silk gowns of the judges, and the piebald costume of the people's representatives.

January 29. — I dined with Mr. Grinnell, who lives in handsome style, has his family here, and his carriage, and gives capital dinners. Our party to-day was a delightful one, consisting of the *élite* of the Whigs, and a more jovial set is not often to be met with. It consisted of Mr. Webster and Mr. Preston, of the Senate, Mr. Bell, Mr. Graves, Colonel Dawson, Mr. Hoffman, Mr. Curtis,

Mr. Rice, Mr. Garland, Mr. Granger, the host, and myself. Mr. Webster was in the midst of his friends, and delighted us with an account of his travels, of the places he saw, the visits he made, the attention he received, and the result of his deep searches into the characters of the eminent men of England. Preston is one of the most captivating men I ever saw. His voice is like music, and there is a natural eloquence about him, and a vein of jocund good-humour quite irresistible. Hoffman was in high spirits; Bell, declamatory; Dawson, gentlemanly; and when I came away (which, in consequence of an attack of lumbago I have had for a day or two, and which, once in a while, brings drops of sweat upon my forehead, was earlier than I wished), the elements of good fellowship were admirably mixed up in this little party.

Commodore Chauncey's Funeral. JANUARY 30. — At eleven o'clock I went to the funeral. At the request of Mrs. Chauncey, I followed as a mourner in the carriage with her three sons, and am now wearing the badge of mourning on my hat. She sent for me to her room, took my hand on my entrance, exclaimed, " Here is my husband's old friend ! " and sobbed aloud in the bitterness of grief. I was completely overcome, and left the room without saying a word. Commander Morris, who had charge of the funeral arrangements, told me that Mrs. Chauncey made a point of having Mr. Webster and me pall-bearers until she found it was to be a military funeral. The bearers were General Scott, General Macomb, Commander Morris, Commander Wadsworth, Commander Ridgely, Colonel Henderson, Commander of Marines, and the former and present Secretaries of the Navy, Messrs. Woodbury and Paulding. The President and heads of departments attended, with a splendid array of naval and military officers in uniform, and there was a handsome escort of marines and volunteers; but they had a hard time of it, the ground being covered with ice, snow, and water, and the rain falling at intervals during the tedious march of about three miles to the Congregational burying-ground, where the remains of the noble old sailor were interred.

I had a high gratification in the Senate, where my good-fortune carried me, and I was kept enchained until the hour of their adjournment. The whole Whig strength was brought out in opposition to the report of a special committee, of which Mr. Grundy, the late attorney-general, is chairman, — a report suicidal in its tendency, as are all the measures of the party of which Mr. Grundy may be considered the leader in the Senate ; the object of which is to show to the world the amount of indebtedness of the several States, exaggerated in its statements and uncandid in its conclusions, charging the States with improvidence and extravagance, telling the creditor, foreign or at home, that he has trusted too much, and it is doubtful if he will be paid ; and, like a cruel step-mother, the government seeking to discredit her own children and discourage their future exertions. But what a burst of eloquence was poured from *our* side of the Senate upon the heads of these unworthy forgers of lies ; these tinkers of government jobs ; these false lights of a misguided people ! Speeches were made by Crittenden, Southard, Webster, and Preston. What a host ! There never was a time in the British Parliament when four such men made speeches upon one subject. They were all great, but I was most pleased with Mr. Preston. It was the first time I had ever heard the eloquent South Carolinian. He is a tall man, of a strongly marked expression of countenance and not very graceful manner ; but he pours forth a flood of eloquence like a mountain cataract, — broad and impetuous at one time, and clear and sweet and beautiful at another ; flowing deep and solemn now, and again breaking into myriads of shining particles, illuminated by the sunlight of a poetical imagination, and reflecting the varied hues of classical imagery ; solemn and playful, argumentative and satirical, by turns. His voice is powerful, with occasional touches of surpassing sweetness ; and then, in private intercourse, he is so playful, his conversation so varied, and his spirits so buoyant, that I am of the opinion at this moment that I have never met a more lovable man. I sat near Mr. Preston on the floor of the Senate whilst he was speaking. He came to me after he had concluded. "There!" said he; "I made that speech on purpose for you. I had no idea that you should go home without showing you what I could do."

I am curious to know what the colleague of this noble gentleman, — what Mr. Calhoun thought of his position during the delivery of this and the other speeches on the same side. This is true, honest, legitimate State-rights doctrine; no nullification, no hinting at separation, but an honest, independent standing-up for the rights of the States; an indignant resistance to the arbitrary interference of an unnatural parent with the welfare and prosperity of her children. My eye glanced from the towering height from which one of these men launched the thunder of his eloquence upon the unworthy associates of the other, to the opposite place, where I saw the dark, scowling aspect of disappointed ambition and fallen greatness.

JANUARY 31. — I dined with the President. The party consisted of about five and twenty gentlemen; a splendid affair, and I think in good taste. The President does the honours with dignity and graciousness. There is no fuss in the business, and every guest has his full share of the attentions of his host. I thought myself particularly favoured, and so I presume others did. The President sat oh one side of the table, with Mr. Southard on his right and Mr. Sturgeon, the new senator from Pennsylvania, on his left. Immediately opposite. to him was Mr. Forsyth, Secretary of State, with General Scott on his right and me on his left, — an arrangement which the Secretary informed me before dinner was made by the President's order. The President's first glass of wine was drunk with General Scott, and the second with me.

FEBRUARY 1. — My son Robert writes me that an awful state of consternation exists in the city; business is at a stand; all description of stocks fallen still lower, and the fire-insurance companies refuse to insure any more. I should not be surprised if the companies should break again, and if they do they will never be resuscitated. Poor New York! a garden sowed with sand running fast into desolation.

I dined with Mr. Barnard; a nice little party, consisting of General Scott, Mr. Granger, Mr. Grinnell, the host, and myself. I got along very well, notwithstanding the pain and stiffness of my back; but, wisely I think, declined going to Mons. Bodisco's, who expected me to pass the evening.

Mrs. Brevoort's Ball.

NEW YORK, FEB. 20. — The fashionable folk are remarkably well off just now in the possession of an inexhaustible topic of conversation in Mrs. Brevoort's *bal costumé, costume à la rigueur*, which is to *come off* next Thursday evening. Nothing else is talked about; the ladies' heads are turned nearly off their shoulders; the whiskers of the dandies assume a more ferocious curl in anticipation of the effect they are to produce; and even my peaceable domicile is turned topsy-turvy by the "note of preparation" which is heard. My daughters are all going in character, and I am preparing to play the harlequin, in my old days. If Cardinal Wolsey don't astonish the folk with his magnificence, then have I spent in vain my money in the purchase of scarlet merino and other trappings to decorate the burly person of the haughty churchman.

Death of Mr. Maury.

FEBRUARY 24. — This venerable and amiable old gentleman died last evening, in the ninety-fifth year of his age. He was a native of Virginia. His ninety-fourth birthday occurred about ten days since. Mr. Maury was the first American Consul at Liverpool, appointed by Washington, a distinction of which he was always proud. This office he held for nearly half a century, and was removed by General Jackson (the second Washington, as he was sacrilegiously called by some of his flatterers). On his return a great public dinner was given to him in New York, by the merchants and others, of which I was a vice-president. He settled here with his sons and daughters, where he has resided ever since, in peace and domestic enjoyment.

His daughter seemed to live for him alone, — a pattern of filial affection and devotedness, — and he has now, full of age, and enjoying the respect and veneration of his friends, sunk calmly and without suffering into the grave which seemed to have had a natural claim to him many years ago.

FEBRUARY 25. — There is little dependence upon newspapers in a record of facts, any more than in their political dogmas or confessions of faith.   If they do not lie from dishonest motives, their avidity to have something new and in advance of others leads them to take up everything that comes to hand without proper examination, adopting frequently the slightly grounded impressions of their informers for grave truths, setting upon them the stamp of authenticity, and sending them upon the wings of the wind to fill the ears and eyes of the extensive American family of the *gullibles.*

The great affair which has occupied the minds of the people of all stations, ranks, and employments, from the fashionable belle who prepared for conquest, to the humble *artiste* who made honestly a few welcome dollars in providing the weapons ; from the liberal-minded gentleman who could discover no crime in an innocent and refined amusement of this kind, to the newspaper reformer, striving to sow the seeds of discontentment in an unruly population, — this long-anticipated affair came off last evening, and I believe the expectations of all were realized.   The mansion of our entertainers, Mr. and Mrs. Brevoort, is better calculated for such a display than any other in the city, and everything which host and hostess could do in preparing and arranging, in receiving their guests, and making them feel a full warrant and assurance of welcome, was done to the topmost round of elegant hospitality.   Mrs. B., in particular, by her kind and courteous deportment, threw a charm over the splendid pageant which would have been incomplete without it.

My family contributed a large number of actors in the gay scene. I went as Cardinal Wolsey, in a grand robe of new scarlet merino, with an exceedingly well-contrived cap of the same material ; a cape of real ermine, which I borrowed from Mrs. Thomas W. Ludlow, gold chain and cross, scarlet stockings, etc. ; Mary and Catherine, as Night and Day ; Margaret, Annot Lyle in the " Legend of Montrose ; " John, as Washington Irving's royal poet ; Schermerhorn, as Gessler, the Austrian governor who helped to make William Tell immortal ; Robert, a Highlander ; and our sweet neighbour, Eliza Russell, as Lalla Rookh.

We had a great preparatory gathering of friends to see our dresses and those of several others, who took us " in their way up." I am not quite sure whether the pleasantest part of such an affair does not consist in " the note of preparation," the contriving and fixing, exulting and doubting, boasting and fretting, and fussing and scolding, which are played off in advance of the great occasion ; and perhaps, after all is over, the greatest doubt is " *si le jeu vaut la chandelle.*"   And if ever that question is tested, it must be by this experiment, for never before has New York witnessed a fancy ball so splendidly gotten up, in better taste, or more successfully carried through.   We went at ten o'clock, at which time the numerous apartments, brilliantly lighted, were tolerably well filled with characters.   The notice on the cards of invitation, " *Costume à la rigueur,*" had virtually closed the door to all others, and with the exception of some eight or ten gentlemen who, in plain dress, with a red ribbon at the button-hole, officiated as managers, every one appeared as some one else ; the dresses being generally new, some of them superbly ornamented with gold, silver, and jewelry ; others marked by classical elegance, or appropriately designating distinguished characters of ancient and modern history and the drama ; and others again most familiarly grotesque and ridiculous.   The *coup d'œil* dazzled the eyes and bewildered the imagination.

Soon after our party arrived the five rooms on the first floor (including the library) were completely filled.   I should think there were about five hundred ladies and gentlemen ; many a beautiful " point device," which had cost the fair or gallant wearer infinite pains in the selection and adaptation, was doomed to pass unnoticed in the crowd; and many who went there hoping each to be the star of the evening, found themselves eclipsed by some superior luminary, or at best forming a unit in the milky way. Some surprise was expressed at seeing in the crowd a man in the habit of a knight in armour, — a Mr. Attree, reporter and one of the editors of an infamous penny paper called the "Herald." Bennett, the principal editor, called upon Mr. Brevoort to obtain permission for this person to be present to report in his paper an account of the ball. He consented, as I believe I should have done under the same circumstances, as by doing so a sort of obligation was imposed upon him to refrain from abusing the house, the people of the house, and their guests, which would have been done in case of a denial. But this is a hard alternative; to submit to this kind of surveillance is getting to be intolerable, and nothing but the force of public opinion will correct the insolence, which, it is to be feared, will never be applied as long as Mr. Charles A. Davis and other gentlemen make this Mr. Attree "hail fellow, well met," as they did on this occasion. Whether the notice they took of him, and that which they extend to Bennett when he shows his ugly face in Wall street, may be considered approbatory of the daily slanders and unblushing impudence of the paper they conduct, or is intended to purchase their forbearance toward themselves, the effect is equally mischievous. It affords them countenance and encouragement, and they find that the more personalities they have in their papers, the more papers they sell.

FEBRUARY 29. — As this brilliant affair is not soon to be forgotten, I have gotten my girls to make out from recollection a list of the characters; it is correct as far as it goes, and contains a pretty good portion of all who were present: Mr. and Mrs. Anderson, Turk and Spanish lady; Mr. Austin, Highlander; Mrs. Brevoort, Joanna of Naples; Miss Brevoort, La Juive; and the children, pages and a brigand; Mr. and Mrs. Bryan, Don Juan of Austria and Spanish lady; Miss Boggs, Clemence d'Isaure; Mrs. Brancher, lady of the old *régime;* Mrs. Burns, Madame du Bourg; Mr. and Mrs.

George Barclay, fox-hunter and peasant woman ; Miss Barclay, fine old lady ; Miss M. Barclay, Lalla Rookh ; Miss Bradbury, of Boston, Diana ; Mr. Berry, l'Incroyable ; Mr. Belmont, German postilion ; Mr. Bowdoin, peasant ; Mr. Bell, German miner ; Mr. and Mrs. Gerard Coster, pirate and Clotilda ; Mr. and Mrs. Washington Coster, Arab boy and Leila ; the Misses Cruger, Quakeresses ; Miss Callender, Dutch girl ; Messrs. Gore and Stanhope Callender, Spanish muleteer and Highlander ; Mr. and Mrs. Constant, fox-hunter and Corinna ; Mr. Coolidge, Chinese ; Mr. C. Davis, Quaker ; Mrs. Charles A. Davis, Norman paysanne ; Mrs. Dutilh, Miss De-Rham, and Mr. DeRham, Jr., Greeks ; Mr. Delprat, Don Basilio ; Mr. F. Dorr, Don John ; Mr. Delaunay, Duc d'Orleans ; Mr. and Mrs. Emmet, the former a school-girl, and the latter her brother ; Mr. Thomas Emmet, Dutch woman ; Mr. Robert Emmet, Dr. O'Toole ; Miss Elwell, Greek ; Miss Fleming, Jeffriece ; Mr. Fleming, Highlander ; Messrs. Asa and William Fitch, Mantilini and Arab ; Mr. Frederick Foster, gentleman of the old school ; Mr. and Mrs. Edward Graves, peasant and Lady Grandison ; Mrs. Robert and Mrs. William Gracie, Portia and La Dame Blanche ; Mr. and Mrs. James A. Hamilton, watchman and Quakeress ; Misses Mary and Angelica Hamilton, Fenella and old lady ; Mr. Alex. Hamilton, domino ; Mrs. Haight, two characters, Jemima Jenkins and Lady of the Knight of the Polar Star ; Mr. Haight, Turk ; Mr. E. Howland, mufti ; Mr. and Mrs. Hills, monk and old lady of quality ; Miss M. and Miss E. Hills, Ann Page and Persian ; Mr. C. Hoffman, friar ; Mr. Harmony, Spanish muleteer ; Miss Mary Jones, Diana ; Miss Kearney, Queen Esther ; Mr. P. Hone, Cardinal Wolsey ; Messrs. John and Robert Hone, royal poet and Highlander ; Miss M. Hone and Miss C. Hone, Annot Lyle and Day ; Mr. and Mrs. Jones Schermerhorn, Gessler and Night ; Miss Lydia and Mr. Delancey Kane, sorceress and goldfinch ; Miss Margaret and Mr. Harrison Lynch, Night and Arab ; Mr. D. Lawrence, sportsman ; Mr. G. Livingston, Greek ; Mr. and Mrs. Mortimer Livingston, each half Quaker and half ancient marquis ;

Mr. and Mrs. T. W. Ludlow, Court dresses; Miss LeRoy, Greek; Miss Meredith, Fair Star; Mr. Edward Laight, Roland Graeme; Mr. La Forest, consular uniform; Mr. Laurie, Crusader; Mrs. Anson Livingston, Virgin of the Sun; Misses Langdon, French paysannes; Miss Helen McEvers, Swiss paysanne; Mr. Charles McEvers, Spaniard; Mr. Bache McEvers, William Penn, and afterward Cupid; Miss McVickar and Mr. Messinger, Greeks; Mr. Robert Mason, old gentleman; Mr. McCarty, French marquis; Mr. McKeon and Mr. Major, Indians; Mr. and Mrs. Maroncelli, Dante and Beatrice; Miss Major, nun; Mrs. Norrie, old lady of quality; Misses O'Donnell, of Baltimore, Greeks; Mr. and Mrs. J. W. Otis, old gentleman and Night; Mrs. Jonathan Ogden, Queen Catharine of Arragon; Miss Oakley, Priestess of the Sun; Mrs. Rufus Prime, Esmeralda; Miss Palmer, Italian peasant; Mr. and Mrs. Pendleton, courtier and Spanish lady; Mr. and Mrs. Pearson, uniform and Scotch lady; Mrs. Panon, Folly; Miss Phelps, Spanish lady; Mr. William Robinson, old gentleman; Messrs. Schuyler, peasants; Mr. N. Schermerhorn, Dutch girl; Messrs. John and James Schermerhorn, postilions; Mr. and Miss Russell, Mameluke and Lalla Rookh; Mr. Steiner, Figaro; Mrs. Sheldon, Spanish lady; Mr. H. Sheldon, Paul Pry; Miss Seton, Greek; Miss Watson, Greek; Mr. S. Williams, old gentleman; Mr. Wright, Spaniard; Mr. and Mrs. H. Wilkes, courtier and peasant; Mr. John White, Russian soldier.

The "Herald" of this morning contains a long account of the ball, with a diagram and description of Mr. Brevoort's house; but, as it was an implied condition of the reporter's admission that it should be decent, it was tame, flat, and tasteless.

MARCH 7. — The ancient mansion of the late Mrs.
Real Estate. E. White, No. 11 Broadway, opposite the Bowling Green, was sold at auction one day this week, by order of her executors, and brought only $15,000. The lot is thirty-nine feet front on Broadway, twenty-seven feet wide in the rear, and extends through to Greenwich street nearly two hundred

feet. This is the saddest proof of the fall in real estate in this devoted city that has been realized as yet. There has been no time within my recollection that this lot would not have brought more money, and before General Jackson's accursed experiments it would have been worth double the price it brought.

Arrival of the "Great Western." At noon to-day this fortunate steam-packet made her appearance, after a voyage of sixteen days, having sailed on the 20th of February. None of her competitors have made their trips with equal despatch and regularity. Owing to an unprecedented delay in the arrival of the regular packets, we have been without accounts from England for forty-one days, which gap has now been filled up by the arrival of the "Great Western." There does not appear to have been much doing the other side of the water during this long period. The most important event was the marriage of the Queen.

MARCH 11.—My daughter Margaret received, as a present from London, a piece of the Queen's wedding-cake, enclosed in a letter from Mrs. Stevenson, lady of the American Minister, and brought in the "Great Western" by Mr. Cracroft, who was introduced by the same letter. This is all very well, but nothing to the present which I am told was received by the same conveyance by Miss Rush, daughter of the former Minister from the United States. Hers came from the Queen herself,—a piece of the cake, with a letter enclosed in a beautiful satin-wood box, on which the letter V is emblazoned in diamonds. This young lady was probably a companion of Victoria's in their youthful days, when, perhaps, her childish dreams dared not to soar to the height of her present greatness, and the "Sea of Glory" on which she now "swims" had no place on the map of her imagination.

MARCH 12.—The Marquis of Waterford says that the New York watch-house is the most shocking one he was ever in.

"Evelina" and "Cecilia." MARCH 19.—The following is in the "Commercial Advertiser:" "Among the deaths mentioned in the English papers we notice that of Madame D'Arblay, better known as Miss Burney, author of ' Evelina ' and ' Cecilia,' two excellent novels that were once extremely popular. She died in London, on the 6th of January, in the eighty-eighth year of her age. Her husband was General Piochard, Count D'Arblay." What a rush of the recollections of old times is here! Miss Burney, " Evelina," " Cecilia ; " their palmy days were also mine. When I was a lad, the " young idea " first beginning to put on its percussion-caps, — fond of reading all things, but especially doting on novels, — with what avidity did I banquet upon " Evelina," " Cecilia," and the host of novels, all of that class, with which the British press teemed ! They are dear to my recollection as identified with, and forming part of, the enjoyment of that period of my life when the curtain of futurity was rudely drawn aside by my impatient hands, and I saw a bright and beautiful world before me ; but its brightness dazzled the eyes so that the dark places were not distinguished, and beauty was more pleasant to look upon than deformity.

This class of writings has completely passed away. The plum-cake school of novels, in which love was the raisins and sentiment the citron, has given place to Scottish oat-cake, English ship-biscuit, and French rolls. Walter Scott's glorious prose stories, in which the substantial dish composed of traditional history was charmingly garnished by familiar dialogue and well-known localities ; and more recently the multitudinous offspring of the prolific imaginations of D'Israeli, James, Bulwer, Marryat, and the incomparable Dickens, have created a new and a better taste ; and although at this time of day we may go back to Smollett and Fielding with some remains of our first love, the works of Miss Burney, Mrs. Radcliffe, and Miss Porter afford no more enjoyment than do the marbles and tops of boyhood to the middle-aged man engrossed by the cares of this life.

MARCH 20. — My wife and I dined yesterday at Mr. Peter Schermerhorn's. The party consisted of Mr. and Mrs. Constant, Mr. and Mrs. Henry Parish, Mr. and Mrs. Pendleton, Mr. and

Mrs. Heckscher, Mrs. Brevoort, General Jones, Mr. Khremer, Jones and Mary Schermerhorn, Mr. Maturin Livingston, and ourselves.

Congress and the Legislature. MARCH 27. — The present session of Congress disgraces the annals of the country. It is a constant scene of tumult and disorder ; an unscrupulous majority rides rough-shod over the Constitution and laws, regardless alike of the rules of parliamentary proceedings and of good manners. The decent Loco-focos (if there are any) resign the reins of party government to the greatest blackguards in their number, and silently record their votes in favour of measures which they are ashamed to justify by reasoning.

Dr. Duncan, of Ohio, and Dr. Petriken, of Pennsylvania, are the acknowledged leaders of the administration party in the House of Representatives ; and surely never was poor patient subjected to the treatment of two such political quacks. Yet there are some decent men, high-minded Southerners, too (as we have been wont to call them), who submit to the degradation of mixing the pills, cleaning the gallipots, and administering the glysters of this precious brace of political empirics. Another of those disgraceful scenes which have followed each other in such rapid succession during the whole of the session occurred on Tuesday. The Treasury-note bill was to have been forced through without allowing the minority to be heard, and a scene of disorder, vulgarity, and personal abuse continued without intermission for twenty-nine hours. The House met at twelve o'clock on Tuesday, and continued in session until five o'clock on Wednesday evening, when they adjourned without taking the question. These daily recurring scenes of violence and disorder and the protracted sessions render the situation of the gentlemen of good habits and respectable characters anything but agreeable, and one consequence of the irregularities is the inroad which it begins to make in the health of some of them. That excellent man, Abbott Lawrence, who is beloved by his friends, and respected even by his adversaries, has been at the point of death. He is an amiable man, and a wise man, and a gentleman, and therefore unsuited for the society of the Robespierres, and the Marats, and the Couthons, who constitute the present majority of our modern Jacobin Club at Washington; and of such men as Abbott Lawrence the Whig party in that House is mainly constituted. Never was seen a contrast so great in all the qualities that go to make up a man as is to be seen there; but the gentlemen cannot maintain much longer the contest with the blackguards. The Duncans and the Petrikens — God help us ! — must prevail. Must things grow worse before they get better? I fear it greatly. If so it is to be, so be it !

Whilst these scenes are passing in Congress, the Legislature at Albany is in a state nearly as bad. The registry law has passed the Senate, and is now in the House, unless it passed there yesterday. James J. Roosevelt, the leader of the blackguards, in whose person, as its representative, our poor city is disgraced, takes the lead in opposition to the law, and resorts to every species of vile, disgraceful conduct and language, in which he is supported by the whole pack. Order, decency, and subordination are openly condemned, and they are supported and encouraged by meetings in Tammany Hall, in which such men as Benjamin F. Butler, district attorney, and John W. Edmonds, — intruders among us, — blow up the coals of sedition ; and their Loco-foco followers swear that if the law is passed they will not observe it, but vote as heretofore, and send their own men to the Legislature in spite of it, and carry by personal violence their men and their measures against the laws, if the laws do not happen to suit them.

A member of the New York delegation named Lasak, a German, who cannot write, nor even speak English correctly, but who, it appears, is a little more honest than his colleagues, had the independence the other day, in a speech he made, to differ from his party on some question of national policy, — something relating to the currency. He slipped his neck for a brief moment out of the collar, when immediately he was ordered down to Tammany Hall to give an account of himself; his answers were not satisfactory to his masters, and since his return a committee has been sent up to demand his resignation. What my countryman will do I know not, but it is tolerably certain he will not do for his party.

MARCH 28. — There was a great meeting last even-
Whig Meeting. ing at Masonic Hall, called by the Whigs to approve the registry law. It was made the occasion of one of those scenes of riot and disorder of which we shall have many more unless such a law is passed. A party of Loco-focos, insti-gated by the Butlers and Edmondses of Tammany Hall, and by the accursed newspapers supported by them, got possession of one corner of the room, and on the first movement being made to organize the meeting they commenced a riotous opposition by hissing, shouting, and every kind of violence. In the midst of this tumult Alderman Benson was placed in the chair, with a large number of vice-presidents and secretaries. The address and reso-lutions were read and passed unheard, and everything done in " most admired confusion." Finally this could be no longer borne. The Whigs, who behaved with great firmness, put the whole rascally gang of banditti out of the room, and order was so far restored that Prescott Hall was suffered to go on with an unanswerable argument in favour of the law, and David Graham, being called for, addressed the meeting. At this stage of the proceedings, the room being exceedingly hot, I came away. On leaving the hall I found my-self in the midst of a crowd of several thousands, who filled Broad-way from the Hospital to Duane street, and one of the friends and disciples of Benjamin F. Butler addressing them from a temporary elevation, and scattering firebrands in this mass of human com-bustibles. When the meeting in the hall was about to adjourn, the banditti returned with a strong reinforcement, broke the furniture of the room, and the heads of some of our people, and had theirs broken in return ; and so ended the first scene of a frightful drama which is to be enacted in this devoted city. As for myself, " I like this rocking of the battlements." I consider it an evidence of the

conscious weakness of the enemy. As long as they felt strong in the power of numbers they did not marshal their forces to interrupt the meetings of the Whigs, and their leaders professed themselves in favour of this most righteous law until they found it was likely to be passed. We have gone too far to retreat; the word must be onward now, or we must " ever after hold our peace."

MARCH 30. — Our friends have been alarmed by a report, which was brought down from Albany yesterday, that Governor Seward hesitates in signing the bill. It passed the Legislature on Thursday, and was not returned on Saturday. This hesitation gives new courage to the opposition, and fresh ferocity to the bloodhounds who are instigated to hunt down the Whigs. The very delay is appalling to our friends in the city; but if the Governor refuses his assent, he and his political friends are ruined, the State lost, and the glorious sun which " gave promise of a goodly day to-morrow" will set in the darkness of Loco-foco misrule and party despotism.

The Registry Law.

John Duer and Amory went up this afternoon. At their request I wrote a letter to the Governor, in strong and urgent terms, but, I trust, a respectful one. This is an alarming crisis. Seward has proved himself an able man; but he has in some things evinced an unworthy courting of popularity, an affectation of independence fraught with danger to his party, and I fear he is somewhat obstinate. He has probably some doubts about the power of the Legislature to pass a law so local in its application; but Duer has gone armed with legal authorities to remove all constitutional scruples. I wish His Excellency had heard Prescott Hall on this branch of the subject, on Friday evening. They tell me that I have some influence with him; if it be so, my letter will do no harm. The news by to-night's boat will be anxiously looked for. Governor Seward has the destiny of the country in his hands. God grant he may make a proper use of his power!

APRIL 1. — To our surprise, this morning's boat brought the news of the Governor having signed the bill as it passed the Legislature.

April 10. — The Whigs are more ardent and active, and, they say, better organized than usual, for the charter election, which is to be held on Tuesday. Immense meetings take place every night at the general and ward places of rendezvous. Processions parade the streets at night with music, torches, and banners; the prevailing device for the latter is the *log-cabin;* and we had hard cider, which has become the fountain of Whig inspiration. In an evil hour the Loco-focos taunted the Harrison men with having selected a candidate who lived in a log-cabin and drank hard cider, which the Whigs, with more adroitness than they usually display, appropriated to their own use, and now on all their banners and transparencies the temple of Liberty is transformed into a hovel of unhewn logs; the military garb of the general, into the frock and the shirt-sleeves of a labouring farmer. The American eagle has taken his flight, which is supplied by a cider-barrel, and the long-established emblem of the ship has given place to the plough. Hurrah for Tippecanoe! is heard more frequently than Hurrah for the Constitution! "Behold old things are passed away, and all things have become new." Thus is it that our opponents have, by their silly, disparaging epithets applied to the Whig candidate, furnished us with weapons, the use of which is understood by every man in our ranks; and, whatever may be the result of this election, the hurrah is heard and felt in every part of the United States.

Albany, April 19. — I went to the Governor's this morning, and accompanied Mrs. Seward and him to St. Paul's Church, — a beautiful edifice in South Pearl street, which was formerly the theatre. The rector is the Rev. Mr. Kip, son of Leonard Kip of this city, and son-in-law of Isaac Lawrence. He gave us a good sermon, and appears to be a favourite of a very respectable congregation. The temple of Thespis is greatly improved since it has been dedicated to the worship of the Most High, and sanctified by the name of the great apostle of the Gentiles. There is no theatre at present in Albany; and it is somewhat remarkable that in this large city, the resort of persons from all parts of the State, the seat of the Legislature and of the Supreme Court, during a large portion of the year the theatre has never been successful.

Having no other day to give to my excellent friend, the Lieutenant-Governor, I dined with him to-day at his lodgings, at Mrs. Lockwood's, in Pearl street, and a most delightful dinner it was. Our party, besides the host and hostess, consisted of the Governor, who came in soon after dinner, Sibley, Ruggles, John A. King, E. Townsend, of New York, and myself. We sat until nine o'clock; talked wisdom and nonsense, law and poetry, puns and politics; drank deep of delicious wine, the venerable resident for thirty years of the Lieutenant-Governor's wine-room in Pearl street, near our Battery, and broke up a protracted sitting, each with the conviction that "it was well to have been there."

AT HOME, APRIL 20.—I left Albany at seven o'clock, in the " North America." She is a fine new vessel, and burns Lackawanna coal, which answers exceedingly well, and only costs half as much as wood. The use of coal for steam navigation must inevitably become general; all the boats built hereafter will be adapted to its use. Travelling on the North river is cheaper than anything I know of, except American shirtings at five cents a yard. Passengers are conveyed one hundred and fifty miles in a vessel with every convenience and luxury, and get a good breakfast and dinner, all for two dollars. I wonder people do not live on board instead of going to the Astor House. We arrived in New York at half-past five o'clock.

APRIL 23.—One of those scenes occurred in the House of Representatives on Tuesday, the almost daily occurrence of which has, of late, called up the blush of shame upon the cheek of every American who retains the least regard for the honour of the country. That superlatively dirty dog, Jesse A. Bynum, whilst Mr. Salstonstall was speaking, left his seat, went near to that of Mr. Garland, of Louisiana, whom he designated by the *courteous* appellation of a " damn'd liar," whereupon Gar-

Congress.

land seized Bynum by the collar and struck him. The latter seized a knife, which he was prevented from using by the interference of the members. This new outrage upon the small remains of dignity in the people's own representatives was submitted to a special committee, consisting of Underwood, Cooper of Georgia, Briggs, Butler of Kentucky, and Clifford, with power to send for persons and papers, light up a little fire whilst the indignation lasts, and then smother it in party smoke.

APRIL 24. — My daughter and I went last evening to a party at Mrs. Van Rensselaer's, the lovely Mary Tallmadge of other times. They reside with the General, in Waverly Place. The party was very pleasant, and I found many agreeable people there. My going to a party has become quite a notable event.

MAY 3. — The " Great Western" arrived this morning, in eighteen days from Bristol, with a great number of passengers, among whom are the celebrated opera-dancer, Fanny Ellsler, and her sister, who are engaged for the Park Theatre. She has been anxiously looked for, and will create a sensation like that which marked the advent of George Frederick Cooke. She is second only in Europe to the immortal occupant of mid-air, the Taglioni. Madame la Comtesse de Merlin, the biographer of Malibran, is also a passenger, and Mr. and Mrs. C. F. Moulton, Mr. Cunard of Halifax, and the widow of Stephen Price.

The news by the " Great Western " is unfavourable. Cotton is dog-cheap; and American securities, owing, I suppose, to the rascally conduct of the Pennsylvania Legislature in refusing to provide for the payment of the interest on their loans, are in bad odour in England. It must be an embarrassing thing to a true-hearted American (if there is such a one in Europe) to know how to act when he hears his countrymen designated as a nation of swindlers, to which he must be hourly exposed.

> " 'Tis true, 'tis pity — and pity 'tis, 'tis true."

MAY 11, 1840. — On my return from Long Island I found two

letters, which were brought by Fanny Ellsler, she who has set New York agog for marvellous saltatory exhibitions, and whose heels are to turn all our heads. They are from Christopher Hughes, at Stockholm, and Samuel Welles, at Paris. Hughes asks me to give " to this really excellent and kind-hearted stranger the benefit and the honour of your kindness and protection," and adds, " I can assure you that Miss Fanny is as good as she is graceful." Welles's letter is as warm as Hughes's, making the proper allowance for the difference in the temperament of the two writers. I could not, therefore, do less than call and pay my respects to the fair *danseuse* as early this morning, after my return, as possible. I went to the American Hotel at twelve o'clock, sent my card, and was told the lady was not dressed, but would be charmed to see monsieur at four o'clock ; now I think, four o'clock being his dinner-hour, " monsieur " will not find it quite convenient to visit mademoiselle at that hour.

Whig Convention.

The papers are filled with accounts of the great Whig Convention held in Baltimore on Monday last. The number of delegates was prodigious, — thirty thousand, it is said. There was a grand procession, with banners, log-cabins, cider-barrels, balls in motion, and every device which the fancy could suggest. All the States were represented, and each endeavoured to outvie the others in the loud, exulting shout of " Hurrah for Harrison ! " Several distinguished members of Congress came on from Washington to attend this affair, which is represented, in one of the accounts from Baltimore, as " the most remarkable assemblage, in point of numbers, character, harmony, and zeal, ever gathered together in these United States." Messrs. Webster, Clay, Graves, Hoffman, Cost Johnson, and Salstonstall were of the number, and made speeches in Monument square and at the Assembly Rooms, where the meetings were held. It could hardly be supposed that the Loco-focos, goaded to madness by such an overwhelming foreshadowing of defeat, could be restrained from acts of violence. The procession was assaulted by some wretches with stones and brickbats, and a respectable carpenter of Baltimore, a delegate to the convention, named McLaughlin, was killed by one of those missiles, and the body of another, with a Harrison badge, was found, with marks of violence, in the basin. Amongst the other proceedings of the convention a resolution was adopted to raise a subscription for the relief of McLaughlin's family, to which none were allowed to contribute more than a dollar ; and with this restriction an amount of between $7,000 and $8,000 was raised, of which the Massachusetts delegation contributed $1,000.

A Van Buren Convention was organized in Baltimore, on Tuesday, at which General Carroll presided.

Van Buren Convention.

It appears to have been a sickly concern, a creeping plant, withering under the shade of the mighty Harrison tree, which overshadows the land, and keeps the sun of popular favour from shining upon its "unwholesome neighbour." At this meeting, on the motion of Mr. Buchanan, it was resolved to dispense with a ballot for President, no opposition having been raised to Mr. Van Buren ; but not so with the Vice-Presidency. On this subject the demon of discord had already lighted his torches. The Tecumseh killer, the present incumbent, has not by any means so clear a title, and the claims of Mr. Forsyth of Georgia, and Mr. Polk of Tennessee, presented obstacles so formidable to the necessary appearance of union, that further drilling was thought necessary, and it was voted inexpedient to nominate a candidate for the second office in the government. This result was so unpalatable to the Southern pride of Mr. Forsyth, the Secretary of State, that he has since come out with an address to his party, under his proper signature, in which he retires from the contest with a very bad grace, snarling and showing his teeth, and retreating tail foremost, like a disappointed cur who has been driven from the bone for which his mouth watered.

MAY 12. — I called yesterday upon Miss Fanny Ellsler. She is an exceedingly fascinating person, not very handsome. Her face has lost its bright bloom,

Fanny Ellsler.

and her complexion appears to be somewhat faded, — the result, probably, of the violent muscular exertions which are required in the profession; but her manners are ladylike. She is gay and lively, and altogether the most perfectly graceful lady I have ever seen; further the deponent saith not. She is to make her first appearance at the Park Theatre, on Thursday evening, in the ballet of " La Tarantule," which all the world will witness, who can gain admission to the theatre. Fashion and taste and curiosity are all on tiptoe to see her on tiptoe, and the pocket of many a sober pa will be drained to furnish the means to his wife and daughters to witness her *pas*.

MAY 14.—A *déjeuner à la fourchette* is something of a novelty in this country, and the last imitation of European refinement. This series of breakfasts given by Mr. William Douglass, at his fine mansion, corner of Park place and Church street, can hardly be called an *imitation;* for in taste, elegance, and good management it goes beyond most things of the kind in Europe, and seems to be placed as a bright object in the overwhelming flood of vulgarity which is sweeping over our land. The first of these breakfasts was given last Thursday, and they are to be repeated weekly until further notice. My daughters went then, and their favourable account induced me to join the throng of beauty and fashion this day. The company assembles at about one o'clock, and remains until four. Breakfast is served at two o'clock, and consists of coffee and chocolate, light dishes of meat, ice-cream and confectionery, with lemonade and French and German wines. The first two floors, elegantly furnished, of this spacious house are thrown open; the dining-room opens into a beautiful conservatory, in which, amongst other pleasant objects, is an aviary of singing-birds, the delicate notes of the canary mingling sweetly with the shrill pipe of the foreign bullfinch, and the whole concert regulated and stimulated by the great leader of the feathered orchestra, our own native mocking-bird. A band, also, of a more material nature, plays at the head of the stairs during the whole time of the entertainment, and after the young folk have partaken of their breakfast-dinner, cotillons and waltzes are danced until the hour of reluctant departure. The honours of the house are performed in good taste by the bachelor host, assisted by his sisters, Mrs. Douglass Cruger and Mrs. Monroe, and his cousin, Mrs. Kane.

The Great Début. Many and many a night has passed since the walls of the Park have witnessed such a scene. Fanny Ellsler, the bright star whose rising in our firmament has been anxiously looked for by the fashionable astronomers since its transit across the ocean was announced, shone forth in all its brilliancy this evening. Her reception was the warmest and most enthusiastic I ever witnessed. On her first appearance, in a *pas seul* called *la Cracovienne*, which was admirably adapted to set off her fine figure to advantage, the pit rose in a mass, and the waves of the great animated ocean were capped by hundreds of white pocket-handkerchiefs. The dance was succeeded by a farce, and then came the ballet " La Tarantule," in which the Ellsler established her claim to be considered by far the best dancer we have ever seen in this country. At the falling of the curtain she was called out; the pit rose in a body and cheered her, and a shower of wreaths and bouquets from the boxes proclaimed her success complete. She appeared greatly overcome by her reception, and coming to the front of the stage, pronounced, in a tremulous voice, in broken English, the words " A thousand thanks," the *naïveté* of which seemed to rivet the hold she had gained on the affections of the audience.

All the boxes were taken several days since, and in half an hour after the time proclaimed for the sale of pit tickets the house was full, so that when we arrived, which was a full hour before the time of commencing the performance, placards were exhibited with the words " Pit full," " Boxes all taken." This wise arrangement prevented confusion. The house, although full in every part, was not crowded, and a more respectable audience never greeted the fair *danseuse* in any country she has charmed.

Hyde Park. MAY 29. — This splendid estate on the North river, formerly the property of the late Dr. Hosack, has been sold by his heirs to Mr. Langdon, Mr. Astor's son-in-law, for $45,000. The ground sold with it is all on the west side of the Post road, and extends to the grounds attached to the cottage which belongs to Mrs. Hosack. The creek and water-power are reserved by the heirs. This is the finest place on the North river; indeed, I never saw one anywhere which possessed natural advantages so great.

JUNE 2. — The career of the infamous editor of the "Herald" seems at last to have met with a check, which his unblushing impudence will find some difficulty in recovering from. Some of his late remarks have been so profane and scandalous as to have drawn out the other editors from the contemptuous silence which they have hitherto observed toward the scoundrel. In one of his late attacks upon the editors of the "Evening Signal" and another paper, in alluding to some personal deformity in each of them, he uses the shocking expression that they are "cursed by the Almighty." The evil has reached a pitch of enormity which renders further forbearance criminal, and a simultaneous attack is made upon the libellous paper, its editor, and those who, from fear or a fellow-feeling, support it. The "Evening Star" has several excellent articles on this loathsome subject. Bennett is absolutely excoriated in the "Signal;" and all the other papers, without regard to party, have joined the righteous crusade. This is the only thing to be done; the punishment of the law adds to the fellow's notoriety, and personal chastisement is pollution to him who undertakes it. Write him down, make respectable people withdraw their support from the vile sheet, so that it shall be considered disgraceful to read it, and the serpent will be rendered harmless; and this effect is likely to be produced by the united efforts of the respectable part of the public press.

JUNE 5. — The steamer "Unicorn," the first of Mr. Cunard's line, which is to run from Liverpool to Halifax and thence to

Boston, arrived at Halifax on Monday, the 1st instant, and departed thence the same evening for Boston, where she arrived on Wednesday evening. She left Liverpool on the 16th of May. This is an important event for Boston. The new-comer was received there with firing of guns and other rejoicings. The establishment of this line will take from New York a considerable part of the great passenger business, which she has heretofore exclusively enjoyed. The British officers can go all the way to Quebec in these steamers, and the people of the British North American colonies, naturally preferring an enterprise of their own, and finding it less expensive, as they avoid transshipments and land travelling, will no longer spend their money in New York hotels or help support the New York packets. Boston, too, will come in for a share of this lucrative business, and with the assistance of their great railroad, which is nearly complete to Albany, will soon crow as loud as we do; but it is to be hoped there is enough for all.

June 11.—The sixteenth volume of this journal is placed upon the shelf, and I now open up the window which looks upon a long vista of pages yet unsullied to constitute the seventeenth. Shall I live to fill them; or, if alive, will the ability and the inclination remain? If the first be granted, I fervently pray the latter may not be withheld. Life without the power of indulging in a habit so pleasing, which, while it gratifies me, injures no one, would scarcely be worth enjoying. Before this volume is filled I shall have completed my sixtieth year, and with some cause for repining at my altered circumstances, I have much to be thankful for. My health is good, except some occasional twitches of lumbago, which causes me to grunt a little and make wry faces when I arise from my chair. I live pleasantly with all my family around me, but it grieves me to see three grown-up sons out of employment.

The hard times (of which I participate largely) still continue with unabated severity. Business of all kinds is completely at a stand; the productions of the country at the lowest ebb; flour four dollars a barrel; cotton a drug in foreign markets; American securities, by the bad management of some of the State governments, are in the worst possible repute in those countries where formerly they were relied upon with full confidence; party-spirit prevailing over the land and obstructing the course of justice and wholesome legislation; and the whole body politic sick and infirm, and calling aloud for a remedy.

The only comfort in this dismal state of affairs is, that a remedy does seem to be at hand in the daily increasing confidence that the administration, whose bad measures lie at the root of all evil, is about to be put down. The Whigs are sanguine in their hopes of electing General Harrison to the Presidency, which happy event, by restoring public confidence, will go far to bring about a better state of things, and individual enterprise will naturally grow up alongside of national prosperity. If I live, the volume I now commence will record this " consummation devoutly to be wished," or its pages will bear the melancholy intelligence of hope destroyed forever.

JUNE 12. — Strange inconsistency! It is hard reason-
Fanny Ellsler. ing against facts; every word I have said in the preceding pages about hard times and pecuniary difficulties is strictly true, and yet the fascinating creature whose name heads this article finished last evening her engagement at the Park Theatre, having danced fifteen nights, and brought to the house something like $24,000, at the ordinary prices, of which sum she puts $9,000 or $10,000 in her own pocket. The seats have all been taken every night, and it appears to me if the theatre had been twice as large it would have been equally full. She took her leave last evening in the ballet of " La Sylphide," and two of her favourite dances, smothered under a shower of wreaths and bouquets of flowers. Amidst the waving of handkerchiefs and three full, thundering rounds of hurrahs, she came and, in a short speech of sweet, broken English, expressed her gratitude, the regret with which she left New York, and her determination soon to return.

She is to dance in Philadelphia on Monday evening, where she has made an engagement at the *moderate* price of $500 a night ; her receipts here being predicated on the amount in the house each night, and that amount being greater than ever was received for the same number of consecutive nights, has produced more than what she has stipulated for in Philadelphia. Her success has been increased by the certainty of her stay being short. She is determined to visit Niagara and other places after her engagement is completed, and must sail on the first of October, as she is engaged in Paris the middle of that month. It is well for us that it is so. If she were to continue long enough in this country, and the popular fever remain at its present height, she would carry back to France all the indemnity money which Brother Jonathan squeezed out of his " ancient ally."

Hone Club. There was a sort of informal revival of the club yesterday at John Ward's, who succeeds his brother Samuel, at the corner of Bond street. The old club, with four or five supernumeraries, dined together in our ancient pleasant style. Of the members, eight were present : viz., John Ward, William G. Ward, Simeon Draper, Charles H. Russell, Roswell L. Colt, J. Prescott Hall, S. H. Blatchford, Jonathan Amory, and myself. We agreed to dine with Mr. Colt at Paterson next Friday.

Death of Mr Lydig. JUNE 16. — Another link is broken in the chain of my social relations, another warning given of the passing away of my generation. My old and valued friend, David Lydig, died this morning, at six o'clock. He has been in bad health the last two years, but had rallied of late, and appeared to be gaining strength until his last illness. He died in the seventy-sixth year of his age, much older than I, but an intimate friend and associate for nearly forty years. He was one of a set who, although my seniors, were my intimate companions about the time of my entrance into society, and with whom I continued in pleasant association until they dropped away one by one, and now I am almost the only one left. How many good dinners I have eaten at poor

Lydig's expense, and how many hours have I passed in his society! He was a just man, prudent and careful in the management of his affairs, unexceptionable in his deportment, with some old-fashioned aristocratic notions, an exceeding good liver, fond of fine wine, which, however, he drank in moderation, but less prudent in the enjoyment of the other pleasures of the table. He was, in short, a gentleman of the old school, — a race which is nearly extinct; for as the old oaks decay and die off, their places are supplied by an undergrowth less hardy, majestic, and graceful.

Log-cabin Meeting.

The great log-cabin in Broadway, near Prince street, was dedicated this evening to Harrison and Reform.

It is a large edifice, constructed of unhewn logs, in the most primitive style, with a large pavilion connected with it. The whole occupies the entire area of ground, fifty feet by one hundred, and will hold an immense number of persons; its capacity was tried on this occasion; every part of the spacious cabin was full. The meeting was organized by the appointment of General Bogardus as president, with seventeen vice-presidents and three secretaries. There were capital speeches from gentlemen of Ohio, Indiana, and Kentucky, amongst whom Mr. Ewing, the former distinguished United States senator from Ohio, whose hand was warm from the recent pressure of General Harrison's, was exceedingly interesting. Joshua Spencer, of Utica, was one of the speakers. Blunt, also, made a speech, and Hoxie. The whole affair was cheering and enthusiastic. Never did the friends of Mr. Van Buren make so great a mistake as when by their sneers they furnished the Whigs those powerful weapons, " log-cabin " and " hard cider; " they work as the hickory-poles did for Jackson. It makes a personal hurrah for Harrison, which cannot in any way be gotten up for Van Buren, and which will, from present appearance, carry him into the Presidency.

Federalism.

JUNE 18.— It is strange that this term, by which was designated in former times the purest, the wisest, and the most patriotic political party which ever existed, should continue to be a term of reproach, and the means of exciting the bad feelings and prejudices of the people, even now, when it has ceased to be a bond of union or badge of party, and when all but those who use it for sinister purposes are more ignorant of its meaning than they are of the Talmud. The fact is, that the Federal party, as it was originally constituted, embraced nearly all the great and glorious spirits of the Revolution, and all the real friends of the people. It numbered its Washington and Greene in the field of battle, its Ames and Morris in the halls of Legislature, its Jays and Ellsworths on the bench, and its Hamilton and Marshall at the forum. But this great party is extinct; the disinterested and patriotic part of its members stand upon their original ground as the advocates of national liberty and sound principles, and are opposed to the present corrupt administration, which sacrifices the rights of the people to the maintenance of the party's supremacy; whilst the men whose ultra-tory principles brought into disrepute the name *Federalist* are odious in the eyes of the people. Both parties apply the word as a term of reproach to their adversaries; the poor term, which abstractedly means everything good and gracious in America, and in its application sought only the good of the people and the preservation of Republican principles, is bandied about like a shuttlecock by the public press on both sides, and by partisan declaimers from the Senate chamber down to the log-cabins, where the sovereigns assemble to prove their patriotism by abusing their political opponents.

Even General Harrison, in whose support all the good men of the country are banded together under the name of Whigs (a name, by the bye, to which I stand godfather, having been the first to use it at a political meeting, of which I was president, at Washington Hall), and on whose success the permanency of Republican institutions mainly depends, deems it necessary, in order to gain the favour of the people, to repudiate, as the greatest calumny with which he has been assailed, the charge of having formerly been a Federalist. In his speech at the recent great Whig celebration on the battle-ground of Fort Meigs, where thirty thousand persons are said to have been assembled, his renunciation of the charge of having belonged to a party of which Washington was the leader, was thus indignantly made, and thus responded to by the assembled multitude : " I have been called a Federalist (here was a loud cry of 'The charge is a lie, — a base lie ; you are no Federalist !') Well, what is a Federalist? I recollect what the word formerly signified, and there are many others present who recollect its former signification also. They know that the Federal party was accused of a design to strengthen the hand of the general government at the expense of the separate States. That accusation could not, nor cannot, apply to me. I was brought up after the manner of Virginian anti-Federalism. St. Paul himself was not a greater devotee to the doctrines of the Pharisees than I was, by inclination and a father's precepts and example, to anti-Federalism."

JUNE 24. — Dined at R. B. Minturn's, where we had a famous party of Whigs, with a great deal of joviality, for we had good wine and good company ; much speaking, for we were composed of congressmen, senators, and lawyers principally ; and entire unanimity, inasmuch as we were all of one mind on the only subject which divides men now-a-days, and excites personal asperity. We had Grinnell and two fine Georgians, members of the House of Representatives, Dawson and King, Verplanck and Sibley of the State Senate, and a fine, fat fellow, Swain of New Bedford, who goes amongst his friends by the title of " Governor," famous for hospitality and kind feelings, and all sorts of qualities for endearing himself to them, and with a most authentic certificate in his broad, good-natured face of the possession of all the good qualities imputed to him.

JULY 3. — There is an admirable letter published of Mr. Webster's "the defender of the Constitution," in reply to an Letter. invitation from the Whigs of New Hampshire to attend their convention, which he declines. Nothing more able than this letter has ever issued from Mr. Webster's pen ; it is the best, the clearest, and the most condensed exposition of the measures of the administration, and their effects upon the present prosperity and future prospects of the country, I have seen from any quarter, and must produce conviction, even in poor, misguided New Hampshire. Mr. Webster speaks in terms of the greatest confidence of General Harrison's election.

ALBANY, JULY 17.— In the morning I went to see the two glorious pictures, which are nearly finished, of the series my friend Cole is painting for Mr. Samuel Ward's family (they having been ordered before his death). These pictures are glorious. The series, when completed, will form an allegory of the four stages of life.

JULY 22.— The United States Hotel, large as it is,
Saratoga Springs. and capable of accommodating so many, is now quite full. A large proportion, however, are persons whom I have never seen before ; a few are agreeable, but much the largest proportion consists of awkward women and stupid men. A little yeast, however, has been infused to-day into this mass of unintellectual dough by the arrival of several of our clever New York lawyers, who have come up to make *motions,* —not such *motions* as people generally make who come here, but motions in the Chancellor's little house up the road. There is William Kent, Dudley Selden, Prescott Hall, Charles O'Connor, Samuel A. Foot, and General Sanford. The first two have brought their agreeable wives with them. They are quite a pleasant accession to the circle in the ladies' drawing-room.

JULY 23.— I passed a couple of hours this morning
Chancellor's Court. in the Chancellor's Court, and was much pleased ; it is held in a small office in a wing in his dwelling-house, which serves as a law library, very extensive, and I should judge well selected. His Honour sits at his desk, on a platform raised about a foot, his habiliments not remarkably neat, pantaloons drawn half-way up to his knees, drinking most intemperately of water (his only drink, as he is president of the tee-totallers), talking familiarly with the lawyers on points as they

arise in the case, and frequently interrupting the speaker, in what appeared to me rather an abrupt manner, which I think must be a stumbling-block in the way of young counsellors; but I liked it very much. There were about twenty lawyers, seated without order, some at a green table, but the greater number on chairs with their backs against the wall, and their legs cocked up; everything was easy and unconstrained, but quiet and decorous. The Chancellor does a great deal of the talking himself, but is treated with great respect. It looked very like a schoolmaster and his pupils, only the boys were a little too big to answer the description of the latter.

The cause before the court whilst I was there was a motion for an injunction to prevent a man named Lance from selling a famous nostrum called " Brandreth's Pills," or, rather, from using a counterfeit label, with a signature and device of the " real Simon Pure." Mr. Muloch argued the cause for the defendant, and the motion was sustained in an able speech by Mr. O'Connor, a distinguished member of the New York bar, and a very clever fellow. The nature of the cause gave occasion to some mirth, in which even the grave Chancellor was compelled sometimes to join. In one of his interruptions he asked Muloch some question about the pills. " We'll take the pills directly," said the counsellor, quite innocently. — " Not I," said His Honour; " I shall not take any of your pills." — " If he does," said General Sanford (who was employed for the complainant), " I trust they will be the genuine ones."

In the course of the argument a printed paper was produced, which caused some amusement. It was one of those stupendous puffs of Dr. Brandreth, in which was enumerated all the diseases, fifty-two in number, which were cured by the pills, and which leads me to wonder why mankind should stupidly refuse to render themselves immortal at so trifling an expense. To these modest credentials was affixed the signature of B. Brandreth, M.D., with the additional letters in capitals, M.E.V.P.L.V.S. This gave room for sundry learned and philological inquiries into the meaning of these cabalistical letters, which unfortunately for the cause of science led to no successful results. Whilst this was going on, I wrote with my pencil and handed to Mr. O'Connor the following solution, which was handed amongst the lawyers, and was very near getting up to the schoolmaster's desk, — in which event my impertinence might peradventure have been rewarded with the ferule, — Most Excellent, Veritable Pills, Laxative, Vomitive, Sudorific.

On the whole, I was favourably impressed with the colloquial manner of transacting business in this great court of little form, the objects of which seem to be, to elicit truth and administer justice.

JULY 27. — The friends of Van Buren and arbitrary rule have had a great jollification this afternoon, in Castle Garden, to celebrate the passage of the sub-treasury bill. And so they would, if Mr. Van Buren, like the Austrian Governor Gessler, had succeeded in placing his cap upon a pole, to receive the homage of his Swiss followers. John Targee presided at the meeting, and Aaron Vanderpoel and a celebrated Van Buren serf, Rantoul of Boston, addressed them ; and a hundred guns were fired, and caps were thrown up, and shouts rent the air at the prospect of the people of these United States, by the grace of God, free and independent as the formula prescribes, having been brought under subjection.

Sub-Treasury Jubilee.

The good people of Boston are so delighted at the prospect of rivalling New York, that they are in perfect ecstasies at the arrival of the steamship " Britannia," and have made a glorification of my little friend Cunard, the enterprising proprietor of the line, of the most magnificent proportions. He was fêted and feasted, and toted and toasted, to his heart's content. A grand pavilion was erected at South Boston, where the line of packets have their wharves. Two thousand persons partook of the good cheer ; Mr. Webster and Mr. Grattan and other eloquent men made speeches ; and Mr. Cunard did not make a speech, because (as he said) he didn't know how. The

Cunard Jubilee.

bright eyes of hundreds of the fair daughters of Boston enlightened the brilliant scene, and the roar of cannon might have been heard, had the wind been easterly, by the unwilling ears of the chopfallen New Yorkers. Among the toasts was the following, "not so bad either," as Fanny Kemble said of my poetry: "Mr. Cunard, the only man who has *dared* to *beat* the 'British Queen!'"

SEPTEMBER 1. — Power made his first appearance last evening, at the Park Theatre. I went this evening to see him in a new farce, "Last Legs," and enjoyed it most heartily. He is the very life and soul of genuine, unadulterated humour, and if laughing be wholesome his acting is a panacea of more value than the far-famed pills of " B. Brandreth, M.D., M.E.V.P.L.V.S." It is a great evidence of Power's powers in the art of *drawing* that he brings good houses now in this dull season, and when the playgoing people have been so heavily dragged by Fanny Ellsler. But the fact is, the roast beef and plum-pudding of Power does not relish the worse for our having feasted on "*volaille au suprême*" and "*ailes de pigeon*." His "Last Legs" pleased me quite as much as the last legs I saw of the divine *danseuse*, and his Irish brogue is quite effective, if not so fascinating, as her "tousand tanks."

BOSTON, SEPT. 9. — Here I am, to join the Whig Convention to be held to-morrow on Bunker Hill, and from appearances it will be the grandest spectacle I ever witnessed. I left Newport in the steamer "Massachusetts," and arrived at Providence at half-past eight, having two hours and a half on my hands before the time of starting of the cars for Boston. I employed the time in walking through the town with Mr. Ruggles, a gentleman of Newport, and viewing the fine houses and noble establishments of the nabobs of that wealthy and prosperous place.

On my arrival in Boston everything was in commotion; the Whig delegations were pouring in from every quarter; the streets were crowded, and happy was the man who had a permit to sleep in the market. I soon found that my good star was in the ascendant. I had notes and messages from several friends to say that they had lodgings provided for me; amongst others, Mr. Otis brought me an invitation from Mr. Cabot. Mr. Sargent was the most pressing; he had provided beds for Ogden Hoffman and me. Hoffman accepted; but Mr. Belknap having vacated his room for me in the kindest manner, I took possession of it, and remained at the Tremont House, where I was lodged like a prince. One of the most remarkable things about this great Whig festival, and which proves most clearly the spirit with which it is entered into, is the noble hospitality with which the first people in the city have opened their doors, spread their tables, and vacated their bedchambers for the accommodation of the delegates. Mr. Otis is to have a table spread for all comers. The committee of arrangements are constantly receiving notices from the most respectable of the citizens: "I have so many beds;" "I shall have a luncheon;" "Send me so many strangers to take care of!" It is so like Boston.

September 10. — The great day is over, and how shall I attempt to describe it? The weather, which was doubtful last night, was bright this morning, and the delegates from other States and from the different towns in Massachusetts began to assemble on the Common at nine o'clock, with their standards, badges, and other paraphernalia. The scene began very soon to be of the most exciting character. Crowds were pressing toward the spot from every quarter. The windows of the fine houses which surround the Common were filled with well-dressed ladies. Horsemen were galloping to and fro, and old men of the Revolution tottering toward the places allotted to them. The marquee of the chief marshal, Franklin Dexter, was placed in the centre of the Common, whence issued troops of handsome young men on horseback and on foot, with their badges of office, conveying his orders to distant points and completing the general arrangements. I was directed to join the other invited guests at the State House, where

I met Webster, the president of the day, and many other distinguished men. The procession did not begin to move until twelve o'clock. It was headed by an escort of men on horseback to the number of more than two thousand; then followed forty or fifty carriages, containing the Revolutionary soldiers and some others who were too aged to walk; after which the chief marshal and committee of arrangements, the president of the day, members of Congress and invited guests, and then the different delegations, with flags and banners "floating the skies," devices of all kinds, and mottoes, some excellent, others so-so, and others displaying more party zeal than either wit or good sense. Of those I saw I was most pleased with a whale-boat from New Bedford, with all the apparatus for taking the whale and extracting the oil, manned by six old masters of whale-ships, and drawn on a car by six gray horses; and with a colossal shoe from Lynn, in which were seated a number of sturdy shoemakers from that celebrated town of Massachusetts, in which shoemaking is the *sole* occupation. The procession moved up Beacon street and down the other side of the Common; thence through several of the principal streets in that part of the city, by Faneuil Hall, around which it made a complete circuit, and so by the wharves and streets occupied by working-people, to Charlestown Bridge, which it crossed, proceeded through Charlestown, and arrived at Bunker Hill after a march of two hours and a half.

The president and invited guests occupied a stage, and the delegations were marshalled in their allotted places as they severally came on the ground, — a work which occupied a long time, and before they all got to it the ceremonies commenced by a short address from Mr. Webster. The Bunker Hill declaration (copies of which had been printed and distributed on the route) was then read by Mr. Winthrop, after which several of the distinguished visitors were introduced to the audience, and each, in turn, made a short speech much to the purpose. This honour was conferred upon me. Mr. Webster presented me as his friend, and informed the people that I was the person who first distinguished the party by the appellation of Whigs. I spoke a few minutes, and concluded by saying that it appeared to me that all the men in the United States were present, and that they had better cut the matter short by going into the election at once. "As many of you, therefore," I said, at the top of my voice, "as are willing to have William Henry Harrison for your President will please to say Aye." This was responded to by a shout that rent the skies, and I came off with flying colours.

The skies, which had been threatening for some time, waited until the ceremonies were over, and then burst into a shower which set the mighty mass scampering. I went with Mr. Webster and a few other gentlemen to the house of a Mr. Pratt, near the place of assemblage, where we had a cold collation, and plenty of cool, refreshing drink ; and, to crown the whole, were waited upon by the ladies of the family, which, I understand, has been the fashion of the day.

The most remarkable part of this most splendid spectacle was the appearance of the streets through which the procession passed, and the enthusiastic participation of the people in the triumph. It was, after all, only a party affair, not one of general or national import, in which the current of public opinion may have compelled some reluctantly to join. We took nothing by compulsion ; nobody was compelled to shout, and yet the whole line of march was enlivened by the cheers of the men and the smiles of the women. The balconies and windows were filled with women, well dressed, with bright eyes and bounding bosoms, waving handkerchiefs, exhibiting flags and garlands, and casting bouquets of flowers upon us ; and this, too, was not confined to any particular part of the city, or any class of inhabitants ; young children were exhibited in rows, with flags in their little hands, and, whenever their greetings were returned, mothers and daughters, old women and beautiful young ones, seemed delighted that their share in the jubilee was recognized.

The stores and shops were all closed; flags were suspended over the streets; arches were erected, with suitable devices and inscriptions, at the entrances into the several wards, and " Welcome, Whigs!" met us at the corners of the principal streets. When we had crossed the bridge and entered Charlestown, the same cheering spectacles were presented, and an arch of triumph and welcome, with an extract from one of Mr. Webster's speeches, received the procession. It was Whig all over; there are certainly Loco-focos in Boston, but I am puzzled to know what became of them on this occasion.

I returned to town with Mr. Webster in a carriage, and went at a late hour, with Ogden Hoffman and Prescott Hall, to dine with Mr. Sargent. In pursuance of the directions of the committee of arrangements I went, at seven o'clock, to Mr. Webster's lodgings, at the United States Hotel, where I found a number of gentlemen, and we accompanied him to Faneuil Hall, where he was to preside. When we came to the hall it was crowded to suffocation, and it was extremely difficult for him or the speakers to get to their places. Mr. Webster opened the meeting with some remarks, and Mr. Leigh, Governor Pennington, Governor Ellsworth, and others spoke. It was allotted to me to speak; but I was overcome with fatigue and the crowd and the heat of the room, and I made my escape before I was called.

SEPTEMBER 11.—I found Gardiner and Samuel Howland and their wives, Samuel's daughter, and Lydia Van Schaick, yesterday, at Mr. Robert G. Shaw's. They are on their way home from an excursion to the White Mountains of New Hampshire. I was invited to dine to-day with Mr. Benjamin Welles, in Boston; but my coming away prevented me. Judge Warren and Joseph Grinnell of this place having made arrangements for Ogden Hoffman and me to visit New Bedford, we left Boston at half-past four o'clock. Judge Warren remained in Boston, and Mr. Grinnell and his wife came on with us. We came on the railroad, with an enormous train of cars, having the Whig delegates from this town and Nantucket, and a large number of those from New York returning. There was shouting and hurrahing all the way.

The Loco-foco Meeting. To counteract the effects of the overwhelming Whig meeting all over the country, a meeting of merchants, supporters of the administration and friendly to the sub-treasury, was held yesterday, at two o'clock, in Wall street, in front of the new Exchange. The call for the meeting was signed by some dozen respectable merchants, and filled up by names never heard of on 'Change. A Mr. George Douglass presided. The meeting was addressed by Silas Wright, senator, and Benjamin F. Butler, maid-of-all-work in the administration kitchen, who essayed to convince the merchants that the times are very good; that all government has been doing is good for us, and that the banking business will operate very nicely when it is all in the hands of Mr. Van Buren; that gold and silver is more portable and handy than bank rags, and that the safety of the country depends upon a continuance in power of the present dynasty.

Great Meeting of Merchants. SEPTEMBER 28. —The great meeting of Whig merchants took place to-day, at two o'clock, in Wall street, at the Williams-street corner of the Exchange. I got a place in a third-story window of the new building occupied by the city bank. I could not hear; but the appearance of the mass of people below was perfectly sublime. It was a field of heads, occupying a space about six times as large as the area of Washington hall, from which I calculated the number at fifteen thousand; all respectable and orderly merchants and traders, intent on hearing the words of wisdom and patriotism from the lips of "the defender of the Constitution," capable of understanding their meaning, and determined to follow where they led.

Jonathan Goodhue was president, with twenty-six vice-presidents and five secretaries. The resolutions were read by Moses H. Grinnell, and at twenty minutes past two o'clock Mr. Webster rose to address the most numerous and attentive audience I ever saw assembled. It was agreed by all who heard him (which was, indeed, a small proportion of the number) to have been one of his very best speeches. I have reason to know that he was better prepared than usual, for I lost the pleasure of his company at dinner on Friday, from his keeping close to his task on that day. He spoke until five o'clock.

Loco-foco Meeting. As a set-off against the merchants' meeting, the administration leaders ordered a muster of their forces at the same hour, in the park. A large number assembled; not one-third, however, as many as the opposition party, and as inferior in quality as in quantity; but they greatly outnumbered the Wall-streeters in orators. Their principal speaker was a Mr. Hunt from somewhere; but his harangue was too dull to suit the fiery tempers of his auditory, many of whom went away whilst they were yet awake, and the rest broke up into squads to listen to more animated appeals from a Colonel Hepburn, — a noisy, frothy demagogue from Savannah, — Colonel King, of the Custom-House, and that exemplary sprig of Loco-focoism, John T. Munford, each of whom got up his own little "line of battle," and all blazed away at the same time; by this means there were four sets of lungs playing at once, and of course four times as much wisdom went simultaneously into the ears of the sovereigns than at the gathering in Wall street.

Boston Munificence. OCTOBER 16. — The chairman of the Bunker Hill Monument Association acknowledges the receipt of a donation of *ten thousand dollars* from Amos Lawrence, towards finishing the work, which, together with the money collected at the fair, will amount to about $40,000, including Fanny Ellsler's contribution. The Bostonians do these things better than any others in America, and this family of Lawrences are noble fellows, and deserve, from their business habits, liberality, and patriotism, to be styled the Medici of Boston.

Great Loco-foco Discovery. OCTOBER 23. — A gunpowder plot has been brought to light, of which the horrid Whigs were the conspirators. The administration papers are filled with awful details of this nefarious conspiracy against the rights of the people and the majesty of the laws. It appears that, previous to the fall election of 1838, some of the leading Whigs employed a fellow named Glentworth to go to Philadelphia, and procure men to come to New York and assist in detecting illegal voters, who, it was understood, had been brought to vote here. This Glentworth had been appointed by Governor Seward, with the consent of a Locofoco Senate, to the office of tobacco inspector (the only appointment of his of any consequence which was confirmed by that Senate), with an understanding, as appears now, that he should divide the spoil with a man named Steverson, a devoted Locofoco who had held the office. How Seward should make such an appointment is not easily to be understood ; but when Glentworth lost it he communicated to his partner the fact of his having been to Philadelphia, and falsely charged the Whigs with having sent him to procure men to vote at our election, for which they were paid $30 each. As soon as these facts came out, a conclave, consisting of Benjamin F. Butler, attorney-general, Jesse Hoyt, collector, and John W. Edwards, a man formerly in the Senate, who has been imported into New York to do the dirty work of the administration, was held at Hoyt's house, where they got Stevenson and Glentworth, and got from them affidavits charging the crime of procuring illegal votes upon Moses H. Grinnell, Simeon Draper, Robert C. Wetmore, Richard M. Blatchford, and James Bowen. The Loco-foco papers of this morning are full of the horrible plot, with the addition that Governor Seward is arrested, and Grinnell and Wetmore absconded. The Recorder, R. H. Morris, Attorney-General Butler, and Justice Marshall held a sort of Star-Chamber inquisition, in which the affidavits are taken and Glentworth sent to prison. In the mean time the Whigs charged make their affidavits denying any participation in the frauds, and produce a copy of a letter written by them to Glentworth, ordering him to desist from doing anything and to come home, as soon as they were led to suspect that he was exceeding his orders and getting men to vote, instead of watching voters. There is a great deal of excitement in the city. The Whigs were great fools to employ a lying coxcomb like Glentworth in any business requiring secrecy and good faith, and especially in anything which might be liable to misconstruction; but it does not appear that they were guilty of the crime imputed to them, and the conduct of Butler in attempting to implicate the Governor and other honourable men in a disgraceful transaction, upon the testimony of two scoundrels, is infamous; and so everybody except his infamous associates seem to think. The affair is an unpleasant one, but the Whigs will gain more than they will lose by it. It discloses a disgusting scene of villany in the conduct of our elections, and proves that universal suffrage will not do for great cities. It proves also the necessity for a registry law, which is a Whig measure, and has been violently opposed by the very men who are now so sensitive on the subject of illegal voting, when it works against them.

OCTOBER 24.—Grinnell, as I have stated before, declined a renomination for Congress with Hoffman and Curtis, and a new ticket was nominated last evening, when the charges were brought against him which his affidavit so successfully repelled. Tallmadge, who has consented to run, withdrew from the ticket. The committee nominated Grinnell by acclamation, and went down in a body insisting upon his consent, which, urged by these circumstances, he gave, and is now before the public for condemnation or approval. It was an excellent move, which cannot fail to benefit the party.

Butler has been addressing his followers this morning in the park, with his characteristic, hypocritical cant. He talked to them about the interposition of Divine Providence in making him the instrument to bring to light this wicked plot. They laughed at the impious assumption, but threw up their caps and hurrahed for Butler, and damned the Whigs, according to orders.

OCTOBER 25.—My birthday; I am sixty years old. It is no cause of rejoicing. I feel old, and have certain pains which indicate that threescore is a pretty heavy score against a man; but as to health and strength, and preservation of my faculties, I have great reason to be thankful. If my circumstances were such as they were four years ago, I should be a tolerably happy elderly gentleman; but I am doomed to vexations and trouble arising from pecuniary embarrassments for the remainder of my life. God grant I may have firmness of mind and strength of body to meet it all!

OCTOBER 26.—There is a remark in one of the Philadelphia papers about a prisoner in the State prison, condemned to the utmost punishment of the law for fraud,—if he wished to escape punishment, he should have committed murder. There is much good sense and truth in this severe remark. Any offence against men's pockets is sure to be punished, because every juror has been cheated at some time, and rejoices in an opportunity to revenge himself upon his fellow-men. But none has ever been murdered; and then there is always some provocation, some palliation,—insanity, drunkenness, or something of the kind,—as if a man must be proved free from vice, a stranger to habits, and not influenced by malevolent passions, to entitle him to the privilege of being hanged. The truth is, human life is not held in as high estimation as money, and he who takes the first has a better chance of escaping than he who makes free with the other.

NOVEMBER 3.—The greatest excitement prevails; men's minds are wrought up to a pitch of frenzy, and, like tinder, a spark of opposition sets them on fire. The vote for presidential electors in Pennsylvania is so close, that out of two hundred and eighty thousand votes it is probable that neither will have five hundred majority. Both parties here claim the victory, and every hour the wheel turns each uppermost. Betting is going on at an enormous extent. Riot and violence stalk unchecked through the streets, and lying is no longer considered a crime. A gang of several thousand Loco-foco ruffians paraded the streets last night with clubs, and assaulted and drove off several of the Whig processions. The police seem to be afraid to oppose the majesty of Democracy; and the Mayor, with oracular wisdom, says, " If the people will be peaceable, there is no danger."   Right, Mr. Sands !

Meeting in Wall street.   There was a great meeting of the merchants, at two o'clock, in Wall street, in front of the Exchange, to express their opinion in favour of Moses H. Grinnell, the commercial representative to Congress, who has been so shamefully traduced by the district attorney and his associates in the Titus Oates plot.   James G. King was president, with a number of vice-presidents, of whom I was one.   The resolutions were presented and read, partly by Mr. Perit and partly by myself.   I introduced them with a speech, as he did also.   An excellent speech was made by Daniel Lord, Jr., and Mr. John R. Hurd made a short address. Mr. Lord's was in the nature of a law argument against the abominable proceeding of the recorder and his Star-Chamber, in seizing the papers of Glentworth and exposing them to the public, — a most tyranical and illegal attack upon the rights of the people, which ought to subject him and his coadjutor, the Mayor, to the indictment of a grand jury, and the former to impeachment by the Legislature.   When the chairman put the question for adjournment it was clearly lost; the meeting would not break up, but insisted upon more speaking.   I was called upon and made a second speech, short and to the point, which was well received, and they went away well pleased.

City Election.   NOVEMBER 4.—The fire is out, the powder expended, and the smoke is passing away.   The election throughout the State ended when the sun went down. Ours was held only to-day, and, thanks to the registry law, forty-three thousand men went to the polls, voted, and came away without confusion, and generally without riot or opposition.   In some of the Loco-foco districts crowds of violent men assembled, but not to the extent formerly experienced.   This beneficial change has been produced by dividing the wards into election districts, so that not more than about six hundred are taken in one place, and all in one day.   Instead of seventeen polls, as it used to be, there are now eighty odd, and the elements of riot and disorder are weakened by being divided. The polls are opened at sunrise and closed at sunset, and by ten o'clock two-thirds of all the votes in the city were in. The number of votes registered in the second district of the fifteenth ward, in which I reside, is six hundred and seventy, of which six hundred and sixty-four voted.

I was selected by the general committee to act as chairman this evening, at Masonic Hall, where the mighty mass of Whigs assembled to hear the reports. It is hard duty, and I am hoarse and sore, and jaded as a horse in an omnibus. I took the chair at seven o'clock. The interval of time before the reports came in was filled by speaking and singing Whig songs. By and by messengers began to arrive with reports from the several wards, which soon satisfied us that we had lost the battle. Many of our people had been sanguine enough to calculate upon our gaining the city, and it was most desirable that we should have sent again to Congress a Whig delegation, particularly Grinnell, whose election would have so severely rebuked the men who assailed him on the eve of the election, and the State senator and members of Assembly would have been a prodigious gain; but, although many of us hoped for such a result, none acquainted with the state of the parties calculated upon it, and the result is, in fact, a cause of triumph. The administration majority is not over twelve hundred; they reckoned upon three thousand. We were beaten a year ago by about eighteen hundred; that was the majority against me for the Senate. The State will go for Harrison, I think, without a doubt; but his majority will not be so great as was expected. The contest has been violent; every effort which a party, unscrupulous at all times, but desperate now, could make to sustain themselves in power, has been resorted to; but it will not do. The sceptre has departed from Mr. Van Buren.

Scenes of violence, disorder, and riot have taught us in this city that universal suffrage will not do for large communities. It works better in the country, where a large proportion of the voters are

Americans, born and brought up on the spot, and where, if a black sheep comes into the flock, he is marked immediately. But in the heterogeneous mass of vile humanity in our population of three hundred and ten thousand souls the men who decide the elections are unknown ; they have no local habitation or name ; they left their own country for ours, to better their condition, by opposing everything good, honest, lawful, and of good report, and to effect this they have banded themselves into associations to put down, at all hazards, the party in favour of order and good government. A mighty army of these banditti paraded the streets last night under the orders of the masters, who, no doubt, secretly directed their movements, attacking every place where the Whigs met. National Hall, in Canal street, the conservative headquarters, was besieged by this army of Jack Jades, and its appearance this morning is a melancholy sample of the effects of unrestrained power in the hands of a mob of political desperadoes. All the windows of this large building are broken ; bushels of brickbats cover the floors, and the doors show where the ruffians endeavoured to gain admission by setting fire to the house. This evening, thus far, has been quiet in my part of the city. I came home from Masonic Hall as soon as the result was known, and did not witness any disturbance. Having beaten us in one way, they don't think it worth while to do it in another.

NOVEMBER 5. — The same subject day after day ; but
Elections.   this week settles all. At present it swallows up everything else. No business is done ; the hammer is suspended on the anvil ; the merchant neglects his counting-house, and the lawyer his office. Nobody invites a friend to dine, and no topic of conversation is permitted but election.

NOVEMBER 10. — The election returns come in from all quarters in favour of Harrison and the Whig cause. It is thought that Mr. Van Buren cannot get more than fifty votes out of two hundred and ninety-four. In our own State, though the city went against us by a greatly reduced majority, and the first accounts from the river counties were somewhat discouraging, all has been redeemed by the North and South. The Harrison electoral ticket is elected by twelve thousand majority. Seward and Bradish are reëlected, and the Whigs have majorities in both branches of the Legislature. Seward runs behind the other tickets several thousand, owing to his having recommended the free bill, which has disturbed the political consciences of the lawyers through their pockets, and more especially by the ill-judged favour which he has shown the Catholics, by which he has lost many of his friends, and not gained the votes of those whom he sought to propitiate. His motives were, I believe, correct; but his policy in this latter affair is justly condemned.

NOVEMBER 16. — There is a chasm of three days in this journal, and, gracious heaven, how has the time been filled! ·My strength fails me when I attempt to account for it, and yet I feel that it will afford me a sort of melancholy consolation. My heart sinks within me whenever my thoughts are concentrated upon the greatest grief which has ever oppressed it. May the indulgent Father of mercies sustain me and my bereaved family in our great affliction, and teach us with resignation to exclaim, " Father, thy will be done !" My dear, beloved Mary left this world of trouble and affliction, and, as I firmly and confidently believe, joined her sister angels in heaven, on Friday morning.

DECEMBER 2. — This is the day which decides the
Presidential Election. fate of Mr. Van Buren and his administration. The electors of President and Vice-President meet simultaneously in each of the States of the Union, and will quietly, and in discharge of the constitutional rights of the people, deposit two hundred and thirty-four votes for William Henry Harrison for President, and John Tyler for Vice-President, and sixty votes for Martin Van Buren for President, and Richard M. Johnson, or some other person, for Vice-President. And thus the dynasty is changed. The party which has been in power forty years yields the sceptre to its adversary, and the policy under which the country has hereto-

fore been governed will be abandoned for one more consonant to
the opinions and wishes of the present majority. This is a beautiful illustration of the operation of a popular government. If Mons.
De Tocqueville should publish a new edition of his excellent work
on the Democracy of America, he will have in this event a striking
confirmation of his principles, and our institutions will be the subject of a new and merited eulogium from his able pen. The late
election, and its consequences, afford a field for deep reflection.
There is not probably a country in the world where a change of
such prodigious magnitude could have been effected in the same
time, with so little apparent machinery, and in so orderly and decorous a manner. It does, indeed, afford encouragement and hope
to those patriotic Americans who are Republicans in feeling and
judgment, but may, at times, have doubted of the continued practi-
cability of the operation of self-government in a country of so great
an extent as the United States.

Levi Woodbury, at present Secretary of the Treas-
Loco-foco
Movements. ury, has a good place provided when he receives
notice to quit, which will be as soon after the fourth of
March as may be. The State of New Hampshire, immovable as
her granite hills in bad political principles, has elected him a Senator in Congress, and thereby given him a chance to vote on the
question of his own ejectment from office. If he makes as indifferent a senator as he did a secretary, he will be a suitable representative of the party which sends him to Congress.

The Legislature of South Carolina (the only State in the Union
in which the people are not immediate electors of the presidential
electors) have given the vote of the State to Martin Van Buren and
Richard M. Johnson; and this they did, not from any predilection
for the *great rejected,* but to be in opposition to the Northern and
Eastern States. The high-minded Carolinians (as we have been in
the habit of coaxingly calling them) are the most clannish, selfish
people in America; they have no affection for anything except
South Carolina; their patriotism is centred in themselves, and

Union means nothing more than their own sticking together. Their apostle, John C. Calhoun, would coalesce with the Devil (as he has with one for whom he has not much greater affection) if he saw in such a course the smallest chance of bringing down New York to the level of Charleston, and would rejoice in a revolution of nature which should cause the Atlantic to recede from our shores, and leave her ships rotting in the mud of her harbours.

DECEMBER 5. — A monument has been erected at Rockaway over the remains of the unhappy sufferers on board the ships " Bristol" and " Mexico," wrecked on the Long Island shore in the winter of 1836–7. The Hempstead people have done well to evince their sympathy in this manner ; but it was too bad, after the cruel suffering and miserable deaths of these poor strangers, that their memory should be handed down to posterity in such wretched poetry as the following inscription, which graces one side of the monumental stone : —

The Rockaway Muse.

> " In this grave from the wide ocean doth sleep
> The bodies of those that had crossed the deep,
> And instead of being landed safe on the shore,
> On a cold frosty night they all were no more."

DECEMBER 23. — Mr Clay came in town on Saturday, to visit (as he gave out) his grandsons, who are at school in Jamaica, Long Island, and returned on Tuesday to Washington. I passed half an hour very pleasantly with him on Monday morning. He told me some of the arrangements of the next Cabinet. Mr. Webster is to be Secretary of State, and Mr. Crittenden, of Kentucky, Attorney-General. A glorious beginning ! The United States do not contain two better men for those respective stations. The other heads of departments are not yet designated. Mr. Clay was offered by General Harrison, for himself, a *carte blanche ;* but he declines office, proposing to retain his place in the Senate, where he thinks he can most effectually serve the new administration, and to be ready to enter the field four years hence, to which I say, Amen, and success attend him !

Visit of Mr. Clay.

1841.

JANUARY 1.—I cannot find a spot on the page of history marked in the margin 1840 on which to place a "white stone." My debts have increased, and my property is reduced in value, while those who owe me cannot or will not pay, and there is but little hope that they ever will; for the most sanguine anticipations of a return of prosperity, the result of the late political revolution, seem to be founded upon the calculation of a sponge being applied to all foregone engagements and a free course to enter again upon the race of commercial speculation.

Great as has been the bereavement we have sustained in the death of our beloved Mary, and melancholy the void it has occasioned in my domestic circle, I am not without many sources of happiness, and have great cause for thankfulness in the present condition of my family. My health is good, although I have occasional attacks of gout, rheumatism, or lumbago, as the case may be, and my limbs have had to submit to many hard rubs. I wish they were the only ones I have to submit to. But welcome, 1841! Let not the storm which marks thy advent prove prophetic of thy course.

JANUARY 16.— Yesterday was an important day in the money annals of the country. The banks of Philadelphia were compelled, under a law of the State, to resume the payment of specie. Some apprehensions were entertained that the Bank of the United States, from the crippled state of her affairs, might find a difficulty in complying with the law, from which cause alone the other banks would be embarrassed; but that institution, having effected a loan in England of 500,000 pounds sterling, by negotiating their bills, were enabled to meet their demands, and all things went on well, so far. Further south they hold out yet; the Baltimore banks say that they can pay, but will not, unless those of Virginia come into the measure of resumption.

JANUARY 20. — I dined yesterday with Mr. William G. Ward, — a sort of revival of the " Hone Club," with all its pleasant rules and social observance. Dinner at five to the instant, the stragglers coming in within five minutes after the time, and ere the soup was gone, each, with watch in hand, disputing the edict which, like the laws of the Medes and Persians, never changes : a strict observance to the limitation of four dishes, so strict that by gastronomic sophistry it extends to a dozen; brant being transformed into fish, oysters coming under the denomination of vegetables, and veal sweet-breads being pronounced of the genus confectionery. The " Ode " was sung by Major Tucker, with a full chorus; and other songs and pleasant converse and good fellowship made us forget the bad times which have caused a suspension of our meetings.

JANUARY 30. — There was a brilliant ball last evening

City Ball.   at the City Hall, — a sort of revival of the old city assemblies, which were formerly held in that time-honoured saloon. It was gotten up by the young men. Heads of families were not allowed to subscribe, but were invited, with their wives and daughters. The whole affair was conducted in a genteel manner; the ball was well attended by the most respectable of our citizens, and gave great satisfaction. Another is to be given, probably on Washington's birthday. The managers are Abraham Schermerhorn, Edmund H. Pendleton, James W. Otis, William Douglass, Henry Delafield, Henry W. Hicks, Jno. Swift Livingston, Jacob R. Le Roy, Thomas W. Ludlow, Charles McEvers, Jr., William S. Miller, Charles C. King.

FEBRUARY 4. — There is a panic to-day in the money

Financial
Panic.   market. The great bank in Philadelphia, falsely called the " United States Bank," after having resumed specie payments with the other banks in that city, a few days since, finds itself compelled to suspend again, and has refused payments of drafts from this city. The effect of this, it is apprehended, will be

to compel the other banks to suspend again. Baltimore, Charleston, and other Southern cities will have to follow suit; and all the horrors of a disturbed currency and ruinous exchanges, of which we thought we were relieved, will be returned upon us for a period of time for which no one can form any opinion of the duration.

FEBRUARY 5.—The suspension of the United States Bank is confirmed to-day. The stock of that institution fell nearly ten per cent. Large quantities were sold at from forty to forty-two per cent.; and, from the opinions of persons better informed than myself, I am induced to believe that it is as much as it is worth. Indeed, it was sold "ahead," as the brokers call it; that is, to be delivered within a certain time, at the option of the seller, as low as thirty-four. Taking the cash price to-day, there is a loss to the stockholders from the par value of $60, of $21,000,000,—equal to that occasioned by the great fire, to say nothing of all that was bought at 120 or 125 before the charter expired, and was transferred into the State institution. This enormous loss falls heavily upon the European holders, who will not in the future be disposed to trust us; but there is a great deal held by widows and children, public institutions, and trustees. When Jackson, the old despoiler, crushed the national institution under the iron heel of vindictive power, the plague-spot upon commercial prosperity first made its appearance; but the disease was not incurable until the bank attained, at an unwarrantable expense, a charter from the State of Pennsylvania to do mischief to the nation, without the ability or the obligation to do good in any but a local sense. At that time, if the concern had been wound up and rested peaceably in the tomb to which party rage and personal malignity had consigned it, the loss to the stockholders would have been comparatively small, and an obstacle in the way of the establishment of a sound national bank would have been removed: a bank solid and uncrippled, whose benignant sphere of action would have been coextensive with true bonds of union; whose duty, as well as its interest, would have been directed to the preservation of a sound currency and the accommodation and support of honest commercial enterprise ; and such a one we must have. The necessity becomes more apparent every day. The prejudices created by the violent measures of the Attila of Tennessee and his furious partisans begins to give way before the light of reason, and if the downfall of the Pennsylvania bank should be necessary to give place to such an institution, it had better be brought at once to that issue. The present vessel is rotten and unseaworthy, and must be broken up as soon as may be, and a new one, the property of the whole, and not a part of the partners in our great national concern, be set upon the stocks without delay, launched, rigged, and set upon her voyage with none but a *national* ensign at her mast-head ; and if John Bull will not ship on board her, we must endeavour to make the voyage on our own hook.

FEBRUARY 8. —There has been a dreadful panic to-day among the brokers and " money-changers " in Wall street. The suspension of the Bank of the United States has been followed by that of the other banks of Philadelphia. Some of them continue to pay specie for their notes of $5 ; but it is only the faint flickering of the expiring candle. Baltimore, also, has suspended again. This unhappy state of things has caused a fall in prices of every description of stock in New York. Delaware and Hudson Canal stock, which has nothing to do with Philadelphia financial operations, fell from ninety-five to eighty-eight per cent. A panic in money matters is like one in an army during a battle : when a part runs away, others follow and prick onward with their bayonets those who may be disposed to stand firm, until a general rout is the consequence. United States Bank sold to-day at twenty-five per cent. Here is wholesale ruin. Here is a loss from the par value of $26,250,000, to be borne by all classes of our citizens, and an utter destruction of American credit in Europe. How happy would it have been for all parties if, when the national institution was killed, it had stayed killed !

FEBRUARY 9. — General Harrison made a sort of triumphal entry into Baltimore on Saturday, where he was
received by crowds of citizens, who formed a procession to conduct him to his lodgings ; and he made a speech which,
in my judgment, he might better have let alone.   Preparations are
making to receive him to-morrow with similar honours at Washington, where he is to remain two or three days.   He then goes to
Virginia to visit his friends, returns to Washington toward the close
of the month, will be inaugurated on the 4th of March, and then
his troubles (not few nor small) will begin.

> " I vow 'tis better to be lowly born,
>   And range with humble livers in content,
>   Than to be perked up in a glittering grief,
>   And wear a golden sorrow."

SATURDAY, FEB. 13. — The day after General Harrison's arrival in Washington he visited President Van
Buren, who received him with the greatest politeness.
They passed half an hour in agreeable conversation, and the next
day the President, accompanied by the heads of departments, returned the visit at the apartments of the President-elect, at
Gadsby's Hotel.   This compliment was the more marked as the
etiquette is for the President not to return visits.   General Harrison was also to dine with the President to-day, and the dinner will,
no doubt, be a very pleasant one, for nobody knows better than
Mr. Van Buren how to do such things.   His tact is admirable, and,
whatever may be his feelings in regard to the success of his distinguished rival, he will never afford his political opponents the triumph of letting them be known.   Calm and unruffled as the bosom
of a lake under the tranquil influence of a summer's sun, there is
nothing to indicate the storm which may have passed over it.   This
is in far better taste than the petulant conduct of the elder Adams,
who left Washington in the night to avoid the mortification of wit-

nessing the accession of Mr. Jefferson; or of General Jackson, when the people in an evil hour wrested the sceptre from John Q. Adams to place it in his ruffian hands. General Harrison visited also the ex-President, Adams.

WASHINGTON, FEB. 18. — Left Baltimore in the nine-o'clock train, and arrived here about the opening of the houses of Congress; got a tolerable room at Gadsby's, that caravansary of long, cold galleries, never-ceasing ringing of bells, negligent servants, small pillows, and scanty supply of water. I am better off, even in these particulars, than three-fourths of the people in the house; but, if a man wishes to appreciate the comforts of home, let him come to Washington. As for the eating part, I am fortunately situated. I am regularly entered of Mr. Granger's mess, with his daughter and Meredith, which promises well, if I should have any chance to enjoy their society.

Journey to Washington.

I found an invitation to dine with the Russian Minister, which he had politely sent in anticipation of my coming, and accordingly rode over to his residence at Georgetown, where I met a large party of distinguished gentlemen, embracing most of the leading Whigs. The dinner was a magnificent affair, a ponderous set-out; it was like dining in a gold mine; immense, lofty, and massy gilt candelabras on the table, in which I counted eighty wax candles burning, besides others in different parts of the room; rich ornaments of every description; a great variety of wines, some of which were good, but the *cuisine* not comparable with an every-day dinner at my own house. Servants below stairs with gilt-laced cocked hats, and surrounding the table with tarnished liveries, which, from their variety, would seem intended to represent all the provinces of Russia; but the host did the honours with great propriety, and treated me with marked attention. The number was about four and twenty, of which I remember the following: Mons. Bacour, French Minister; Mr. Fox, British Minister; Mr. Stockel, Russian Secretary; Mr. Webster, Mr. Clay, Mr. Crittenden, Mr. Tallmadge, Mr. Rives, Mr. Merrick, Mr. Henderson, Mr. Bayard, Mr. Southard, Mr.

Dawson, Mr. Cushing, Mr. Meredith, Mr. Reverdy Johnson, Mr. Austen of Massachusetts, Richard Peters, Mr. Mangum, Mr. Sargent, and Colonel Stuart. There was whist after dinner. I got at a table with Messrs. Bodisco, Fox, and Clay, and sat until we were the survivors of the large party.

FEBRUARY 19. — I called this morning upon President Van Buren. He received me alone in his study, in the kindest and most gracious manner; talked a little about the late political contest, professed an undiminished friendship for me, notwithstanding my opposition, which he said he had been gratified to learn had been unaccompanied by the use of any expression of personal disrespect. He is fat and jolly, with the same self-satisfied smile upon his countenance. A stranger would be greatly at a loss to discover anything to indicate that he was a defeated candidate for the high office which he is about to vacate.

The Supreme Court was for two hours the point of Mr. Webster. superior attraction. Mr. Webster was engaged in one of those great arguments on a constitutional question in which he stands unrivalled, the interest of which was enhanced from its being one of the last in which he will be engaged. He has resigned his seat in the Senate, of which he will take leave on Monday, and on the 4th of March he commences a new sphere of action as Secretary of State in General Harrison's Cabinet. The Supreme Court presented a sublime and beautiful spectacle during Mr. Webster's argument. The solemn temple of justice was filled with an admiring auditory, consisting of a large proportion of well-dressed ladies, who occupied the seats within the bar; the nine judges, in their magisterial robes, attentive and thoughtful; and all minds and bodies bent upon one great object, and that object a single man, of commanding presence and intellectual aspect, not remarkably correct in his costume nor graceful in his action, but commanding, by the force of his giant intellect, an irresistible control over the minds of all who heard him, and enchaining all their faculties to one point of observation and attention. It was, in truth, a noble illustration of the power of mind over the material faculties of humanity.

FEBRUARY 20. — I dined with Grinnell and Hoffman. We had a good dinner, fine wine, and a very pleasant party, consisting of Mr. Hoffman, Mr. Grinnell, Mr. Southard, Mr. Habershaw, Mr. Bayard, Mr. Holmes of South Carolina, Mr. Graham of North Carolina, Mr. Sargeant, Mr. Winthrop, Mr. Lincoln, the Speaker, Mr. Tallmadge, Mr. Henderson, Mr. Lowe of New York, and P. H.

FEBRUARY 22.—I have been all day in the Senate, and greatly interested. The principal business was an animated debate on a motion made by Mr. Crittenden to bring a bill, formerly presented by him, to prevent the interference of office-holders in elections. This motion was supported in an eloquent speech by the mover and the leading Whigs, and opposed by Messrs. Buchanan, Calhoun, Wright, etc., and defeated by a strict party vote. They could not stand the implied odium which the passage of such an act would cast upon the party going out of power, nor acknowledge the magnanimity of their successors in binding themselves in advance not to use the same means to secure a continuance of their own, which have heretofore been employed against them. Mr. Preston's speech in support of this measure gave rise to an incident of considerable excitement. He closed his speech with an eulogium upon Mr. Crittenden, on the occasion of his quitting the Senate to assume the office of Attorney-General in General Harrison's administration. Never did human voice utter anything more beautiful than this well-merited panegyric. It was warm and glowing, tender and touching, by turns. The Senate was full, and the galleries crowded to the utmost. I was seated on the floor, behind the eloquent Carolinian. The audience seemed to be rapt in mute attention until the close, when the effect was irresistible, and there was a pretty general applause in the galleries. This unwonted outbreak gave great offence to the *Loco-focos*. Several arose at once, and with loud screams and violent gesticulation demanded the clearing of the galleries. "Turn them out!" said

Clay of Alabama, Sevier Cuthbert, and even Calhoun.   "Turn out
the blackguards!" exclaimed the refined Mr. Benton, striking the
desk with great vehemence; and the Vice-President, with evident
reluctance, proceeded to give the harsh order.   Mr. Clay, with his
wonted suavity, interposed to save the ladies.   He was "sure they
could not have joined in the offence, and ought not to be included in
the punishment;" and the Vice-President, nothing loath, saved them
and the men in their gallery from being turned away to gratify the
spleen of half-a-dozen demagogues who are forever talking about the
dear people, and let no opportunity escape of affronting them.   There
was an easier way for them to clear out the galleries: let either of
them arise to make a speech, and the object is accomplished without a resort to violence.   But what a glorious triumph of eloquence !
I would have given the world at that moment to have been Preston ;
but I would have given such worlds to be Crittenden !   The latter
was greatly moved ; those that were near him say that he wept vis-
ibly.   He is beloved by all parties.   Mr. Buchanan, a political
opponent, but the most gentlemanly senator on that side, paid him
a handsome personal compliment in a speech in which he opposed
his motion.   This exhibition of vulgar rage gave occasion to the
following *jeu d'esprit*, which was handed to me the next morning
by a senator : —

> "'Turn out the blackguards!' If they do,
> Friend Benton, what becomes of you?"

As soon as this affair was ended, a new excitement was created,
which continued until the adjournment.   Mr. Webster having
retired from his place, a letter addressed to the Vice-President
was read, in which he resigns his seat, and took leave of the Senate ;
immediately upon which a firebrand from Georgia, Mr. Cuthbert,
arose and attacked him.   He regretted that the senator from Massachusetts had not made a verbal valedictory, as he had intended
to put certain interrogatories to him touching his doctrines on the
subject of the transmission of slaves from one State to another, —

doctrines which Georgia's senator denounced as " damnable here-
sies." He evidently desired to get up a quarrel. His manner and
his language were equally insulting, and there was something so dis-
courteous, so unkind, in his taking that moment to vent his spleen
against the absent senator, when the tide of generous feeling was
flowing so strongly in his favour, that there was not an individual of
Cuthbert's party who, by word, look, or action, seemed disposed either
to countenance cr support him. Mr. Clay rebuked the ruffian in a
manly and eloquent speech, in which the character and principles
of his friend were ably defended, and Mr. Rives and Mr. Preston
followed in the same strain. The former gentleman came in for an
undue share of the wrath of the Hotspur of Georgia ; his manner
toward him was provoking and insulting, and met with haughty
scorn and defiance. Mr. Rives, at the commencement of his
speech, happened to apply to Cuthbert the parliamentary term,
" My honourable friend." — " No, sir ; no friend," was the uncivil
reply. — " So be it," retorted Mr. Rives ; and it is not likely the term
will be repeated very soon. Mr. Rives defended Mr. Webster with
great ability, approving, though a Southern man, his opinions on
the exciting subject of slavery.

FEBRUARY 26. — Rufus Choate is elected a senator
New Sena-
tors.
from Massachusetts, to fill Mr. Webster's place ; and
Mr. Morehead, after several ballots, was elected, by
the relinquishment of two of his Whig opponents, to fill that of
Mr. Crittenden, as senator from Kentucky. It is a fearful ven-
ture for those gentlemen to undertake to supply the void occasioned by the setting of those two " bright particular stars " of
the Senate.

I dined with Mr. Barnard ; a small and very pleasant party,
and an excellent dinner of French cookery and good wine. The
party consisted of Mr. John Quincy Adams, Mr. Richard Bayard,
Gouverneur Wilkins, Abbott Lawrence, Mr. Jackson of Philadelphia, and myself. Mr. Adams was, as usual, the fiddle of the
party. He talked a great deal ; was gay, witty, instructive, and

entertaining. It is a privilege, and an era in one's life, to see him as he was on this occasion. A man must be stupid, indeed, who can listen to this wonderful man for three or four hours, as I have done to-day, without being edified and delighted.

The President's Dinner to General Harrison.

We had an account before I left home of some amiable passages of courtesy between the outgoing and the incoming Presidents, in which the former had great credit for courtesy extended to the latter, particularly in inviting him to dine. I have heard since I came here some particulars about this dinner, which have satisfied me that it was not the kind of compliment which we gave him credit for. Instead of inviting to meet the General his personal and political friends, such as Webster, Clay, Crittenden, Southard, etc., the party consisted, besides General Harrison and Colonel Chambers and Mr. Todd, his personal suite, of the following: the cabinet ministers, Mr. Gouverneur Kemble, Silas Wright, and Aaron Vanderpoel,—all Loco-focos of the bitterest stamp, and his most decided political opponents. He was in the camp of the Philistines; it seemed as if they were there to take advantage of the old man's kind, benevolent openness of disposition, and treasure up for future use anything which may have fallen from him in an unguarded moment.

News from Home.

They write me from home that times are hard in New York, despondency prevails among men of business, and melancholy forebodings of worse times to come. The State of Illinois will not pay the interest of her debt, and doubts are entertained of the great State of Pennsylvania. Stocks have fallen very much; Delaware and Hudson down to eighty per cent.

MARCH 1. — I went yesterday to St. John's Church, where I caused some remarks to be made by my sitting in the President's pew, for which I had afterwards to stand some shots from the Whigs, who have not the taste to understand how a man may continue on good terms with a gentleman whose election he has worked hard to defeat. The truth is, the President passed me in his carriage on his way to church, and when I arrived I found his son Smith waiting for me at the door, to take me to his father's pew, — a civility which I accepted most willingly, and did not find my devotions interfered with, nor my political principles contaminated, by the company I had the honour to be placed in.

MARCH 2. — Broadway on a fine Sunday, when the churches are emptied, does not present a more animated spectacle than Pennsylvania avenue on this bright and beautiful morning; there are men here from every State in the Union. Our good city of New York has its full proportion. I have remarked, and heard it remarked by others, that there is not a country in the world where in such a crowd, so gotten together, there could be found so large a proportion of good-looking and well-behaved persons. I was talking about it with Mr. Bell yesterday, and he remarked that he was here at the time of General Jackson's inauguration, when the same objects and motions brought together a greater crowd, and the difference in appearance and deportment of the people is most striking; but now they are Whigs and gentlemen, then Loco-focos and ——

I was forcibly stricken this morning by a characteristic circumstance, of which an American may well be proud. Passing through the crowd of which I was just speaking was to be seen an elderly gentleman dressed in black, and not remarkably well dressed, with a mild, benignant countenance, a military air, but stooping a little, bowing to one, shaking hands with another, and cracking a joke with a third; and this man was William H. Harrison, the President-elect of this great empire, whose elevation has been produced by a severe throe which has been felt in the most remote corners of the land, which has destroyed and elevated the hopes of hundreds of thousands, and which is destined to effect a change of principles and policy to which the whole world looks with interest; and there he was, unattended, and unconscious of the dignity of his position, — *the man* among men, the sun of the political firmament. People may say what they will about the naked simplicity of Republican institutions; it was a sublime moral spectacle.

MARCH 3. — This city is an immense mass of animated Whig matter; every hole and corner are filled; thousands have arrived to-day, and happy is the man who finds "where to lay his head." A large building has been erected in the court at Gadsby's, in which four hundred breakfast, dine, and sup; and the dining-room is a vast camp-bed. This has been a day of confusion; everybody running against his neighbour, all full of business, and nobody accomplishing any.

I witnessed the last moments of the 26th Congress. At twelve o'clock the refractory old lady terminated the career which she so naughtily began. The Speaker sang a requiem to her departing moments in a very respectable speech, somewhat too long and a little too school-boyish. He is an amiable man, and has acted with impartiality, but no more fit to be Speaker than I to dance on the tight rope. On the whole, the scene was imposing, and more orderly and decorous than I had anticipated. The aforesaid old lady behaved with propriety, " and, like immortal Cæsar, died with dignity."

MARCH 4. — The affair is consummated. General Harrison has taken the oaths, and is President of the United States. The day was fine. A great procession, consisting of several militia companies in uniform, Tippecanoe clubs, and citizens from different States, under the orders of marshals on horseback, with sashes and batons, escorted the President to the Capitol. He was mounted, and passed through the streets amidst the shouts and hurrahs of fifty thousand men, and almost as many women waving their handkerchiefs, whilst he, like the haughty Bolingbroke, —

> " Mounted upon a hot and fiery steed,
>   Which his aspiring rider seemed to know,
>   With slow but stately pace kept on his course,
>   While all tongues cried, 'God save thee, Bolingbroke!'
> You would have thought the very windows spoke."

The Inauguration.

As for Van Buren, " No man cried, God save him ! "   He was snug at the house of the Attorney-General, McGilpin.

Inauguration Ball.
I attended the great inauguration ball last evening, at the National Theatre. The crowd was very great ; all the great men of the nation were there ; an exceedingly brilliant collection of ladies, of whom Mrs. Reverdy Johnson, of Baltimore, a mother of nine children, was preëminent.   The President came in about half-past ten o'clock, with a numerous escort, and was marched through files of ladies up and down the room. This ceremony, with his previous visits to two other public balls, added to the severe labours of the day, has tried the old soldier's stamina ; but he appears to stand it very well.   If the opponents of the administration expect to make capital out of his imbecility of either body or mind, they make a woful mistake.   He'll do his duty well and faithfully.   The gentlemen had a supper in the lower regions of the theatre, from which in former times ghosts and hob-goblins and infernal spirits made their " exits and their entrances." I was escorted by the managers to this subterranean banquet-hall, where I found senators, cabinet ministers, military officers, and common men like myself, eating, drinking, laughing, and joking in a strain somewhat uproarious.

The nominations of the new cabinet have, it is said, been con-firmed, all but that of Mr. Granger, against whom charges of that crying sin, abolitionism, having been brought by the opposition, his friends consented to let it lie over until to-morrow.   This is a base and ungentlemanly proceeding ; but it will have no other effect than that of misrepresenting his principles, for he will certainly be con-firmed to-morrow.

NEW YORK, MARCH 23. — Dined with Mr. Blatchford. The dinner was given to Mr. Edward Curtis, the new collector, who was there, and his brother, George Curtis ; Mr. Tallmadge, the new recorder ; Grinnell, Minturn, Prescott Hall, Charles King, Ruggles, John Ward, Bowen, etc. There was talk about the appointments and other political matters.   I am pestered to death to sign recommendations and write letters to the collector, in behalf of applicants for office in the Custom-House. It is distressing to see how many worthy people are compelled to be suppliants for little, contemptible situations, the emoluments of which are hardly sufficient to keep life and soul together.

MARCH 24. — *The friends of the people*, the real Loco-focos, had a grand triumphal entry of their chieftain, the ex-President, yesterday, on the arrival of the cars from Philadelphia. The man of the people, whom the people have rejected by an electoral vote of two hundred and thirty-four to sixty, was received by the people on foot, on horseback, and on carts. The *conquering hero*, who was elected by sixty votes, the other two hundred and thirty-four having been thrown away upon one William H. Harrison, was escorted up Broadway to Bleecker street, and down the Bowery to Tammany Hall, where he was addressed by the people in the person of ex-Recorder Morris, that immaculate Republican who, under the sanctum of official station, enters men's houses at night and steals their private papers, to which address of the people the aforesaid people's President (who was elected as aforesaid by the unanimous voices of the people, not counting those votes which were improperly cast for his opponent) read a feeling and suitable reply, after which he and Mr. Forsyth, his Secretary of State (whose place has been recently usurped by one Daniel Webster, an obscure individual from the rebellious State of Massachusetts, against the will of the people, expressed as aforesaid), were escorted, amidst the shouts and huzzas of the people, to the quarters provided for them at the Carleton House, named in honour of the Prince Regent of England ; and in the evening the people were gratified with a view of the men of their choice, and permitted to cheer them again at the Bowery Theatre. The worst of this affair was, that it rained " cats and dogs " during the progress of the procession ; but this was as it should be. His *reign* being over in Washington, New York's favourite son was entitled to *rain* here ; and he stood it, as if, like his friend Benton, he had been born a *veteran*. His followers, too, enjoyed the joke, albeit not a *dry* one ; their begrimed skins expanded and were softened by the unwonted ablution, whilst the spirits *within* happily remained undiluted by the water *without*.

MARCH 27. — I dined with Mr. G. G. Howland, where I met Mr. and Mrs. Abbott Lawrence, after which Mr. Lawrence and I went to Moses H. Grinnell's, where we had also been invited to dine. Here we met a large party of good Whigs, "full on mirth and full on glee," as Billy Taylor says, and sat until midnight. There were Mr. Crittenden ; Mr. Berrien, the new senator from Georgia ; Messrs. Barnard, Hoffman, Ruggles, Blatchford, Bowen, Minturn, Griswold, John Ward, Davis, Prescott Hall, Aspinwall, etc.

MARCH 30. — Mr. Webster came in town this morning, with his wife, to see Mr. Herman Le Roy, her father, whose long and virtuous life is drawing to a close. He is compelled to return to Washington to-morrow morning. I saw him a few minutes this evening, by his appointment. The object of the interview was to acquaint me that a certain affair in which I am deeply concerned might be considered settled, and to my satisfaction.

APRIL 2. — There is a pretty good hit in one of the Southern papers upon the rather redundant introduction of classical illustrations in the President's inaugural address ; for, if there is a fault in it, it consists of a little too much interlacing of Greece and Rome with its sound principles and honest professions. The writer says that General Harrison was prevailed upon to consent to the appointment of Edward Curtis as Collector of New York, by being told that he was a lineal descendant of the Curtius of Rome.

The Curtii.

APRIL 3. — There was a rumour yesterday of the illness of our worthy President, General Harrison, which has assumed to-day a shape somewhat alarming. He has a severe attack of pleurisy, or inflammation of the lungs. The report to-day speaks of danger, which, until now, was not apprehended, but adds that he is better. God grant that

Illness of the President.

he may recover ! His death just now would be, indeed, a severe national calamity.

APRIL 5. — With a mournful heart and trembling hands I record the sad and unexpected (unexpected, at least, until yesterday morning) event which will fill this country with sincere grief and melancholy forebodings. The noble and virtuous old man whose recent elevation to the chief magistracy so lately established the triumph of our popular institutions, and lighted up the hope of a dispirited people ; the honest patriot, whose acts during the brief period in which he held the reins of government gave the fullest evidence of his intention to pursue that policy which was best calculated to redound to his country's glory and secure the happiness of her citizens, — has, by an inscrutable decree of Providence, to which we are bound to bow with cheerfulness and resignation, been called away from the exalted station which he has occupied during the space of one little month. On the 3d of March I took his hand in Mr. Granger's parlour, at Gadsby's, in Washington, and congratulated him, but more especially his country, on the auspicious event of his election ; and on the following day I witnessed, at the capitol of the nation, the consummation of the people's will, in his solemn pledge before the Almighty to devote all his faculties to the just government of the Republic. And I heard the accents in which " the old man eloquent " poured forth the aspirations of his honest heart for the prosperity of that people, and the preservation of the free institutions of that Republic ; and in one short month — one month of unremitted labour and ceaseless anxiety, in which he was taught the painful truth that " uneasy lies the head that wears the crown " — that heart has ceased to beat, the account so auspiciously opened has been suddenly closed, and his virtuous intentions now sleep with him in the silent grave.

General Harrison is the first President who has died in office, and Mr. Tyler will be the first Vice-President who has ever exercised the executive functions. He will be President, if he lives, during the long period of three years and eleven months. If he carries out the government on the principles avowed by his illustrious chief, and to which his able cabinet stands virtually pledged, all will go well, for Governor Tyler is an able man and true patriot; but there is some danger that his opinions in the leading measures, which we in this part of the country consider important to the restoration of public confidence, such as the establishment of a national bank, and the annulling of the sub-treasury system, do not coincide with theirs. He is a Virginian, and we think their policy on these subjects fraught with danger. If this, unfortunately, be the case, the cabinet must, of course, be dissolved, and all our bright hopes, in their virtuous and patriotic administration of the government, be overthrown. May we not trust in the goodness and mercy of Heaven, that the blow we have experienced may not be rendered more afflictive by the occurrence of so disastrous an event.

General Harrison, in his last moments, expressed much solicitude on this subject, and his last words expressed a confidence in the wisdom of his successor. Governor Tyler was absent at the time of this melancholy event, and an express was immediately sent to him.

There seems to be very little doubt that the President's illness was brought on, and its severity increased, by the constant labour and deprivation of comfort brought upon him by his new duties. He told his friends that his time was so much occupied that he had been prevented from performing the necessary functions of nature. The sudden change from the quiet occupations of his life for several years past to the turmoil of public business, and the sacrifice of his personal convenience and comfort to the impracticable task of attending to every man's business, had been too much for the debilitated frame of a man nearly seventy years of age; the strength of the mortal covering of clay was not commensurate with the ardour of the immortal spirit within.

April 6. — On the receipt of the news here yesterday morning a spontaneous exhibition of the badges of woe was seen throughout the city; the flags on all public places, as well as on the shipping in the harbour (not excepting Tammany Hall), were exhibited half-mast, and some of them shrouded in black. The courts in session immediately adjourned. The newspapers were clothed in mourning, all but the " Evening Post," whose malignant, black-hearted editor, Bryant, says he regrets the death of General Harrison only because he did not live long enough to prove his incapacity for the office of President. Most of the places of amusement were closed in the evening. The last words uttered by the President, as heard by Dr. Worthington, were these : " Sir, I wish you to understand the true principles of the government ; I wish them carried out, nothing more."

APRIL 7. — This volume of my journal commences at a moment when great grief overspreads the American nation, and doubt and uncertainty, mingled with some degree of solicitude, has taken possession of the public mind in regard to the political prospects of the country, and the bearing they must inevitably have upon individual interests. The patriotic ruler of this great country, called from the bosom of retirement to carry out the great measure which a large majority of the people deem essential to their welfare, has just been called from his elevated station to render an account of his stewardship while upon the earth, the most important part of which was comprised in the little month immediately preceding his lamented decease, and which, according to my imperfect judgment, was calculated not only to secure the approbation of all good men, but to give a bright presage for a better condition of things.

The mantle of rule falls suddenly and unexpectedly upon the shoulders of the Vice-President for a period, if he should live so long, nearly equal to a full presidential term, — for good, or for evil. We may be permitted to hope for the former, of which the honourable character of Governor Tyler would seem to be a guarantee ; but the times are so ticklish, that the effects of this change are looked to with deep anxiety. Never was there a time when political measures were brought so closely home to men's bosoms, and men are compelled to be politicians in despite of their natural dis-inclination.

The news of the break-down of the Bank of the United States and of the confinement and indictment of McLeod caused great excitement in London, and poor Brother Jonathan gets all he deserves, and something more, from his brother, Mr. Bull. The greatest dissatisfaction was caused by the violent and ill-judged report of Mr. Pickens, in the House of Representatives, and its having been adopted by a strong majority ; but, if they would only suppress their rage and wait a while, they would see the gentleman who was foremost in the opposition to that report placed in the cabinet as Postmaster-General under the new administration, which might be considered an evidence that the principles of that ill-judged report were not to be adopted by the present ruling party. But the English papers say that an absolute demand has been made on our government to surrender the mischief-making loafer, and in case of refusal that Mr. Cox is to demand his passport. It is also reported that a squadron is ordered off our coast to carry their hostile measures into effect. If this be so, the difficulties in the case may be greatly increased ; but it is likely that the love of mar-vellous and startling subjects, which are sought for with equal avidity by British and American readers, is gratified there, as here, by the unscrupulous writers for lying newspapers.

Funeral Ceremonies. This is the day set apart in Washington for the funeral of the late President. It has been observed here with great solemnity, and a sort of gloom has overspread not only the appearance of the city, but the countenances of the citizens. In accordance with the programme published by the joint special committee of the common council, all business was simultaneously suspended at noon. The banks and insurance offices, with the stores generally, throughout the city were closed. The flags were suspended from the public places, theatres, and hotels, half-mast, and some tastefully enshrouded in black. The vessels in the har-bour bore a similar badge of grief until two o'clock.

APRIL 9. — I am invited by the committee of arrangements of the corporation to assist in the funeral ceremonies of to-morrow as pall-bearer at this great affair. The following are the names of the pall-bearers ; the number, twenty-six, was made to correspond with the number of States in the Union : Gen. Morgan Lewis, John W. Hardenbrook, Major William Popham, Peter R. Livingston, Stephen Allen, Isaac Lawrence, Aaron Clark, John Rathbone, Cornelius W. Lawrence, Edward Taylor, Walter Bowne, Philip Hone, Chancellor Kent, George Griffin, Richard Riker, John L. Morgan, John Targee, Sylvanus Miller, Peter A. Jay, Leffert Lefferts, John Wyckoff, Jeremiah Johnson, Daniel Winship, William Furman, Peter Bonnet, Robert Bach.

APRIL 10. — This was the day designated by the joint special committee of the common council of New York and Brooklyn for the grand funeral solemnities to commemorate the death of Gen. William Henry Harrison, late President of the United States, who, after having responded to the call of his fellow-citizens, and worthily fulfilled the high functions of the exalted station to which their suffrages have called him, during the brief period of a little month, was called by the sudden mandate of divine power to lay down his earthly honours, and seek in another and a better world, it may be hoped, a brighter reward of his virtuous actions.

The corporation of the city, a large majority of whom were political opponents of General Harrison and his party, have done themselves great credit by the zeal and spirit with which this great affair was planned and carried into execution. The arrangements of the committee were made upon the grandest scale, and the citizens of all ranks, professions, and parties entered into their measures with a full and spontaneous expression of the most profound grief. Business of every description was suspended ; all the public places, markets, hotels, the shops, and many private houses on the route of the procession, were covered with festoons and hangings of black, and other mournful devices. Minute-guns were fired, and the bells tolled during the four hours' progress of the melancholy parade.   Flags were suspended intertwined with black crape across the streets, and the whole city was clothed in the habiliments of woe.   Ours is a remarkable population in such matters; once satisfy their judgment that the call made upon them either to mourn or to rejoice is a proper one, and their spontaneous expression of feeling bursts forth without bonds or limitation.   On this occasion, as in the reception of Lafayette, the populace seemed to take the affair into their own hands.   The committee of arrangements published in advance an admirable programme, and the people, one and all, became the actors in the great drama.   All was order and regularity in the tremendous mass of humanity which formed the greatest civil and military procession ever witnessed in the city, for spectators occupied every window, and the house-tops, or covered the entire streets, leaving only a space sufficient for the passage of the procession.

APRIL 17. — Mr. Biddle, late president of the Bank

Bank of the
United States. of the United States, he who so lately was incumbered with the load of his greatness, to whom men's knees were bent, and the beavers came off of their own accord, and who is now so fallen that there are " none so poor to do him reverence," — this financial Lucifer has published three letters on the subject of his connection with the bank, in which he seeks to prove (and, it would appear, with tolerable success) that the ruin of the institution is not attributable to him, but to the jealousy, cupidity, and negligence of the directors; that when he said, on leaving the office of president, that its affairs were prosperous, they were so in fact, and that the loss of its immense capital was all brought about in the short space of time subsequent to his abdication.   If this be so, these gentlemen cannot be charged with a want of industry, for certainly the road to ruin, smooth and easy as it is, was never before travelled with half the speed.   Railroad progression is a snail's pace to this.   These letters are admirably written, like everything that comes from the pen of the last president of the bank, and are calculated to make warm blood in Philadelphia, and to cause

astonishment elsewhere. One precious disclosure is made which must brand with infamy the whole concern. Mr. Biddle asserts distinctly that certain money operations planned and executed sometime since by the committee of directors, but since he relinquished the presidency, were intended to compel the New York banks to suspend specie payments at the time when those of Philadelphia were compelled to adopt that measure, or rather, to use Mr. Biddle's more emphatic language, "to ruin the New York banks."

This neighbourly operation was to be effected by drawing bills on the house of Hottinguer & Co., in Paris, without funds and without advice, and with a knowledge that they would not be accepted for any amount beyond the funds in hand. These bills were sold in New York for any price they would bring for New York funds, the specie drawn from the banks to be remitted to meet the bills ; and thus the New York banks were to be broken, and brought down from their high and honourable position to a level with themselves. But the attempt was signally frustrated ; demands were suddenly and unexpectedly made in one day for $1,200,000 in specie, and notaries were ready to protest the drafts if (as was supposed) they could not be promptly met ; but they *were* promptly met ; those drafts and all others were paid without a moment's demur, and our friendly neighbours were left to mourn over their unsuccessful attempt to *equalize the currency*, and to make good the loss upon this hopeful speculation.

MAY 27. — Yesterday the great Conservative dinner was given to Nathaniel P. Tallmadge, United States senator, at the saloon, Tivoli Gardens. Five or six hundred persons, Whigs and Conservatives, were present. George W. Bruen presided; the intended president, John L. Lawrence, being detained in Albany. A great many toasts were drunk, speeches and letters of excuse from great men read, and the affair appears to have gone off with enthusiasm and good feeling.

Dinner to Mr. Tallmadge.

JUNE 2. — There is much difference of opinion amongst the wiseacres of the Whig party about the message; some say it is not sufficiently explicit on the leading measures to be adopted by those who rule the roost in Congress. I think otherwise; it is a plain, sensible speech. The President says there must be a new fiscal agent, a sort of Jupiter to help the State wagon out of the mud. Pet banks, sub-treasury and treasury notes have been repudiated by the people, and now he leaves the matter with their representatives, and whatever they agree upon shall have his sanction, provided he does not deem it unconstitutional. If this does not mean a national bank, it is difficult to say what it does mean. Mr. Tyler is a good, old-fashioned Republican, and with his able cabinet will do all that can be done to get things right.

I find, on referring to my journal, that on the 12th day of March I dined with a party at Mr. Robert B. Minturn's, and remember well the dreadful walk I had from his house, pretty late that night. It snowed and rained very hard, and the wind blew with such violence that I found it almost impossible to navigate up Broadway; and to carry an umbrella was out of the question. In referring to that walk, I have always said it was the most tempestuous night to which I was ever exposed.

JUNE 10. — The same party which dined on Tuesday at Mr. Russell's (excepting Mr. Kernochan) dined to-day at James G. King's, at Highwood, in addition to which we had Mr. Daniel Lord, Jr., and Dr. Wilkes. Everything about this magnificent place is in the finest order; our dinner was capital, the weather superlatively fine, and the entertainment in all respects worthy of the host and hostess.

JUNE 14. — Fanny Ellsler appeared this evening at the Park Theatre, after her long tour of triumph and profit to Havana, New Orleans, etc. She performed in the ballet of "Nathalie," and danced the Cachuca. The house was so full that it could hold no more. She was well received and much applauded, and on being called out after the performance made a very neat little speech in broken English, which every one in the audience thought was worth his dollar. I went with our lovely neighbour, Eliza Russell. Some of the newspapers — the " Commercial Advertiser," " Evening Signal," and " Tribune " — have, with a degree of insufferable arrogance, undertaken to write down this amusement, and abuse those who go to see it, calling them fools and idiots, and lying abominably about the proofs of admiration bestowed upon this graceful *danseuse*. This sort of interference between men and their consciences, and dictation as to matters of taste, has become very common of late, and people seem determined not to submit to it. I have no doubt that many, like myself, went to the theatre to evince their disapprobation of this kind of impertinence.

JUNE 15. — The House of Representatives is all in
Congress.   confusion. Mr. Adams has thrown a firebrand among
the combustibles of the South, and Mr. Wise, the most inflammable among them, blazes away, to the utter destruction of all that is orderly and dignified in legislation. The vote by which the twenty-first rule was rescinded, which rejected without reading all petitions on the subject of slavery (which vote was carried through by the pertinacity of Mr. Adams), has been rescinded, and another vote carried, which annuls the resolution adopting the rules of the last session; so that, after being in session a fortnight, and the most violent proceedings having taken place, the House is precisely in the same situation it was at the commencement of the session, with no organization and no rules to govern their proceedings. The Whigs neglect the urgent business which occasioned the meeting of Congress at this unusual season, and indulge in violence and recrimination against each other, and the Loco-focos take every occasion to " fan the embers." The South is arrayed against the North. Mr. Adams brings forward " in season and out of season " his anti-slavery opposition; and Mr. Wise drives over friend and foe, calling the best men of the party, with which he pretends to act, nullifiers. He spoke yesterday six hours on this

exciting subject, to the bitter annoyance of all the members, who wish to get through the important business of the extra session. He is either crazy, or has not so good an excuse for his conduct. He apes John Randolph, without a scintillation of the genius which gave to that talented and eccentric man so great a popularity. He pretends to think for himself, and act as he pleases, regardless of the opinion of his friends and of the bonds which should unite together gentlemen who are honestly engaged in a patriotic cause, and virtually pledged to honest measures. It would be happy for the country, and I doubt not agreeable to their colleagues, if the fox of Massachusetts and the wild-cat of Virginia were both tied up in some menagerie for the remainder of the session.

JULY 5.—This has been celebrated as the sixty-fifth anniversary of American Independence : the usual military parade ; booths at the park ; ringing of bells ; firing of guns in a regular way, and " Independence file firing " (as we used to call it in the artillery) of muskets, pistols, and crackers from the juvenile lazzaroni of the city, to the bitter annoyance of all persons of quiet habits and sensitive nerves. Added to all these, and the divers amusements at theatres, gardens, and other public places, there was a great procession of temperance societies, with banners, water-carts, and other diluting emblems and devices, with Benjamin F. Butler in the midst, who was the orator of the day, and enforced, no doubt, by his own precept and example, sound doctrines of temperance, in all things but politics, and honesty, too, when it is not crossed by party discipline. Another gentleman, a Mr. Brownson, delivered an oration to another section of the teetotallers. This is all very well, and may be made productive of good, if it be not perverted by designing men to improper ends, or led by mistaken zealots out of the paths of cool reason, in which case reaction may be produced highly injurious to morality, temperance, and good order. Governor Seward came in town to review the troops, which ceremony I witnessed in front of the Astor House. His Excellency did us the honour of a visit yesterday, and I called upon him just in time to "see the review" (as Caleb Quotem says) from the window of his room. I dined at Blanchard's Globe Hotel, with the State Society of the Cincinnati.   The dinner was capital, but the interest of the occasion was lessened by the absence of the little band (only five or six in number) of original members.   Their venerable limbs have no longer the strength to bear them to the festive hall, and the independence they fought for must in future be celebrated without their presence.

"Courier and Enquirer."   Webb, after sundry mutterings of distant thunder foretelling a storm, and suppressing with considerable difficulty an occasional outbreak of his mortification at not being appointed postmaster of New York, has at length broken ground in his papers of yesterday and to-day in the regular attack upon President Tyler, his cabinet, and several of the leading Whigs and Conservatives.   There is certainly some reason to complain of timidity and something like a time-serving policy on the part of the cabinet who enlisted under General Harrison, and do not find it so entirely conformable to their principles to adopt the half-and-half Virginia policy of his successor.   But it is ungenerous to charge them with sacrificing their principles in order to retain office.   God knows they sacrifice enough in remaining where they are, and deserve the people's gratitude for their patriotism.   What would be the situation of the Whig party, and what would become of the reforms, which their elevation to office gave the country a right to hope for, if they were to resign at such a time as this? Every day brings us fresh cause to lament the untimely decease of the "good President."   It was, to be sure, the signal for all the discordant materials of the Whig party to ferment and boil over, or, rather, the Conservatives, for the true Whigs are all true men yet; but the agitation is about to subside, the scum and froth will soon settle down, and the political pot boil once more heartily and quietly, notwithstanding the Loco-foco fire *which, without the slightest regard to the people's welfare and the nation's health, is treacherously supplied to keep it in uneasy motion.   In the mean

time here comes this Colonel Webb, a *soi-disant* leader of the Whig
daily press, a self-created fugleman of the party, who has not been
long enough in the ranks to entitle him to command, with language such as this to feed the flame of discord, and cause (so far
as he has influence to effect it) the pot to boil over.

Bank for
Savings.

JULY 12. — I was elected yesterday president of the
Bank for Savings, in the place of Mr. Pintard, whose
resignation was accepted at the last monthly meeting
of the trustees.   I cannot but feel gratified at having been elevated
by the unanimous vote of my associates to the honourable station
of president of the greatest associated institution in the United
States, — greatest in the influence which it exerts over the community; greatest in the amount of business which it transacts, and
by which it is drawn into intimate contact with the people; and
greatest (I think I may from experience assert) in the good which
it has already done and all it may hereafter (with a continuance
of the blessings of Almighty God) be the means of doing.

JULY 19. — On Saturday, Mr. and Mrs. Howland, my wife and
I, went on a visit to Mr. Thomas W. Ludlow's, below Yonkers, —
a drive of eight or nine miles, principally along the valley of the
Saw-Mill river; a more beautiful drive is not to be found anywhere.   The trees are glorious, the lands diversified by hills and
valleys, and the whole in the highest state of cultivation.   Mr.
Ludlow has lately taken possession of his new house on the bank
of the Hudson, — a cottage in the true Gothic style of architecture,
replete with every convenience and elegance, and the situation
splendid.   We were kindly entertained by old Mr. Robert Morris
and his wife until Mr. and Mrs. Ludlow returned home from a
drive.   We had a pleasant visit, and returned to dinner, after
which the same party, with the addition of Mr. and Mrs. William
H. Aspinwall (who were visitors, like ourselves) and the young
folks, went on another pleasant excursion up the valley to Tarrytown and around by the river.   In the course of our drive we
went to see Mr. Paulding's magnificent house, yet unfinished, on

the bank below Tarrytown.   It is an immense edifice of white or
gray marble, resembling a baronial castle, or rather a Gothic mon-
astery, with towers, turrets, and trellises; minarets, mosaics, and
mouse-holes; archways, armories, and air-holes; peaked windows
and pinnacled roofs, and many other fantastics too tedious to
enumerate, the whole constituting an edifice of gigantic size, with
no room in it; great cost and little comfort, which, if I mistake
not, will one of these days be designated as " Paulding's folly."   But
the situation, the prospect, and the form of the grounds are all
admirable; with good taste and a great deal of money it may be
made to equal Hyde Park.   As for the splendid marble house, I
would not exchange Howland's plain, respectable, airy mansion,
embosomed in one of the most charming groves I ever saw, for a
dozen of it.

On Sunday morning we all went to the Episcopal Church, near
the landing, where the service was performed by the respectable
pastor, my old acquaintance, Dr. Creighton, who officiates alternately, morning and afternoon, there and at Tarrytown.   We found
a great number of our friends, residents in the neighbourhood, who
form the congregation of this pleasant little temple of the Lord,
whose kind greetings and pressing invitations gave us abundant
reason to believe that our visit in these parts might be very agreeably and advantageously prolonged.   After a hasty dinner of cold
meats, the usual Sunday fare at Howland's, we attended the afternoon service in the Presbyterian Church, situated near to that in
which our morning's devotions were performed, but less to my satisfaction.   Returned home to the well-regulated, cheerful, happy
place of our sojournment, ate a good supper, united in the religious
services of the family, which are performed in a devout, unostentatious manner every morning and evening, and retired to rest.

> "And thus did pass away, brightly as it began,
>   A rural Sabbath day."

After an early breakfast this morning, Mr. and Mrs. Aspinwall,

my wife and I, drove to Dobbs's Ferry, took the " Kosciusko " at
half-past eight o'clock, and in two hours we were at home.   Our
visit has been exceedingly pleasant ; everything at my friend Howland's wears the aspect of comfort, happiness, and elegant hospitality. God grant that the estimable inmates may live long to enjoy
the blessings of which they are so well deserving !

JULY 30. — The long agony is over. The man who
Bank Veto.   was elected by the Whigs to the second office in the
government, and has by the death of the *good Presi-
dent* been unfortunately elevated to the first, has put his veto upon
the most important measure of Whig policy. The bank bill having
been in his possession ten days was returned to the Senate yesterday, with the President's objections, in a message, which, in my
humble judgment, is one of the weakest and most puerile State
papers we have ever had from the Executive Department. It is
all his own ; for every member of the cabinet is opposed to its principles, and not one of them (if it were not so) would be desirous
to claim any part of the paternity of this confused, egotistical, in-
conclusive argument. It wants more talent than Mr. Tyler has
evinced in this document to " make the worse appear the better
cause." " He has always been opposed to a bank," and therefore
to sanction one would " be to commit a crime which he would not
willingly commit to gain any earthly reward, and which would justly
subject him to the ridicule and scorn of all virtuous men." If this
is not the quintessence of " twaddle," I know not what is. Why
did he accept the nomination for Vice-President, involving the
dreadful contingency which has occurred, opposed, as he says he
was, to a national bank in any form, — one of the cardinal points to
which was directed the ultimate success of the party which nominated him. Governor Tyler has, however, succeeded in making
friends of the mammon of unrighteousness. Tammany Hall was in
ecstasies on the receipt of the news. Mr. Walker, of Mississippi,
when that jackass Benton was making a fuss about some fellow in
the gallery of the Senate who hissed on the reading of the veto

message, begged his *friend* to withdraw his motion. "His heart was so full of joy and gratitude to the acting President" for his course in this business, that he could not bear to have those feelings interrupted by anything of a less pleasant nature. Poor Tippecanoe! it was an evil hour that "Tyler too" was added to make out the line. There was rhyme, but no reason, in it.

AUGUST 19. — Washington Irving is very ill with a bilious fever, at his cottage at Tarrytown. I regret exceedingly to hear that his case is considered dangerous. A newspaper, giving an account of his illness, attributed it to his excursion with me to the coal-mines and Honesdale. It may be so; but he certainly was never better in health and spirits than during the whole time of our pleasant trip, and he and I separated on our arrival here, delighted with all things we had done and seen, and with no indication that either of us was the worse in health, spirits, or experience. As the boys say in such cases, he will die *after* it, but I should say, not, by any means, of it.

AUGUST 26. — Died, on Saturday last, at the great age of ninety-four, Mr. Henry Brevoort. He lived all his life upon his farm, now in Broadway, a short distance above my house, which cost him a few hundred dollars, and is now worth to his heirs a half million.

Edward Everett's Nomination.   AUGUST 30. — One nomination has not been acted upon by the Senate, and rumour says that it will be rejected, — that of Edward Everett, of Massachusetts, as Minister to England. The result of this, in my judgment, is of more consequence than President's Tyler's veto of the bank, the rejection of all the great Whig measures, the dissolution of the cabinet, and all the other mischievous consequences realized and anticipated as the fruits of Whig inconsistency and Southern impracticability. If Mr. Everett's nomination is not confirmed it will be upon the ground that he is a Northern man, and, by the inference, an Abolitionist. And some general observation on the subject of slavery in the abstract, which was used by the gentleman whilst Governor of Massachusetts, is now brought up to strengthen the unholy cabal. This rejection cannot be accomplished except by the votes of two or three *soi-disant* Whigs or Conservatives from the slaveholding States, united with the unflinching profligate phalanx of the opposition, who would reject the great apostle of the Gentiles if he came before them (and no doubt he would) covered with the mantle of Whig principles.

This dreadful question comes now broadly and clearly before the American people; all extraneous matter is cast away from it, and Edward Everett stands forth the embodiment of a principle upon which is to be made an issue of the deepest solemnity, one on which the union of the States and the prosperity of the country depend. Governor Everett is acknowledged on all hands to be perfectly qualified in every respect for the dignified appointment to which he has been nominated. No mere party objections can be brought to bear against him, for the opposition cannot hope or expect by defeating him to get a man of their own; nor is it possible that any predilections in favour of Mr. Stevenson, the present Minister, if such existed strong enough to overcome party preference, could have any influence in this case, for that gentleman has solicited his recall, and is waiting in London for the arrival of his successor. The case, therefore, stands in its naked beauty or deformity. If the nomination is rejected it will be by the union of pseudo-Whigs with exterminating Loco-focos, to punish a patriot and a statesman because he is in favour of the right of petition, which it would be treason in a public man to deny, and because he refused to exclaim with Mr. McDuffie and the other hotspurs of the South, that slavery is a positive blessing to the land. Perhaps it is well that this star of baleful influence should appear now when the political horizon is enveloped in darkness, and " the planets shoot madly from the spheres." Let us settle all the hash at once. If Everett's nomination is rejected upon the grounds above stated, and the people of the East and the North and the Northwest submit to it, they deserve to change places with Mr. McDuffie's troops in South Carolina, Virginia, Georgia, and Alabama.

SEPTEMBER 6. — On my arrival in Albany I found **Second Veto.** bad news from Washington. President Tyler sent in to the House of Representatives, where the bill originated, his veto message of the act to create a fiscal corporation, a national bank, framed, as was thought, to make it acceptable to the fastidious palate of the accidental executive. The message is weak and devoid of argument as the former one. He was always opposed to a national bank, and therefore his oath and conscience forbids him to sanction one. A very good sort of Jacksonian argument, which, being the only one, we are bound to abide by. Congress has done all they can, and will adjourn on Monday, unless the measures necessary to be adopted in relation to a disgraceful occurrence, which I am about to have the mortification of recording here, should render a longer session necessary.

Thursday is distinguished by another black mark in **Fracas in Congress.** the congressional proceedings of the President's veto. On that day a fracas occurred between two of the hotspurs of the South, which caps the climax of vulgarity and violence, so common of late, and which have rendered the American Congress little better than the National Assembly of France during the reign of terror, when *poissardes* and *sans-culottes* controlled their proceedings, and the guillotine carried their bloody edicts into execution. In the course of a debate on the bill making appropriations for diplomatic services, a motion being before the House to dispense with the *chargé* at Naples, Wise, of Virginia, whose conduct of late has been that of an infuriated madman, charged Stanley, of North Carolina, who is nearly as rash and hot-headed as himself, with inconsistency, and applied to him the *gentlemanly* and *parliamentary* epithets " little and contemptible ; " to which Stanley, of course, replied in language equally mild and conciliating ; soon after which Wise left his seat, crossed over to Stanley, and renewed the dispute in vituperative terms. Warm words passed. Wise invited Stanley to follow him into the lobby, which he declined. Wise told him he was " beneath his contempt."

Stanley called him a liar. Wise struck him; the blow was returned, and the hall of the House of Representatives was defiled by a thumping match between two men who call themselves gentlemen, and represent the chivalry of the South. The House became a scene of confusion; the Speaker in vain attempted to restore order. Whilst the main battle was raging, several agreeable little codicil fights were gotten up between the friends and champions of the combatants, the principal one of which was enacted by Colonel Butler, of Kentucky, and Mr. Arnold, of Tennessee. I blush to acknowledge that all four of these ruffians call themselves Whigs. Such a weight is sufficient to break down any party.

After the fight was over, Mr. Wise apologized to the House for his conduct, which he attributed to his having received the lie from Stanley (a pretty hard word to swallow), and offered to make any atonement. Mr. Stanley said he had no apology to make; they might do with him as they pleased, or he would resign, but he gloried in having punished his assailant, and regretted that interruption prevented him from giving him all he merited. A committee was appointed to investigate the circumstances and report. Many members were in favour of expelling Wise *sur le champ*, which, in my judgment, would have been the best course, but not that perhaps which comported best with the dignity (if any may be left) of the House.

Mr. Wise's conduct and deportment, during the whole of the last and present sessions, has been unruly, arrogant, and ungentlemanly, and if he is not crazy he has no excuse; his expulsion would give equal satisfaction to all parties. He calls himself a Whig, but he has done the Whig party more injury than any half-dozen of their most violent political opponents. These men may escape punishment, from the anxiety of the members to adjourn and return to their families, after this painful and vexatious session; but if I were one, I would never consent to rise until this committee reports, and the House shall have taken suitable steps to vindicate their own characters and that of the country.

SEPTEMBER 14. — The prediction of Mr. Webster is verified. The cabinet, with the exception of Mr. Webster and Mr. Granger, sent in their resignations on Saturday, which were accepted by President Tyler, and their successors nominated to the Senate.

The select committee, of which that prince of demagogues, Ingersoll, of Philadelphia, was chairman, reported on Saturday on the case of Wise and Stanley, and Colonel Dawson announced to the House that the business had been amicably settled between the parties. The House accepted the report, which slurred over the matter in the most approved manner; the dignity of the people's representatives remains insulted, and in future every well-behaved man, whose abilities and patriotism may entitle him to take a part in the deliberations of the House, and is ambitious of serving his country and justifying the choice of his constituents, must do it at the risk of being bullied, brow-beaten, and perhaps otherwise beaten, by Mr. Wise and other Southern hotspurs.

SEPTEMBER 15. — Edward Everett's nomination as Minister to England has been confirmed by the Senate by a vote of twenty-three to nineteen; so that dark and portentous cloud is happily removed from our distracted political horizon. There is enough to excite angry feelings, and disturb the tranquillity of the country, without leaving that firebrand unquenched.

SEPTEMBER 20. — The " New York Herald " is now understood to be the champion of President Tyler; and, if report speaks true, its correspondent in Washington (a person named Parmely) is his confidential adviser, enjoys in the most enlarged degree the run of the presidential kitchen, and is favoured with copies of his messages and other public acts before they have been submitted to his cabinet ministers. For these high privileges and distinguished favours he, of course, evinces his gratitude, and does his share of the dirty jobs about the palace, by abusing in the most gross and vulgar language the members of the late cabinet; and Mr. Ewing, the late Secretary of the Treasury, having been the most prominent among the abdicators, comes in for the largest share of this reptile's venom. A long article is published in the " Herald," filled with the grossest vituperation against this gentleman, against whom the tongue of slander has never until now been raised.

SEPTEMBER 2. — The ex-Postmaster General came to see me on Monday evening, when I was not at home ; and I called upon him yesterday, and had a long and interesting talk with him about the unhappy state of things which had lately existed at Washington, and the difficulties and mortifications to which he has been subjected in the discharge of his official duties by the faithless and wayward conduct of Mr. accidental President Tyler. To the embarrassment which this conduct has caused him, more than to the famous veto of the bank bill, the resignation of the Postmaster General is to be attributed. The most active and violent opposers of the Whig administration have been retained in important post-offices against his most urgent remonstrances, to serve the ulterior views of the President and to create personal partisans out of political adversaries ; by which temporizing policy our friends have been disgusted, and their accustomed exertions in the " good cause " been paralyzed and rendered ineffectual, and for the sins of omission the head of the department has received all the blame. Mr. Granger mentioned several cases of this kind of the most flagrant nature. His representations have been disregarded. Assurances have been given from time to time and promises made, which have been violated and broken with a want of good faith and the comity supposed to exist between official characters standing in so intimate relations with each other, for which no excuse can be found but in the utter inability of the present Executive for the discharge of his high and responsible duties. Among other matters, of which I have now been for the first time made acquainted, is one in which I was concerned, and which satisfies me that Mr. Granger has been true to me ; he informed me that on one occasion he succeeded so far in obtaining

Mr. Tyler's consent to the removal of Mr. Coddington, and my appointment, that he was about to leave him, with directions to send up my name, when he was called back and told that more time was wanted to determine upon the propriety of removing an active and violent political opponent from the important office of postmaster of New York, and putting in his place a true and undoubted Whig. This vacillating and time-serving policy has broken up the party, and my friend Granger could not remain in a place where he was exposed to contumely and deprived of power.

SEPTEMBER 23.— Having received from the President and Directors of the New York and Erie Railroad Company an invitation to attend the ceremony of the opening of the first section of the road from Piermont, on the North river, through the county of Rockland, to Goshen, Orange county, I was one of four hundred and fifty guests who assembled yesterday morning on board the steamboat "Utica," and started on our excursion at eight o'clock. Such a crowd of important and distinguished men, official and unofficial, I have seldom or never seen collected. An accident like that of the "Lexington" on the Sound, or the "Erie" on Lake Erie, would have vacated more offices, broken up more establishments, and broken more hearts than a seven-years war or a general conflagration of the city. We had the Governor, judges of all grades, the bishop of the diocese and other clergymen, the Mayor, Recorder and members of the Common Council, ex-mayors, merchants, bankers, generals, distinguished men from other States, Whigs and Loco-focos, pipe-layers and editors of newspapers; and thus huddled together, with scarcely standing-room on the deck of the steamer, we arrived at the company's pier at Piermont, twenty-five miles from New York, were stowed away as close as Loco-foco matches in a box (but happily not rendered equally combustible by attraction) into the cars prepared for the occasion, some of which were temporary platforms with seats of rough plank, calculated for one hundred persons each, and exposed to a constant shower of sparks and cinders like those which accompany a visit to Vesuvius or Ætna, only not half so romantic and worthy to be talked and written about. Thus placed, and *toted* by two whizzing, snorting, fire-and-smoke-vomiting locomotives, we set off under the discharge of cannon, the hurrahs in English and Irish of the men, and the occasional waving of handkerchiefs (when they had them) of the women, by which we were also saluted on the whole line of the road. We went on rather slowly, to be sure, but fast enough, perhaps, for so great a weight on a new and untried road, and arrived at Goshen, forty-six miles, at two o'clock. Here the cannon were firing, bells ringing, and such a collection of people from the adjacent country as were probably never before assembled in the "land of Goshen."

SEPTEMBER 29. — The noble steam-frigate which was built in New York, on the plans and under the direction of Robert and George L. Schuyler, sailed (I must write sailed until some other word is invented ; but how can it be called sailing when no sails are used?) this morning. I was one of a large party of gentlemen invited to go down in her. We assembled on board a steamboat at the foot of Liberty street, at eleven o'clock, whence we were taken to the " Kamschatka," lying in the stream, and by noon the anchor was weighed and the tremendous mass of timber and iron put in motion down the bay. It had been raining in the morning, but the sun came out about this time, and her voyage down to the Hook was very pleasant.

Sailing of the "Kamschatka."

SEPTEMBER 30. — Mr. Stanley, Wise's competitor in the disgraceful fracas which lately occurred in the House of Representatives, although a clever man and a good fellow, is fiery as a Loco-foco match, and as easily ignited by hard rubbing ; and so small and boyish in his appearance that Pickens once contemptuously called him Cock-Robin, and he in return let out a broadside of cannon-balls, bomb-shells, and chain shot, each apparently larger than the calibre of the gun itself. It must have been funny to hear this little man with a big heart

Congressional Lyrics.

boast of the fisticuffs he inflicted upon Mr. Wise, and what he would have done if they had not been separated. These remarks are suggested by reading the following nursery lines, taken from a Western paper, as a sort of heading to an account of the congressional battle : —

> " Stanley, you should never let
>   Your angry passions rise;
> Your little hands were never made
> To pummel Mr. Wise."

Columbia College. OCTOBER 5. — The Commencement of Columbia College took place to-day, in St. George's Church, Beekman street. I walked in procession from the college, and remained in the church until nearly four o'clock. The medals were presented, the degrees conferred, and most of the other ceremonies performed by President Duer, whose feeble health and sickly appearance created a strong sensation of sympathy and apprehension among his friends that he was risking too far his impaired powers ; but he got through it, and boasted that he was not fatigued ; but I am afraid there was more pride than sincerity in the declaration. The speaking was generally very good ; the valedictory, especially, was a fine composition, well delivered, but too long, and the music, a double dose. Thirty-one of the senior class graduated, of whom the following delivered exercises: James Emott, Jr., George W. Collord, Oliver Wolcott Gibbs, James H. M. Knox, H. T. E. Foster, John J. Townsend, John Rankin, Robert Le Roy, Jr., T. B. Dibblee, and Robert D. Van Voorhis.

Picnic Dinner. OCTOBER 16. — The following gentlemen dined with me : Francis March, J. T. Brigham, Charles H. Russell, M. H. Grinnell, J. de Peyster Ogden, James W. Otis, Charles A. Davis, Charles A. Heckscher, John A. King, Robert Tyler, son of the President. This was a picnic for wine ; each gentleman sent his bottle of Madeira. I decanted and numbered them in such a way that nobody could recognize his wine but by its taste. There was a great display; it is not extravagant to say that such another could not be made out of an equal number of other wines. After tasting around, a vote was taken, and a bottle furnished by Mr. Grinnell bore off the palm by all the votes except two; this was wine formerly belonging to Mr. John B. Coles. Besides this, our board was graced by Kirby wine, March and Benson, 1809; Butler, Helicon, etc.

Ogden Hoffman, Butler King, of Georgia, Prescott Hall, and Judge Kent were kept away by sickness or business. The latter gentleman is working like a slave in his new vocation, to clear away the accumulation of business in his court, caused by his predecessor being less active and industrious than himself; but I fear it will be the labour of Sisyphus, — the more work he does the more he will make to do, for there is always burden enough for the back of the willing horse. Judge Kent was employed in the morning in sentencing one wretch to the gallows, and another to the State prison, and I should have thought that was grave work enough for one day; but he proceeded in the afternoon to try civil causes, and so lost his dinner, but sent his bottle to represent him. Mr. Grinnell brought Mr. Robert Tyler, who, by his request, I had previously invited; he is the young man who married Miss Penelope Cooper, remarkable for nothing, that I could discover, but a very strong resemblance to his father.

Governor Marcy said once, in the Senate of the **Spoils.** United States, "To the victors belong the spoils." This is a maxim acted upon by the political parties in our country, but not usually avowed so openly as in this instance. But the Romans, in the plenitude of the power of the mighty republic, when she was mistress of the world, when monarchs bowed at her footstool and no nation existed except by her sufferance, had the prettiest notion of spoils; not such as our American senator had in his eye, which are extorted from one portion of the citizens to be bestowed upon the other, but those acquired from foreign nations as the fruits of victory, the price of peace, and wages of corruption.

This was the time of Rome's greatest power, but not of her greatest glory; *that* had departed with her Catos, her Ciceros, and her Fabii. Honour and patriotism had been succeeded by rapine and corruption, and the Roman name, though still feared, was no longer honoured. The only consolation humanity derives from the lesson is, that the very spoils which she wrung with their liberties from tributary nations was the cause of her downfall.

OCTOBER 25. — My birthday, — I am sixty-one years old; and it does not require a record in " black and white " to remind me of it. It appears to me that I am more than a year older than I was last year on this day. How much faster we go down than up hill, and how much less time there is to stop and gather flowers by the way !. There are not so many flowers, either, or perhaps we cannot see them, or want the taste to enjoy them. Stones and ruts and jolts there are enough, and sorely do our bones feel the effects of them; but on we go ! The downward impetus cannot be resisted, and our best hope is that we may find a quiet, comfortable spot at the foot.

OCTOBER 28. — The new church recently erected at the corner of Tenth street and the Fifth avenue for the congregation of the Rev. Dr. Eastburn, who were burned out in Canal street, is a noble Gothic building, upon the same plan, but of smaller proportions and less elaborate workmanship than the new Trinity Church, or rather cathedral, which is slowly raising its massive walls, its beautiful arches, and graceful turrets, at the head of Wall street. The exterior of the Church of the Ascension is of hammered stone. Trinity is of polished stone, and the material more beautiful; but the proportions of the former are faultless, and the interior is finished in a style of appropriate solemnity and excellent taste. The church is so nearly finished that notice is given of the consecration, to take place on Friday of next week.

Church of the Ascension.

Mr. Franklin and I went out to the reservoir on Murray Hill, — a short drive from the city, — which I have not seen for more than a year. I fortunately found

Croton Water-Works.

on the spot Mr. Thompson Price, the contractor, who showed and explained to us everything about the gigantic work, which is nearly completed; and the whole work is in such a state of forwardness that the fourth of July next is already fixed upon for the ceremony of letting in the water. The principal reservoir, which will contain a surface equal to thirty acres of water, is near Yorkville, about four miles farther from the city, from which the water is conveyed by double rows of enormous iron pipes to this, which is called the distributing reservoir; of less extent, but of more costly workmanship. This is divided into two equal compartments, which, together, will contain nineteen millions of gallons. The walls are of granite, of prodigious thickness, finely wrought on the exterior, and affording a pleasant promenade on the top, from whence to view these two Mediterranean seas, so well calculated to carry out the object of the temperance teetotallers. Some idea may be formed of the whole expense of this great work, from the fact that the contract for this one item amounts to half a million of dollars. The Philadelphians may boast of their Fairmount works; they are no more to be compared to this than the Schuylkill to the Hudson. I doubt whether there is a similar work in Europe of equal extent and magnificence with the Croton aqueduct, — its dams, bridges, tunnels, and reservoirs.

OCTOBER 30. — The excitement in relation to the school fund, and its distribution for the exclusive benefit of the Catholics, *per se* (as President Tyler would say), is increased to fever heat by the proceedings of a meeting of citizens of that religious faith held last evening at Carroll Hall, at which the Catholic Bishop Hughes was the prime mover and generalissimo, and at which he made an inflammatory speech, urging his flock to come out at the election "upon their own hook," repudiating the candidates on both sides who were opposed to the alteration of the school system as at present conducted, and presenting a new ticket, composed of those who were supposed to be in favour of such a law as they desire. The senators

on both sides came under the ban of the Right Reverend regu-
lator, and Charles O'Connor and a Mr. Gotzberger are nominated
in their places; and a ticket for Assembly, containing the names of
ten of the Loco-focos, whom the Bishop says are favourable to his
views, and three new ones in place of that number of impracticable
heretics. This is certainly a most impudent interference with the
rights and privileges of native Americans; an unblushing attempt
to mix up religion with politics, — an unpalatable dish in this country, — but it may be the means of assuring the success of the Whigs,
particularly the Senate ticket. Good may come of evil; but evil
it undeniably is.

NOVEMBER 5. — The people will be amused; they
Lectures.   must have some way of passing their evenings besides
poking the fire and playing with the children. The
theatre does not seem exactly the right thing; when it revives a
little and raises its head, the legitimate drama—good, honest tragedy, comedy, and opera — has to encounter a host of competitors
ready to administer to a vitiated public taste. The good is mixed up
with the bad; Shakespeare and Jim Crow come in equally for their
share of condemnation, and the stage is indiscriminately voted im-
moral, irreligious, and, what is much worse, *unfashionable*. But the
good folks, as well as the bad, must be amused, and at the present
time lectures are all the vogue. Regular courses have commenced
at the Mercantile Library Association, the Mechanics' Institute, the
Lyceum, and the Historical Society, at all of which some of the
ablest and most distinguished men of this and other States have
agreed to contribute their learning and eloquence. Jared Sparks,
for the Historical Society, is engaged in a course of eight lectures
on the " Events of the American Revolution," to which crowds so
numerous are attracted that the chapel of the New University cannot hold them, and they have had to adjourn to the Tabernacle,
the *omnium gatherum* and hold-all of the city. Concerts, vocal
and instrumental, are also well attended. Mr. Knoop fiddles and
Braham sings to large audiences, whose $400 or $500 a night is

made as easily as a broker's commissions; and ladies' recitations come in for a good share of public patronage. This is all right; it is more rational than the expensive parties for which New York was formerly celebrated, where friendly intercourse was stifled in a crowd of oyster-eating parasites, modest merit put to the blush by reckless extravagance, and good fellowship voted vulgar by parvenu pretension; but I cannot help thinking that the theatre, well conducted, should come in for a better share of support: its morals will always be regulated by the countenance it receives from the respectable part of the community. Vice naturally shrinks from the contact with virtue. If good plays are encouraged and decent theatres frequented by respectable people, none but such will be presented to the public.

NOVEMBER 17.—The rotunda of the Merchants' Exchange in Wall street, the magnificent room in which the merchants of New York are to "congregate," was opened this day for their use. The façade wants three columns to be complete, and the offices are all occupied by brokers, banks, money-changers, and those who deal in *pigeons*, if not "those who sell doves." The following memoranda are taken from an account in one of the morning papers of this superb edifice, which will be an ornament to the city, but a very bad concern for the stockholders, of which number I am one to the amount of $2,500. I may say as Gomerts, the Philadelphia Jew, said to me, when I congratulated him on the news of peace, "Thank you, thank you, Mr. Hone; but I wish I had not bought them calicoes." The ground on which the building stands cost $750,000. The cost of the building will be about $1,100,000, so that the whole expense will not be much short of $2,000,000; and it is doubted whether the revenue of all kinds, with all the advantages of situation and contiguity to the great centre of business, will be more than sufficient to pay the interest on the foreign debt contracted over and above the amount of subscriptions raised from such simpletons as myself for the erection of this costly temple of mercantile pride.

NOVEMBER 23. — This nobleman came in town on
Lord Morpeth. Thursday.   I called this morning, with Mr. Buchanan,
to see him, at the Astor House, and invited him to dine
with us on Saturday next.   He is a plain man, ill-dressed, rather
undersized, with gray hair, which makes him look older than his
age (something under forty), with fine teeth and good eyes.   In
his manner he is, like most of his countrymen, fidgety and ill at
ease, a forced vivacity, a desperate determination to do "the
agreeable," come what may; all of which would seem to indicate a
want of polish which intercourse with good society alone can impart, did we not know that in this case no such question can arise.
No individual in England can claim higher breeding from ancestral
blood, high connections, finished education, and dignified employment.   He is evidently what is called in his country "a clever
man."   He talks much and well, forms no ridiculous pretensions
upon his rank, and is delighted with everything he has as yet met
with in this country.

NOVEMBER 25. — I was at a dinner given by Mr. Buchanan, the
British Consul, to Lord Morpeth.   The party consisted of the host
and his two sons, Lord Morpeth, Chancellor Kent, Mr. Morris, the
Mayor; Mr. Fanshaw, Dr. Wainwright, Mr. Thomas W. Moore,
Mr. Jephson, Col. Nelson, a West Indian; Judge Oakley, Judge
Betts, Mr. Curtis, the Collector, and myself.   It was a pleasant,
cheerful dinner.   His lordship improves upon acquaintance.
Chancellor Kent was very agreeable, and the judges gave good
opinions.   I advised his lordship to accept an invitation he has
received from the corporation to the Joinville dinner on Saturday,
and agreed to postpone mine until Wednesday of next week.

The following statement is copied from an article
Record of in the "American," the object of which is to prove
Ruin.
that the ruinous depreciation of personal property is
mainly to be attributed to the party warfare which terminated in
the destruction of the Bank of the United States.   This frightful
exhibit relates only to the fall in the value of certain stocks here

in New York ; it is even worse in some of the other States, in which banks are broken, the solemn obligations of the State repudiated, and the mass of the people standing ready to avail themselves of the new bankrupt law as soon as it goes into operation. And yet the prostituted press of the party which is about to resume its ascendency has the impudence to tell the people that the country is as prosperous as ever. "To convey some idea of the immense amount of money sunk in stocks within the last three years, we give below a list of the prices that a small portion only of those bought and sold at our stock-board alone, within that period, have ruled at, and their prices at the present day. The difference, in many instances, seems incredible ; but unfortunately it is true."

	Prices within three years past.	Present prices.
United States Bank	122½	4
Vicksburg Bank	89	3
Kentucky Bank	92	56
North American Trust . . .	95	3
Farmers' Trust	113	30
American Trust	120	nothing
Illinois State Bank	80	35
Morris Canal Bank	75	nothing
Mohawk Railroad	76	63
Paterson Railroad	75	53
Harlem Railroad	74	18
Stonington Railroad . . .	70	23
Canton Company	54	23
Long Island Railroad . . .	60	52

NOVEMBER 27. — The great affair given in honour of
Mrs. Mott's Ball.
the French Prince de Joinville, by Dr. and Mrs. Mott, at their elegant house in Bleecker street, formerly the residence of Washington Coster, came off last evening, in a style of magnificence which we have not witnessed for a long time. Cut-

ting of limbs has been a better business of late than trade, and the doctor, having been absent in Europe during the dark days of New York, has had no temptation to invest his money in stocks which have become worthless; "*tant mieux pour lui*." I rejoice in the worthy doctor's ability to honour his royal guest, and do credit to our city in a manner equally worthy of himself and the occasion. My wife and daughters and myself were invited, but I alone represented the family. I called and took Mr. Hughes to this "Doctor's mob," for such, in fact, it was. The house is curiously constructed, with a great number of small rooms, but none large enough to accommodate such a great crowd; and the fine women and lovely girls, dressed in a style of taste and splendour for which they are remarkable, were squeezed in corners by fat men in black, and boys with long beards which the bloodthirsty Venetian Jew might have envied in his day. And as for dancing, one cotillon was all that could find room, and that only the one in which the Prince and his happy partner were exhibited from time to time to the admiring multitude who gazed upon him, the tall ones over the heads of the short ones, and the short ones under the arms of the long ones. I came away before supper, which I am told was in equal splendour with the rest of the entertainment. It was a superb, hot-pressed edition of New York's "good society," elegantly bound, with gilt edges and rich illustrations. Lord Morpeth divided the notice of the company with the distinguished guest of the evening. His society and conversation were much courted.

The Corporation of New York gave a grand dinner Civic Feast to the Prince. this day to the Prince de Joinville, at the Astor House. The company, for so large a one, was very select, including none of the vulgar hangers-on of the corporation, who are apt to creep in and ungentlemanize the company on these occasions. The company, about two hundred in number, consisted, besides "their honours," of the prince and officers of the Belle-Poule and Cassarde; the French committee; officers of the Army and Navy of the United States; militia officers of the rank of general; members and ex-members of Congress; chancellors and judges; ex-mayors, which dignified corps was confined to C. W. Lawrence, Aaron Clarke, and myself; Lord Morpeth; Colonel Clive and Colonel Percival; Mr. Bacourt, French minister; Christopher Hughes, *charge d'affaires* at Stockholm; Francis Granger, postmaster-general, out of place; Bishop Onderdonk; Dr. Knox and Rev. Mr. Verrin; and a fair representation of the respectable gentlemen of the city, Whigs as well as Loco-focos. The Mayor, of course, presided, with Aldermen Bennett and Shaler as vice-presidents; there was good material in the company, but the president had not the tact to bring it out, until after the French guests retired, which was soon after the regular toasts were done, when affairs took a livelier turn, and the usual amount of speech-making and toastifying came into play. The Mayor, in his toast, the first after the regular ones, paid a handsome compliment to Lord Morpeth; to which he replied in a short speech, in excellent taste and fine language, evidently prepared, however, and committed to memory, and delivered in the strained, awkward, sing-song style of elocution which characterizes most of the parliamentary orators. The handsome dining-room of the Astor House was tastefully decorated with the flags of France and the United States, and devices and inscriptions appropriate to the two nations; and the dinner, which cost the good people of Gotham $2,000, was gotten up in Stetson's best style.

DECEMBER 1. — We had a very pleasant dinner-party, consisting of the following gentlemen: Lord Morpeth, Henry Brevoort, Mr. Charles H. Russell, Peter Schermerhorn, Washington Irving, E. H. Pendleton, John Duer, Dr. Wainwright, Dr. Francis, Ogden Hoffman, James G. King.

His lordship has been so *fêted* and lionized at large public dinners, and has been so thrust forward to make speeches and be stared at, that he declared himself delighted with the ease and sociability and repose of this little party of talented and agreeable men. He left at ten o'clock to attend an evening party at Mr.

Isaac Jones's; but some of my guests remained until half-past
eleven.   Lord Morpeth grows upon us amazingly; his fine talents,
improved by education of the highest sort, and the frank urbanity
of his social intercourse, makes us overlook his awkwardness of
manner, and a half-hour's conversation almost persuades us that
he is a handsome man.

Launch of the " St. Nicholas."   DECEMBER 6. — This being the anniversary of the
tutelar saint of the New Netherlands, the new ship
built for a Havre packet, which bears his name, was
launched, at three o'clock, from the ship-yard at the head of Cherry
street.   The ceremony was delayed a fortnight to grace the anniversary, and she was launched into her destined element, with all
her masts standing, — a beautiful specimen of naval architecture.
At the appointed time, in fine style, Alderman Benson, the president of the St. Nicholas Society, in full Dutch costume, with
a cocked hat and orange ribbon, performed the ceremony
of the christening, by pouring the mystical libation of Holland
schnapps over her bows.   The owners of this noble vessel provided
an appropriate banquet for the members of the society, in a warehouse from which an excellent view of the launch was obtained.
We were treated with coffee, spiced rum (known in the Dutch
nomenclature as hot stuff), nice bread and butter, Dutch cheese,
herrings, doughnuts, New Year's cookies, crullers, mince pies, and
waffles.   The ship bears on her bow a full-length figure of the
patron saint, in full canonicals, and her stern is ornamented with
a representation of the same worthy in his better-remembered
capacity of the friend and benefactor of our early days.   He is
represented here entering a chimney loaded with his annual gifts
for " good children," which he is supposed to have brought from
Holland, *via* his aerial railroad, in less time than is required in
these boasted times of rapid locomotion to get up the steam of the
" Great Western ; " and in another portion of the same carving we
see the kind-hearted saint filling the stockings with his far-fetched
treasures, the thoughts of which are preventing the slumbers or

employing the dreams of their expectant recipients. The latter scene is copied from Weir's admirable picture on this subject.

Greenough's Statue.

The marble statue of Washington, executed in Italy, by the American artist Greenough, was placed in the rotunda of the Capitol at Washington on the first instant. It is pretty severely criticised by some of the newspaper correspondents, one of whom goes so far as to condemn it as another of the caricatures which disgrace that spacious apartment; but these folks are so much in the habit of furnishing lies to their employers about living subjects, that they cannot tell the truth when marble is to be treated of.

Mr. Biddle.

DECEMBER 14.—Bills of indictment have been found by a grand jury of Philadelphia against "Nicholas Biddle, Samuel Jaudon, John Andrews, and others to the jury unknown," for robbery, cheating, swindling, and all the other crimes, true and technical, known to the criminal law, and described in its exuberant phraseology. "How are the mighty fallen!" The great financier, the golden calf of Chestnut and Wall streets, at whose approach the well-brushed hat of the cosey millionnaire, or the business-like cap of the money-broker, instinctively came down from its empty eminence, and the pliant knee could with difficulty restrain its idolatrous genuflection, the "monster" of General Jackson's imagination, and the very "Old Nick" in the path of Locofoco politicians,—"fallen, fallen, from his high estate," now "none so poor to do him reverence." Indicted for high crimes and vulgar misdemeanors by a secret conclave of greasy householders, who, a few short months ago, reflected back the complacent smile from his good-natured visage as he ascended the marble steps of the classical temple of Mammon, of which himself was the highpriest, and, marking the animated step and comfortable rotundity, wondered and exclaimed with the jealous Cassius : —

> " Now, in the names of all the gods at once,
> Upon what meat does this our Cæsar feed,
> That he has grown so great? "

But these worthy men, influenced, no doubt, by a zeal for justice and a regard for the public morals, had each of them a sharper prompter to those holy impulses stowed away in his little morocco pocket-book in the shape of an unredeemed five-dollar note, or had been compelled to write off in his stock account a reluctant line on the dark side of the profit and loss account, where first his jocund pen had caused a ray of light to play around the consolatory word *dividend*.

DECEMBER 15. — I attended the sale of Commodore Chauncey's wine, at the City Hotel, to-day. The fine old sherry of 1786 and 1789 brought four to four and a half dollars per bottle, much less than I expected; but I doubt if it is *the* wine which we used to extol so highly. He had several kinds, all good; but the great wine, probably, is all gone the way of all wine. I felt melancholy when reminded, by seeing this wine under the auctioneer's hammer, of the delightful days when this liquor was an adjunct of the hospitality and good cheer of which I have so often partaken at the table of the noble old commodore. Peace to his ashes, and revered be his memory! The race is dwindling away; when will my turn come?

DECEMBER 20. — President Tyler's plan of a ma-
Fiscal Agent. chine to go without wheels, a mill without water, a steam-engine without fuel, a sort of bank and no bank, has been received and referred in the Senate to the standing committee of ways and means, of which Evans is chairman; and in the House of Representatives to the special committee, of which Cushing is chairman. The Whigs, who have yet respectable majorities in both Houses, seem disposed, now that their own schemes to regulate the currency and provide the means to carry on the government have been defeated by the President, to give those he offers a fair chance, and will do nothing under the influence of party-spirit to obstruct the administration of public affairs. At present, things at Washington are calm and quiet.

DECEMBER 21. — I came out last evening in a character which I had laid aside for a long time : I went to two parties; first, to one at Mrs. Hammersley's, in the handsome new house, her share of the Mason row, above us in Broadway, where everything was in the finest style of elegance and good taste; and afterward to Mrs. Charles Heckscher's, where the party was given in honour of the bride, Mrs. Washington Coster, late Miss Elizabeth Oakey, where I found many agreeable people, a capital supper, and fine wine. I was very well pleased at both places; in these cases *c'est le premier pas qui coûte;* the difficulty is in saying, " I will go," and going upstairs into a cold room to dress at an hour when you ought to undress to go to bed. I went to Mrs. Hammersley's at ten o'clock, and found half-a-dozen ladies collected in the receiving-room; and at eleven, when I came away, it was difficult to make my way through the crowd.

DECEMBER 23. — This society celebrated their anniversary yesterday, by an oration at the Tabernacle, from Professor Hadduck, of Dartmouth College, and afterward a dinner at the Astor House. The last was remarkable for two circumstances, — Yankee inventions, — one wise and in good taste, the other exceedingly doubtful in both those characteristics. The tables were graced by the presence of ladies, but chilled by the exclusion of all beverages but water, — the " pure element," as they call it. The water, it is true, was brought from the neighbourhood of Plymouth; but the *spirit* of the Pilgrims has evaporated long since, and I suspect that those on whom the duty devolved of making speeches and singing songs would have gotten on better if a substitute had been provided in the shape of a glass of Stetson's good Madeira, or the spur to intellect which is found in a sparkling tumbler of champagne. The Pilgrims could not boast of many such stimulants, and were compelled to drink " water from the rock; " but I shrewdly suspect that if from the rock streams of champagne had issued, instead of water, it would not have been suffered to run to waste or sink untasted into the earth. There is a scandalous report prevailing, that after the dinner was ended, and the company had dispersed, the bar-rooms and oyster-cellars in the neighbourhood of the Astor House had an unusual run of custom, and soon gave evidence that this grand temperance jubilee was to them at least an *empty* boast.

I dined to-day with Prescott Hall. The party consisted of Messrs. Curtis, Grinnell, Minturn, De Wolf, Draper, Gerard Coster, Brigham, Dr. Sparks, etc. Several of these gentlemen were leading men yesterday at the New England dinner. They made ample amends to-day for their unwonted abstinence on that occasion; their libations gave evidence of a " foregone conclusion " destructive to the capital wine furnished by our hospitable entertainer. This descendant of the Pilgrims has no particular predilection for the " pure element."

1842.

JANUARY 1.—If the moral, social, and political year which has now commenced shall take its features from the earth, the air, and the heavens this day, it will be all bright sunshine, balmy air, and cloudless skies. Never was there a more beautiful New Year's Day, and never did people seem disposed to make more of it. Broadway, from ten o'clock until the shades of evening, was animated by pedestrians of all ranks, sexes, and ages, and by every description of vehicle that ever was contrived as a substitute for legs. I entered upon the spirit of the game, was fairly on the go from noon until five o'clock, and paid many agreeable visits.

The year comes in under gloomy auspices and discouraging forebodings. We are, as a community, much worse off than we were at the commencement of the year which has just passed off forever. And the aggregate of individual loss, embarrassment, and disappointment is most fearfully increased. Real and personal property is diminished greatly in value, and the confidence which promotes success in the dealings of men seems to have fled.

Here, in the city of New York, trade is stagnant. Local stocks are lower than ever. Real estate is unsalable at any price; rents have fallen and are not punctually paid, and taxes have increased most ruinously. The general government has, by a course of bad management and corrupt measures in the last administration, and a want of harmony and concert in the present one, been reduced to bankruptcy; there is not enough money in the treasury to pay the members of Congress, nor patriotism and honesty enough in the rulers to agree upon any feasible plan to make matters better. And, to add to this babel of enormities, several of the States are holding meetings, to deliberate upon the propriety of repudiating State debts. Elections have gone in favour of this damnable principle, and we shall stand before a jury of nations, a nation of swindlers, not entitled to the ordinary courtesies of the civilized world, and a by-word and a reproach ; all of which, New York, Massachusetts, and Ohio must suffer for the rascality of Mississippi, Michigan, and, I greatly fear, Pennsylvania.

JANUARY 17. — Died in Philadelphia, on Saturday, in the seventy-third year of his age, Francis L. Hopkinson,

Death of Judge Hopkinson.

Judge of the U. S. Circuit Court for the State of Pennsylvania.   Few men in this country have enjoyed, during a long life, so good a name, or deserved it more ; he was a man of taste, learning, and public spirit, an agreeable companion, and a gentleman, as such things were formerly understood in this country, before it was Jacksonized.   Judge Hopkinson has been more celebrated as the author of the national song " Hail Columbia," than for many more important services rendered to the people, and higher evidences of talents.

JANUARY 22. — We had a pleasant dinner-party of young folk, viz., Mr. and Mrs. Delancey Kane, Miss Eliza Russell, Miss Emma Meredith, Mr. Charles Brugière, Genevieve Anthon, Edward Laight, Emily Hone, Frederick Foster, Caroline Howland, and William Schermerhorn.

Arrival of Charles Dickens.

JANUARY 24. — The steamer " Britannia " arrived in Boston on Saturday evening, having left Liverpool on the 4th inst.   She brings news thirty days later than we had before.   Among the passengers in the " Britannia " are Mr. Charles Dickens and his wife.   This gentleman is the celebrated " Boz," whose name " rings through the world with loud applause," — the fascinating writer whose fertile imagination and ready pen conceived and sketched the immortal Pickwick, his prince of valets, and his body-guard of choice cronies ; who has made us laugh with " Mantilini," and cry with poor "little Nell ; " caused us to shrink with horror from the effects of lynch law, as administered by the misguided Lord George Gordon, and to listen with unmitigated delight to the ticking of " Master Humphrey's Clock."   The visit of this popular writer has been heralded in advance. He was expected by this packet, and I signed, three or four days ago, with a number of other persons, a letter to be presented to him on his arrival in this city, giving him a hearty welcome and inviting him to a public dinner, which, from the spirit which appears to prevail on the subject, will be no common affair.

The news by this arrival is of a more sunny nature than we have been accustomed to of late. The language of the quotations from the public papers is more conciliatory, and there seems to be a greater disposition to shake hands than to crack crowns. Every favourable symptom on this side of the water is made the most of. The temperate tone of President Tyler's message has contributed to produce this effect, and Lord Morpeth's reception, and the attentions he has received in this and other cities of the United States, have not been without their influence upon public opinion. But the best evidence of a return of good feelings, and a sincere desire on the part of the British government to adjust the unpleasant difficulties between the two countries, is the appointment of Lord Ashburton on a special mission to the United States (which appointment he has accepted) to settle, if possible, the points in dispute. This is an unusual piece of condescension on the part of our haughty elder sister. It will make Brother Jonathan feel his importance, and the devil is in it if it does not put him in a good humour. Besides the gracious nature of the act itself, the choice of the messenger of peace may be considered highly complimentary. Lord Ashburton is better known as Mr. Alexander Baring, head of the great mercantile house of Baring Brothers & Co., closely identified with American commerce, and long known as the bankers of the American government; and it would be strange if he had not some predilections in favour of a country whose blood runs in the veins of his children, Lady Ashburton being an American lady, the daughter of Mr. Bingham, of Philadelphia.

Happy will it prove for us that Mr. Webster has remained in

the office of Secretary of State when this special Minister shall
have arrived, and great will be the triumph over those who abuse
him for remaining at his post when his colleagues resigned, if he
shall prove to be the happy instrument in settling the painful difficulties between the two countries in an honourable manner, and
averting a war so little desired by either. Let these two men get
fairly together at Washington, and, if the sores are not speedily
healed, they may be pronounced incurable.

JANUARY 25. — Isaac Iselin, formerly of the house of Le Roy,
Bayard, & Co., and more recently connected with that of De Rham
& Moore, died on the 10th of December, at his residence in Bâsle,
Switzerland, in the fifty-eighth year of his age. I visited Mr.
Iselin, at Bâsle, in the year 1821. He was a banker, deal-
ing largely through Paris in exchange and stocks, and lived in
the dull, aristocratic style of the dullest and most aristocratic
city of Europe.

The House of Representatives presents every day a
Congress.   scene of violence, personal abuse, and vulgar crimina-
tion, almost as bad as those which disgraced the
National Assembly of France in the early stages of the " Reign of
Terror." Mr. Adams, with the most provoking pertinacity, continues to present petitions intended to irritate the Southern members, and by language and manner equally calculated to disgust his
friends and exasperate his enemies, and does something every day
to alienate the respect which all are disposed to render to his consummate learning and admirable talents. To those outbreaks of
ill-temper Wise replies in language which the veriest demagogue
of a porter house would blush to use to his vulgar associates.

Among other insane movements of the ex-President, he has presented a petition praying *for a repeal of the Union*, because the
petitioners are deprived of the privilege of agitating the terrible
question of slavery ; and their right to bring forward a proposition
so monstrous, and his to be their organ of communication with the
Congress of the nation, is enforced with the indomitable obstinacy

which marks all his conduct of late. Wise calls him "black-hearted traitor;" and Adams, in return, pours out the vials of his wrath upon the fractious Virginian. Happy would it be for the country if these two firebrands were expelled from the House! Indeed, a motion has been made to expel Mr. Adams for subordination of treason in the presentation of the obnoxious petition above mentioned; and in the present temper of the members, it will require all the reverence which is felt for his age, his talents, and the exalted office which he formerly bore, to save him from that or some other signal mark of disgrace. In the course of this unprofitable debate Mr. Gilmor made a happy application of a well-known couplet to Mr. Adams, who expressed his regret at seeing that gentleman play the *second fiddle* to Mr. Wise. Mr. Gilmor said he played second fiddle to no man; all he wished to do was to stop the music of a man

> " Who, in the space of one revolving moon,
>   Was statesman, fiddler, poet, and buffoon."

While scenes are represented in one part of the great chamber in which " the collected wisdom of the nation " is presumed to be assembled, in another, one of this kind is enacted : " Mr. Dawson, of Louisiana (who, by the bye, always goes armed), deliberately took his seat by Mr. Arnold, and, after applying to him a number of most violent and abusive epithets, told him that if he rose from his seat he would cut his throat, at the same time significantly pointing to the bowie-knife he carried in his bosom." How long will it be before the people of this abused country will begin to look with favour on the sad alternative of a master? If we had a Julius Cæsar at the head of his victorious legions, now would be the time for him to march to the Capitol. . . . We are a factious people and a conceited people; but we are also a calculating people, and have sense enough to know that in such a dangerous experiment the chances are fearfully against us.

JANUARY 27. — In addition to the dinner which it
is intended to give Mr. Dickens on his arrival at New
York, a grand ball is to be gotten up for him and his
lady, at the Park, where it is proposed to have *tableaux vivants*
and other devices illustrating some of the prominent scenes in his
admirable stories. For this object a meeting was held last evening at the Astor House, which was attended by fifty or sixty very
respectable gentlemen.

Reception of "Boz."

The Mayor presided, and a letter, of which I was selected to be
the author, was agreed upon, signed by all present, and intrusted
to David C. Colden to be delivered by him in person to Mr. Dickens, in Boston, inviting him to the *fête*, and requesting him to
name the day on which it shall take place. This is all well, but
there is danger of overdoing the matter and making our well-
meant hospitalities oppressive to the recipient. We are a people
of impulse ; when we get fairly mounted upon the back of a *lion*,
we are apt to drive with might and *mane*, until the " royal beast "
is fain to escape from the menagerie.

JANUARY 31. — Another sign has been exhibited
in the House of Representatives ; another movement
toward the accomplishment of my recent melan-
choly prediction. That indomitable, pugnacious, wonderful man
of knowledge, without tact, John Quincy Adams, has presented a
petition from some people in Haverhill, Mass., praying for a
separation of the Union, as the only means of obtaining the right
of petition, the maintenance of which they consider of more importance than the union of the States. A monstrous doctrine, the
very whispering of which has a sound as of thunder, more awful
than that of foreign war ! But, after all, it is precisely the same
threat, founded on better ground, as that made by the Southern
anti-tariff nullifiers ; but now that the brat is born of Northern
parents, these patriotic hotspurs are horrified beyond all example ;
their indignation knows no bounds. " Treason ! " " Expulsion ! "
" The guillotine ! " resound from the whole slaveholding part of the

Signs of the Times.

House, both Whig and Tory. Wise vomits fire like the Dragon of Wantley. Gilmor and Marshall seem ready, like Curtius, to spring into the gulf to save the Constitution, when such parts of it as happen to suit them are thought to be in danger ; and all the little dogs — Tray, Blanche, and Sweetheart — join in the cry, and snap at the heels of the sturdy mastiff of Massachusetts, who growls on and guards with pertinacious obstinacy all approaches to his kennel. A motion to censure the ex-President is now before the House, with amendments more or less violent, which he combats inch by inch, and which probably, after consuming the time of the House (which the people pay for) a week or so, and increasing the flames of discord, which may be seen issuing from every crevice in the political volcano, will end in smoke and the foreboding sound of internal thunders.

FEBRUARY 1. — I went to two *Boz* meetings last evening; one at the Carlton House, of the dinnerites, at which Chief Justice Jones presided. A committee of arrangements was appointed and the officers of the dinner selected. They consist of Washington Irving, John Duer, John A. King, Judge Betts, and myself, and we are to determine on the presiding officer and the names of the vice-presidents. The other was a meeting of the ballites, at the Astor House, the Mayor in the chair. A long report from the committee was adopted. This affair is in a forward state, and promises to eclipse the Lafayette ball at Castle Garden.

FEBRUARY 3. — Dined with Mr. George Curtis, Washington place : a pleasant party, good dinner, and fine wines ; after which I joined the girls at a party at Mrs. Archibald Gracie's, Waverly place.

FEBRUARY 9. — After I came from the committee last evening, I went to Mrs. Ray's fancy ball, by special favour, as nobody. It was a beautiful affair. The house and furniture and everything thereunto appertaining is new and splendid, — the greatest thing, by common consent, in the city. The party consisted of about ninety, all (with two or three exceptions) in fancy characters, some of which were mag-

Mrs. Ray's
Ball.

nificent and others highly characteristic.　The scene was extremely brilliant.

Mr. Adams Acquitted.　The vote of censure in the House of Representatives, which has caused so great an excitement, was laid on the table on Monday, by a vote of one hundred and six to ninety-three.　This is a triumph for the pertinacious ex-President, who, it is to be feared, will be encouraged by it to keep the floor, to the exclusion of all other business but the presenting petitions, for the remainder of the session.　The Southern men are so exasperated at their failure in the attempt to punish Mr. Adams for presenting a petition praying for a dissolution of the Union (a proposition, horrible though it may be, yet one which these Southern men have regarded with no small share of favour themselves), that some of them are unwilling to work in the same team with him.　Messrs. Gilmor, Hunter, Rhett, Proffit, and W. Cost Johnson, members of the important committee on foreign affairs, have been excused from serving on that committee, because, as they say, they " are unwilling to work with a chairman who has shown himself an unsafe repository of the public trust, and who has not the confidence of the members of the committee."　All this the old hero takes very coolly, and moves for the appointment by the Speaker of members to fill the vacancies.

Minister to Spain.　Washington Irving is nominated Minister to Spain, and will be, or has been by this, confirmed by the Senate.　In many respects this is a good appointment. Mr. Irving has spent some time in Spain, and some of his best works were written in that country, from materials collected on the spot.　The appointment, he says, was altogether unexpected by him ; but I have no doubt, from his manner of speaking of it, that he is pleased, and will accept it.　The place has been vacant since the return of Major Eaton.

Bennett's Sentence.　FEBRUARY 14. — This impudent disturber of the public peace, whose infamous paper, the " Herald," is more scurrilous, and of course more generally read, than any other, has been tried in the Court of Oyer and Terminer, and convicted on two indictments for a libel on the Judges Noah and Lynch, of the Court of Sessions; he was sentenced this morning to pay a fine of $250 on one, and $100 on the other. This will do him more good than harm; he will make money by it; the vitiated appetite for slander which pervades the mass of the people will be whetted by the notoriety which this trial will give him, for dearly do people love the scandal of which themselves are not the subject! The court consisted of Hon. William Kent, president, and two Loco-foco aldermen, Purdy and Lee; the two latter " birds of a feather" overruled the judge in making up the sentence, of which he took care to inform Bennett in the address which he made to him in announcing it, telling him plainly that if he had had his way he would have sent him to the penitentiary, and intimating that whenever he gets a chance he may expect it at his hands, on the commission of another such offence.

Death of
Mr. Barhyte. Old Mr. Barhyte died, one day last week, at his farm near Saratoga Springs, where he lived so long that " the memory of man runneth not to the contrary." He was closely identified in my memory with many pleasant trout dinners and card-parties at his plain Dutch house, situated on the brow of a hill, at the foot of which was his fish-pond, surrounded by a beautiful forest of dark-green pine-trees, whose tall, spiral tops seemed to bow into the clouds. This was formerly a favourite resort of Governor Clinton, whose moments of ease and hilarity I have often shared. Many a joke of his have I enjoyed, when he laid aside his state to be a boy once more, and many a good dinner have I helped him to eat in the old Dutchman's house. Here, too, have I enjoyed pleasant intercourse with Mr. Otis, Mr. Van Buren, Colonel Drayton, Louis McLane, Governor Lewis, and many other distinguished men; listened to the charming notes of poor Dom Lynch, and enjoyed the enjoyment of my brother John. Old Barhyte would permit us to use his house and eat his trout as a special favour, and charge us double price for everything, with a fair understanding, fairly expressed by him, that if we did not like it we need not come again. His civility was extended rather sparingly, and only to those to whom he had a liking, of which number I was always one. Presidents and governors, judges and generals, all fared alike. He sold his trout, his cool drink, and his pleasant seat on the piazza, only to those who found favour in his eyes, and as for the rest, "they might go whistle."

FEBRUARY 15.—"The agony is over;" the "Boz"

The "Boz" Ball. ball, the greatest affair in modern times, the tallest compliment ever paid to a little man, the fullest libation ever poured upon the altar of the muses, came off last evening in fine style; everything answered the public expectation, and no untoward circumstances occurred to make anybody sorry he went.

The theatre was prepared for the occasion with great splendour and taste. The whole area of the stage and pit was floored over, and formed an immense saloon. The decorations and ornaments were all "Pickwickian." Shields with scenes painted from several stories of Dickens, the titles of his works on others surrounded with wreaths, the dome formed of flags, and the side walls in fresco, representing the panels of an ancient oaken hall. A small stage was erected at the extreme end, opposite the main entrance, before which a curtain was suspended, exhibiting the portly proportions of the immortal Pickwick, his prince of valets, and his body-guard of choice cronies. This curtain was raised in the intervals between the cotillons and waltzes, to disclose a stage on which were exhibited a series of *tableaux vivants*, forming groups of the characters in the most striking incidents of "Pickwick," "Nicholas Nickleby," "Oliver Twist," "The Old Curiosity Shop," "Barnaby Rudge," etc. The company began to assemble at half-past seven o'clock, and at nine, when the committee introduced Mr. and Mrs. Dickens, the crowd was immense; a little upward of two thousand tickets were handed in at the door, and, with the members of the committees and their parties who came in by back ways, the assembled multitude numbered about two thousand five hundred. Everybody was there, and every lady was dressed well and in good taste, and decorum and good order were preserved during the whole evening.   Refreshments were provided in the saloons on the several floors, and in the green room, which was kept for the members of the committees and their families.   This branch of the business was farmed out to Downing, the great man of oysters, who received $2,200.   On the arrival of the " observed of all observers " a lane was opened through the crowd, through which he and his lady were marched to the upper end, where the committee of reception were stationed.   Here I, as chairman of that committee, received him, and made a short speech, after which they joined in the dancing.

The author of the " Pickwick Papers " is a small, bright-eyed, intelligent-looking young fellow, thirty years of age, somewhat of a dandy in his dress, with " rings and things and fine array," brisk in his manner, and of a lively conversation.   If he does not get his little head turned by all this, I shall wonder at it.   Mrs. Dickens is a little, fat, English-looking woman, of an agreeable countenance, and, I should think, " a nice person."

FEBRUARY 16. — Charles Aug. Davis invited a number of us yesterday to meet Dickens at dinner ; but, lo and behold ! an apology was received from him, stating that he was confined to his room by a sore throat, and was inhibited by the doctor from going out.   Two very good-humoured notes were received from him, and so we had to perform the tragedy of " Hamlet," the part of Hamlet omitted ; but we made a good thing of it, notwithstanding the hiatus in our ranks. The major and his charming wife were agreeable, as usual, and if any party could get along without missing Mr. Boz it would be one formed of such materials as the following : Mr. John Duer, Judge William Kent, Samuel B. Ruggles, F. G. Halleck, Dr. De Kay, J. Prescott Hall, William B. Astor, Washington Irving, John A. King, Gulian C. Verplanck, Judge Betts, David S. Kennedy, Henry Brevoort, P. Hone.

FEBRUARY 19. — The great dinner to Dickens was given yesterday, at the City Hotel, and came off with flying colours.   Two hundred and thirty persons sat

Dinner to
Dickens.

down to dinner at seven o'clock. The large room was ornamented with two illuminated scenes from the works of " Boz," busts of celebrated persons and classical devices, all in good taste ; and the eating and drinking part of the affair was excellent. The president was Washington Irving (I beg pardon, " His Excellency "). " Non Nobis " was sung by Mr. Horn and his little band of vocalists, who gave several glees during the evening. After the unintellectual operation of eating and drinking was concluded, the president rose and began a prepared speech, in which he broke down flat (as he promised us beforehand he would), and concluded with this toast : " Charles Dickens, the literary guest of the nation." To this the guest made his acknowledgment in an excellent speech, delivered with great animation, and characterized by good taste and warm feeling.

An unusual feature in this festivity was the presence of a coterie of charming women, who were at first stowed away in a small room adjoining the upper part of the hall, and who, with a laudable and irrepressible curiosity to hear me, and others equally instructive and agreeable, at the lower end, edged by degrees into the room, and finally got possession of the stage, behind the president, to the discomfiture of certain pleasant old bachelors and ungallant dignitaries, but to the great delight of us who profess to have better taste in such matters. This flying squadron of infantry consisted of Mrs. Davis, Mrs. Colden and Miss Wilkes, Mrs. Dickens, Miss Sedgwick, Miss Wadsworth, the Misses Ward, Mrs. Burns, Mrs. Parish, Miss Anna Bridgen, Mrs. McCrackan, Mrs. Brevoort, and others, all of whom were greatly pleased, and some of whom seemed to regret they could not take a more active part in the business of the evening. This dinner, with the ball on Monday night, is a tribute to literary talents greater than any I remember ; and, if the English people do not repay it in some shape to our eminent men, they are no great things.

WASHINGTON, MARCH 15. — Dickens and his wife are here. There has not been much fuss made about him. They laugh at us in

New York for doing too much, and have gone upon the other extreme. He has been invited to dine by several gentlemen to whom he brought letters. Amongst the rest Mr. Adams invited him and his wife to dinner on Sunday, at half-past two o'clock. (This early hour was fixed, I suppose, to keep up the primitive beauty of New England Republican habits.) Some clever people were invited to meet them. They came, he in a frock-coat, and she in her bonnet. They sat at table until four o'clock, when he said, " Dear, it is time for us to go home and dress for dinner." They were engaged to dine with Robert Greenhow at the fashionable hour of half-past five ! A most particularly funny idea to leave the table of John Quincy Adams to dress for a dinner at Robert Greenhow's ! He is to be here on Tuesday or Wednesday, and Kennedy has written to Mr. Gilmor to take charge of him and keep him out of bad hands ; as I also have urged him to do, but I don't think he will. He detests humbug. Washington Irving, Ogden Hoffman, and Moses H. Grinnell came here last evening ; the former to receive his instructions previous to his departure for Spain, and to read up, as he expressed himself to me, to the political state of affairs, and to the nature of his official duties. He is a charming good fellow, a feather in the literary cap of his country.

Mr. Granger gave us a grand dinner to-day at Gadsby's. I did not think it possible to get up anything so genteel in this house. The service was beautiful, the dinner excellent, the attendance unexceptionable, and the guests of the highest grade. The party consisted of Mr. and Miss Granger, Mr. Webster, Washington Irving ; Legaré, Attorney-General ; Martini, Dutch *Chargé ;* Rives ; Bodisco, Russian Minister ; Mr. and two Misses Hone, Fletcher Webster ; Lerruys, Belgian *Chargé ;* Barnard, Van Rensselaer, Grinnell, Gouverneur Wilkins, and Nordin, Swedish *Chargé.*

Mr. Webster was in his happiest mood ; I had a nice talk with him. He is seriously impressed with the melancholy situation of the domestic affairs of the country ; not entirely free from solicitude about his own position, but full of hope regarding the issue of the vexed questions between us and Great Britain. They will be settled before September, he said to me, with a solemnity of manner and emphasis of expression, with the volcanic fire flashing from out of the caverns of his dark eyelashes, which struck to my soul and which I never can forget. "They will be settled if they will give me a fair chance!" And I believe it! All I fear is that the people do not deserve such a man as Daniel Webster, and that Justice rather than Mercy will be awarded to us.

We went this morning to Mrs. Webster's drawing-room, Tuesday being her day for receiving company. It is a good arrangement; it makes one of those pleasant places of resort for ladies and gentlemen which serves to take off the rough edge of party violence and Republican vulgarity. From Mrs. Webster's we went to call upon Mrs. Madison, who was not at home. She is a *young* lady of fourscore years and upward, goes to parties and receives company like the " Queen of this new world."

This has been a day of great business. After our dinner-party broke up, we went to the President's levee,— the last of the season, and the crowd was great. The east room, which is one of the most splendid I ever saw, was a complete jam ; but, considering the facility of access, the sort of people who do the honours and those who receive them, the company was highly respectable ; the first people in the land were there, and the women were well dressed. I witnessed no gaucheries, no vulgarity, and I doubt if any society in any country so organized could have turned out so decorous and respectable an assemblage. As for the host and his immediate satellites, they seemed to be in the situation of King George's apple in the dumpling, — wondering how the devil they got there. It struck me that a majority of all the men over the age of thirty were more fit to be President than Mr. Tyler. He walked from one magnificent apartment to another, holding a little child by each hand, to show, I suppose, how amiable he was, how simple in his habits, how affectionate in his feelings. Shades of Washington, Adams, Madison, Monroe, do turn aside your heads from such an exhibition! Even the hickory face of Jackson would smile, and the courtly nose of Van Buren turn up, at such an absence of dignity.

Dickens was at the levee, and Washington Irving, and, as far as I could judge, Irving out-bozzed "Boz." He collected a crowd around him; the men pressed on to shake his hand, and the women to touch the hem of his garment. Somebody told me that they saw a woman put on his hat, in order, as she told her companions, that she might have it to say that she had worn Washington Irving's hat. All this was "fun to them," as the frogs said, but "death" to poor Irving, who has no relish for this sort of glorification, and has less tact than any man living to get along with it decently. I was, however, rejoiced to see it; it showed that the refreshing dew of popular favour could be shed upon the indigenous, as well as the exotic, plants of literary talents.

MARCH 24.— I passed the morning in walking through the streets of Philadelphia. Notwithstanding the dreadful times they have experienced, many new buildings are going up; the shops exhibit their accustomed display of costly merchandise. The markets are well supplied with provisions, and there seems to be no lack of customers. The marble fronts of the houses in the fashionable streets are kept bright and clean, as usual, and the noble portico of the Bank of the United States looks down proudly as ever upon the ruin which the institution has occasioned. Such of the banks as are not hopelessly crippled have resumed the payment of specie, and the Philadelphians clap their wings and crow at the triumph of exchange on New York being a quarter per cent. below par. But the merchants are suffering. There is no business, and the Western exchanges are worse than ever.

AT HOME, MARCH 25. — We left Philadelphia at nine o'clock this morning, and got home at three. Washington Irving joined us on starting, and made a very pleasant addition to our little party. He is more gay and cheerful than he is wont to be, and talks a great deal, enlivening his conversation with stories of old times, literary reminiscences, and pretty fair jokes. He is evidently much gratified with his unexpected elevation to diplomatic dignity, and is making his preparations to sail for England on his way to Spain, in the packet of the 7th of April.

APRIL 4.—The anniversary of the death of William Henry Harrison, the good President. The flags are suspended at half-mast from the Whig public-houses and some other conspicuous places ; and well may they be ! The bells should be tolled, and if the people were to put on sackcloth and ashes such manifestations of grief would not transcend the cause. The decease of the good old man, much to be lamented by his personal and political friends, was to him of small importance. He had arrived at the summit of a man's ambition in this country, and could not have died at a better time for himself; but how little did the American people comprehend the extent of their bereavement ! One year of the rule of imbecility, arrogance, and prejudice has taught them the folly of selecting for Vice-President a man of whose fitness for the office of President they had no reasonable assurance. The " New York Herald," which is said to be high in favour with Mr. Tyler, and considered a sort of semi-official, says that he is about to resign. God grant it may be true ! but if he does, he will gain no credit for it. He would undoubtedly serve his country more effectually by such a step than by all the actions of his previous life, and would for once be entitled to the gratitude of his fellow-citizens ; but he would not receive it. No credit would be given to him for a motive so patriotic ; it would rather be attributed to that sort of patriotism which caused Hull to desert his post and surrender Detroit when he spied out in the cloud which darkened the horizon a hostile force approaching. But the report can have no foundation. It is only raised to keep Bennett's hand in, who lives by lying. John Tyler resign ! Why, he is just *weak* enough to believe himself the *strongest* man in the United States ! He has all the self-conceit of him who announced in the plenitude of his arrogance that " he would administer the laws as *he*" (not the Supreme Court) " understood them ; " while at the same time he does not possess a tithe of his force of mind and strength of intellect.

APRIL 5. — The British ship of war, "Warspite," with Lord Ashburton, the special Minister on board, arrived at Annapolis on Saturday, and his lordship was to depart immediately for Washington ; so that by this time it is probable he and Mr. Webster have gotten *toe to toe*, and put their *heads* together, by which means it is to be hoped they may reëstablish matters on a friendly *footing*, and preserve their respective countries from cracked crowns and bloody noses. The sending out on this mission so distinguished a man, nay, the sending a special Minister at all, ought to be considered a strong proof of the desire on the part of the British government to preserve friendly relations, if possible, with this country. So it is distinctly understood by Mr. Webster, with whom the negotiations will of course be conducted, and who assured me the other day that he had the fullest confidence in being able to settle *all* the differences with England before the first of September. If these two men cannot effect this important object, none can, and then the Lord have mercy upon John Tyler and Queen Victoria, and all their men !

APRIL 21. — A terrible hubbub has been going on in the redoubtable little State of Rhode Island for some time past ; a party of disorganizing, radical demagogues, unable to accomplish their object of changing the politics of this steady State and bringing themselves into office, by fair means, have set about defeating the will of the people (of which, when it suits them, they pretend to be the champions and supporters), and, having made a constitution of their own, have elected a governor (one Mr. Dorr) and State officers ; whilst the sober part of the community, proceeding according to law and the' Constitution, have reëlected the present governor (King) and the State officers as at present constituted ; so the smallest State in the Union is the only one which can boast of *two* governors, and the sword of civil commotion is likely to be drawn in a quarter hitherto distinguished for good order and obedience to the laws. The incendiaries, headed by Dutee J. Pierce, and other such warriors, many of whom are auxiliaries from other States, impelled solely by a love of liberty and reverence for other men's rights, swear that the State belongs to them, and that they will govern it; whilst the other party swear that it does not, and that they shall not, and so they are preparing to go to blows about the matter. President Tyler, on being applied to by the regulars, has written a letter, which is published, in which he avows his intention, in a manly, frank manner, to carry out the duty prescribed to him in the Constitution of the United States, by supporting the Constitution of the State and standing by the right, and, if more gentle means are unavailable, United States troops will be sent to settle the hash. What acts of tyranny are committed now-a-days under the name of *liberty*, and how the people's will is defeated by those who profess to be their best friends. The Rhode Island rebels, as well as the New York Loco-focos, have no notion of heeding the *vox populi*, when that *vox* fails to raise the one to power in the State, or to secure to the other the patronage and emoluments of municipal supremacy.

APRIL 25. — This patriotic song, which, like the Hail Columbia! "Song of the Rhine," in Germany, and "The Marseillaise Hymn," in France, has been adopted as the national anthem, and still continues a sort of "smoke-pipe" for overheated patriotism, was written by the late distinguished Judge Hopkinson, who died in Philadelphia on the 15th of January last. It was first sung at the theatre at the benefit of a young actor, whom the author was desirous of serving. This was in the summer of 1798, during John Adams's administration, when a war with France was supposed to be inevitable, and party-spirit raged with great violence, the American people being divided into an English and a French party. The object of the author was (as he himself expresses it in a letter to the Rev. Rufus W. Griswold, now published) "to get up an American spirit, which should be independent of and above the interests, passions, and policy of both belligerents, and look and feel exclusively for our own honour and rights." These were the famous black-cockade times, when the wisdom and patriotism of Washington were insufficient to control the " madness of the people," who, in espousing the quarrels of the Europeans, had almost ceased to be Americans. Judge Hopkinson was then, and continued always to be, one of that noble " band of brothers joined," a true American Federalist; not of that section of the band who have since been Jackson Federalists, or Harrison Conservatives, but a true American Whig Federalist, born of the Revolution, educated in the school of Washington, Jay, and Hamilton, and acknowledging no party but his country.

APRIL 26. — When I returned home I found that Dr. Wainwright had called in the course of the morning to invite me to a family dinner, to meet Mr. William H. Prescott, of Boston, — the accomplished author of the " History of the Reign of Ferdinand and Isabella," — who had just arrived in town on a very short visit. I joined the pleasant little party after they had dined, and enjoyed a highly intellectual treat. The party consisted of the doctor, Mr. Prescott, Henry Brevoort, George Griffin, John C. Hamilton, Henry Cary, and myself. Mr. Prescott is rather a handsome man of about six and forty, of intellectual appearance, good manners, agreeable conversation, and much vivacity. Mr. Prescott reminded me that we had met before, at dinner at General Lyman's in Boston.

APRIL 28. — Our city was disgraced by a meeting, last evening, at Tammany Hall, called by Alderman Purdy, Messrs. Slamm, Vanderpoel and such persons to approve the proceedings of the insurrectionists in Rhode Island, who are in arms against the constitution and laws of the State, and to encourage them in their factious opposition to the constituted authorities, and their contempt for the expressed opinion of the general government. Aaron Vanderpoel (the Kinderhook roarer, as he is familiarly called by those who have listened to

the dulcet tones of his voice in the House of Representatives),
was most appropriately chosen chairman of the meeting, and
addresses were made by Mr. Parmenter, a Rhode Island Jacobin,
and Mr. Davezac, Mr. Edmunds, and other New York patriots,
and resolutions were passed suited to the occasion. What would
these fellows have said if the people of Providence had held a
meeting to denounce the law of the last Legislature of New York,
repealing the late salutary registry act, or that which destroyed the
beneficial influence of the public schools to propitiate the Irish
Catholics and secure their votes at the expense of the rights of
native Americans? That would have been stigmatized as an impertinent interference in other people's affairs, whilst their meeting
last night was a generous ebullition of patriotic sympathy in favour
of the oppressed victims of official tyranny.

Steam.
This powerful agent, which regulates just now the
affairs of the world ; this new element, which, like the
other four, is all-potent for good and for evil, — has
not only almost annihilated distance, and overcome the obstacles
which nature seems to have interposed to locomotion, and reduced
the value of most of the articles in use for which we formerly
depended upon the labour of men's hands, but it has become a
substitute for war, in the philosophical plan of keeping down the
superabundance of the human race, and thinning off the excessive population of which political economists have from time to
time expressed so much dread. Scarcely a day passes that we do
not hear of some steamboat being blown up, and hundreds of
human beings suddenly summoned to give an account of the
" deeds done in the body," and hurried off, " unanointed, un-
annealed," to another world, for which most of them are unprepared ; or of a locomotive running off the railroad, and thus
bringing many to an unexpected termination of their journey.
These are some of the wholesale operations of steam ; the retail
business is of comparatively no importance, and we only hear of
those cases which occur in our immediate neighbourhood ; but they

are most deplorably frequent. One day last week a young man jumped from the car on the Harlem railroad, to recover his hat, which had blown off, fell on the rails, and was killed in a shocking manner ; and yesterday a fine lad, eleven years of age, son of Mr. John Steward, Jr., an old acquaintance of mine, was killed, near Elizabethtown, New Jersey, by a similar act of carelessness, and in the same manner.

MAY 2. — The following gentlemen dined with us : Mr. William H. Prescott, Dr. Wainwright, Mr. Brevoort, I. S. Hone, W. B. Astor, D. C. Colden, Lieutenant-Governor Bradish, James G. King, and Charles A. Davis. Mr. Prescott is exceedingly pleased with the attentions he has received in New York, and in truth he deserves them all. He is agreeable in manners, and bright in conversation, free from pedantry, and modest, as we always wish to find a man of such talents. He is engaged at present in writing a history of Mexico, which requires about a year to be finished. His " Ferdinand and Isabella " has been eminently successful, it having passed through eight editions since it came out in 1838, and is still a very salable book.

MAY 3. — To-morrow is the day appointed by the Rhode Island. Rhode Island insurgents for the organization of their pretended government under the officers illegally elected by what is called the " free suffrage party." In expectation of the violence which it is feared will attend these insurrectionary proceedings, United States troops have been sent on to Providence from the different stations ; two companies went from Governor's Island a day or two since, and yesterday a detachment from Norfolk passed through this city. General Wood is on the spot prepared for *business*, and it is hoped that the prompt interference of the general government to " keep the peace " will prevent bloodshed for the present ; but finally it will result, as it always does, in the " fierce democracy " getting the better of law and good order. Downward, downward, is the tendency of all political affairs in this country ! If old King George the Third, who so reluctantly released us from colonial bondage, could raise his obstinate head, and take a look at us, how would he rejoice to contemplate the probable failure of our experiment of self-government.

MAY 13. — The Union Club is now pretty well
Union Club. settled in its new quarters, — Mr. William B. Astor's large house, in Broadway, higher up the street, and on the opposite side from the former situation. The house is exceedingly well calculated for the club, or will be, after a new building is finished in the rear, intended for the public dining-room, and kitchen below. It has been newly furnished and put in handsome order at an expense (including the new building) of $7,000, —an excellent lounging place for old and young beaux, each of whom would fain wish to be thought what the other is; where horse-racing and politics are discussed by those who know little about either of those abstruse sciences; where the " young idea " is taught to shoot billiard-balls, and study the mystery of whist; and where I frequent, notwithstanding the satirical tone of the present remarks. Such is the inconsistency of man's desires! Happy at home, I seek amusement abroad; and, preferring my library to all other places, I join the society of men who know nothing of books but "the history of the four kings."

MAY 19. — The face of affairs has changed in Rhode
Rhode Island. Island. Governor Dorr, the supernumerary governor of that redoubtable little State, who came to New York a lamb, and was sent on to Providence a lion, by the Tammany sympathizers, drew his sword, planted his cannon, fortified his castle, issued his proclamation, and doomed to death, without " benefit of clergy," every man opposed to him. But finding that his friends fell from him, and his enemies gathered strength and courage, he sheathed his Durandina, withdrew his bloody sentence, as he did his own person, and, his cannon refusing to *go off*, went off himself in the middle of the night; and when Governor King, accompanied by the sheriff, went to arrest him yesterday morning, he had "absquatulated," "mizzled," "made tracks" (either of

which terms may be used, each being considered equally classical
in the slang nomenclature of the day, and particularly appropriate
and expressive in the present case), —

> " And Governor Dorr
> Was seen no more."

The first accounts from Providence led us to suppose that, with
the retreat of the leader, the opposition to the laws and the constituted authorities had ceased; but it appears that a body of his
followers still retained possession of the cannon, and had thrown
up a sort of redoubt for their defence; but this was probably intended as a means of securing a favourable capitulation, and the
steamboat to-morrow will, it is hoped, bring us the agreeable tidings
that the civil war is at an end.

Now, what a pretty figure do the men cut who encouraged the
Rhode Island rebels, and denounced the general government for
the interference to which it was enjoined by the Constitution!
Some of them begin already to back out.   Stephen Allen has published a sort of half-way disavowal.   He only meant " to *advise*
the President, not to interfere."   " He did not mean to take sides
with the insurgents," — not he, good, easy man !   " He was engaged,
and did not attend the meeting."   Most virtuous citizen !   But he
did allow his name to be used by a set of fellows of whose companionship he was ashamed, for a purpose which he knew could come
to no good; and so he will again, whenever his tools say he must,
and so will Walter Bowne, and John J. Morgan, and Churchill C.
Cambreling, and Campbell P. White; but they have done a deed,
the bad odour of which they will never be able to shake from their
garments.   If, hereafter, any of them shall go to Newport or Providence, the finger of scorn will be pointed at them, as incendiaries
who threw from a distance a brand to light the flames of civil discord
in a sister State, and put weapons in the hands of misguided men
to shed the blood of their brethren and neighbours.   I record with
pleasure the fact that some of the leading men of the Loco-foco

party refused to be made parties to this nefarious proceeding. My old acquaintance, John Targee (whose orthodoxy nobody can doubt), told me to-day that he refused to sign the call for the meeting, as an affair which he did not understand, and an interference which he could not justify; and, furthermore, if they used his name he would come out publicly and disavow it.

MAY 30.—Robert C. Winthrop has resigned his seat in Congress, as representative from Boston, in consequence of the illness of his wife. This is a great loss at such a time as the present, but one which can be repaired, as it is understood that Abbott Lawrence, whose health is restored, will consent to resume his place if he should be elected, of which, for the credit of Boston, there is no doubt.

MAY 31.—Ex-President Van Buren, who is on an
Courtesy of Rivals. excursion to the South and West, accompanied by Mr· Paulding, late Secretary of the Treasury, after having paid his respects, as in duty bound, to his " illustrious predecessor " of the Hermitage, went to Lexington, Kentucky, where, as the account states, " he was immediately called upon by Mr. Clay, with an invitation to go to Ashland (Mr. Clay's residence). On the next day, in company with Mr. Paulding, he went to Ashland, in compliance with Mr. Clay's invitation, where he remained for a day or two." I wonder if they talked about Tyler.

Departure of the "George Washington." JUNE 8.—Yesterday was quite a day of jubilee with me. On coming down to breakfast I found a kind note from Mr. James G. King, to attend, with one of my lady folk, a parting breakfast, given at Highwood, to Mr. and Mrs. Dickens. Margaret and I went over at ten o'clock, where we found the Boz and Bozess, Mr. and Mrs. Archibald Gracie, Miss Wilkes and the Doctor, Mr. and Mrs. Colden, Miss Ward, and the charming family of our host and hostess. We had a breakfast worthy of the entertainers and the entertained; and such strawberries and cream ! The house, and the grounds, and the view, and the libraries, and the conservatory were all more beautiful than I have ever seen them. Having been favoured with an invitation from Grinnell, Minturn, & Co., the owners of the ship "George Washington," to accompany Mr. and Mrs. Dickens to Sandy Hook, I left Margaret to take Mrs. Colden and Miss Wilkes in the barouche to town, and was driven down to Jersey City, where, by previous arrangements, a steamboat was sent to take us on board, and we embarked with a "hurrah" from the people assembled on the dock. We found on board the steamboat a large party of gentlemen, among whom were the owners, Rev. Dr. Wainwright, Drs. Francis, Cornell, and Wilkes; Mr. Chapman, Mayor of Boston; Judge Warren, of New Bedford; Mr. Crittenden, the distinguished Kentucky senator; Charles King, D. C. Colden, Simeon Draper, James Bowen, Henry Cary, J. Prescott Hall, R. M. Blatchford, and his son, and other gentlemen, — a right pleasant merry company. We went delightfully down to Sandy Hook, where the ship lay at anchor. Soon after we came on board a cold collation was spread, to which and to an infinite number of bottles of champagne wine the utmost justice was done. Speeches and toasts and bright sayings went around, of all which Dickens was the most fruitful theme. I gave his health in the following toast: "Charles Dickens: the welcome acquired by literary reputation has been confirmed and justified by personal intercourse." At the conclusion of this jolly repast we took leave of the passengers with many hearty shakings of the hands and good wishes, returned to the steamer, towed the ship to the point off Sandy Hook, and having cast her off and given three cheers, which were returned in proper style, she went "on her way rejoicing," and was soon out of sight, and the party returned to the city about six o'clock.

I was invited to dine at Mr. Charles A. Davis's; but my attendance at the Bank for Savings prevented my being there at the commencement of the dinner, and I thereby escaped the dull part, that is, the eating part, of such entertainments. The dinner was given to the great financial giants who arrived in the "Great Western," — Messrs. Horsley Palmer and Sampson Ricardo; besides whom we had Mr.

Labouchère, and a gentleman whose hard German name I cannot recollect, who represents the great house of Hope.

I was placed by Mr. Davis in the lady's seat after she retired, where I had an opportunity of talking a great deal with Messrs. Palmer and Ricardo. The former gentleman is the governing spirit of the Bank of England, which governs England ; England governs Europe, and Europe governs the world, etc.

This world was made for Horsley Palmer ; his solid, portly presence, and the bright, shining face of Mr. Ricardo, seem to be the suitable representative and embodiment of the bank-notes and the gold and silver of Great Britain. It is their first visit to this country, of which they appear to have favourable predilections, notwithstanding they have pretty considerable quantities of unpaid coupons for interest on State loans. The rest of our party consisted of Judge Oakley, the Collector, William B. Astor, Moses H. Grinnell, Blatchford, Parish, John I. Palmer, James G. King, Cornelius W. Lawrence.

JUNE 14.—I went from court yesterday to dine with Mr. Robert B. Minturn. It was a most delightful dinner. We had Mr. Crittenden, Mr. Horsley Palmer, Messrs. Griffin, Grinnell, George Curtis, John C. Hamilton, Russell, Cary, Depeyster, Ogden, etc. At nine o'clock Dr. Wainwright (who had also a dinner-party, to which I was invited) joined us, with several of his guests ; viz., Ogden Hoffman, Daniel Lord, Jr., Mr. Curtis, of Boston, and Judge Warren, of New Bedford. The whole party sat and drank fine wine, and had conversation of the most brilliant kind, until the "noon of night."

FIRE–PLACE, JUNE 24.—The weather being fine this morning I determined to make a visit to my old friend Sam Carman. I got Mr. Crandell to send me alone, in a nice little wagon, with a man to drive a pair of horses ; alone, for I could not get a single companion, the rest of the party having planned another excursion to the bay. Won't the blue-fish be glad when they are gone ! I got here at one o'clock, tried for trout in the pond before dinner, and again all the afternoon, and took only two ; the water is full of grass, it is too late in the season, and, if the truth was known, I do not believe there are as many trout in the pond as there used to be ; at any rate, I will console myself with the reason that unsuccessful fishermen generally give for bad luck. I had, however, a good dinner and supper, and after an hour's gossip with Carman and his son Joe, I retired to a comfortable bed in the little back room in which I have so often in the olden times courted "Nature's soft nurse." This will be a short visit, mayhap the last. It is about forty-five years since the first.

JUNE 27. — Affairs in Rhode Island between Governor King and the friends of law and good order,

Rhode Island.

and the spurious Governor Dorr and the insurgents, with the aid of their auxiliaries from this State and Connecticut, on the other side, have drawn to a crisis. The rebellion, after being apparently smothered for a while, has broken out afresh. Governor Dorr, as he is styled, is regularly encamped at a place called Chessacket, between Providence and the Connecticut line, and about six miles from the latter, with a force of about eight hundred ragamuffins, of which a large proportion are volunteers, sympathizers from New York and Connecticut, instigated by such men as Walter Bowne, John J. Morgan, and Stephen Allen, none of whom are understood as yet to have gone to the wars. Perhaps they will, when the first heroes shall have been killed in battle, or hanged, as they certainly will be if " the King " (I mean Governor King) " comes to his right." The insurgents have twenty pieces of cannon, principally ships' guns, planted on a hill which commands the Providence road, and the barns, cattle-sheds, and hen-roosts of the farmers are laid under contribution to keep out "the foul fiend" from the stomachs of this heterogeneous mass of rebellion and rapine.

In the mean time Governor King and the regularly constituted authorities of the State are adopting the most energetic measures, which are nobly supported by the citizens. A proclamation was issued on Saturday by the Governor, declaring the State under martial law ; banks are closed by the same authority ; the students of Brown College are dispersed, and the college turned into barracks.   No person is allowed to cross the river after eight o'clock, to enter or leave Providence without a permit, and all shops and houses must be closed before ten o'clock.   The citizens are armed and doing military duty ; troops come in hourly from other parts of the State ; a force of three thousand men is organized, under the command of Major-General William Gibbs McNeill, an old acquaintance of mine (and a sort of cousin, his wife being Mrs. Charles Cammann's daughter), who has assumed the command, with a strong staff of the most respectable men in the State ; and the city of Providence, one of the most pleasant, and hitherto most orderly, cities in the United States is suddenly transformed into a garrison, and the noise of drums and trumpets and the " pride and circumstance of glorious war " have succeeded the hum of business and the tranquillity of elegant retirement for which this capital of " the Providence Plantations " has always been celebrated.

JUNE 28. — Yesterday the ceremony took place of letting in the waters of the Croton river into the upper reservoir at Yorkville, from which the city is to be supplied with " pure and wholesome water," at an enormous expense, which is felt by the present, and will be by all future, generations of our posterity.

JUNE 30. — The civil war in " the Providence Plan-
Rhode Island. tations " seems to be suddenly brought to a conclusion.

The friends of law and good order, full of fight and good spirit, as they certainly were, marched out from Providence to the enemy's entrenchments at Chessacket, but could not get a fight, because " they found no enemy to fight withal," and Major-General McNeill has gathered laurels none the less bright for being guiltless of blood.   On the arrival of the troops at Governor Dorr's " headquarters," the hero had again run away, and left his adherents to shift for themselves and make the best terms they could with the conquerors. There was some little skirmishing between a portion of the insurgents and the regular troops, in which one man was killed and two wounded; but the camp was taken quiet possession of, with the arms and ammunition, powder and pumpkins, guns and geese, pikes and potatoes, and by this time the good people of Providence have returned to their peaceful pursuits, for which happy deliverance they are mainly indebted to their own gallant conduct, and the wisdom and determination of their rulers. Dorr escaped, nobody knows where. It is said that he has been seen here in New York, — not very unlikely, for he makes this his "City of Refuge." Here are friends to sympathize in his misfortunes, and stimulate him to future "deeds of daring." Tammany Hall infuses in his manly bosom a certain quantity of valour with which, from time to time, he marches to the field of battle, but which, like a Yankee clock, is only warranted to go for a certain short period, and, like a bottle of champagne manufactured for a specific market, is sure to evaporate as soon as the cork is started at his "Headquarters, Gloucester, R.I."

The friends of law and order are indebted for this happy and bloodless result of the dangers with which they were threatened, to their own manly spirit and uncompromising devotion to the true interests of their gallant little State; they marched out to fight the insurgents with courage and promptness worthy of their sires, and besides the actual citizens of the State, many of her native sons resident in other States rallied around her in the "hour of her need." I saw young Blatchford, who was sent by Governor Seward to ascertain if any of the arms or munitions belonging to the State of New York had been surreptitiously conveyed to Rhode Island, or any of our citizens taken in arms among the insurgents. He told me he saw my neighbour, Charles H. Russell, with his sword at his side and spurs on his heels, serving as *aide-de-camp* to General McNeill, with whom he rode out to the camp of the insurgents when a battle was expected, and returned the same night after the enemy had fled. Insurrection and rebellion have no terrors when met thus, and boldly confronted by patriotism and loyalty, and the spirit now manifested will be the best security from future attempts against the peace of the State.

JULY 12. — My wife and I drove out this afternoon to see the two reservoirs in which the Croton water was introduced a few days since. This great work is thus completed, with the exception of the magnificent aqueduct by which it is intended to convey the water across the Harlem river, where pipes are now temporarily laid down from one bank to the other on a level with the water. We visited first the receiving reservoir near Yorkville, consisting of two basins which cover about thirty acres, a solid fabric, erected on a height sufficient to convey the water to the tops of the houses in the city. The outer walls are of handsome wrought stone, the basins lined with a dry slope wall, one twenty and the other thirty feet in depth. They are at present about half full, and the clear, sweet, soft water (clear it is, and sweet, and soft; for to be in the fashion I drank a tumbler of it, and found it all these) is flowing in copiously, and has already formed two pretty, limpid, placid, Mediterranean seas, of wholesome temperance beverage, well calculated to cool the palates and quench the thirst of the New Yorkers, and to diminish the losses of the fire-insurance companies. There were a great number of visitors at this place, — pedestrians, horsemen, railroad travellers, and those who, like myself, came in their own carriages (which, if they had no more right than me to do, was very reprehensible), — for it has become a fashionable place of resort; and well it may, for it is well worth seeing.

We then came down and stopped at the lower, or distributing, reservoir, at Murray's Hill, about two miles above my house, which I had not seen since the arrival of the waters. The two basins here have about one-third of their quantity of water, and the distributing pipes are filled and the waters being supplied to such places in town as are prepared for it. This great enterprise will cost $10,000,000, and it is somewhat remarkable, and an evidence of its acknowledged utility, that with the certainty of a tremendous increase of taxation consequent upon it, to the present generation and its posterity, and in party times, too, when men are so hard to please, not a voice has been raised against it, and all parties hail the advent of the " pure and wholesome water," after its journey on the earth, and under the earth, and across the watercourses of miles, as a proud event for our city, and one which enables the Knickerbockers to hold their heads high among the nations of the earth.

JULY 13. — The splendid edifice fronting on Wall,

New York
Custom-House.
William, and Pine streets is now entirely completed, and has been occupied as the New York Custom-House, in all its manifold and complicated departments, since the first of May. It is intended to collect the import revenue upon the commerce of the nation ; but how if it should prove that, the commerce being annihilated, there will be no revenue to collect? A splendid reservoir has been prepared, with fountains whose streams are to irrigate the land in all quarters ; but how melancholy would it be to discover that, after all these preparations, the springs are to be dried up and the waters have ceased to flow. It looks awfully like it just now. The natural earth is sufficiently soaked, in all reason ; but the exchequer is dry, — dry as powder. The waters are stagnant, but the government *runs* in debt alone. The building of the Custom-House was commenced in May, 1834, and the edifice finished, with its furniture complete, in May, 1842 ; cost, $985,000.

The statement of the cost of this magnificent *winding sheet* of departed commerce is taken from an elaborate and well written description published in the " Commercial Advertiser," of this afternoon. A stranger walking from Broadway down Wall street would laugh heartily at these lugubrious expressions of mine, and be apt to remark, " If these are the grave-clothes of commerce, of what materials were her bridal garments composed?" With his back to " New Trinity," the most beautiful structure of stone in America (and I know of none more beautiful anywhere), he passes the

Custom-House, which cost a million; eight or ten banks, each a palace for the worship of mammon; and the New Exchange, with a portico of granite columns such as Sir Christopher Wren had no notion of; worthy, indeed, of Palladio or Michael Angelo,—an edifice the cost of which sunk all the money of myself and other fools who subscribed for it, besides contracting a debt of which nothing but the interest will ever be paid out of the income. These, with brokers' offices and the " seats of money-changers " (there are none who " sell doves," that I know of, though there may be many *pigeons*), some of which have cost extravagant sums, would convey to the mind of the wayfaring man an image wholly different from that of commercial distress and pecuniary embarrassment; and yet that these do exist at this moment, in a degree altogether unprecedented, there can be no doubt. Verily, the good people of New York, and especially the merchants, like the apothecary in the " Honey Moon," have " new-gilded their pestle and mortar in the jaws of bankruptcy." The cage is splendid, but the bird has fled. The setting is costly enough, but the jewel is lost, or has been pawned or gambled away. There must be a recuperative principle in this great country to restore things some time or another, but I shall not live to see it.

JULY 27. — I was grieved to see, in a New York paper, that my old friend, Goold Hoyt, died at Sharon Springs, on Friday, 22d instant. He was in the seventy-third year of his age.

Negotiations
with
England.

AUGUST 2. — Mr. Webster's emphatic declaration, which he made to me in March, that all the negotiations between us and Great Britain would be settled before September, seems to be in a fair progress of accomplishment. The ugliest knot is now said to be disentangled. Nothing official has been published; but it is generally understood at Washington that the basis of a treaty in relation to the Maine boundary · has been settled between Lord Ashburton and the Secretary of State, with the concurrence of the commissioners who represent the States of Massachusetts and Maine.

The terms, no doubt, are mutually honourable and advantageous, notwithstanding some of the demagogues in Congress who would consent to see the ship of state a wreck, rather than that she should be saved by a Whig pilot, are making a clamour about the terms of the settlement agreed upon before they know what it is, and condemning measures which they could not understand, to minister to the morbid appetite of party-spirit. It is reported and believed that the terms agreed upon are a cession by the United States of a portion of the disputed territory sufficient to give Great Britain a transit from New Brunswick and Nova Scotia to Canada, for which a portion of land, I believe, in the vicinity of Lake Champlain is ceded to us. For this relinquishment Great Britain is to pay $400,-000 or $500,000, which will probably go to quiet the two States which claim the territory, and there is very little doubt that they will sell their worthless swamps and barren hemlock lands at a good round price; and, what is of more consequence, a joint participation in the navigation of the St. John's river is secured to the United States, which, by giving an outlet to the lumber, will increase the value of the remaining lands.

In confirmation of the report that this difficult question is in a certain train of amicable adjustment, Mr. Webster gave a dinner the other day to Lord Ashburton, at which were present the President, the cabinet ministers, and the commissioners of Massachusetts and Maine, at which much mutual good-will was exhibited, and loving toasts and tender speeches were made by the reconciled lovers. Lord Ashburton gave "The President," with a complimentary sentiment to " Brother Jonathan; " to which the Secretary responded, coaxing " John Bull " through his lovely queen; and the President gave "The Commissioners," with " Blessed are the peace-makers ;" from which latter circumstance it may be inferred that no danger is to be apprehended in that wayward and unreliable quarter.

AUGUST 17. — A letter has been published in some
"Boz."   of our newspapers, signed "Charles Dickens," dated
July 15, and addressed from " Devonshire Terrace,

Parkgate," "To the Editor of the ' Morning Chronicle,' " which contains some sentiments so derogatory to our country, in which the writer has been so recently honoured to the full extent of his deserving, that nothing is left for Mr. Dickens but to deny its authenticity, to save himself from the merited charges of wilful misrepresentations and gross ingratitude. I have written him a letter, calling for his avowal or denial of this unworthy piece of splendid impudence, which is copied in my letter-book ; and he must stand or fall, in my estimation, by his answer, if he chooses to make one. If the following sentiments are, indeed, Mr. Dickens's, he has proved himself a slanderer more vile than any of his predecessors, in the disreputable trade of misrepresenting the United States and their people : —

"Though in my travels from city to city I, of course, found much to be pleased with and astonished at, yet the total difference between our good old English customs and the awkwardness, the uncouth manners, and the unmitigated selfishness which you meet everywhere in America, made my journey one of a good deal of annoyance. I do not think the Americans, as a people, have much good taste. To a person brought up among them, and in their own way, of course the glaring faults that strike a stranger do not appear ; but to any well-bred man from abroad, the effect of the prevalent features of the American character is by no means agreeable." The following is a part of this letter, so arrogant and so ungrateful that I am led to hope the whole may be a forgery : " It may be said that I, of all persons, ought to be blind to the dark spots of American character, treated as I have been by the American people. I do not agree with this view of the case. I did not seek their attentions, their dinners, and their balls. On the contrary, these things were forced upon me ; many times to the serious inconvenience of myself and my party. The kindness of a friend, if it is troublesome and officious, often annoys as much as the injuries of an enemy. The Americans have most of the faults both of the English and French, with very few of their virtues. I never thought that I was petted, merely for *myself ;* but as a kind of *monster*, to look at, and imbue my keepers with somewhat of the notoriety that enveloped myself. I can freely and confidently say that this was the case, almost without exception."

Treaty and Tariff.

AUGUST 23. — This day should be marked with a white stone. Two gleams of sunshine have broken through the dark clouds which obscure the political horizon, and men look round upon each other, as who should say, " May not these things lead to better times? " This day we have two pieces of agreeable intelligence : the treaty with England is ratified by the Senate and promulgated, and the tariff bill has passed the House of Representatives.

Lord Ash-burton.

His mission of peace having been accomplished, this distinguished nobleman, who has " bought golden opinions " during his sojourn in Washington, came this way on a short excursion, previous to his sailing for England in the " Warspite " frigate, which has been lying in our harbour to await his departure. His lordship came to New York on Monday, where the " Governor's Room," in the City Hall, has been handsomely appropriated by the common council to his use ; but which, from his short stay, he did not avail himself of. He dined yesterday with a party of gentlemen at James G. King's splendid seat at Highwood, Weehawken. Mr. King took much pains to find me, to partake of this handsome feast and to pass the night at Highwood, where I should probably have gone if I had known of it ; in which case I should have avoided Francis's dose, and perhaps not have been so well as I am to-day.

Tariff Bill.

AUGUST 26. — " The deed is done : " the revenue bill, or the tariff bill, or whatever it is called by men of different opinions, passed the Senate on Saturday evening, with some trifling amendments, which will probably be instantly adopted by the House ; and Monsieur Veto, it is thought, will not exercise his oft-used and abused privilege by refusing his assent. *Laus Deo*, however, I rejoice that this great question is likely to be settled. This and the Webster and Ashburton treaty will make matters easier in this poor country, unless the patient has been brought so low that no remedies can save her. The circulation ! the circulation is stopped !

SEPTEMBER 2. — The dinner to Lord Ashburton was given last evening, at the Astor House. Mr. Peter A. Jay presided, with James D. P. Ogden and Moses H. Grinnell as vice-presidents. Among the guests besides his lordship were the following: Messrs. Mildmay and Bruce, of the Legation; Mr. Buchanan and Mr. Grattan, British consuls at New York and Boston; Lord John Hay and the officers of the " Warspite; " Mr. Horsley Palmer and Mr. Speddings; Rev. Dr. Wainwright and Rev. Dr. Potts; the Mayor; Hon. George Evans, senator for Maine; Colonel Bankhead, U.S. Army; and Commodore Perry, of the Navy.

The dinner was exceedingly good, and the decorations of the room in admirable taste; and everything went off successfully, although some of the papers find fault with the committee of arrangements for some alleged neglect to that tenacious body of gentlemen, the reporters, who went off in a huff after the fourth toast; for this, and because the toast to the President was not cheered, some of them (especially the abusive " Herald ") are pouring out the vials of their wrath upon the devoted heads of the committee of arrangements as if it was their business to indicate to the company the amount of approbation with which the toasts they had prepared should be received by the company, and to regulate the amount of their enthusiasm. It is true that a dead silence was spread over the room on the drinking of that toast, and it is equally true that the next one, "The Queen," was differently received; and I could have wished it otherwise. Mr. Tyler certainly had no claims upon the affection or respect of the individuals present; but I am quite sure that a sentiment of respect for the exalted office he holds would have prompted all present to receive the toast with the accustomed honours if the Chair had set the example, whose duty I think it was; and as there was none of that spontaneous feeling in favour of the individual, which sometimes sets a company in the humour to cheer and applaud, the toast passed off with the ominous silence which has been complained of; but it certainly was not the fault of the committee. The following are the names of the gentlemen composing the committee of arrangements, — and things have come to a pretty pass in our heterogeneous city, if such men, most of whom have devoted their lives to the gratuitous service of their fellow-citizens, should be thus abused by a foreign blackguard, who gains a livelihood by administering to the bad taste and worse morals of an ungrateful public: James D. P. Ogden, Prosper M. Wetmore, James Lee, Benjamin L. Swan, George Griswold, James G. King, Robert B. Minturn, Stephen Whitney, William B. Astor, Cornelius W. Lawrence, and Theodore Sedgwick.

SEPTEMBER 14. — The amusement of prize-fighting,

Boxing. the disgrace of which was formerly confined to England, to the grief and mortification of the moral and respectable part of her subjects, and the disgust of travellers from other countries, has become one of the fashionable abominations of our loafer-ridden city. Several matches have been made lately; the parties, their backers, betters, and abettors, with thousands and tens of thousands of degraded amateurs of this noble science, conveyed by steamboats chartered for the purpose, have been following the champions to Staten Island, Westchester, and up the North river, out of the jurisdiction (as was supposed) of the authorities of New York; and the horrid details, with all their disgusting technicalities and vulgar slang, have been regularly presented in the " New York Herald," to gratify the vitiated palates of its readers, whilst the orderly citizens have wept for the shame which they could not prevent.

One of those infamous meetings took place yesterday on the bank of the North river in Westchester, the particulars of which are given at length in that precious sheet and others of a similar character. Two men, named Lilly and McCoy, thumped and battered each other for the gratification of a brutal gang of spectators, until the latter, after one hundred and nineteen rounds, fell dead in the ring, and the other ruffian was smuggled away and made his escape from the hands of insulted justice.

SEPTEMBER 17. — The people seem at last to be a little aroused at Mr. Tyler's tyrannical and proscriptive administration of the government. His last act is intolerable, and if there was any spirit in the people it would be visited with impeachment. He has removed from the office of Collector of Philadelphia a fine old American gentleman, — Jonathan Roberts, a man of his own appointment, who has acted in all things upon the very principles in relation to political matters in the discharge of his official duties which our inconsistent President laid down on his entrance into the office which he so unworthily fills.

Executive Proscription.

Mr. Tyler orders the collector to turn out of office thirty inferior officers, tide-waiters, measurers and weighers, for the alleged crime of being friendly to Mr. Clay, and to appoint in their places others whom he designates, — Tyler men. This mandate is given in a tone worthy of the Grand Sultan, — "for reasons satisfactory to myself." When Mr. Roberts attempted to remonstrate with the President, saying that the present incumbents are capable and honest, and that they are men of family, and come up to the President's standard of non-interference in politics, the savage order is further enforced by the sapient son and secretary of the unfeeling despot, who closes his official rescript in the following language, worthy of that amiable autocrat, Paul of Russia, " He, therefore [his honoured papa], has ordered me to say to you that he desires the requisition he has made on you in the matter to be at once and to the letter complied with."

This is *le roi le veut* with a vengeance. But Mr. Roberts is not pliant and subservient enough for the times and for Mr. Tyler. He goes on to Washington, and, after much contumelious treatment from the satrap of the palace, is admitted to an audience by Kouli Khan, who cuts him dead, as the saying is, and tells him plainly, " Turn these men out, or I shall turn you out." The old veteran does not understand this language. He refuses to obey the order, saying, in his honest heart, " I'll see you d—d first." He returns to Philadelphia, where he has hardly arrived when a supersedeas is handed to him by a Mr. Smith, who is appointed in his place, and stands ready, no doubt, to do this or any other dirty work to which he may be ordered. In the mean time Mr. Roberts is applauded for his firmness and honoured for his independence. Meetings are held in Philadelphia to condemn the President and to exalt his victim, of whom it will be said in his retirement : —

> "Great Cincinnatus, at his plough,
> With brighter lustre shone,
> Than guilty Cæsar e'er could show
> When seated on a throne."

Phelps in Limbo. SEPTEMBER 30. — My old friend, Thaddeus Phelps, having been cited to appear before the grand jury to testify in the examination of the facts in the duel case between Webb and Marshall, appeared, but refused to give evidence, on the ground that information was derived from another person in confidence, and that he was in honour bound not to betray him. He stated, however, that his informant was not Colonel Webb, nor any other person concerned in the duel. This, I think, should have been satisfactory to the grand jury; but they thought otherwise, and Phelps was taken before the court, where he persisted in his refusal, but disclaimed any intentional disrespect, and was ready to " bow to their mandate ; " on which he was sent to prison for ten days. But his confinement is only a technical sort of affair, for I find his wooden leg is still stumping its way in Wall street ; in custody, I presume.

Mr. Webster's Speech. OCTOBER 1. — Great interest has been excited in the political circles, by a promised speech to be made by Mr. Webster to his friends in Boston. He had declined the offer of a public dinner, expressing his preference for a meeting of the Whigs, before whom he might define his position in relation to Mr. Tyler's cabinet. This meeting took place, and the great speech was made yesterday in Faneuil Hall, the cradle of liberty, and the theatre of many of the proudest triumphs of the accomplished orator and patriotic statesman who now appeared before the assembled multitude of Whigs. The speech is published in several of our newspapers, reporters having been sent from this city, who appear to have done justice to the important subject. It is a *great* speech ; on such an occasion, and from such a source, it could not be otherwise, but it will throw the whole Whig party into confusion. Mr. Webster defends his continuance in the cabinet, and gives good and sufficient reasons for it, in the labour he has performed and the success he has achieved in the negotiation of the British treaty ; and in this all the good men of his party, and all candid men in the nation, would now willingly bear him out ; but, unfortunately, he goes further. He intimates pretty clearly that he means to remain, and justifies in many particulars, to which his friends will not consent, the course of Mr. Tyler's administration. For these causes moderate Whigs are sorry, and violent ones abusive ; and the latter description of politicians are for hauling neck and heels out of the party the man who has heretofore been its ornament and pride, — the theme of their extravagant panegyric, as he is now of their violent denunciation. How uncertain is the favour of the people ! How unsatisfactory the calling of politics ! Such a man as Daniel Webster may be in an instant blown down by the same breath which set him up. There is no breathing-spell in the popular voice between the last vibrating shout of " Hallelujah " and the first appalling cry of " Crucify him ! "

Mr. Webster's recent movement will, no doubt, be prejudicial to the prospects of the Whig party ; but for himself personally there is much palliation. The flood which has set in with a force so irresistible for Mr. Clay as the next candidate for the Presidency can never convey Mr. Webster on its bosom to personal honour or political distinction. These two eminent men are undeniably rivals; their talents, public services, and exalted rank in the great Whig army of the Union have raised for each a personal party, and, their pretensions being equal, the elevation of one forbids that of the other; the sun of popular favour shining on one must inevitably throw the other into the shade; and, whatever simulated expressions of good-will may pass between them, it is impossible they should be friends. It is, perhaps, unfortunate for the party that it has two such men in its ranks; their political opponents are not so troubled.

Mr. Webster is not a party to his unceremonious ejectment from the cause, nor from among the men with whom he has been so nobly identified during his whole brilliant career of political service. He only differs on the best means of serving them; he deprecates the measures of the administration in some particulars, avows his steady opposition to the fatal exercise of the veto power, but submits to his hearers whether the cause they support and the principles they advocate cannot be better served by *him* as a member of the cabinet, than by some other person who may be appointed his successor, less acquainted with their interests, and less capable of promoting them. In short, shall he, a tried friend, leave his place at the risk of seeing it filled by an enemy? Plausible, certainly, if not convincing; but, whatever may be his determination on the subject of his own course in relation to his continuance in the cabinet, which constitutes the main ground of difference between him and the other friends of Mr. Clay, he thus expresses himself proudly and emphatically as to his undeviating adherence to what he considers Whig principles. And if Daniel Webster does not understand the meaning of the term, where shall we look for its exposition? "I am a Whig," he says; "I always have been one, and I always shall be one; and if anybody undertakes to turn me out of the pale of that communion, let him see to it who gets out first! I am a Massachusetts Whig, — a Faneuil-Hall Whig, — breathing her air now for twenty-five years, and meaning to breathe it on the spot so long as God shall please to give me life." On the whole, this speech is one of the most important incidents that ever occurred in the political history of the country, and as such will be referred to in all future times of the Republic. Daniel Webster stands alone in the Whig party.

OCTOBER 4.—The annual commencement of Co-
College Commencement. lumbia College was held this day, in the middle Dutch Church,—an Episcopal literary institution, endowed by the church and established upon its principles, compelled to resort to the liberality of the seceders for a place to hold its anniversary exercises, because an intolerant bishop and a subservient rector (both of whom are trustees of the college) have made the mighty discovery that such exercises are a desecration of the holy temple of God, the main support of which depends upon a successful system of moral and religious education, such as is imparted by Columbia College to the youth of our country. The attendance was greater than usual. Many distinguished persons were present (among whom was the Governor of the State) ; and the inauguration of the new president, Dr. Nathaniel F. Moore, with the address made to him by the president of the board of trustees, Peter A. Jay, Esq., and his own in reply, formed an interesting feature in the exercises of the day.

Thirty members of the graduating class received the degree of Bachelor of Arts, of whom fourteen delivered orations, in the following order: Abram Stevens Hewitt, William L. Kernochan, Robert Jaffray, Jr., William Henry Ebbetts, William Pinckney Stewart, Robert M. Olyphant, John Lyon, Wheelock H. Parmly, David R. Stanford, Silas Weir Roosevelt, Oliver Everett Roberts, W. Rodman, Zebedee Ring, Jr., Edward E. Potter.

OCTOBER 7.—I found, on my return last evening, the following letter from Mr. Dickens, in reply to one I wrote him on the 19th August. It turns out as I supposed. The scurrilous remarks on the United States, to which his name is subscribed, and which were so promptly taken up by the rascally penny papers and published through the country, were a base forgery, gotten up probably by one of the craft on this side of the water.

Broadstairs, Kent, England,
16th September, 1842.

My dear Sir : — I am very much obliged to you for your friendly letter, which I have received with real pleasure. It reached me last night, being forwarded from London to this sea-side fishing town, where we are enjoying ourselves quietly until the end of the month. I answer it without an hour's delay, though I fear my reply may lie at the post-office some days before it finds a steam-packet to convey it across the ocean. The letter to which you refer is, from beginning to end, in every word and syllable, the cross of every *t* and the dot of every *i*, a most wicked and nefarious forgery. I have never published one word or line in reference to America, in any quarter whatever, except the copyright circular, and the unhung scoundrel who invented that astounding lie knew this as well as I do. It has caused me more pain, and more of a vague desire to take somebody by the throat, than such an event should perhaps have awakened in any honourable man. But I have not contradicted it publicly, deeming that it would not become my character or elevate me in my own self-respect to do so. I shall hope to send for your acceptance next month my " American Notes." Meanwhile, and always, and with cordial remembrance to all friends,

I am, my dear sir, faithfully yours,

Charles Dickens.

October 8. — Dr. Doane, the health-officer, sent me a fine little turtle the other day, which he has had fattening for me at the quarantine, and I invited the following party to assist us in disposing of the delicious soup : Mr. D. S. Kennedy, Mr. J. P. Giraud, Mr. F. C. Tucker, Mr. Charles A. Davis, Mr. J. D. P. Ogden, Mr. Moses H. Grinnell, Mr. R. M. Blatchford, Mr. Samuel B. Ruggles, Mr. W. G. Ward.

Dinner-party.

October 12. — Nothing is talked of or thought of in New York but Croton water ; fountains, aqueducts, hydrants, and hose attract our attention and impede our progress through the streets. Political spouting has given place to water-spouts, and the free current of water has diverted the attention of the people from the vexed questions of the confused state of the national currency. It is astonishing how popular

Croton Water.

the introduction of water is among all classes of our citizens, and how cheerfully they acquiesce in the enormous expense which will burden them and their posterity with taxes to the latest generation. Water! Water! is the universal note which is sounded through every part of the city, and infuses joy and exultation into the masses, even though they are out of spirits.

OCTOBER 14. — The fine weather, which has continued without interruption twenty-four days, held out one day longer, to smile upon the great pageant. The other elements, with becoming politeness, united to do honour to the triumph of water, and nothing occurred in "the heaven above, nor the earth below," to mar the splendid scene; as for "the waters under the earth," they were all brought to the surface on this occasion, and made a great *spouting* about their emancipation. I was invited, as "ex-Mayor," to take a place in the procession, for which purpose I went to the City Hall at nine o'clock. At this time the whole population of the city, and as many more from other places, were in motion. At ten the procession began to move. I was placed in a barouche with Aaron Clark, another ex-Mayor; Mr. Hart, ex-Mayor of Troy; and Mr. Murphy, Mayor of Brooklyn. This detachment consisted of about a dozen barouches, in one of which was Governor Seward; his staff was under the orders of Mr. Morris, the Mayor of the city. We went down to the Battery, where we were placed in the line immediately after a splendid military escort, and proceeded up Broadway to Union place, where the Governor reviewed the troops. Thence the procession continued down the Bowery to Grand street, through Grand street to its junction with West Broadway, and down the latter street to the Park, where the whole was reviewed, in front of the City Hall, by the Mayor and Common Council.

The whole line of the procession extended about five miles; it embraced, besides the different regiments of troops, the firemen, of whom there were fifty-two companies, including several from Philadelphia, Brooklyn, Newark, and Poughkeepsie. This part of the procession was a mile and a half in length, and beautiful it was, with the machines, banners, and other devices; and a finer-looking set of men, nor a more orderly one, I never saw. Then there were the butchers on horseback, the temperance societies, the different scientific and civic institutions, mechanic associations, among whom were the printers, with a car on which was placed the identical press at which Dr. Franklin once worked. This was employed during the transit of the procession in printing and distributing an ode written in honour of the occasion by George P. Morris, which was sung in front of the Hall by a choir of two hundred male and female performers, who were placed on a stage erected for the purpose.

The whole of this great " turn-out," which embraced everything and everybody, did not finish its round until five o'clock, when an address was made by Mr. Samuel Stevens, president of the old board of water commissioners, and a reply made by Mr. John L. Lawrence, president of the new board. Such of the dignitaries and guests as had tickets, and could get in, were then taken to the large court-room, where a collation had been provided, not by any means the best feature of the day's festivities. Here the Mayor made a speech and toasted the Governor, who made a very good speech in reply. By this time it was night, and the public gardens, theatres, and fountains completed the great celebration of the triumph of Croton water.

It was certainly a great affair; but nothing struck me with more pleasure and surprise than the perfect order and propriety which prevailed among the immense masses of male and female spectators on the route of the procession; not a drunken person was to be seen. The moral as well as the physical influence of water pervaded everything. Ardent liquors were not proof against its predominating power; there was no quarrelling, no resistance to authority, no unruly behaviour; the people stood and looked on delighted and unfatigued during the three hours occupied in the passage of the pageant. It was a day for a New Yorker to be proud of.

OCTOBER 25. — This is my birthday, — I am sixty-two years old.

Sixty-two years of active life, not always, I may hope, uselessly employed, prosperous during the greater part of this long period, and always in the enjoyment of more of the blessings of this life than I was thankful for. Sunshine has illumined my path for many of the years that are gone by, and my journey has not been impeded by more obstructions than are usually met with; and even now, when I have my share of the darkness which overspreads the land, I can enjoy some rays of light which are denied to others who are not less deserving than myself.

OCTOBER 31. — Now that this gentleman is about

Governor
Seward.

retiring from office, the people of the State seem willing to give him credit for the talent which he certainly possesses in an eminent degree, and some of his own party cease to cavil at some of his public acts, and pass complimentary resolutions at their political meetings. It has been said (and I think not without reason) that he has courted popularity a little too much, especially in some injudicious concessions to the Roman Catholics; but I believe he was always influenced in those measures by good motives, by a sincere desire to serve the cause which is supported by his political friends, and which we Whigs at least must uphold as the people's cause. There can be no doubt, however, of Governor Seward's talents, especially as a writer of pure English. His style is perspicuous and nervous, free from the tawdry and unmeaning embellishments of our modern public documents, and equally fitted for the good taste of the scholar and the comprehension of the plain man of sense.

NOVEMBER 2. — Mr. Hamilton Fish, the Whig can-

Hamilton
Fish.

didate for Congress in the Sixth District, gave a supper last evening to the nominating committee and other Whigs. I was one of the invited, but other engagements prevented me from going. It will require sundry good suppers and something stronger than his father's fine old wine to make my friend Fish swim into Congress; and, if he should, I hope he will not be out of his depth. These good things, moreover, would have a more efficacious influence if administered to the other party. "Who cares for our friends?—we are sure of them." That is the true political morality, of which the Whigs are not unmindful. But it requires a new miracle of loaves and *fishes* to feed such a multitude.

NOVEMBER 3.—A noble ship of one thousand one hundred tons, built for Grinnell, Minturn, & Co.'s line of packets, was launched yesterday morning with the good taste and patriotic feeling of those fine fellows. They have called her the "Ashburton,"—a handsome name, and a suitable compliment to the British negotiator of the treaty with England.

Launch.

NOVEMBER 4.—This has been a great day for the Secretary of State. He has recovered much of the ground he lost by his late speech at Faneuil Hall, and his continuance, against the wishes of his Whig friends (such at least as go for Mr. Clay), in the cabinet of Mr. Tyler. The common council having assigned to Mr. Webster the use of the Governor's room in the City Hall for that purpose, he received the visits of the citizens from eleven until two o'clock. An immense crowd waited upon him, the number of which was probably enhanced by the announcement that the Chamber of Commerce were to attend his levee in a body, agreeably to a resolution which had been previously adopted. At one o'clock the members were received by the Secretary on the platform in front of the hall, when an address was made by the president, Mr. James D. P. Ogden, on presenting the resolution of the chamber. It was a pleasing coincidence, that during this interesting ceremony one hundred guns were being fired in the Park on account of the news, which had just been received, of the ratification of the treaty by Great Britain, which were answered by an equal number from several other places in the vicinity of the city. This was, no doubt, a kind of interruption, not less agreeable to the orator than the applause of the thousands of spectators who listened to the address. Whatever may be the opinion of Mr. Webster's Whig friends as to his political position, they cannot deny him the credit of being the

Mr. Webster.

main instrument in effecting this important measure, the value of which posterity will appreciate.

Dinner to Mr. Webster. This gentleman having declined the invitation to a public dinner, which was signed by seventy of our most respectable citizens, a select knot of four-and-twenty Whigs had him all to themselves yesterday at the Astor House. I was one of the fortunate number, and "it was well to be there." This dinner was an event not soon to be forgotten. The party consisted of the following: Mr. Webster, Moses H. Grinnell, Charles A. Davis, Simeon Draper, Ogden Hoffman, Edward Curtis, Russell H. Nevins, Mr. Wetmore, M. C. Patterson, Robert B. Minturn, R. M. Blatchford, John I. Palmer, Samuel G. Raymond, George Curtis, Mr. Lyman, Mr. Stone, Hiram Ketcham and his brother, James W. Gerard, John Ward and myself, and two or three others whom I do not recollect. By previous arrangement, Messrs. Grinnell and Davis were placed at the head and foot of the table, and Mr. Webster in the centre, with Mr. Palmer on his left hand and I on his right. The dinner was capital; Stetson's heart was in the matter. The honoured guest appeared to be delighted, and was in turn delightful, full of anecdote and pleasant gossip; his expressive eyes shone with unusual lustre from under the dark canopy of his overhanging brows, and the infection of his brilliancy pervaded the whole table, and made the occasion a feast of reason and a flow of soul.

After the cloth was removed there was a temporary pause in the conversation, and I was requested by two or three to say something which would bring out the lion of the day. This I did. After this Mr. Gerard made a short speech in his usual good taste, with a sentiment complimentary to the Ashburton treaty and to the American negotiator. Then the dark brow at the head of the table became contracted; the noble intellect began to arrange itself and the bright eye to gather up its lightnings, piercing but benignant as those which irradiate the darkness of a summer evening.

Mr. Webster, after having gained the attention of the company, began a *talk*, not a *speech*, without rising from his seat, with no declamation, no oratorical nor rhetorical ornaments ; without gesture, in a plain, business-like, colloquial strain ; but in language pure as the dew of heaven, and full of such instruction as might proceed from such a mind as his to the minds of men to whom he paid the high compliment of considering his equals.   He gave a full history, in all its stages, of the negotiation which resulted in the treaty, from his first interview with Lord Ashburton at Washington.   He took up each point separately : the Eastern boundary, the case of the " Carolina," that of the " Creole," the subject of impressment, the right of search, the suppression of the slave-trade, and other incidental questions ; stated the difficulties which had occurred, the mutual concessions arising out of a sincere and earnest desire on both sides to consult the interests and honour of both nations in a spirit of good feeling and honest intention, rather than to resort to the exploded arts of diplomacy or to insist upon advantages merely technical.   It was agreed, said the eloquent speaker, that such arts were unworthy of two such nations as Great Britain and the United States.   They had met in a spirit of unity to settle important questions, and went to their work like men of business.   This exposition lasted an hour, and left every auditor as well acquainted, in his own mind, with the treaty, and all that appertained to it, as he who made it.   This branch of his subject being finished, Mr. Webster turned to me, and, meeting my bow by a graceful one of his own, he said, " And now as to my friend Mr. Hone, and in reply to his allusion ; if I mistake not, that gentleman gave its name to the Whig party.   I was christened at his font, and have continued firm in his faith.   I am too old to change my politics or my religion."

He then went on in a strain similar to that which had characterized his former remarks.   He attributed the unhappy divisions which exist at present in the Whig party in relation to the course of the Executive, to the unfortunate alteration of the Constitution which made it necessary to designate in the presidential election the candidates for President and Vice-President.   Previously to this change, which, like all others, has been productive of great mischief, the candidates were selected with reference to the fitness of both for the highest office, to which either was equally liable to be elected; and since that change, the second officer was usually selected with a view to personal predilections, sectional interests, or party preferences, to fill an office of no political importance (except in such a melancholy contingency as has now occurred) and devoid of personal responsibility. He then defined his position in relation to Mr. Tyler's administration. In his judgment it was better for the people and for the Whigs to make the best of existing circumstances during the remainder of the present term of the President; to secure the appointment of wise and patriotic Whigs in the foreign diplomatic department, rather than, by opposition, to throw the Executive bodily into the arms of our opponents.

The whole of this exposition of his sentiments was given in a frank and confiding manner; the interest excited was intense, and a stillness prevailed in the room during its delivery such that you might literally "hear a pin-drop;" not a word was lost, not a glance passed unnoticed. A sketch of the speaker and his audience at the moment when the former said, "And now one word for Mr. Hone," would have been a sublime moral study, a noble illustration of the omnipotent power of intellect. When he had finished, I bowed low and said, "Mr. Webster, as one of this delighted and instructed company, I thank you for the history you have given of your important negotiation; and, for myself, I feel honoured over-much by the notice you have taken of my remarks and the explanations they have been the means of eliciting." The company continued in delightful session until midnight.

NOVEMBER 7.—The "Great Western" brings out the much-talked-of "Notes on America, for General Circulation," by the celebrated author of the "Pickwick Papers." I am much afraid that the desire of the illiberal and malevolent penny-paperists and other fault-finders, who confidently expected to find "offence in it," will be disappointed. I have not

Dickens's New Work.

read the book; but one of the extracts, which is much abused in the "Herald," and held up as its greatest montrosity, viz., a most glowing picture of the mischief affected by just such papers as this "Herald," and the national disgrace attending their wide circulation, is precisely to my taste; it is true, every word of it; and if there is nothing worse in the book, I say, with all my heart, "ditto to Mr. Burke."

NOVEMBER 12. — Mr. John Delmonico, the respectable proprietor of the great hotel and restaurant in William street, died on Thursday morning, in a strange and awful manner. He was with a party, deer-hunting at Snedecors, Islip, L.I. He was placed on a stand up the creek, and a deer coming, he fired. The deer, badly wounded, took to the water, and was killed by one of the number on another stand. After some time his companions, going to join him, found him lying on his face in the same spot where he had fired, quite dead, of apoplexy, probably produced by the excitement which the sport of deer-hunting always occasions with persons unaccustomed to it. Mr. Delmonico was an amiable man, very obliging in his house, and will not fail to be remembered as long as good dinners dwell pleasantly upon the recollection.

"American Notes for General Circulation." NOVEMBER 14. — This is the somewhat singular title of Dickens's new book, which has just been received here. Its advent was expected with a vast deal of curiosity, and no *notes* have ever had a more prompt or rapid *circulation*, nor, in my opinion, has any writer been more unfairly treated by my countrymen. Lies were circulated in advance; sentiments were attributed to him which he never uttered. His name was forged to papers which he never saw; his distinct and indignant disavowal was refused the publicity which was accorded with satisfaction to the slanders regarding the unworthy character of the present work. These slanders have been refuted by the appearance of the book itself. Because a few hospitable people here and in Boston made a little too much fuss about him on the occasion of his late visit to the United States, but more especially because

Mr. Dickens saw with an unprejudiced eye the horrible licentiousness of the daily press in this country, and uttered in the language of truth his denunciation of the stupendous evil, and would fain assist in wiping out the foul blot from our national escutcheon (for all which I humbly conceive we ought to be greatly obliged to him), this lively writer, whose works have been hitherto so popular in this country, is now vilified and misrepresented. And so will any man be who has the moral courage to make battle against this frightful monster, who stalks unrebuked through the land, blasting with its pestiferous breath everything bright and lovely which is too sensitive to resist its influence, and receiving the daily homage of those who, like the men who cater for their depraved appetites, have no sympathy for virtues and accomplishments which they themselves do not possess, and whose insignificance affords them an immunity from the attacks which they enjoy so much in the persons of their superiors.

The truth is, that, contrary to the predictions of the conductors of the vile penny press, and greatly to their disappointment, Mr. Dickens has written a very fair and impartial book about this country; not very creditable, I think, to its author as a literary production, and not by any means so amusing as might have been expected from a writer who, in his previous works, has afforded us so much and such highly wrought and varied amusement. It is written carelessly; his sketches are drawn from hasty observation, and it is evident that his volatile wing has not rested long enough in one place to enable him to understand its peculiarities, nor to discourse wisely upon its characteristics. But the public institutions of the country, its manufacturing establishments, hospitals, prisons, courts, and colleges are praised and censured with equal justice and impartiality, and not unfrequently most favourably contrasted with similar institutions in his own country.

Singular Ad
vertisements. " Business is business," as some man says, in some play. The following notice, which was published the day after the funeral of poor Delmonico, is very much in the style of the inscription on a tombstone in Père-la-Chaise, which runs somewhat in this form: " Here lies the body of Pierre Quelquechose, who died so and so. This monument is erected to his memory by his widow, who takes this occasion to inform her friends and customers that the pastry-cook establishment is continued at such a number Rue Saint Honoré, where she will be happy to receive their orders."

This is the counterpart : —

" A card. — The widow, brother, and nephew Lorenzo, of the late much respected John Delmonico, tender their heartfelt thanks to the friends, benevolent societies, and Northern Liberty Fire Engine Company, who accompanied his remains to his last home. The establishment will be reopened to-day, under the same firm of Delmonico Brothers, and no pains of the bereft family will be spared to give general satisfaction. Restaurant, bar-room, and private dinners No. 2 South William street; furnished rooms No. 76 Broad street, as usual."

Death of Wm. Ellery Channing, D.D. William Ellery Channing, D.D., the great apostle of the Unitarian faith, the eloquent divine, the philanthropist, and the champion of religious and political freedom, died at Bennington, Vermont, on the 2d of October, aged sixty-three years. A funeral ceremony was performed on the 13th ult., in the church of the Messiah in this city, on which occasion a eulogy on the character, writings, and Christian labours of the deceased was pronounced by the Rev. Henry W. Bellows, of which I received a copy to-day. It was warm, glowing, eloquent, and metaphorical, as I am inclined to think all the productions of that gentleman are, and which I suspect are the characteristics of most of the eloquent divines of the Unitarian church.

Webb's Sentence. NOVEMBER 26. — James Watson Webb was brought up in the Court of Sessions this day, and sentenced by the Recorder on his plea of guilty of the charge of leaving the State to fight a duel, and fighting a duel with Thomas Marshall. The sentence was two years imprisonment in the State prison, — the shortest term prescribed by the statute. There is very little doubt that this sentence will be followed immediately by an unconditional pardon from Governor Seward, to whom petitions to that effect have been forwarded, signed by fourteen thousand citizens of New York. In this large number are included most of the leading men of the party in politics opposed to Colonel Webb, fourteen of the seventeen members of the grand jury who found the bill, every alderman and assistant of the city except one, a great many of the clergy, judges of the several courts, and members of the bar. The roll was upward of four hundred feet in length. This is all very flattering to the delinquent who has fallen into the law's danger; but there is good reason to believe that Governor Seward did not require this strong appeal to incline him to exercise the most agreeable prerogative of executive power. The pardon is, no doubt, prepared already, and all reasonable men will justify it on the present occasion.

NOVEMBER 28. —The trial in Westchester before Judge Ruggles, of Sullivan, McCluster, and Kensett, seconds in the battle fought at Hastings by Lilly and McCoy, which resulted in the death of the latter, closed on Saturday. The jury brought a verdict of " guilty of manslaughter in the fourth degree," which will probably subject the accused to two years imprisonment in the State prison. It remains to be seen whether executive clemency will find the same extenuating circumstances in this case as in that of Webb. We are deplorably in want of an example to break down the ruffianism which has been growing up amongst us; but it will puzzle His Excellency to draw a distinction in favour of a pistol, which in most cases is intended to produce death, and the fist, from which it may incidentally occur. Webb, to be sure, stands acquitted, by the letters which he wrote before the duel, from the murderous intent which characterizes such meetings on ordinary occasions; and an ounce of lead is an argument so much more genteel than a handful of knuckles. But, after all, the " *quo animo* " is not so bad in the latter case as in the former.

I was wrong, the other day, in stating that Lilly, the principal in the fight, was on trial at White Plains. That worthy "absquatulated" immediately after the "Olympic games" were over at Hastings, and the paper this day announces his arrival in Liverpool by the "George Washington," on the 30th of October. He will be all the fashion in that refined country, whose sensitive tourists faint at the recollection of the tobacco chewing and spitting Yankees, and lose their delicate appetites at our vulgar substitution of the knife for the fork. The man who killed his man here will, by that heroic exploit, have un-Yankeeized himself there. He will become an associate of the magnates of the land. His name will be enrolled in the court calendar, with the Belchers and the Springs, the Cribs and the Dutch Sams, and his portrait will adorn a page of the elegant literature of British science; the Yankee *Lilly* alongside the black champion in a hot-pressed volume, in superb binding, — one of a set which sells at a guinea and a half a volume, such as I saw last evening at Prescott Hall's, and which occupy a place in the boudoirs of the British fair alongside of "Flowers of Fancy" and "Mills's Chivalry."

DECEMBER 13. — The late Minister to France is all General Cass. the fashion in New York. He receives company in presidential and gubernatorial style at the City Hall. He has defined his political sentiments in a letter to Governor Dickinson, of New Jersey, which is published with a flourish of trumpets for the benefit of all good Republicans who may have been troubled with doubts and misgivings on that important subject. He professes to be a Democrat of the Jefferson school, and opposed to a national bank. The return of General Cass at this time, his reception, and the declaration drawn from him in the above-mentioned letter seem to indicate pretty clearly that he is to add one to the number of candidates for the Presidency. He will be a thorn in the side of Mr. Van Buren, whose chances will be more affected by this new aspirant than by that of the Southern candidate. Whether all will work together for the benefit of the single Whig candidate remains to be seen.   It is pretty difficult for me to find out the claims of General Cass.   But in that respect he stands about on a par with General Harrison at the time of his nomination.   If Mr. Clay cannot be elected, I do not know that I shall not be prepared to hurrah for Cass.   Anybody but Calhoun, even Van Buren.   I am a Northern man, and a New Yorker.   As such I can never consent to be ruled by one whose paramount principle is one of opposition to the interests and prosperity of this part of the Union.   Mr. Calhoun has talents of a superior order.   So much the worse; for his enmity is the more effective.   The canker of envy, hatred, and malice against the Northern and Eastern States lies deep in his heart.   He would prefer that the cotton of Carolina should go to Europe in British vessels rather than in those of New York, Boston, or Philadelphia.

DECEMBER 17. — On our return to-day we found the

city excited by the development of a dreadful story, of which there were some rumours when we went away. The United States brig "Somers," Captain Alexander Slidell McKenzie, arrived in this port on Wednesday night from a cruise on the African coast, and last from St. Thomas, from which latter port she had only eight days passage.   During the whole of Thursday there was a strange mystery about this vessel.   She lay in the bay; nobody, not even the near relations of the officers, was permitted to visit her; the brother of Lieutenant Gansevoort was forbidden to approach.   The cause of all this is now explained.   A dreadful mutiny had been formed when the brig left the coast of Africa, which was discovered soon after she sailed from St. Thomas.   Of this conspiracy, Philip Spencer, a young man of twenty years of age, son of the Hon. John C. Spencer, Secretary of War, was the ringleader.   The plan was to murder the captain and lieutenant, convert the brig into a pirate, and come to the American coast for the purpose of intercepting and robbing the packets, which were supposed to have large quantities of specie on board.   The crew of the vessel consisted of about seventy-five young men from the naval schools, who had been sent out to complete their education. The mutiny was disclosed by one of the conspirators, when measures were immediately taken for its suppression. Two-thirds of the crew were engaged in the plot; but Captain McKenzie appears to have acted with the utmost decision and bravery. The mutineers were confined under hatches, a court-martial was held, and young Spencer, with two of his confederates, were hung *at the yard-arm;* the rest of the mutineers put in irons, in which situation they were brought home, and have been transferred to the " North Carolina."

A messenger was sent to Washington, and nothing was allowed to transpire until the return of the mail from that place. The imminent danger of the captain and lieutenant, with so large a proportion of the crew in a state of insubordination, no doubt rendered this dreadful and summary exercise of power unavoidable, as an example and measure of safety. If it should so appear (as there seems to be no doubt), public opinion will support, and the government will approve, the conduct of Captain McKenzie. But if it should prove otherwise, he will have assumed an awful responsibility, and his reckoning with the distinguished individual, the father of the principal sufferer, will be fearful, indeed.

Captain Slidell McKenzie is a brave, gallant young officer, son of my old friend Mr. John Slidell, of this city, brother of John and Thomas Slidell, of New Orleans, the latter of whom is husband to Fanny Callender. Young Spencer was a worthless fellow, who would have been cashiered for some misdemeanour on a former cruise but from feelings of delicacy for the respectable character and high station of his father, whose severe affliction is entitled to the deepest sympathy.

DECEMBER 19. — Further particulars of the mutiny and execution on board the brig " Somers " are published this morning, not differing importantly from yesterday's statement. The plot was disclosed to Captain McKenzie by Wales, the purser's steward, on the 29th of November, and the three ringleaders executed on the 1st of

December. The conduct of Wales is highly commended by the captain and lieutenant. He pretended to give into the plot until he obtained all the plans of the conspirators, when, at a risk of his life, he made the disclosure. The two men who shared the miserable fate of Spencer were Samuel Cromwell, boatswain's mate, and Elisha Small, seaman. Twelve men and boys are now confined in irons on board the " North Carolina," awaiting the action of the navy department. The public, with the exception of the editor of the " Herald," appear to approve the captain's conduct.

DECEMBER 21. — A statement is published in the
The Mutiny. " Washington Madisonian," signed S., which will occasion some revulsion in the public mind in relation to the melancholy tragedy on board the brig "Somers." This statement, which the author asserts is " not made to excite prejudice, but to repel the attempt to create it, and to enable the American people to see what mighty principles are involved in this unheard-of proceeding," is evidently written by Mr. Spencer, the Secretary of War. It is one of those strong, forcible documents for which he is celebrated ; fierce in style, rigid in argument, and certainly presents the subject of his son's execution in a light somewhat different from that in which it was received at first. If there exists any reasonable doubt of the absolute necessity for this awful exercise of power, Captain McKenzie may wish sincerely that he never had been born to meet such a responsibility. A more dangerous opponent than John C. Spencer could not be found in the United States ; stern, uncompromising, obstinate in temper, determined and energetic in action, and with talents equal to any effort which his feelings may prompt, or his duty may call him to execute. It is officially announced that the navy department is not in possession of information sufficient to form a statement for the public eye. This would appear unfavourable to Captain McKenzie. If his official report were not so clear as to leave " no hook on which to hang a doubt," the doubt, the hesitation alone would be fatal to him. If the cabinet should take part with the bereaved parent, who is one

of its prominent members, in denying the existence of the necessity for the execution of the ringleaders of the mutiny, and if the laws should not support the measure, Captain McKenzie is ruined past redemption.

DECEMBER 24. — The following party, most of whom were members of the Hone Club, dined with me to-day, and passed a merry Christmas eve ; we sat honestly until twelve o'clock, and ate and drank, and laughed and talked, as if the times were as good as ever : R. M. Blatchford, Moses H. Grinnell, John Ward, William G. Ward, Simeon Draper, Jr., Samuel Jaudon, J. W. Webb, Edward Curtis, James Bowen, Dr. J. W. Francis, Robert B. Minturn.

DECEMBER 28. — I dined at Judge Pendleton's. The party consisted of Mr. and Mrs. Schermerhorn, Mr. and Mrs. Hammersley, Mr. and Mrs. Edward Jones, Mr. and Mrs. James J. Jones, Mr. Ray, Mr. Boreel, Maturin Livingston, James Thomson, and P. H.

Court of Inquiry.

DECEMBER 29.—Great interest is excited by the proceedings of the court of inquiry, now sitting at the navy yard, on the affair of the " Somers." The first testimony was the production of the report sent on to the navy department by Captain McKenzie, immediately after his arrival in New York ; and well would it have been for him if it had never seen the light. " Oh that mine enemy should write a book ! " was the vindictive exclamation of some such person as the Secretary of War. I have learned by experience and observation, that nine-tenths of all the scrapes men get into are occasioned by writing or saying *too much.* Here is a document ten times longer than was necessary, written without consultation with any judicious friend, who, from not being immediately interested in the event, would have been better able to look at the consequences, full of public details of trifling circumstances and irrelevant conversation, and interspersed with sage reflections with which the public and the navy department had no more to do than with the cogitation of the Emperor of China on the invasion of the "outside barbarians," or the speculations of London stockbrokers on the fall of American securities. He has aimed to be very impartial, and has conceded so much that the confidence of his friends and the public, who would fain be on his side, is shaken in the belief of the imperative necessity of the dreadful example which he felt himself called upon to make.

Not only the character of Captain McKenzie, but that of the flag under which he sails and of the nation which he serves, is deeply concerned in his making out a complete justification. There is no middle ground in this business; it was altogether right, or altogether wrong. And here, instead of a concise, manly statement of his proceeding on the discovery of the mutiny, the necessity which, in his judgment, existed for his summary exercise of power, and his regret that he had been called upon to adopt measures so painful to his feelings, we have a long rigmarole story about private letters discovered on the person of young Spencer, orders to blow out the brains of "refractory men," religious ceremonies, cheers for the American flag, and conversations with the accused, in one of which he said to Spencer that " he hung him, because if he took him to the United States he would escape punishment, for everybody got clear who had money and friends,"—a national reproach, which, even allowing it to be true, came with a bad grace from an officer of the American navy.

He makes an apology, it is true, for this indiscreet expression. But, in the name of all that is wonderful, why should he stigmatize himself by relating such a conversation in a document which will be carried on the wings of the wind to the most distant part of the earth? The truth is, there is much to be seen, in this statement, of the pride of authorship. Captain McKenzie, when he was Alexander Slidell, wrote a clever book called " A Year in Spain," which gave him some reputation as an author, and he disdained to take advice in regard either to the matter or the manner of the narrative. Even in this particular it is a failure; it will add nothing to his literary renown.

The oral testimony of his officers thus far is greatly in his favour,

and I trust he will stand justified before God and his country, notwithstanding his ill-judged report ; but, as the Unitarian divine said
of St. Thomas's exclamation, " My Lord and my God," I wish he
had not said it. There is abundant testimony of the utter depravity
of young Spencer ; but doubts are freely expressed by many reflecting people of the guilt of Cromwell and Small, and of the sufficiency
of the evidence on which they were condemned.

1843.

JANUARY 2. — Yesterday was the regular New Year's Day; but being Sunday, it was only observed by the moral and religious sentiments which this occasion never fails to inspire, and which were inculcated by the Christian zeal and forcible eloquence of our clergymen. My excellent pastor, Dr. Wainwright, gave us on this occasion, as he did on Christmas Day, an exceedingly interesting sermon, which it is to be hoped some two or three of his congregation may remember to their own edification and the honour of the reverend orator, during the year 1843.

The festivities of the New Year were reserved for to-day, and there appeared to be no falling off from the time-honoured observances of our city. There were two snow-storms in the course of the morning, neither of which continued long enough to prevent the visiting, and, as the sleighing was excellent, all but the horses enjoyed it exceedingly. I started in a sleigh at twelve o'clock, and made forty odd visits, which occupied me until five. The ladies smiled and looked beautiful, the fires sparkled and looked warm, the furniture shone and looked comfortable, the whiskey-toddy smoked and looked strong, and everything was gay as it used to be in good times. The heads of the people were *up* to-day, however certain it may be that many of them will be bowed down by misfortune, and some laid low, before another year calls them to similar festivities.

The old year was marked by public calamity and individual misfortune, the former relieved only by the successful termination of the negotiations with England, and the latter by abundant harvests and the consequent low prices of provisions; but business is unprofitable, confidence impaired, stocks and other personal property of little value, taxes nearly doubled, rents reduced, tenants running away, debts wiped out by the bankrupt law, and Locofocoism triumphant. So ends the year 1842, and so begins the year 1843. In all these particulars the latter will not only "tread in the steps of its predecessor," but tread so much harder on the "road to ruin" as to leave no remembrance of its footsteps; or I am a false prophet, that's all. Amongst the other calamities which mark the advent of the New Year, Governor Seward retires from office, and leaves Governor Bouck to fill his place — if he can.

JANUARY 3. — The survivors of the Hone Club had a pleasant dinner to-day, at Moses H. Grinnell's. The party consisted of the following old members: Grinnell, Blatchford, John Ward, William G. Ward, Draper, Prescott Hall, and myself; besides whom there were Robert B. Minturn, Edward Curtis, James Thomson, James W. Otis, Ogden Hammond, James W. Webb, M. Brigham, and James Bowen.

JANUARY 5. — I went over this morning to the navy yard, and after visiting Commodore Perry, and inspecting, greatly to my satisfaction, the library and museum of the navy lyceum, I attended for two or three hours the court of inquiry on board of the "North Carolina." The cabin was filled with spectators and newspaper reporters, for the examination is conducted by the greatest publicity. I was received with flattering respect by the president and members of the court, who invited me to a seat at their table. The proceedings are characterized by the utmost dignity and decorum. The witnesses examined to-day were Mr. Leycock, the surgeon, and Mr. Rodgers, senior midshipman; the latter a fine, sturdy fellow, a sailor out and out. I was amused by his seamanlike reply of "Aye, aye, sir," on two occasions when requested by the judge advocate and commodore to raise his voice. The witnesses are made to give a narrative, in their own words, of the events attending the mutiny and execution on board the "Somers," after which questions are put to them in writing by Commander McKenzie, and orally by the judge advocate.　Their answers are prompt and manly.　The evidence looks well for the commander.　He looks careworn and anxious, as well he may.　God send him a safe deliverance !

JANUARY 24. — I was greatly surprised and pleased "Kent's Commentaries." to learn from the gifted and amiable ex-chancellor of the continued sales and large profits afforded by this highly popular work.　Ten thousand copies have been printed in four editions, which are sold by him at $9 a copy.　His profits ever since the work came out have been $5,000 a year, — double the amount of the chancellor's salary, — and from the undiminished demand for the work from all parts of the United States, as well as from England, where it is established as a text-book, the learned author does not apprehend any diminution of the profits of the sale for twenty years to come.　I doubt if any American book has ever produced so much money.　It gives the author a noble and most honourable independence for life ; and that God may grant that life to be extended to its utmost term of usefulness, and to the full measure of his family's desire, is my most sincere and fervent prayer.　I venerate him as a father, while I love him as a brother ; and the reverence I feel for him as an instructor is sanctified by my affection for him as a friend.　The hour I pass in the twilight of every Sunday evening with Chancellor Kent and his amiable family (including the " wise young judge " from next door, and his wife) afford me the highest gratification, and I come away delighted with my visit as a young lover from the society and the smiles of his mistress.

JANUARY 27. — The English papers do abuse us National Character. shamefully for swindling, repudiation, cheating, and other trifling departures from rectitude, which abuse is all the harder to be borne from the difficulty we have in many of the cases of contradicting the truth of the charges.　A man may know his wife to be a ——, but if he has the spirit of a man he will not allow others to call her so.　We are not the less disposed to resent an injurious epithet from the consciousness of meriting it ;

but, on the contrary, our revenge is stimulated in proportion as we are deprived of the proud satisfaction of condemning a charge which we know to be false. John Bull, smarting under the loss of his money, charges the whole of us, indiscriminately, as a nation of swindlers; and such of us as are honest, besides defending our own characters, are bound, by a sort of family pride, to a much more difficult task, that of palliating the rascality of our brethren. Pennsylvania, Mississippi, Ohio, Indiana, and Illinois have more to answer for at home than abroad. It is as much as we in New York and hereabouts can do to keep on our legs, without having the burden to carry of the disgrace of the dishonest part of the family.

FEBRUARY 1. — This is the quarter-day of the ruin of landlords. Rents are fifty per cent. lower and taxes fifty per cent. higher; nearly the whole burthen of taxes falls upon real estate, for it is the only tangible property. The pressure is severe enough upon the owners of houses and stores who are out of debt; but if the property is mortgaged, and the seven per cent. interest must be regularly paid, the Lord help the owners! Several of my tenants are unable to pay the rent of last year; all the good ones are going away, and the reduction of rent in the few cases where they remain is ruinous. Clinton Hotel, the lease of which to Mr. Hodges, at $4,500 per annum, expires on the first of May, is rented to the same person for another year at $2,500; but this year must determine the fate of New York; the patient is in extremity, and must die or be relieved before another comes round.

FEBRUARY 14. — The noble old Commodore Isaac Hull, the *Hull of the Constitution*, died yesterday morning, in Philadelphia, where he has resided since his return from the cruise in the "Ohio." He was the oldest officer in the navy, with the exception of Barron and Stewart. He it was that "plucked up drowning honour by the locks" on the ocean at the same moment that his namesake on the land was shoving it under. Hull's capture at Detroit, and Hull's capture of the "Guerrière," stood side by side in the chronicles of the day, and the exultations of John Bull and Brother Jonathan were equally restrained by the one and the other.

FEBRUARY 21. — I am grieved to record the decease of Peter Augustus Jay. Few more learned and accomplished men, and none more upright and honourable, are to be found in this city than Mr. Jay, the son of the illustrious John Jay, the purest of patriots and the wisest of statesmen. Mr. Jay inherited a large share of those noble qualities which distinguished his sire. He was a gentleman of the old school; he adorned society by the example of his deportment and manners; by his strict integrity he rebuked the corruption of the times, and by his religious principles he set an example to his professional brethren. I was associated with Mr. Jay at the board of trustees of Columbia College, of which he was president, and as a vestryman of Trinity, of which he recently became a member. The deceased was sixty-seven years of age.

Death of Mr. Jay.

FEBRUARY 23. — There is an absolute plethora of specie in this country; no more certain indication of the prostration of commerce and disordered state of trade. The banks in New York have two dollars in gold and silver for every dollar in circulation, lying like an ingot in the vaults, producing nothing and unable to get into circulation. What must be said by the croakers about an occasional scarcity of specie (which shows that something good is doing), when they read the following list of consignees by the steamer "Acadia"! She brings out 200,000 pounds sterling, and the "Great Western" will have 300,000 pounds, — two millions and a half of dollars; I wonder if Mr. Benton has a purse large enough to contain all this humbug personification of national prosperity; 850 pounds to Charles Hill; 1,700 pounds to George Pratt; 300 pounds to Joseph Shaw; 413 pounds to Heard & Welsh; 10,000 pounds to Sands, Fox, & Co.; 1,250 pounds to T. W. Ward; 20,000 pounds to J. E. Thayer & Bro.; 7,000 pounds to J. Dixon & Son; 3,000 pounds to Gossler & Co.; 20,000 pounds to order; 2,200 pounds to J. Shillaber;

Specie.

2,000 pounds to J. & H. Thayer & Co.; 5,280 pounds to Boorman, Johnston, & Co.; 100,000 pounds to Brown Bros. & Co.; 300 pounds to De Rham & Moore; 1,000 pounds to C. H. Upham & Co.; 20,000 dollars to T. Patten; and several smaller sums.

FEBRUARY 25. — The court-martial at Brooklyn, on the "Somers" case, drags along its tedious length so slowly, and there is such an everlasting sameness in the examination, that the public here appears to have lost all interest in the matter, and you scarcely hear an inquiry made as to its progress, or the probability of its termination.   Not so with our kind, officious brethren in the "mother country."   One universal burst of vituperation comes from the pack of hireling papers published in London; not only is Commander McKenzie saluted with the epithets of "murderer," "coward," "fool," "bully," and all others which may be supposed to be most offensive to a gentleman and an officer, but the navy is vilified, the civil institutions of the country derided, and the country itself insulted by the blackguards of the British press, and their coadjutors and supporters here.   The editor of the infamous "Herald" blazons these offensive articles in the public view with evident satisfaction, and makes their publication the ground of insulting remarks to the court.   When the court's actions were subject to the supervision of the American people only, it was not of much consequence how the proceedings were conducted; but now that they come under the notice of the "British press;" that the Bennetts of St. Paul's churchyard have honoured the country by their animadversions, and established a tribunal in the slums of St. Giles for the trial of the triers, — it behooves them to be circumspect.   They must blacken the character of McKenzie if they wish to preserve their own, and hang him if they would escape the gibbet themselves.   So says Mr. Bennett.   The vile bribe, which there is good reason to believe has set him in motion, shines through every line he now writes on this melancholy subject.   The interest of the protracted affair has given place in the public mind to new subjects, and the character of an honoured American officer is left to be worried and mangled by as filthy a cur as ever barked in foreign accents at the bidding of a corrupt employer.

I am not as clear as I could wish to be in my opinion of the absolute necessity of the dreadful act of discipline resorted to by McKenzie, and for his sake, as well as for the sake of national justice, I sometimes think I should like to have evidence of some clearly overt act of mutiny; but I do most entirely believe that he proceeded in his extremity with good motives, in a full conviction of the existence of the mutiny, and a persuasion that the execution was necessary for the safety of his vessel and the preservation of his men. Be this, however, as it may, I am indignant that this "scum of Britons" should avail themselves of this distressing occurrence to cast the contents of their "stink pots" upon my country, and that a wretch should be found among us base enough to ladle them out to the last loathsome drop. But, above all, am I humiliated that my fellow-citizens should give to this infamous journal a circulation greater (if the mendacious sheet may in any sort be believed) than that of any other daily newspaper in the country.

MARCH 6.—The House of Representatives and the Senate adjourned on Saturday; so there is an end of the Congress which floated into power on the great Harrison wave of 1840,— the people's Congress, from which so much was expected, but which, by untoward circumstances, by treason, misplaced confidence, and unchastened ambition has been thwarted and checkmated at every move; which has done little to redeem its pledges, and of that little has undone much. Like a goodly vessel, the pilot lost overboard, the rudder broken, and several of the crew in a state of mutiny, but with timbers sound, chart accurate, and a voyage planned which could not fail to prove profitable to the owners, she was soon cast adrift, made no headway, and has at last returned into port to refit, and, if possible, to recommence her voyage under better officers and crew. Much of this, however, will depend upon the owners, and they are not much to be relied upon. The closing scene in the House of Representatives was marked by less asperity of feeling than might have been expected, from the previous squabbles of the members. They seemed to be afraid to trust themselves, and so, like wise men, they opened the galleries and laid themselves under petticoat government.

MARCH 9. — I dined with Mr. William B. Astor, in his noble mansion in Lafayette place, one of the finest houses in the city. The party consisted of Mr. and Mrs. Peter Schermerhorn, Mr. and Mrs. Philip Van Rensselaer, General Tallmadge, Captain and Mrs. Bolton (Mary Lynch formerly), Mr. and Miss Ward, Mr. Havers, Dutch *chargé;* Messrs. West, Blunt, Brevoort, etc.

MARCH 10. — I witnessed yesterday the launch of the " Liverpool," a noble ship of one thousand one hundred and fifty tons, built for the new Liverpool line of Woodhull & Minturn. She was built by Bell & Brown, and launched from their extensive dock-yard, foot of Houston street, East river. It was a beautiful exhibition. She is the largest packet-ship yet built; her figure-head is a fine full-length figure of Jenkinson, late Earl of Liverpool, in his peer's robes, taken from an accurate likeness of that distinguished British minister. What must John Bull think of these superb specimens of Yankee skill and enterprise, arriving in his ports one after the other, and each more admirable than all that went before it? If we run in debt in some States of the Union more than we can pay, we have something to show for it by sea and by land, and, like Dickens's raven, we say, " Never die yet."

MARCH 14. — Died last evening, John Rathbone, aged ninety-two years. His son died a few weeks since. The deceased was father-in-law of Robert Chesebrough and Samuel B. Ruggles.

The " Madisonian," the organ of President Tyler in Washington, which speaks his language, supports his doctrine, and registers his edicts, has the following semi-official notice on Saturday: " Mr. Webster has expressed a wish, because of certain considerations, well understood between the

President and himself, and which did not in the least affect their public or private relations, to retire from the cabinet. *The President has been pleased to grant him permission to retire.* This fact was publicly stated in the Senate; and it was declared by a senator authorized to do so, that Mr. Webster *would* retire in thirty days after Mr. Cushing's confirmation."

O Gog and Magog! John Tyler pleased to grant Daniel Webster permission to retire from office! Daniel Webster, the personification of pure Whig principles, consorting with treachery and corruption,— a giant shrinking before a dwarf,— Daniel Webster standing, cap in hand, before John Tyler, like a hard-pressed school-boy, asking from the pedagogue permission to *go out!* But it may be that necessity, which, we are told, knows no laws, and which bows the neck of pride to the footstool of imbecile power, may have something to do with this humiliation of intellectual greatness.

MARCH 21.—General Harrison was sung into the Presidency, and, if Mr. Clay should succeed, it will be effected in some degree by dancing. The *voices* of the people in advance were clearly in favour of the former, and the latter has established a favourable *footing* with them. Clay balls are quite in vogue. They answer a good purpose; for while they assist by a little surplus of funds to furnish the ways and means for electioneering, they enlist the women on our side, and wives and daughters are famous auxiliaries in a righteous cause, and good supporters of a tottering conscience.

Clay Ball.

I went last evening, by invitation, to one of those political jollifications given by the Clay Club of the third ward, at Washington Hall. The large ball-room was handsomely decorated and well filled. There was a fair collection of ladies, some of whom were fair, dressed generally without much pretension, and of modest deportment; but the male division of the dancing part of the company would hardly have passed muster in former days at the Bath assemblies, when Beau Nash was the *arbiter elegantiarum*, or at present in the courtly saloons of Almack's. Colored handkerchiefs and unpolished boots declared the determination of their wearers not to be laid neck and heels by the mandates of fashion; and, O Terpsichore! how they did dance! Their independent ears scorned to be controlled by the arbitrary measures of the music, and their pliant legs described every letter in the alphabet from A to Z. But it went off very well. The elderly ladies were pleased with their children, the young ones with their beaux, and the beaux with themselves. The Whig common councilmen and other politicians gave their august countenance with solemn jocularity to the affair, as a piece of political machinery, and the third ward gets $250 towards the charter election.

MARCH 22.— This interesting trial, which has dragged Court-martial. out a tedious existence of six weeks, has at last come to a conclusion. As long as hopes were entertained that Commander McKenzie might be brought within the power of a civil court and jury, and the court-martial be thereby nullified, every artifice was resorted to by Mr. Norris, the judge advocate, to procrastinate the proceedings, exhaust the patience of the court, and worry out the accused and his counsel; but now that the learned and virtuous decision of Judge Betts has frustrated all hope of revenge from that quarter, the judge advocate consented to let the affair come to a close, and forego any longer his emoluments of ten dollars a day and ten dollars for engrossing every fifteen pages of his notes of evidence, which have extended, I am told, to five hundred and fifty pages, nine-tenths of which consist of the merest repetitions and the dullest technicalities that ever helped to swell a bill of costs. The examination closed yesterday, and as this was the day assigned for the reading of McKenzie's defence, the chapel in the navy yard, where the court has been held, was filled at an early hour by anxious spectators, including a large number of ladies. My daughters went over with Mrs. Depeyster, Mrs. John Hone, and Emily. I also formed one of the delighted audience; prejudiced, I acknowledge, in favour of the accused, and anxiously desirous that a clear case of justification might be made out, but never until now so fully and thoroughly satisfied that his innocence has been established and the character of the navy redeemed.

The defence, which had been prepared by Mr. George Griffin, was read by that gentleman; the reading occupied about an hour and a half. Never was an audience more attentive, and, from all the indications I observed, never was there one better prepared for a verdict of complete and honourable acquittal, — a result of which I think there cannot be a shadow of doubt. Mr. Griffin has done himself immortal honour in this able document. Many new and striking points were presented, circumstances hitherto doubtful were elucidated, the most convincing and appropriate authorities produced; and occasionally scope was found for a display of the most thrilling eloquence, while throughout the whole defence the utmost taste and soundest discretion prevailed. There were no vindictive charges against the prosecution, no angry recrimination, no seeking after technical or legal advantages, but a straightforward appeal to the judgment and patriotism of the court, worthy of its dignity, the character of the accused, and the professional reputation of the learned advocate.

I cannot refrain from recording here the following thrilling and graphic picture, drawn toward the close of the address, of the case as it might now have stood if a different line of conduct had been pursued under the awful circumstances in which Captain McKenzie found himself placed. " To enable the court the better to judge of the necessity of the execution, permit me to bring the case to another test. I suppose that the execution had not taken place; that the unconfined malcontents had risen and released the prisoners; that the mutiny had triumphed, and the brig been turned into a piratical cruiser; that the faithful officers and members of the crew had been all massacred, except the commander alone; that, from a refinement in cruelty, the pirates had spared his wretched life, and sent him on shore that he might be forced to wend home his solitary way, and become himself the disgraced narrator of what would then have been, indeed, 'the tragedy of the "Somers."' With what a burst of indignation would the country have received his narrative!   How would the American press, with its thousand tongues, have overwhelmed him with exclamations and interrogations like these: 'You were seasonably urged, by the unanimous voice of your trusty officers, to save their lives, the lives of your faithful seamen, and the honour of your country, by the timely execution of these malefactors, who deserved to die, and whose immediate death was imperiously demanded by the exigencies of the case.   Why did you not heed the counsel, the earnest counsel of your associates in authority, your constitutional advisers, with whose opinion your own, too, concurred?   You did not, because you *dared* not.   You faltered in the path of known and acknowledged duty, because you wanted moral courage to tread it.   On you, in the judgment of conscience, devolves the responsibility of those murders, which you might and ought to have prevented; on you recoils the disgrace of that flag which never sustained a blot until it was committed to your charge.'   To finish the picture, permit me to fill up another part of the canvas.   I suppose that the 'Somers,' now turned pirate, while cruising off our coast had been permitted by Heaven, in an evil hour, to capture some vessel plying between this port and Europe, freighted with the talent and beauty of the land.   The men are all murdered, and the females, including perhaps the new-made wife, and maidens just blooming into womanhood, are forced to become the *brides of pirates*.   A universal shriek of agony bursts from the American people throughout their vast domains, and the wailing is echoed back from the whole civilized world; and where then could the commander of the 'Somers' have hidden his head, branded as it would have been by a mark of infamy as indelible as that stamped on the forehead of Cain?"

The court-martial will require two or three days to read the minutes of evidence, and close up their work.   Their decision will then be sent to Washington, until which time the anxious public must remain in ignorance of these interesting proceedings.

MARCH 30.—The finest pair of capons I ever saw formed the ostensible motive for a very agreeable dinner to-day at Prescott Hall's. The guests were Robert B. Minturn, Henry Grinnell, R. M. Blatchford, James Thomson, Gerard Coster, Mr. Dutilh, Mr. Post, and myself.

MARCH 31.—A similar call to that of yesterday, in the form of a fine mess of trout, brought together Moses H. Grinnell, R. M. Blatchford, Ogden Hoffman, Prescott Hall, Simeon Draper, and myself, at a cosey dinner at Robert B. Minturn's.

APRIL 10.—The agitation of the public mind in
Naval Court-martial. relation to the trial of Commander McKenzie is put to rest by the promulgation of the decision of the court-martial. The character of the navy is sustained and the majesty of the laws vindicated by the full and honourable acquittal of the accused from all the charges brought against him. This verdict is approved and confirmed by the President of the United States, and the gallant officer who has been the subject of those investigations is relieved from the anxiety which his unpleasant situation has caused him, except the painful reflection arising from the necessary act of severe discipline which he was called upon to perform by the circumstances in which he was unfortunately placed. It remains now to be seen whether the vindictive feelings of his enemies can find further means of annoyance and persecution.

APRIL 12.—*Tout perdu, sauf l'honneur.* Francis
The Election. the First, when beaten by the imperial Loco-focos at Pavia, and a prisoner in the power of his inexorable enemy, the Emperor, Charles the Fifth, had a right to console himself by the saving clause in this celebrated and often-quoted passage in his letters to his mother. But the New York Whigs, who have *perdu* everything, have not, I fear, equal reason to claim the merit of having *sauvé* even their honour. Certain it is that in the election yesterday, though deficient in odd tricks, they have revoked

shamefully, and lost the game, — double, single, and the rubber. Morris is elected mayor by six thousand majority, and the Loco-focos have carried twelve aldermen and fourteen assistants out of seventeen in each board. The first ward gives Mr. Smith only one hundred and forty majority, and has elected a Loco-foco assistant by a division among the Whigs. The majority even in the great fifteenth (my ward) is reduced to six hundred. This was occasioned by a split on the collector; but my man, R. C. Wortendyke, got in by a very small majority. The eleventh gives Morris the unheard-of majority of thirteen hundred. There has never been an election in which frauds have been so openly and shamefully practised. Under the present system no restraint nor check upon illegal voting can ever be rendered available. I am thoroughly convinced that it is impossible for the country to sustain itself against the desolating effect of universal suffrage. Public virtue is the only foundation of a republican form of government, and that is utterly swept away. The edifice must fall; what comes next? And through what scenes of blood and violence are we to pass before we settle down into the death-like paralysis of despotic power? The old-fashioned honest men of both parties (for there are honest men in both) have nothing to say in the matter. The power is in the hands of a rabble, vile and savage as the *canaille* of the Faubourg St. Antoine at the commencement of the French Revolution; and in the number of red-flannel-shirt and turned-up-trousers men are thousands ready to cry "*À la lanterne!*" and Marats, Robespierres, and Le Gendres ready at hand to lead them on to works of blood and violence when the time shall come.

APRIL 25. — I landed from Long Island just in time
Ashburton
Dinner.   to fulfil an engagement to dine with Moses H. Grinnell and Robert B. Minturn on board their splendid ship the "Ashburton." Our party consisted of Messrs. Grinnell, Minturn, Colden, Ogden Hoffman, James Thomson, Captain Rogers, Gibbes, Draper, Bowdoin, Mr. Barnard of Albany, John

Stevens, James W. Otis, James W. Webb, Charles King, Nicholas Low, Charles L. Livingston, Captain Huddleston, and myself.

May 11.—A letter is published, signed by three hundred merchants and others of our most respectable citizens, addressed to Commander Alexander S. McKenzie, *Commander McKenzie.* expressing their approval of his conduct in the unhappy affair of the mutiny on board the "Somers," and their congratulations on his honourable acquittal by the court of inquiry and court-martial. His answer to this high compliment is much better written, and in better taste, than his unfortunate statement made to the government on his arrival. If he had said no more then, and said it as well, his case would have stood better before his fellow-citizens; particularly that portion of his friends who lament the necessity, while they justify the motives, of the dreadful act of discipline which he was called upon to perform. The merchants have raised a sum of money by subscription to pay the lawyers' fees and other charges attending the trials; but this fact is delicately kept out of view in the correspondence.

May 23.—Died this morning, at his seat in Westchester County, Mr. Peter Lorillard, in the eightieth year of his age. He was last of the three brothers of that name, himself the eldest,—Peter, George, and Jacob,—all rich men; he the richest. He was a tobacconist, and his memory will be preserved in the annals of New York by the celebrity of "Lorillard's Snuff and Tobacco." He led people by the nose for the best part of a century, and made his enormous fortune by giving them that to chew which they could not swallow.

May 24.—Mr. Webster, accompanied by some of *Mr. Webster.* the Le Roys, went down on Long Island fishing yesterday. His object, I suppose, is to get away from the crowd who press upon him here, and to prepare his thoughts in retirement and quiet for the address which he is to deliver next month on the occasion of the celebration of the completion of the Bunker Hill Monument, on which occasion President Tyler, the heads of departments, and many other distinguished characters are expected to be present. Mr. Tyler's office-holders must hold themselves in readiness to receive him with all due reverence on his transit through New York, for woe be to him whose stubborn knee and ungrateful neck refuse to do proper homage to the master whose livery they wear !

Death of Noah Webster. MAY 30. — Died on Sunday evening, at his residence, New Haven, Conn., Noah Webster, LL.D., in the eighty-fifth year of his age. He was lawyer, schoolmaster, grammarian, and lexicographer; a man of great learning, deep research, and laborious investigation; a patriot of the Revolution, in which he took part as a volunteer while yet a junior student in Yale College; a stiff Federalist and Washingtonian, a cause which he supported by his writings with great ability in his younger days, and in which good, old-fashioned faith he was content to die. As an author, he was best known by his works on elementary education, and his fame will rest principally on " Webster's Spelling-Book " and " Webster's Dictionary."

JUNE 8. — In the packet " George Washington," which sailed yesterday for Liverpool, went passengers Thurlow Weed and Mr. Schoolcraft, of Albany. The former is the able and influential editor of the " Albany Evening Journal," a firm supporter of the Whig cause; somewhat of a radical, however, and in Whig times Governor Seward's conscience-keeper.

President Tyler's Visit. JUNE 12. — The accidental President, attended by the Secretary of the Treasury, the Postmaster-General, and young Mr. Tyler, made a triumphal entry into the good city of New York this 12th day of June, on his way to Boston, where he is to be present at the great Bunker Hill jubilee and the delivery of Mr. Webster's oration, on the 17th. Great preparations were made for this auspicious occasion by the civil and military authorities. I was honoured by an invitation from the joint committee of the corporation.

But " my arrangements would not permit." I did *not* go, be-

cause I did not choose to pay homage to the man who has deceived
his friends, and betrayed those who spent time and money, and
comfort and lungs, to place him where he is.   Now, when old
Jackson visited New York, I cheerfully helped to swell the loud
hurrahs in honour of the President of the United States.   We
were opposed in politics, and had a right to be.   I tried to keep
him out, and had no right to expect any favour from him ; and,
moreover, with all his tyrannical notions of government, and reference of public matters to private considerations, there was a man-
liness of character about the old warrior which commanded respect.
But this man has played false to his friends, and is of no use to
any but his enemies ; and well may Mayor Morris, and Alderman
Purdy, and the rest of the crew, fire the guns, and ring the bells,
and make speeches to him, and tender him the tenderest welcome,
for in truth he is the best friend their party ever had.

JUNE 19.—The papers are filled with accounts

Bunker Hill
Celebration. of the great Bunker Hill celebration, on Saturday.
The heavens, and the earth, and the works of man all
conspired to render the affair equal in all respects to the anticipations of those who planned and executed it.   The storm of the
preceding day (that on which the President of the United States
made his *entrée* into Boston) cleared away during the preceding night ; the sun rose bright on Saturday, and the lofty summit
of the monument erected on the sacred spot (the completion of
which was the object of the jubilee) pierced the unclouded canopy
of a New England sky.

The procession was formed on Boston Common.   The military
display consisted of troops from all parts of New England, and a
beautiful corps of National Guards from New York, who went on
as an escort to a body of two or three hundred Yankees, residents
of this city, who made (as they say themselves) a splendid appearance ; and, if anybody should be disposed to gainsay it, I will refer
him to Moses H. Grinnell.   Then there was the President of the
United States, John Tyler, and Robert Tyler.   There was enough

of " Tyler too," but unhappily no " Tippecanoe ; " Mr. Upshur,
Secretary of the Navy; Mr. Spencer, Secretary of the Treasury;
Mr. Porter, Secretary of War; Mr. Legaré, Attorney-General; and
Mr. Wickliffe, Postmaster-General; and then there was Mr. *Brim-
mer*, Mayor of Boston, *overflowing* with patriotism; and Mr.
Quincy, whose throat was sore with huzzaing on the great occasion ;
and Mr. Cushing, whose diplomatic fame is about to be emblazoned in *china*. And there was the immortal Dan, the orator of
the day, who added the brightest and the greenest leaf to the
chaplet which adorns his brow, by the oration in which he invested
with the *toga virilis* the monument, the offspring of New England
patriotism, in strains of eloquence bright and impressive as those
in which he announced its birth. And there were one hundred
and seven soldiers of the Revolution, of whom thirteen fought in
the battle of Bunker Hill on the 17th of June, 1775 ; and three,
namely, A. Bigelow, L. Harrington, and P. Johnson, were present and mingled in the fight when the first blood of the Revolution was shed at Lexington in the month of April preceding, when,
in the inspiration of prophetic patriotism, Samuel Adams exclaimed
to his brother patriot, John Hancock, " Oh, what a glorious morning is this ! " All accounts agree that this jubilee was a great
affair, even for Boston, where they certainly do excel in such
matters ; and as for Webster's speech, no praise can do it justice,
no extract can be fairly made, no passage can be selected as
unequalled, while all are unsurpassed by others in the same
great oration.

JUNE 22.—Such an Irish howl as we had in New
York the other day was gotten up in Boston in honour
of their "distinguished visitors," and Mr. Robert Tyler,
son of the President, heir apparent of his office as he thinks, heir
presumptive of his vanity, and heir *de facto* of his talents, made a
violent inflammatory speech, in which England and her throne,
her government and her constitution, were attacked with all the
fury of big words, sharp epithets, and senseless declamation. The

son of the Executive of the United States, under the eye of his father, and as is understood with his sanction, uniting with rebels and disorganizers in opposition to their government, and exciting civil war in a country with whom we are on terms of amity and friendship, is in the worst possible taste, to say the least of it; but there is reason to fear it is something worse than that. I wish with all my heart that the people of England knew what fools these men are, — father and son; it might be the way to turn their anger into contempt.

JUNE 23. — Died this day, Christian Bergh, aged eighty-one years, the oldest ship-carpenter in the city, the father of that great system of naval architecture which has rendered the city of New York famous throughout the world. He was the first to send on the great waters the models of packet-ships which have borne the palm from all other commercial nations; others have followed in his career, and of late some may have exceeded him, but Christian Bergh was the first to raise the character of Yankee packet-ships to a height which as yet has been unapproached by any foreign nation.

JULY 4. — I spent a delightful Fourth of July at Mr. Grinnell's, at Throgs-neck; the old club set had been duly warned, and at ten o'clock Prescott Hall and Gerard Coster called to take me out. On arriving at Mr. Grinnell's we found our party engaged in pitching quoits under the noble trees, with a flowing bowl of champagne punch to prepare them for the labours of the day. The party consisted of Moses H. Grinnell, Simeon Draper, Jr., Edward Curtis, George Curtis, J. Prescott Hall, Gerard Coster, R. M. Blatchford and his son Bloodgood, Ogden Hoffman, John Ward, and myself. Our dinner was, of course, excellent, and the drink capital, and we left the quantity of the latter considerably diminished on coming away.

JULY 12. — This distinguished artist died at his
Washington
Allston.
residence, in Cambridge, near Boston, on Saturday evening last, in the sixty-fourth year of his age. He

was a native of Charleston, South Carolina ; was educated at Harvard University, went early in life to England, where he became a pupil of Benjamin West, and an associate of Reynolds, Fuseli, and the other eminent painters of the day. He spent several years in Europe, and returned to this country one of the most distinguished painters among us. It may not be too high praise to say the *most* distinguished. The last twenty-five years of his life were spent in Cambridge, where he has been employed in his profession, painting not much, but well. For many years he has had in hand a great work, " Belshazzar's Feast," which was gotten up by the liberal subscriptions of some of the rich men of Boston. Great expectations were formed of this painting, which was intended as a national specimen of American art ; but the unaccountable dilatoriness of the artist has left the subscribers nothing but " hope deferred " to repay them their advances, and many of them have died without seeing the picture, as it is feared the artist has, without finishing it. Money spent does not excite to exertion so much as money expected. Mr. Allston was equally successful in his literary as in his artistical labours. His writings are marked with the same stamp of excellence as his paintings. He published, many years since, a volume of poetry, which has been well spoken of, and a novel of great merit, entitled " Monaldi."

SARATOGA, JULY 21. — My first glass of Congress water was drunk this morning, at six o'clock precisely, bright as the sun gilding the hill-tops of Vermont, and restorative as Brandreth's pills. The effect of my morning draught has been found in a hearty breakfast and good spirits. I am in a mess with James DePeyster Ogden and Daniel Giraud, — a pleasant arrangement. The former contributes to my *intellectual*, as the latter does to my *material*, wants ; the superabundance of words at Mr. Ogden's command makes up for Mr. Giraud's taciturnity ; and as for ideas, I flatter myself that, without drawing largely upon the last-named gentleman, the average is tolerable.

Several of my acquaintances are here : Bowne, Haggerty and

his wife, Carow, James Thomson, a large lot of Le Roys, William Edgar, John Cox Morris, D. L. Haight and family, Mr. and Mrs. Richard Haight (by the bye, I have taken a liking to this lady; she is conceited, but in truth she has much cause for it). The Haights have with them a young lady who is to accompany them to Europe, a daughter of Dr. Jarvis, about twenty-one years old, an uncommonly lovely girl, bright, beautiful, and intelligent. Then there are Mr. Wetmore, the tall man, Mr. George Griffin, the taller, and Mr. Sterling, the tallest. The latter is an old Ballston acquaintance; he might regulate the town clocks without going up into the belfry. There are also Mr. and Mrs. Arnold of Rhode Island, — a charming woman she, and a clever fellow he ; and Mrs. Vandenheuvel and Miss Morris, Mrs. McGregor, Mrs. Hart, Mrs. Ingersoll of Philadelphia, daughter of Jacob Ridgeway, the millionnaire who died the other day. Last, but not by any means least in anything but size, Daniel Lord, Jr., and his wife and daughter.

AT HOME, JULY 29. — Mr. Ogden, Mr. Daniel Giraud, and I, after dining yesterday at the Springs, arrived here early this morning; the rapidity of travelling astonishing us who remember how it worked before the use of steam and the invention of railroads, when a week was consumed in the voyage to Albany, and it was a day's journey (and a hard one, too) from thence to Saratoga. Now we dine at Saratoga, and arrive in New York before people are stirring.

Another great change has taken place, one which I do not like as well. The superior enterprise and public spirit of the Trojans have drawn away travel from Albany. Here have I been up the river and returned, stopping for a few minutes at the wharf in Albany, but not even landing, and continuing my voyage to Troy in going up, and embarking there in returning, turning "a cold shoulder" upon the good old city of the Van.

Dickens has just published, as one of the chapters of "Martin Chuzzlewit," an account of the arrival of his hero in New York, and what he saw, and heard, and did, and suffered, in this land of pagans, brutes, and infidels. I am sorry to see it. Thinking that Mr. Dickens has been ungenerously treated by my countrymen, I have taken his part on most occasions; but he has now written an exceedingly foolish libel upon us, from which he will not obtain credit as an author, nor as a man of wit, any more than as a man of good taste, good nature, or good manners. It is difficult to believe that such unmitigated trash should have flown from the same pen that drew the portrait of the immortal Pickwick and his expressive gaiters, the honest locksmith and his pretty Dolly of Clerkenwell, and poor little Nell, who has caused so many tears to flow. Shame, Mr. Dickens! Considering all that we did for you, if, as some folks say, I and others made fools of ourselves to make much of you, you should not afford them the triumph of saying, "There! we told you so!" "It serves you right!" and other such consolatory phrases. If we were fools, you were the cause of it, and should have stood by us. "*Et tu, Brute!*"

JULY 31.—This glorious old man, the type of the Revolution, the apostle of pure, exalted, genuine Republicanism, has been making a tour, for the first time, to the Falls of Niagara and Canada; and to the honour of our people, and all the people with whom he has come in contact, he has been received wherever he went with demonstrations of respect. Committees have waited upon him to usher him into the bosom of their respective communities; honours, unbought and spontaneous, have been tendered, and the eloquent, wise, and patriotic old man has been petted and caressed by men of all parties, and women with their hearts in their hands. Not like John Tyler, who has offices to bestow. He had nothing to return for the homage of the heart and the incense of sentiment, but the recollection of a long life spent in the service of the country and devoted to the best interests of the people. There is a redeeming grace about all these demonstrations, which puts one in good-humour with the popular impulse. His career of triumph began at Saratoga, continued across the lines, and has followed his footsteps on his return ; he cannot be otherwise than gratified ; it is the only reward which such a man can be ambitious of receiving from his countrymen.

Tribute to Chancellor Kent. AUGUST 4. — Proud am I to record the proceedings of the New York bar in relation to my venerated friend, Chancellor Kent. Here is another octogenarian receiving the spontaneous tributes of his fellow-citizens without distinction of party ; the honours are not so general as those lately bestowed upon Mr. Adams, but more complimentary even, as coming from the members of the profession of which he is the acknowledged ornament, — that class of citizens who are best able to appreciate his talents and his virtues. The members of the bar of the State of New York, being " desirous of once more meeting the venerable and honoured patriarch of the profession, and of testifying their respect, gratitude, and affection for his profound learning, eminent services, and private virtues," have tendered to Chancellor Kent a public dinner. The letter of the committee to the Chancellor is published, and is signed by the following New York lawyers : David B. Ogden, John Duer, George Wood, Daniel Lord, Jr., George Griffin, Beverly Robinson, Benjamin F. Butler, Charles O'Connor, J. Prescott Hall, Samuel B. Ruggles, F. B. Cutting, James W. Gerard, B. D. Silliman, George W. Strong, Thomas L. Ogden, David S. Jones, Samuel A. Foote, Ogden Hoffman, James R. Whiting, James T. Brady, David Graham, Jr., A. L. Robertson, Theodore Sedgwick, John Anthon, Murray Hoffman, A. Crist, John W. Edmonds, Edward Sanford, J. S. Bosworth, A. L. Jordan. It is a beautiful letter ; written, I believe, by John Duer.

Licentiousness of the Press. AUGUST 30. — Coming from market yesterday I saw on one of the corners a placard in large letters : " Crim.-con. Reporter, for sale at No. 98 Nassau street. Newsboys supplied at four dollars per hundred." This is only a sample of the literary food supplied daily to the reading public of this great city, — something worse, to be sure, than the run of it ; but the same character prevails in all the transient publications ;

licentiousness, no matter how disgusting, lies however glaring, personal abuse without a shadow of foundation, must be served up to gratify the taste of the people, or the papers will not sell. And this is the case, too, in a church-going community, which boasts of its Sunday-schools and temperance societies. The moral sense of a majority of our people is opposed to this enormous evil; but none have the courage to come out and assist in putting it down. An association for this object, fearless of the attacks of profligate editors and the ridicule of their supporters, would do more good at this time than all the societies for sending missionaries among the Tartars and Scythians, or the total-abstinence men, who are working so hard in their vocation.

SEPTEMBER 2.—Bennett, the editor of the "Herald," is on a tour through Great Britain, whence he furnishes lies and scandal for the infamous paper which has contributed so much to corrupt the morals and degrade the taste of the people of New York. If the following article, which is published to-day in the "Courier and Enquirer," be correct (and it is too circumstantial to admit of its being doubted), it will require all his impudence to get over the effects of it. Such a rebuff, from such a quarter, must have been unexpected as it was mortifying. "The rejected of O'Connell" is not an enviable title. The occurrence took place at a great repeal meeting held at Dublin, on the 7th of August, at which the "great repealer" was, of course, the most prominent actor. The statement relating to Mr. Bennett is as follows: "A gentleman, who had for some time been sitting beside Mr. O'Connell, here addressed Mr. Steele, and, handing him his card, requested an introduction to Mr. O'Connell. Mr. Steele accordingly presented the card, and intimated that Mr. James Gordon Bennett, of New York, was present. Mr. O'Connell replied, ' He is a person with whom I can have nothing to do. He is the editor of the " New York Herald," one of the most infamous gazettes ever printed, and I shall have nothing to say to him.' This was a reception that Mr. Bennett did not count upon, and he forthwith proceeded to take his departure. The room being very full, his movement was much retarded; but, by the aid of the chairman, he struggled out amid the groans of the meeting."

"Queen of the West."

SEPTEMBER 9. — I went with my wife and daughter this morning to visit the last new packet, "The Queen of the West," lately launched from Brown & Bell's yard, for Woodhull & Minturn. She is taking in cargo, and will sail for Liverpool on Saturday next. The improvement in this class of vessels is so uniform that each one is perfect until the next is built, when perfection itself becomes a convertible term. Certain it is that "The Queen of the West" exceeds all others in strength, beauty, and convenience, as she does in size. Her burden is thirteen hundred and fifty tons, and her length, one hundred and ninety-eight feet. The length of the gentlemen's cabin is sixty feet, and that of the ladies eighteen feet. The staterooms are double the size and better arranged than any I have seen. But her superiority is not confined to the cabin accommodations; those in other parts of the ship are equally good; the steerage and forecastle, the kitchens, cooking apparatus, and ice-house are admirable. When I went to Liverpool, in 1821, with my friend Captain Rogers, in the "James Monroe," we thought our ship a splendid affair. She was four hundred tons burden, not one-third as large as "The Queen."

American Commerce.

SEPTEMBER 16. — The fine new packet-ship, "Queen of the West," sailed on her first voyage this morning.

If John Bull is not "knocked in half" by this specimen of Yankee naval magnificence and extravagance he has no sensibility. He will begin to think by and by that there may be some truth in the prediction of Monsieur De Tocqueville that "the Americans were born to rule the seas as the Romans were to conquer the world."

A state of things exists in the commerce of this country unprecedented, and worthy to be noted down among the notable occurrences of the day. This ship has taken out to England a cargo consisting of articles all (with the exception of the naval stores) of Northern production, and the " Ashburton," which sailed a day or two since, has not a Southern article on board. Not a single bale of cotton in both cargoes. The "Stephen Whitney " has only one hundred and nineteen bales of cotton. This fact, which may be the forerunner of important commercial change, is so extraordinary that a list of these three cargoes may prove an interesting subject of reference. The large shipments of provisions may be accounted for by Sir Robert Peel's new tariff. Cotton is higher here than in England, and rising.

The cargo of the " Ashburton " is 3,650 barrels flour, 249 boxes cheese, 62 bales hemp, 345 casks oil, 19 packages hams, 176 firkins butter, 97 barrels ashes, 8 boxes machinery, 480 barrels lard, 39 packages beeswax, 50 barrels beef, 96 packages tallow.

Of the "Stephen Whitney : " 3,200 barrels flour, 1,234 packages lard, 4 packages beeswax, 1,900 barrels turpentine, 1,137 packages cheese, 119 bales cotton.

Of the " Queen of the West : " 4,173 barrels flour, 274 barrels lard, 81 hogsheads and 30 cases merchandise, 2,400 barrels naval stores, 19 tierces beeswax, 212 tierces rice, 360 boxes cheese.

SEPTEMBER 16. — I dined at Mr. Jaudon's with the following party : Mr. Horsley Palmer, Mr. Webster, George Griswold, Samuel Nicholson, Charles A. Davis, Mr. Stebbins, Mr. Morgan, Mr. Blatchford, Mr. Edward Curtis, and P. H.

Mr. Webster came in town yesterday, on his way to Washington. He goes up on Monday to attend the cattle-show at Rochester, when another great speech will be expected, — agricultural, statistical, and perhaps a little political. It is announced that ex-President Van Buren will be there, and Governor Bouck ; but the great Dan will be the lion of the day, and of the thousands who go to hear him none will be disappointed.

SEPTEMBER 21. — An Irish repeal meeting was held at the Tabernacle yesterday : a convention from the different States, to play into the hands of O'Connell, and encourage a portion of the subjects of a foreign country with whom we have relations of amity and good-fellowship to rebel against their government. The whole number of delegates was something over two hundred. Robert Tyler came on from Philadelphia at the head of forty delegates, and was appointed president of the convention. If the disgrace of this miserable affair rested upon the head of this silly young man, and his equally silly father, it would be of little consequence. But every citizen of the United States is concerned in it, and must participate in the shame brought upon the country by this impertinent interference of the Chief Magistrate and his hopeful son, whom he is understood to encourage.

BOSTON, SEPT. 30. — They are preparing to make a railroad from Hartford to Springfield, which is a cheap and easy route. It will be finished next year, and this twenty-seven miles will make a continuous road from New Haven to Boston, by which means travellers will come from New York to Boston by daylight; and then good-by to Stonington, Newport, and Providence, and good-by to my stock.

Arrival of the "Arcadia." BOSTON, OCT. 3. — The steamer from England arrived here early yesterday morning. It is a fact worthy of being recorded here as one of the miracles of steam navigation, that Mr. Dorr, of New York, who sailed from here on the first day of September, arrived in Boston yesterday morning, having been absent thirty-two days, of which he spent seven in England. What next?

BOSTON, OCT. 5. — Mr. Otis called in his carriage to take us out to Brookline to see Colonel Perkins. I was highly gratified. The house and grounds are in the highest taste, the gardens beautiful, and the grapes and other fruits unequalled. It was a pleasant sight to witness the meeting of these two gouty old gentlemen, — fine old gentlemen of the old school; and a capital school it was. Mr. Otis will be seventy-eight years old on Sunday next. We drank his health yesterday in anticipation of his birthday. Colonel Perkins is a year older. We drove around the beautiful country of Brookline, and called to see a new house of General Lyman's. I dined with Mr. Truman, who is famous for giving the prettiest bachelor's dinners in Boston, and has the most exquisite claret. The party consisted of the host, Bishop Eastburn, Mr. Codman, Isaac P. Davis, Commander Nicholson, and myself. In the evening my wife and I went to a party at Mrs. H. G. Otis's, — a travelled lady, a virtuoso, and a lion-hunter.

NEW YORK, OCT. 11. — There was a handsome affair to-day at Highwood, the splendid seat of Mr. James G. King, near Hoboken. I went over at one o'clock, with my daughter, my son, and Miss Callender. But my duty at the Bank for Savings compelled me to leave the gay scene before the company was fairly engaged in the festivities. Everything was arranged with the good taste and elegance which is to be expected from the host and hostess. The day was fine as possible, the house and grounds in perfect order, the company large and of the very best quality, and everything went off so well that I was loath to go off myself.

OCTOBER 12. — Speaking of the United States, Mr. Dickens says in the story which he is spinning out in one of the London periodicals, " That republic, but yesterday let loose upon her noble course, and but to-day so maimed and lame, so full of sores and ulcers, foul to the eye, and almost hopeless to the sense, that her best friends turn from the loathsome creature with disgust." If the scamp had no regard for his own character, he ought to have had for ours, who made fools of ourselves to do him honour.

"Martin Chuzzlewit."

OCTOBER 14. — I dined at Jamaica with Mr. James DePeyster Ogden. The party, besides the host, consisted of Mr. Horsley Palmer, David S. Jones, James Brown, Henry Brevoort, John H. Hicks, Gen. James J. Jones, and myself. Mr. Ogden, who always does such things in the proper style, had an extra car provided for his company on the railroad, which was in attendance to bring us home at our own time.

I went last evening with my daughter to the Park Theatre to see Macready for the first time. He played Claude Melnotte in the pretty play of "The Lady of Lyons;" but I did not like him as well as I expected. The part does not suit him; he is too old for it. His reading is good, but his love wants tenderness, and his sorrow is too obstreperous. The last time I saw this play Charles Kean pleased me more in the part of Claude, and I should like Wallack still better in it. Lear, Macbeth, Richard, and Hamlet are better suited to Mr. Macready. When the age is in, love ought to be out.

OCTOBER 25. — My birthday, — I am sixty-three years of age, a great part of which have been prosperous and happy years; but pecuniary troubles and embarrassments have embittered the few last, and rendered the recurrence of this anniversary anything but a joyous occasion. With the perversity of human feelings I am sometimes tempted to forget the former blessings of my life in my present deprivations, and to overlook those which are still left to me; but I struggle against this rebellion of my nature, and pray that I may be taught to say, in heart and in judgment, "Thy will be done." It is a consolation to me that my wife is better. I think that she will be well again. For this I ought to be thankful. My children walk in the paths of honour and integrity. This demands my gratitude. As far as I know, I am respected by my fellow-citizens and possess the affections of my friends. Why, then, should I despond?

OCTOBER 26. — The members of the club dined to-day at Mr. Draper's. We had a pleasant, jovial dinner, in true club style. Seven of the old members were present, with a number of other gentlemen. The club was reorganized by the election of the following members; the meetings are to take place once a fortnight under the old regulations, and each member drew for the day on which he was to give the dinner: Philip Hone, Moses H. Grinnell, Simeon Draper, Jr., John Ward, William G. Ward, J. Prescott Hall, R. M. Blatchford, Roswell L. Colt,

George Curtis, Edward Curtis, Jaudon, Gerard, H. Coster, Thomas Tileston, Spofford, and James Bowen. Dr. J. W. Francis is physician to the club. Daniel Webster was elected an honorary member.

OCTOBER 27. — This fine old veteran of the army of Napoleon, who fought in many battles at the side of his master and followed him into exile; true to him in adversity as in prosperity, and never forsaking his fortunes until death rendered his services no longer necessary, — this steady follower of the great captain is now in New York. He came here from the West Indies by the way of New Orleans, on his return to Europe. He is a lion of great magnitude in our wonder-loving city. Civil and military honours are showered upon him; the Corporation, Mayor, and all, wait upon him. He receives company in the Governor's room in the City Hall. Troops escort him from place to place. He visits all the public institutions; is received with military honours at the naval and military stations. The theatres are filled by the announcement of his name; the fair of the American Institute exhibits him among their rare productions, and General Morris and General Sanford are in most exalted feather on the occasion. He sent me a letter of introduction from Dr. Niles at Paris, and I called upon him this morning; but did not see him, he having gone out under the charge of the committee. He is described to me as a good-looking old Frenchman, seventy-one years of age, plain in his appearance, with a benevolent and intelligent expression of countenance, but nothing hero-like in his deportment or manner; just such a man as one would wish him to be.

General Bertrand.

OCTOBER 30. — I had a long and interesting visit yesterday afternoon from the friend and favourite of Napoleon. He came to see me, accompanied by Mr. Louis Peugnet. There is much of the affability and *bonhomie* about this veteran soldier which characterized Lafayette, and no more of the warrior in his looks or manner than was seen in him. He likes to talk about his residence at St. Helena, and told me so much of the wonderful man, to whose fortunes in adversity as in prosperity, in death as in life, his devotion was unwavering and unceasing, that I could have listened to him all day long. It seemed to me as if we had been acquainted half our lives. This fine old Frenchman is an interesting link in the chain of recollections of modern events, and revives in his person the image of his great commander.

NOVEMBER 1. — The public dinner given by the French residents to General Bertrand *came off* yesterday at the Astor House. It was the crowning affair of his highly complimentary reception in New York, and was in all respects worthy of the occasion. The best speech of the evening was made by Charles King, in pure, correct, and beautiful *French*.

NOVEMBER 3. — Died this morning, in this city, Edward P. Livingston, of Clermont, Columbia county, in the sixty-fourth year of his age, formerly a senator in the State Legislature, and Lieutenant-Governor of the State. A gentleman in manner and deportment, but a regular, well-trained Democrat, with abilities not above the average of the Livingstons.

NOVEMBER 4. — This demagogue, who has reigned so long over his discontented countrymen, and has made himself the rallying-point of sedition in Ireland, has been stopped in his career by an arrest for treasonable practices with several of his associates, on the eve of a great meeting which was to be held in Dublin. In the mean time O'Connell has left his favourite theme of repeal, and amuses his countrymen by abusing the United States. He opens his battery upon our most vulnerable point, slavery, and advises his disciples here to come out from among us. I wish they would take his advice. There is nothing "we would more willingly part withal." But what say Mr. Robert Tyler and his ridiculous father; Richard M. Johnson, who harangues the repealers in a red jacket which he ostentatiously wears as a trophy of his victory in the pretended killing of Tecumseh; and John McKeon and other patriots, who have lauded this O'Connell at the expense of all honest American

feeling? Let them hurrah in the Park and harangue in the Tabernacle for Ireland and O'Connell. But they should, to be consist-
ent, renounce their allegiance to this country of slaveholders and
tyrants, and stand ready, if needs be, to join O'Connell, if he
should come over to mend our manners. This Mr. Tyler hopes
to be reëlected President, and Colonel Johnson is also an aspirant
for the same office.

Mr. Adams.

NOVEMBER 10. — This eminent statesman, who, with
all his simple habits and unostentatious manners, is as
fond of distinction as other people, was so much
pleased with the honours which were showered upon him wherever
he went last summer, that he is now on a similar tour to Cincinnati,
with the avowed object of assisting in the foundation of a public
work for the promotion of scientific objects. The same glorification attends him wherever he goes; every city and town at which
he arrives sends out its multitudes to welcome "the old man eloquent." Guns are fired, bells are rung, branches strewed in his
path, speeches made and answers returned; and if eating and
drinking may be taken as the criterion of glory, the first Adam,
who was the sole possessor of all the good things in the world,
made a poor figure in comparison with the Adams of these latter
days. The rise of the bright sun of American patriotism was
obscure, and its meridian splendour dim, compared with the efful-
gence of its setting beams. He is a noble specimen of straightforward American Republicanism, firm as a rock in his principles,
as sharp in his angles and as unyielding in his materials, and deserves from the American people all the honours they are so fond
of bestowing and he of receiving.

Death of
Colonel
Trumbull.

NOVEMBER 13. — Col. John Trumbull died in this
city, on Friday last, aged eighty-seven years. He has
been a distinguished man during the whole of his long
life, a patriot of the Revolution, a chevalier "*sans peur et sans
reproche*," a gallant soldier, one of the aides of Washington, a
statesman and diplomatist intrusted with important concerns in

Great Britain at the close of the Revolutionary war. As a painter, his pencil has chronicled some of the great events of the fearful struggle, the issue of which was the liberty and independence of a great nation.

NOVEMBER 17. — One of the great articles of expor-
Sending Coals tation to Great Britain at the present time is cheese.
to Newcastle.
Every packet takes out immense quantities of this article. Who would ever have thought of John Bull eating Yankee cheese? It sells in England at forty to fifty cents per hundred pounds, which pays freight and charges, and leaves Brother Jonathan a pretty good profit. This is a strange turn in commercial operations, but does not illustrate so forcibly the saying at the head of this article as a circumstance of which I am informed. The " Prince Albert," Grinnell, Minturn, & Co.'s splendid new ship, which sails on her first voyage on the first day of next month, takes out as freight a quantity of anthracite coal ! America shipping coal to England ! Who knows how soon we may fit out Chinamen with outward cargoes of tea consigned to the successors of our old acquaintances, Hougua, Chinqua, & Co. !

NOVEMBER 25. — Mr. Wallack and Charles Clinton dined with us. Wallack delighted us with recitations and dramatic readings. He was exceedingly agreeable, more so perhaps than he would have been in a larger party.

NOVEMBER 27. — I went with Grinnell on board his splendid new packet-ship " Prince Albert," which is loading, to sail on her first voyage to London on Friday next. She is equal to the noblest, the best and most beautiful of her unrivalled class. This vessel is taking in one of those anomalous cargoes which we send now-a-days to John Bull, consisting of provisions, oil, lard, oil-cakes, cheese, coals, and Yankee clocks. This last is one of the triumphs of Yankee skill and ingenuity. Five hundred thousand clocks are made annually in Connecticut. I saw one of these clocks the other day in a merchant's counting-house. It was enclosed in a handsome mahogany case, with a looking-glass plate in front, as fair a face as many of its betters can boast, keeps good time and goes well, of which it gives *striking* proofs ; and all this costs one dollar and seventy-five cents. John Bull thought when he first traded in this article at seven or eight dollars that Brother Jonathan had stolen them. They seized some of them at the Custom-House in Liverpool, as undercharged. But Jonathan told them he would supply them with as many as they wanted at half the price.

"An eagle towering in his pride of place." A circumstance occurred on Saturday, which among the ancient Romans would have been considered an omen of high importance. Augurs and soothsayers would have drawn from it presages of victory and triumph, and legions would have marched with confidence under its auspices. A large eagle, after sailing in the air of this busy city, so unlike his usual haunts, until his gyrations had attracted the notice of a large number of spectators, perched upon the truck of the foremast of the " Prince Albert," now preparing for her first voyage, at the wharf in South street, near Fulton market. He sat there for some time, looking down in solemn dignity upon the busy scenes beneath him, and wondering, I suppose, how the "unfeathered bipeds " could make such fools of themselves. After resting himself sufficiently he spread his wings and took to flight again ; not, however, without receiving a shot from some fellow below (privileged to kill game, I presume), which made the feathers fly a little, but did not impede the progress of the " bird of Jove."

The ravishment of the musical *dilettanti* had reached

Ole Bull.   its highest pitch by the power of Monsieur Artot's vio-

lin, when here comes another performer on the same instrument, with the unmusical name at the head of this article, — a Norwegian Bull, who drives monsieur out of the arena, and roars so much louder that his performance is all " fiddle-de-dee." The last man appeared at the Park Theatre, on Saturday evening, and all agreed that his performance is admirable. I presume he is the best violinist (how much prettier that word is than fiddler) now living. Wallack says he plays better than Paganini did.

December 11. — Dined at Mr. Robert B. Mintum's, with Governor Seward, R. M. Blatchford, two Curtii, M. H. Grinnell, P. Hall, etc., — fragmentary parts of the great Hone Club, which is the best thing extant. They are a set of capital fellows; talk well, eat well, sit well, drink well; and Rob. B. M. is a good fellow, though not a member.

December 23. — The anniversary of the landing of the Pilgrims was celebrated in greater style than usual, and the *éclat* of the occasion was enhanced by the presence of Messrs. Webster and Choate, of Massachusetts, and Evans, of Maine. The oration was delivered in the Broadway Tabernacle, by Mr. Choate. The subject, of course, was the landing of the Pilgrims, and never has this fruitful and exciting theme given scope to anything more thrilling, eloquent, and affecting than this splendid address. The other performances, consisting of several original hymns and choruses, were in good taste. The Tabernacle was full, notwithstanding the rain, which was hard and incessant. Having joined in the exercises of the former part of the day, I finished at the great dinner, which was given at the Astor House, and by one o'clock this morning, at which time I came away, was as good a Yankee as ever ate pumpkin pie on Thanksgiving Day.

New England Society.

There was, of course, a great deal of speaking; some very good. Mr. Choate was short, but brilliant and effective; Mr. Evans, not as good as I expected; Dr. Wainwright, happy; and Mr. Henry W. Bellows, the Unitarian clergyman, one of the very best of the day. Being called upon, I gave as a toast: " New England, and New England clocks; their striking qualities enhanced by the modesty which prompts them to place their hands before their faces. They look well, perform well, and speak well, and are less expensive than any others equally valuable of their species."

1844.

THE new year has set in propitiously so far as the weather is concerned. It has been pleasant during the day; cold enough to make excellent walking, with bright skies, and no cutting winds, and the population of our good city of Gotham have availed themselves of these favourable circumstances to an unusual degree. New York seemed to enjoy a general carnival. Broadway, from one end to the other, was alive with private carriages, omnibuses, cabs, and curricles, and lines of pedestrians fringed the carriage-ways. There must have been more visiting than on any former New Year's Day. I was out more than five hours, and my girls tell me they received one hundred and sixty-nine visits.

This fine old custom, almost peculiar to New York, does not lose favour in the eyes of our citizens, and foreigners are delighted with it. There is so much of life and spirit and heartiness in it, that it is to be hoped no new freak of fashion will ever interpose to prevent its observance.

The year which has just closed was one of trouble and difficulty. Lessons of economy have been more taught than practised; but people have, on the whole, been wiser than formerly; they have spent less money than heretofore, for the plain reason that they had not so much to spend. It is for this reason that my family expenses are reduced one-half from what they were seven years ago. The new year commences, however, with brighter prospects than the last. Trade is returning into its old channels, commerce reviving, and confidence gaining strength; and if all these encouraging appearances shall be realized, speculation, extravagance, and rashness, there is reason to fear, will follow in their train. The stream, in this busy, trading community of ours, may run dry for a while, but it never returns without a freshet.

JANUARY 16. — A very good letter of the Hon. W. C. Rives to one of his constituents is published in the Whig papers, in which he declares his determination to support Mr. Clay for President in preference to Mr. Van Buren, and comes down rather savagely upon the latter gentleman. This and other circumstances indicate that the Southern Democrats, and among them Mr. Calhoun, intend to refuse implicit allegiance to the dictation of the packed convention which is to be held at Baltimore. Such a course would be unfavourable to the ex-President.

Mr. Rives's Letter.

JANUARY 18. — The new ship "Yorkshire" sailed to-day on her first voyage to Liverpool. Among her passengers was the interesting dwarf, who has delighted the citizens of New York, under the name and title of "General Tom Thumb." The greatest *little* man I ever saw, handsome, well-formed, and intelligent, eleven or twelve years old, and not taller than my knee.

FEBRUARY 28. — Nicholas Biddle died yesterday morning, at Andalusia, his country-seat, on the banks of the Delaware, eighteen miles below Philadelphia. Mr. Biddle was born in 1786. His father was a worthy of the Revolution, and the family have ever been known as staunch Whigs, of the right sort. In the year 1804 he went out to France with General Armstrong, studied law on his return, was subsequently member of the Assembly and of the Senate of Pennsylvania. In 1819 he was appointed a government director of the Bank of the United States, and in 1823, on the resignation of Langdon Cheves, was elected president of that institution.

Death of Mr. Biddle.

The result of this last responsible trust is a matter of history, and a sad page it is in the history of this country: the record of ruin and distress to thousands here and in Europe, moistened with the tears of widows and orphans, and sullied with reproaches and vituperations which unhappily attach to the national character, and of which every American citizen is compelled to take his share. How much of all this is to be charged to the ungovernable passion

of General Jackson, and how much to the uncompromising pertinacity of Mr. Biddle, is a question in which personal prejudice
and party predilection are so much mixed up that the present
generation can never come to a just decision.   Posterity, not being
so immediately interested, will come to better conclusions on the
subject; one thing is certain : that between them they caused a
shock to be given to commercial credit, a stab to national character, and ruin to innumerable families, which the grave cannot hide,
nor party-spirit palliate.

The great financier is no more.   He whose appearance in Wall
street at a certain period broke like a ray of sunshine through the
clouds of financial difficulty; he whose word established and over-
threw banks, whose fiat governed the rate of exchange and regulated the price of cotton, is now laid low.   "And none so poor to
do him reverence."   He left, amongst a host of enemies, a few
firm friends, who lament the misfortunes which attended his management, but are unwilling to attribute them to his incapacity or
imprudence, and entertain no doubts of his honesty.

Bryant, the editor of the "Evening Post," in an article of this
day, virulent and malignant as are usually the streams which flow
from that polluted source, says that Mr. Biddle " died at his country-seat, where he passed the last of his days in elegant retirement,
which, if justice had taken place, would have been spent in the
penitentiary."   This is the first instance I have known of the vam-
pire of party-spirit seizing the lifeless body of its victim before
its interment, and exhibiting its bloody claws to the view of mourning relatives and sympathizing friends.   How such a black-hearted
misanthrope as Bryant should possess an imagination teeming with
beautiful poetical images astonishes me ; one would as soon expect
to extract drops of honey from the fangs of the rattlesnake.

FEBRUARY 29. — Horrible ! most horrible !   An ex-
The "Prince-
ton" Disaster. press arrived at two o'clock, bringing an account of an
awful catastrophe which occurred yesterday, about four
o'clock P.M., on board Captain Stockton's steam-frigate " Prince-

ton,"— the vessel which was here a few weeks ago, fitted up with
Ericsson's propellers, and carrying an enormous wrought-iron gun,
which threw, by the force of forty-five pounds of powder, a ball of
proportionate size three miles at each discharge.   This murderous
projectile was called the " Peace-maker ; " and most deplorably has
it earned its name, by making, in an instant, the *peace* of several of
the most distinguished men of the country, and sending them
" where the wicked cease from troubling."   As far as the accounts
have reached us, it is certain that in discharging this gun with a
ball, near to Alexandria, on the Potomac, it exploded at a time
when there was a party on board of five hundred ladies and gentlemen, including the President and heads of departments (all
except Mr. Spencer), with their families, naval and military officers,
senators and members of the House of Representatives, and all
the distinguished persons resident and visiting at Washington.   The
effect of this tremendous explosion was the immediate death, under
the most shocking circumstances, of Mr. Upshur, Secretary of State ;
Governor Gilmor, Secretary of the Navy ; Virgil Maxcy, late *chargé
d'affaires* at Belgium ; Mr. David Gardiner, late State senator of
New York, from Long Island ; Commander Beverly Kennon,
United States Navy ; and some others whose names are not yet
given.   Several persons are wounded ; in the number, Captain
Stockton dangerously, Colonel Benton slightly, etc.

There were two hundred ladies on board ; but, fortunately, they
were all below, dining and drinking toasts.   The noise of mirth
and joviality below mingled with the groans of the dying on deck.
By this circumstance they were saved.   Not one of the ladies
was injured.   But oh the anguish of wives and daughters on
the sight of the mangled remains of their husbands and fathers !
Nothing so dreadful has ever happened in this country, except the
shipwreck of the " Rose-in-Bloom " and the conflagration of the
Richmond theatre.   The wife of Governor Gilmor was on board.
The story of her woe is melancholy and touching in the extreme.
Her lamented husband entered upon the office of Secretary of

the Navy a few days since, and the estimation in which he was held is proved by his nomination having been unanimously confirmed without debate by the Senate. Mr. Gardiner's two daughters were also witnesses of their father's death. To-morrow will bring us more particulars of this scene of woe.

Bad Taste.   President Tyler gave a new instance of folly and bad taste in a toast which he gave at the entertainment which terminated so tragically on board the " Princeton." It was : " Oregon, the ' peace-maker,' and Captain Stockton." Oregon is the bone of contention at this time between Great Britain and ourselves, to settle which difficulty a new Minister has just landed on our shores. It is a subject which requires to be handled with the greatest delicacy. The " peace-maker " is the great gun which was to hurl defiance at Great Britain, or any other nation which might stand between the wind and Colonel Benton's popularity; Captain Stockton is the firebrand which was to ignite the whole; and in the excited state of the public mind on this subject the President gives this mischievous sentiment. The " peace-maker " at the same moment broke the peace in the manner which has been described, and amidst the melancholy reflections arising from this fatal day's excursion will be mingled a feeling of contempt for this act of folly.

Appearance of the Bay.   MARCH 6. — Having on my hands a quarter of an hour before going to Mr. David S. Kennedy's to dine, I walked on the Battery, — a luxury which the distance of my residence from the spot does not permit me frequently to enjoy; and a more delightful scene can nowhere be found. The setting sun threw a bright glow over the tiny waves; there was just wind enough to give motion to hundreds of vessels of all sizes; a golden haze was spread over the Jersey shore and Staten Island ; every now and then a steamboat came puffing and blowing with the speed of a race-horse across the Bay, or a barge skimmed rapidly around the corner of the Battery, and vanished under one of the openings of the bridge ; groups of children were sporting under the still leafless trees, and the air was so mild that one might well doubt the authority of the almanac, which points to the 6th of March.

MARCH 18. — I attended the funeral of Mr. John S. Schermerhorn as a pall-bearer ; the service was performed in Grace Church. The following were the pall-bearers : Abraham Ogden, Edward W. Laight, Henry Beekman, Benjamin W. Rogers, John Oothout, Jacob R. LeRoy, Edmund H. Pendleton, and P. H.

MARCH 19. — The annexation of Texas to the United States — a measure which many of our best and wisest citizens have looked at with most anxious apprehension — seems now likely to take place. The Executive incubus of the country, to gain Southern capital for his personal and political objects, has been for some time past flirting with the Texan government, the result of which is said to be a treaty of annexation, signed, and ready to be submitted to the Senate. The belief in this report, and the dread that a majority of the Senate will ratify this alarming act of Executive power, caused a panic in Wall street. Stocks fell; United States six-per-cents fell four per cent. ; men looked alarmed, and shook their heads in fearful doubt. A war with Mexico would be the immediate consequence of this measure, and privateers would be fitted out in the Mexican ports of the Gulf of Mexico, to prey upon the immense commerce of the United States, having themselves little or nothing to risk in return. The Mexican flag would be made to cover a predatory marine fifty times larger than belongs to them, and I fear much that many of my virtuous countrymen are already rejoicing in the chance of expatriating themselves, to appropriate to their use the treasure and merchandise of their fellow-citizens. There are nice pickings in that quarter.

MARCH 22. — I dined yesterday at Mr. Simeon Draper's with a pleasant party (principally clubists), gotten up for Mr. Webster, who came in town Thursday. The great negotiator was in one of his happiest moods. He talked like a book, and was pleasant as the morning twilight; his dark eyes looked like stars in their deep caverns. He has none of those moody fits of abstraction which were wont to come over him at times when his great mind was overtasked with public or professional business. On the contrary, he was the fiddle of the party, full of anecdote and amusing gossip; by turns instructive and amusing, he found his auditors willing to indulge a very natural desire he has to be well listened to; nor did he withhold his fair quota of hearty laughter at the wild, enthusiastic extravagances of our learned and jolly Dr. Francis. Like the school-boy relieved from his daily task, the great Yankee statesman seems to enjoy, " to the top of his bent," his temporary release from the cares and responsibilities of public life.

Death of General Lewis. APRIL 8. — The venerable Major-General Morgan Lewis died yesterday, in the ninetieth year of his age. He was born in this city on the 16th of October, 1754. He was a son of Francis Lewis, one of the signers of the Declaration of Independence (a glorious ancestral trophy), and was educated at Princeton College, where he graduated in 1773. He joined the army of the Revolution in June, 1775, as a volunteer, and assumed the command of a company at Boston. In November he was appointed first major of the Second Regiment, of which John Jay was colonel. John Jay, a soldier, sounds strangely. I never heard of this title of the great statesman and jurist of the Revolution. Mr. Jay did not, however, take the command, and Major Lewis succeeded to it. He went to Canada with Gates, and was at Ticonderoga until its evacuation in July, 1777; he was present at the capture of Burgoyne, and was the officer who received the surrender of the British troops. He served with honour in the valley of the Mohawk, and accompanied Governor George Clinton to Crown Point. After the war he resumed the practice of the law; was soon after appointed Attorney-General, Judge and Chief Justice of the Supreme Court of this State, and was elected Governor, and afterwards a senator. In the last war he also served with distinction; was appointed quartermaster-general of the army of the United States, and saw good service on the Niagara frontier.

Dinner-party. APRIL 10. — I am " spreading pretty considerable canvas" just now, as Captain Salters said of his son Nick. I dined yesterday with Mr. David S. Jones, at his house in Fifteenth street. It was a large, old-fashioned party, of seventeen guests, consisting of a variety somewhat incongruous, and affording some striking contrasts. There was Dr. Wainwright, all mildness and grace, and Mr. Samuel Niell, presuming and blustering; Vice-Chancellor McCoun, portly and plain in appearance, and the exquisite Mr. Westerlo Van Rensselaer; James Gerard, brisk as a bee and loquacious as a whip-poor-will, and Thomas E. Davis, with head full of lands and hereditaments; James G. King and young Mr. Newbold; William B. Astor, who thinks twice before he speaks once, and James Watson Webb, who speaks a great deal and does not think at all; Edmund Pendleton and Charles King, who laugh obstreperously at their own smart sayings, and Charles Clinton and young Mr. Edgar, whose position as family appendages seemed to forbid their making smart sayings themselves, or helping to carry off those of others. But the dinner went off very well. We drank the Judge's old wine, humoured his punctilios, and rejoiced sincerely in the favourable turn of his affairs, of which this dinner was one of the evidences. He is an honourable, high-minded gentleman, and his conduct in temporary adversity has been such as to render him worthy of permanent prosperity.

Supper-party. After leaving the dinner-party, some half a dozen of us came down on the Harlem Railroad. The streets in the upper part of the city were alive with masses of people shouting at the success of the Native American party in the charter election held this day. The returns were not all in this evening; but it is certain that Harper is elected Mayor, and the Whigs and Loco-focos, bundled up together, are thrown overboard. I am very well pleased with the result; but it is the first time I ever rejoiced in the success of candidates for whom I did not vote.

Charles King, Webb, and I, being engaged to sup at Grinnell's, we went there at the time we ought to have gone to bed, and found a pleasant party of Curtises and Hoffmans, Bowens, Drapers, Blatchfords, etc., with plenty of all sorts of good things, provisions enough to sustain a besieged city, and rivers of cool wines to tempt palates already placed by previous indulgence beyond the reach of temptation. Grinnell is an out-and-out Native American party man, and this supper was given to celebrate a victory which he anticipated with great accuracy, as the event proved.

APRIL 11. — I attended, yesterday, the funeral of General Lewis, as a pall-bearer. The deceased was Grand Master of Masons and President of the Society of the Cincinnati, which caused a great display at his funeral. The Masons, in all their ancient paraphernalia, attended; and the Cincinnati, with military officers and martial music, made a grand and solemn procession. The streets were full of people on the whole line of march, from the General's house, on Leonard street, to St. Paul's Church, where the obsequies were performed. The ceremonies in church were very impressive. After the religious service, which was performed by Dr. Taylor, the whole body of Masons, with their insignia, marched in single file up the aisle, and, in passing, each member laid a sprig of myrtle on the coffin; after which some silent ceremonies were performed, and they left the church. The following were the pall-bearers: Chancellor Kent, Chief Justice Jones, Mr. William Bard, Thomas Morris, Walter Bowne, Jonathan Goodhue, E. H. Pendleton, and myself.

The most interesting spectacle on this occasion was the venerable Major Popham, the vice-president of the Cincinnati and the only survivor of the original members of that time-honoured institution, who is ninety-two years of age. He sat in church near the coffin, hale and hearty, deeply impressed with the solemnity of the occasion, but apparently prepared to follow his venerable friend when the brief remnant of his days shall be spent.

Collector
removed. APRIL 13. — A most nefarious instance of the corrupt and tyrannical course of the administration of the man whom accident has placed at the head of affairs (doubtless for the sins of the people) has just been perpetrated. Edward Curtis has been removed from the office of collector, and Charles G. Ferris, formerly Loco-foco member of Congress, nominated in his place. But it is impossible that the present Senate should ever sanction so gross an outrage upon public feelings as to confirm the nomination. Posterity will not believe that the American people would have, in this enlightened period, submitted to be so insulted. Mr. Tyler's son came on to New York, with two of his toad-eaters, bearing the mandate. Charles A. Clinton was called upon, and the office tendered to him, on condition that he should turn out every man in the Custom-House who would not pledge himself to support the pretensions of his papa to the Presidency. This, Clinton promptly and indignantly refused. (He ought to have kicked the puppy.) Ferris, being more conformable, was placed in the gap ; and there let him stick. Shame ! shame ! As an American, I blush.

APRIL 17. — I dined to-day with a pleasant party at Mr. M. H. Grinnell's. The hospitalities of the famous back dining-room were, as usual, freely extended, and the tables abundantly spread with everything good to eat and drink, to honour especially John M. Botts, the great Whig member of Congress, who does not like Mr. Tyler as well as he formerly did. Our party consisted of Messrs. Botts and Taylor of Virginia, Granger, Edward Minturn, R. B. Minturn, David Graham, J. Prescott Hall, Charles King, Edward Curtis, Ogden Hoffman, James Monroe, Simeon Draper, R. M. Blatchford, J. D. P. Ogden, and myself.

In the evening Judge Jones, King, Hall, and I went to Dr. Wainwright's, to a large party of gentlemen, assembled to meet Mr. Prescott, the popular historian, to whom we and the reading world are indebted for " Ferdinand and Isabella " and " The Conquest of Mexico."   We had all the clergy, — Episcopalian, Presbyterian, and Unitarian, high church and low church, Puseyite and liberal ; but there were no Roman Catholics on the one side, nor do I believe that the tolerant principles of my reverend friend went so far as to invite, on the other, his bitter and uncourteous antagonist, the self-sufficient Dr. Potts.   It was a pleasant reunion ; all the literary men of the city were there, all the distinguished men ; the learned and the wise, by their own estimate or that of their compeers, were assembled to honour the man who has raised so proud a monument of the literary glory of his native country.

APRIL 25. — I attended, last evening, a great meeting at the Tabernacle, convened to protest against a favourite measure of the administration, — the annexation of Texas to the Union.   This is one of Mr. Tyler's electioneering schemes, fraught with injustice to others and danger to ourselves.   If this measure is adopted, and if the treaty which is now before the Senate should be approved, it will lead us into external difficulties and endanger the Union of the States.

The venerable Albert Gallatin presided, with the usual array of vice-presidents.   Good speeches were made and strong resolutions passed, and all things would have gone well had not a gang of ruffians, headed by one Mike Walsh, and formed of prize-fighters and pardoned felons, got possession of one corner of the room and interrupted the speakers by groans and hisses and exclamations of Hurrah for Texas ! for Calhoun ! and vituperative epithets of British gold, Wall-street brokers, etc. ; but their number was too small to make head against the immense multitude of respectable persons who were there to condemn the measure which these " minions of the moon " are concerned in supporting.

The spirit of the " fierce democracy," a sample of which is recorded in the preceding article, blazed forth with more lustre on Tuesday, in the House of Representatives at Washington, which is now the " Five Points " of

America. Mr. White, in defending the character of Mr. Clay from the ribaldry of several of the blackguards who represent a portion of the people of this happy land, was insulted by a Mr. Rathbone, and blows passed between these "grave and reverend" senators. A general *mêlée* took place ; a man named Moore (not a member) mixed in the fight and discharged a pistol, the ball of which passed through the door and lodged in the thigh of Mr. Wirt, one of the House police. How long will it be before this *liberty* of ours becomes so licentious that we shall be compelled to take refuge in the arms of despotism ?

PHILADELPHIA, APRIL 26. — In pursuance of my design to attend, as a looker-on and supernumerary, the great Whig Convention to be held at Baltimore on Wednesday next, I left home this morning at nine o'clock, and came by the railroad to Bordentown and thence by steamboat to this city, where I arrived at three o'clock.

WASHINGTON, APRIL 27. — The discomforts of my journey were fully compensated, on my arrival in Washington, by the excellent quarters provided for me, by the care of my good friends Joseph and Moses H. Grinnell, at Mrs. Whitwell's, on the hill near the Capitol. I have never been so pleasantly accommodated in this place. I find myself in a mess consisting of Mr. and Mrs. J. Grinnell, Mr. Evans of Maine, Mr. Winthrop, Mr. and Mrs. Cabot, Mr. Bates, the two senators from New Jersey, Messrs. Miller and Dayton, and some other gentlemen whose names I have not yet learned. Mr. and Mrs. Kennedy went up to Baltimore this afternoon. The loss of their company is not, however, without some consolation, as it gives me possession of their apartment, and I have the prospect before me of an excellent bed, with which I hope in five minutes to be better acquainted.

APRIL 29. — I made a delightful visit yesterday, in the afternoon, to Mr. Adams, who talked as no man ever talked before.

Poor General Scott is in distress. I walked with him from church, and am to see him this morning. I cannot imagine a more severe trial, for a heart susceptible as his, than that which he is about to undergo. His daughter, a lovely young woman, twenty-two years of age, has determined to take the veil in the convent at Georgetown, and shut herself out from the world forever. No entreaties of her parents have the least effect to divert her from her rash resolution, and their tears are unavailing to save her from self-immolation. I know what it is to resign a beloved daughter to the hands of Him to whose bounty I was indebted for the precious gift; but the bereavement had its accompanying consolation : she died in the faith of her sorrowing parents, her Heavenly Father received her back from the arms of her earthly one, and her dying words were not breathed into strangers' ears.

Greenough's colossal statue of Washington has been removed from the rotunda and placed in an octagonal building erected temporarily in the beautiful grounds in the rear of the Capitol. I do not like it as well as I did when I first saw it. It does not give a correct idea of the "Father of his Country;" there is too great an exposure of the naked body. It looks like a great, herculean, warrior-like *Venus of the bath ;* a grand martial Magog, undressed, with a huge napkin lying in his lap and covering his lower extremities, and he, preparing to perform his ablutions, is in the act of consigning his sword to the care of the attendant until he shall come out of the bath.

It strikes me that the sculptor has failed in representing the character by its adjuncts. The Roman toga would have done better, — that grand resort for artists in search of the picturesque ; a suit of ancient armour even, obsolete though it may be, or the ungraceful Continental uniform; either would have been more appropriate than a body naked from the waist upward. Washington was too prudent and careful of his health to expose himself thus in a climate so uncertain as ours, to say nothing of the indecency of such an exposure, — a subject on which he was known to be exceedingly fastidious.

BALTIMORE, APRIL 30. — Mr. Grinnell and I left Washington at six o'clock this morning, and came to this city. We found our kind host, Mr. Morris, waiting for us at the depot, who took us to our delightful quarters, at his house in Mulberry street, opposite the Cathedral. We had an excellent breakfast, and found ourselves in the midst of every comfort which our hearts could desire.

MAY 1. — This has been a day of excitement, of jostling and crowding, in the good city of Baltimore beyond anything I have witnessed elsewhere; and it is not difficult to account for it in the fact that the number of males within a certain space is double, nay, within these precincts, quadruple, that which is usual. At ten o'clock the masses began to move toward the church in which the convention was to assemble, and by the time I reached the spot every avenue to the church seemed to be filled, and I did not entertain a hope that I should be admitted; but by good fortune, or some other cause more flattering to my vanity, I found myself carried forward by two members of the delegation and placed in the midst of that august body of patriotic Whigs, in one of the best seats in the middle aisle.

After the formal proceedings, Mr. Benjamin Watkins Leigh, of Virginia, arose, and with a few remarks presented the following resolution: "That this convention unanimously nominate and recommend to the people of the United States *Henry Clay*, of Kentucky, as President of these United States."

The question on this resolution was put at ten minutes past twelve o'clock, and in the language of the reporters of the ceremonies, "A thousand voices sounded *Amen* and *Amen*, accompanied by such cheers and clappings of hands as the world never heard before. The cheers were prolonged for many minutes, and with such deafening shouts as made the church quake."

This was certainly one of the most sublime moral spectacles ever exhibited: the twenty-six States of the American Union, by their representatives, consisting of the best talents, virtue, and patriotism of that portion of the several communities which constitute the great Whig party, voted by acclamation to present to the people, as the choice of the party for the highest office in the Republic, a citizen who stood so prominent in their ranks as to preclude all the forms usually adopted on such occasions, and without a doubt or the shadow of dissent to place him before the people as their first and only choice; "and the people said Amen." It was all done in less time than I have taken to record it.

Now came the nominations for Vice-President, and Theodore Frelinghuysen was then declared by an unanimous vote the candidate of the convention, and the delegates from the States who had preferred other candidates gave their most hearty concurrence in the choice. Thus, in the most perfect harmony, ended this sublime and exciting ceremony, the remembrance of which will never be effaced from my mind. I shall always rejoice that I was present.

I left the convention before the speaking was over, to prepare for dinner, and went to Mr. Meredith's, where I joined the following agreeable party: Mr. Ewing, Crittenden, Granger, ex-cabinet ministers; Grinnell and Saltonstall, ex-members of Congress; Mr. Chapman and myself, ex-mayors, the former of Boston; a large proportion of *ex's*, with Mr. Grattan, an *ex*-otic of rare fragrance; Mr. Kennedy, of North Carolina; Mr. Quincy, of Boston; and Mr. Robert Gilmor. Meredith's house is so near the scene of action, Monument square, in which the concourse of people was prodigious and the speeches and shouting without intermission, that we were scarcely allowed to *eat our crust* in quiet.

May 2. —I went to bed last night before my companion, Mr. Grinnell, came in, and was fast asleep, when suddenly, about half-past one o'clock, I was awakened by his entrance, accompanied by a man, who stood erect and silent at my bedside. There I was, stuck up in bed like that "wicked Captain Smith" quailing before the ghost of "poor Miss Bailey," unpacified by "the one-pound note." Is this a constable? thought I, with my companion in custody for some nocturnal irregularity committed in this Saturnalia, and shall I be his bail, if required?

"I certainly will," continued I to myself, "for he would do the same for me." But my doubts were soon removed, when, with one more rub of my eyes, I perceived the dark brows of *Daniel Webster* hanging over me. "I have no hat on," said I; "but off goes my night-cap;" and I sat uncovered in the presence of the great man of the East.

The solution of this spectral visitation is, that Mr. Grinnell waited for the arrival of the cars from Philadelphia in which Mr. Webster was expected, and escorted him to Mr. Birckhead's, where he was to be lodged; but at this late hour access could not be obtained, and he brought him to Mr. Morris's to put him to bed in my room, and there he remained, enjoying a good sleep, until six o'clock this morning. Mr. Webster comes to Baltimore at the solicitation of his Whig friends, to give in his adhesion to the nominations. And right glad does he seem to be to have an opportunity to define his position in relation to Mr. Clay and his friends, and to assume the lofty rank among Whigs, from which some have thought he was inclined to swerve. But he told them all about it to-day. His appearance here and the part he has played is one of the most interesting incidents in the great drama.

Yesterday was the solemn formula enacted by the Whigs of the United States in the selection of candidates for President and Vice-President of the United States; but this has been the day of jubilee. Ten thousand men of the other States came to Baltimore to ratify the choice. This great mass of noble, fine-looking fellows, from the granite hills of New Hampshire to the green prairies of the great West, formed in procession this morning; and each State under its proper banner, and each individual swelling out its numbers, with flags and patriotic devices, badges and the weapons of peace, passing under triumphal arches, cheered on by the bright eyes of the prettiest young women in the world, for whose use every window-sash on the route of the procession was taken out, and with handkerchiefs waving overhead and wreaths and bouquets thrown at their feet, did this mighty army march out to the Canton race-course. Being in the procession myself, in the New York ranks, I cannot judge what appearance it made; but the street, the whole of Baltimore street, presented a pageant more bright and brilliant than any I ever beheld. The field to which we marched is about three miles from that part of the city with which I am acquainted. The weather was doubtful and the sun did not shine; the dust was the only annoyance. But everything went off well, and the rain which threatened during the morning had the politeness to keep away until nothing was left undone but a few speeches, which are a commodity so plentiful just now that the people could afford to wait. Of this great meeting John M. Clayton, of Delaware, was appointed president. Mr. Webster was called out by unanimous acclamation, and addressed the people in an excellent speech, approving the nominations without the least reservation, and pledging himself and receiving the pledges of all in his hearing to an unwavering, united, and zealous support of the people's candidate.

Dinner at Mr. Johnson's. At six o'clock I joined a large party at dinner at Mr. Reverdy Johnson's, whose noble mansion, on this occasion, has been the seat of elegant and profuse hospitality. We had at dinner, and afterward at supper, all the great genii of the Whig party; and such an array was never before presented to my view: Benjamin Watkins Leigh, Judge Berrien, Mr. Webster, Governor Morehead, Judge Spencer, Governor Metcalf, Governor Sprigg of this State, Mr. Morgan, Mr. Crittenden, Butler King, Stanley, General Dawson, Governor Johnson of Louisiana, Mr. Ewing, Mr. Granger, Mr. Kennedy, etc. I was never concerned in a more jovial affair, and never heard more small shot fired from big guns. I was eight hours on my legs in the morning of this great day, and eight hours seated at the table, and shall now get eight hours' sleep, if I can.

The Secretary of the Treasury. May 4. — John C. Spencer has resigned his place in the cabinet, and a pretty business he has made of it. Discarded by all parties, and spurned by the hand which he basely condescended to lick, he will have nothing but his own bad feelings to feed upon. As his stern old father said the other day, " He has dug his own grave, and must lie in it." John Tyler could never tolerate the man whose father was the president of a *Clay* convention.

Dined with Mr. Robert Gilmor. Our party consisted of Messrs. Kennedy, Birckhead, Byron of somewhere South, Abbott Lawrence, David Hoffman, Robert Gilmor, Jr., Granger, Grattan, Thomas Oliver, Meredith, and myself. The city has assumed its usual appearance ; Barnum's is approachable and traversable, Reverdy Johnson's shut up, the rostrum in front of the Court-House taken down, Loco-focos beginning to peep out of their holes, and friendship and hospitality assuming their usual quiet habits of entertainment.

NEW YORK, MAY 14.—The annexation of Texas

Texas.   to the United States is now the question which regulates all our politics, the pivot on which party-spirit moves, and the stepping-stone from which presidential candidates rise, or on which they stumble, to rise no more. The discussion of the treaty lately entered into by President Tyler and his cabinet with Texas has laid open a scene of executive usurpation which ought to subject the chief to impeachment, and such of his advisers as remain (some of them were blown up in the " Princeton "), to disgraceful dismissal from their offices. Mr. Tyler has, in this instance, usurped the power of Congress to make war, by ordering naval and military forces to carry out his treaty before its ratification by the Senate, against the anticipated opposition of Mexico,—a nation with whom we have the most friendly relations, whilst we are plotting to steal a valuable part of her dominions.

Here is the great question of severance between the North and the South, which is one day to shake this overgrown Republic to its centre. The Southern States desire the annexation of Texas to the Union, to strengthen their position geographically and politically by the prospective addition of four or five slaveholding

States. We of the North and East say we have already more territory than we know what to do with, and more slavery within our borders than we choose to be answerable for before God and man. So this Texas question is brought up by the man whom accident has placed at the head of affairs, and used by designing demagogues to promote their personal objects at the risk of a separation of the Union, and the downfall of liberty in the Western world. The several aspirants to the Presidency have been called upon to declare their opinions on this distracting question. Mr. Clay, with his characteristic frankness, condemns the project as dangerous to the tranquillity of the country, unjust to Mexico, and dishonourable in the eyes of the world. Mr. Van Buren, in language less explicit, avows the same sentiments. These opinions have left a door open for other would-be candidates, who would struggle upward by means of the most unscrupulous conduct. In this number is General Cass, who, after having made himself ridiculous by interfering in affairs with which he had no concern, comes out now in favour of the measure in all its length and breadth, declaring war against Mexico, threatening Great Britain, and scoffing at all the old-fashioned notions in favour of union and harmony. This is the horse on which this demagogue would ride into power. Clay must beat them all, for the country cannot stand a fourth administration like the present and its two predecessors.

MAY 24.—Seeing in the newspaper this morning a Old Times. statement that in pulling down an old house on the corner of John and Dutch streets some pieces of cannon were dug up from the cellar, it occurred to me that this must be my father's house. So I went that way to the office, and, sure enough, the old house in which my youthful days were passed was no more to be seen, and a shapeless mass of ruins marked the spot. I was born in Dutch street, near by. My father bought the house at the corner something like sixty years ago, and carried on his business there, and thence spring all my early recollections. How the old house stood so long (for it was a slight building) I know not, but whilst I stood gazing at the ruins I mourned over the departure of an old acquaintance.

But how came the cannon there? There are three pieces, which, from the fixtures attached to them, belonged probably to a vessel (a rebel privateer, perhaps), and were secreted in the cellar of this house at the commencement of the Revolutionary war, before my father bought the property. I saw two of these pieces in a black-smith's shop near by (the other had been taken away), and tried to get one, as a relic of old times; and I may yet, if the purchaser consents to part with it. They have been so long in a state of confinement that, like the old man who was released on the destruction of the Bastille, it will be difficult to make them go off.

Chancellor
Kent.

One of those incidents occurred this morning so characteristic of our dear Chancellor. He mystified me completely. Coming suddenly into the insurance office, with a book under his arm, he took a chair beside mine, and the following dialogue took place: " Do you write marine risks? " — " Certainly, sir, it is our business." — " I want some insurance." — " You," asked I ; " what can you possibly have to do with marine insurance? " — " I have an interest in a vessel which I wish insured for nine months." — " Very well, sir, what vessel is it? " — " I suppose that I must disclose everything? " — " Certainly." — " Well, she is as good a vessel as ever floated, staunch and sound ; but I have no confidence in the captain, and am afraid of barratry, which I would insure against." — " Well, sir, what is her name? " — " The good ship Constitution ; John Tyler, master; will you write her?" Acknowledging myself completely taken in, I replied, " Change the captain, stop up the leaks with *clay*, and we will write her upon the most favourable terms." And off went the bright and amiable octogenarian as suddenly as he entered.

Baltimore
Convention.

MAY 28. — The " Monumental City " is again the scene of a great political gathering ; but how different from that I lately witnessed there ! Then all was union, harmony, confidence, and enthusiasm. Now the Loco-focos have possession of the ground; and discord, suspicion, doubt, and apprehension prevail in their ranks. The convention met yesterday. Mr. Hendricks, of Pennsylvania, was elected president, with a vice-president from each State.

The *party* does not seem pleased with either of their numerous candidates. Mr. Van Buren, heretofore the standing candidate, has gotten into *bad smell*, as the Count Lowendahl once said to me, when he attempted to do *mauvaise odeur* into English. Dick Johnson says he won't ride to immortality in the same cart with the New York candidate; and, disgraceful as it would be to the country, there are serious thoughts of that demi-savage being brought forward for the first office. I would prefer that Mr. Van Buren should be the man, for in the present state of parties he would be most easily beaten; and, in the unlikely event of Mr. Clay's defeat, I would rather have him than any other candidate on that side.

MAY 30. — Van Buren is killed (politically), and Cass is no better. The Loco-foco Convention yesterday threw them both overboard, and nominated James K. Polk, of Tennessee, for President, and Silas Wright, of New York, for Vice-President. How it was brought about belongs to the Loco-foco chronicles of the times; but Polk and Wright! Alas for poor Van Buren! He is the best of the bunch by great odds, and to be so repudiated by his political friends who have so long been accustomed to swear by him! *Et tu, Brute!* And then, the idea of running Silas Wright subordinate to General Jackson's chief cook and bottle-washer, Colonel Polk! Some Northern Loco-foco, speaking of the nomination, says very smartly, "The ticket is like a kangaroo, — it goes upon its hind legs."

Mr. Wise.

The United States frigate " Constitution " (dear old " Ironsides ") sailed yesterday for Rio de Janeiro, having on board His Excellency Henry A. Wise, Minister to the Court of Brazil, and his family, and Mr. Sargeant, his secretary. Success attend the new Minister! If he is half as troublesome there as he was here, they will wish to have my old acquaintance, Mr. Hunter, back. Some of his colleagues in Congress would send him on a mission to the antipodes or elsewhere, and keep him there, if they thought there was any chance of his being reëlected to Congress on his return.

MAY 31. — Among the recorded deaths we sometimes see the names of men whose services in the Revolutionary army must endear them to the present, and their memory to all future, generations. Two are recorded in the papers of this day; namely, at Schenectady, on the 23d May, John Jacobus Van Voorst, aged one hundred and three years, four months, and four days; at Fouda, Montgomery county, on the 11th of May, Jacob Van Allstyne, in the ninety-sixth year of his age. He was an adjutant and quartermaster in the Continental army, and was in the service at the taking of General Burgoyne.

MAY 31. — The Polk-Van Buren-Cass Convention, at Baltimore, closed their patriotic labours yesterday. Silas Wright, the nominee for the Vice-Presidency, not liking the position in which he was placed, subordinate to one so inferior to himself, and indignant, no doubt, at the ill-treatment which his friend, Mr. Van Buren, had received at the hands of his party, peremptorily declined the nomination, notwithstanding a committee (of which Benjamin F. Butler, the exponent of New York Loco-focoism, was one) went to Washington to urge his acceptance. Mr. Wright has done himself great credit by refusing to lend his name to prop a sinking cause and give currency to political heresy. In this new dilemma, the convention, after floundering about in a troubled sea of uncertainty, hoisted a new signal of distress, and nominated as Vice-President George M. Dallas, of Pennsylvania, a man who, at the first meeting of this *august* assembly, was no more dreamed of than John Tyler. But it is so; and now the faithful must change their shout from Van Buren to Polk, and from Wright to Dallas. In the midst of these political squabbles at Baltimore, the ridiculous farce has been played of the nomination of the present incubus upon the country. A Tyler Convention (as they called themselves), consisting of a few office-holders and political adventurers, held a meeting simultaneously with the Polkites, and agreed to make Mr. Tyler President, if they can get votes enough. He accepts the nomination in one of those asinine manifestos in which the father's wisdom is so beautifully adorned by the son's erudition.

JUNE 1. — A white stone to mark the closing hours of Picnic Dinner. this week ! Never was there a lovelier day, a brighter sun, and never was nature more daintily decked out to receive their embraces and profit by their influences. Never was there a nicer picnic dinner than that provided by John R. Snedecor, near the Long Island race-course, and never a pleas-anter party than the *nine* (not the Muses, but votaries and wor-shippers of their ladyships) who assembled to partake of it. Our party consisted of Dr. Wainwright, Prescott Hall, David C. Colden, Mr. Macready, M. C. Patterson, Samuel B. Ruggles, Francis Griffin, Henry Brevoort, and myself. We left town at half-past two o'clock, sat down to dinner (previously engaged and the par-ticulars arranged by Mr. Hall) at half-past four, and started for home at ten o'clock, just as the full moon arose from the ocean to light us on our way, and unlike the lamps of us dull mortals, has grown brighter as the oil consumed.

Mr. Macready, for whom this pleasant affair was gotten up, delighted us with his conversation, which was occasionally diversi-fied with his admirable recitations and dramatic readings. The reverend doctor enjoyed the feast, and added to its charm the tribute of his intellectual remarks. Brevoort opened wider than usual the lid of his knowledge-box, and each member of the party was ready and willing to contribute his stock to the entertainment and instruction of his companions.

JUNE 10. — Died on Friday last, at his residence, Geneseo, Mr. James S. Wadsworth, aged seventy-seven years. Mr. Wadsworth was a native of Connecticut, one of the pioneers in the settlement of the western part of the State of New York, to which he removed many years ago. His farm on the Genesee river, above Rochester, is said to be the finest in the State. I have been at his house, — a noble mansion, beautifully situated in the heart of a country rich and fertile as any the sun shines upon, — a country which not only filled his garners with grain and fattened his cattle on a thousand hills, but filled his purse to overflowing with the treasure which buys all things but life, health, and contentment.

JUNE 11. — Mr. Tyler's infamous treaty, by which
Treaty of Annexation. he hoped to rob Mexico of her province of Texas, against the consent of the people of the United States, to promote his political ends with the Southern States, at the risk of plunging the country into an unjust and discreditable war, and to force the country to assume thereby the enormous debts of a set of vagabond adventurers, has received its quietus in the Senate, where it was discussed in secret session several days, and finally rejected on Saturday.

JUNE 14. — One of those astounding Wall-street stock revolutions has occurred, which are occasionally gotten up by gamblers, and by which the turn of a day makes nabobs and beggars, and unsettles the minds of men who watch the brokers' books with anxiety equal to that which of old attended the developments of the sibylline leaves. Within the last week many descriptions of what are called *fancy stocks* were inflated, by the progress of bubble-blowing, to prices double and quadruple those of the previous week. Many who had " sold ahead," as it is called in Wall street, were ruined by the change, and fortunes were made by men who had not sense nor judgment to make a living in an honest calling. This inflated state of things lasted three days, and then came the reverse, which always follows these high-pressure operations. All of a sudden, stocks fell back nearly to the place where the speculation found them ; the sellers became buyers, pocketed their gains, and laughed at their dupes.   Such is the course of stock-jobbing,

—a most profligate and ruinous system of gambling, infinitely worse than any of which the laws take cognizance.

AT HOME, JUNE 25. — Much has transpired during my short absence. Congress has adjourned in "most admired confusion," after a session (I mean of the House of Representatives) more disgraceful to the country, and humiliating to all who continue to love it, than any in the annals of our National Legislature. The Whig majority in the Senate is the salt which has preserved the body politic. God knows how long that conservative principle may be suffered to remain! President Tyler, in the madness of his misrule, has made many removals and appointments at the close of the session, some of which were confirmed, but more rejected. What a patient ass is the American people, and how well he who rides seems to know them!

JULY 2. — Mr. Tyler's broom sweeps clean; there is hardly one important appointment made by General Harrison which has not fallen within the scope of its destroying influence. He seems destitute of the ordinary feelings of respect for the memory of the man under whose mantle he was smuggled into office.

Long Island Railroad. JULY 27. — The road being completed from Brooklyn to Greenport, — its terminus on the Sound, — a distance of ninety-two miles, the first trip was made to-day, with the usual jollifications customary on such occasions. A large number of invited guests were taken down on the cars, partook of an entertainment, and returned early in the evening. Wonderful stories are told of the speed of the steam-team on this occasion. They went to Greenport in four hours; but if they had kept up the speed with which they started, — fourteen minutes to Jamaica, — the distance might have been accomplished in two.

Aquatic Jubilee. JULY 29. — There is a gay, saucy-looking squadron of schooner-yachts lying off the Battery, which excites considerable admiration. About a dozen of these handsome little vessels, owned by gentlemen of fortune and enterprise, are preparing for a voyage to Newport, under the command

of that excellent fellow, John C. Stevens, as commodore, who
hoists his broad pennant and makes his signals in the most approved man-of-war style.   Crowds of people, especially of the
fairer sort, go down to witness this mimic display of maritime
glory; and some of the most favoured of our belles and nice
young men about town are invited to pleasant parties by the Jack-
tars.   The arrival of the squadron at Newport will, of course,
occasion a sensation among the company there, and serve to re-
lieve the monotony of a tolerably dull place of sojournment.

ROCKAWAY, AUGUST 9. — I grieve to record the death

Death of Mr. Coster. of my venerable friend, John G. Coster.   He died at
ten o'clock, last evening, in the eighty-second year of
his age.   Mr. Coster has done me many kind services; and I never
asked a favour of him which was not cheerfully, willingly, and dis-
interestedly granted.   I was grateful to him living, and honour his
memory now that he is removed from those who loved and
respected him.

AUGUST 12. — Mr. Coster's funeral took place yesterday, at five
o'clock.   There was a great concourse of people; for the deceased
was extensively known and greatly esteemed.   The ceremonies
were performed by Dr. Wainwright, in St. Mark's Church, in the
cemetery of which the body was interred in the family vault.   The
following were the pall-bearers: Major Popham, Chancellor Jones,
James McBride, Maltby Gelston, John Adams, David S. Kennedy,
Edward W. Laight, and myself.

The " Commercial Advertiser " comes this afternoon

Death of Wil- liam L. Stone. in mourning, for the death of its editor, William Leet
Stone, who died at the residence of his father-in-law,
the Rev. Mr. Wayland, at Saratoga Springs, yesterday morning,
aged fifty-two years.   Mr. Stone has been editor-in-chief of the
" Commercial Advertiser " since April, 1820.   I have long thought
it one of the best papers in the State.   Its principles were of the
sound Whig kind, its editorial writings sensible, discreet, and moral,
and its matter generally entertaining, without any pampering to a

depraved popular taste. Mr. Stone has written several good books, principally on subjects connected with the early history of the State, manners, customs, and annals of the Indian tribes, and of the public institutions in which he took an interest, and in which he did not shrink from his share of the work.

AUGUST 22. — I had a nice little party at dinner, consisting of John P. Kennedy, R. M. Blatchford (who brought us a basket of delicious fruit), William Wood, Dr. Stevens, our St. Croix friend Delprat, and M. H. Grinnell. They came at three o'clock, and we broke up soon after six.

Whig
Speeches.

AUGUST 30. — I have read the speeches of Mr. Webster and Judge Berrien. Both are excellent. I am much mistaken if that of the Massachusetts man is not the best he ever made on such an occasion. It is a clear, sound, uncontrovertible argument in favour of the Whig doctrines of the present day. On the subject of protection of American industry it is glorious. It carries even me beyond the highest point of conviction to which I had ever reached. It proves that this principle lies at the root of the federal compact ; that it was the broad, deep-laid foundation of the fabric which could never have been erected upon any other, and he was provided with facts taken from imperishable records and statements derived from the most authentic sources to prove every word he said.

Electioneering.

SEPTEMBER 11. — We hear of nothing but great mass-meetings (as they are called) in all parts of the country. The Whigs have collected immense gatherings at Taunton and at Lynn, in Massachusetts, where Daniel Webster, Rufus Choate, Robert C. Winthrop, John M. Berrien, Francis Granger, John P. Kennedy, and a host of the brightest spirits in the land have been instructing the people in the principles for which we are contending, and of which Clay and Frelinghuysen are the index and exemplars. In New Jersey, where the first State election will take place, similar efforts are being made ; and if the sovereigns do not get enough of tariff and Texas, they are the most insatiable gormandizers in the world. We have beaten the Loco-focos handsomely in Vermont; but, on the other hand, their majority in Maine has increased fearfully. It is not so hollow a thing as it appeared a few weeks since; party discipline works well for our opponents, and the prospect of spoils in advance are mighty encouraging for both parties.

SEPTEMBER 19. — A slap at Brother Jonathan. One of the English papers says that the *Iowa* American Indians, now exhibiting in London, must not be confounded with the tribe of *I.O.U.'s*, who are natives of Pennsylvania, and intimates that the former are much the more respectable of the two.

Astonishing Despatch. SEPTEMBER 20. — The go-ahead principle prevails in this country to such a degree that it must be difficult to prove an *alibi* in any case in which locomotion is concerned; for it ought not to excite much wonder that a man should be in two places at once. The "Commercial Advertiser," which I read this day at two o'clock, contains a report, in three or four columns, of a speech made by Mr. Webster yesterday afternoon at a great Whig meeting on Boston Common.

SEPTEMBER 30. — I found yesterday, in overhauling old papers in a chest of my father's which had not seen the light for a quarter of a century, many curious records of the days of my infancy and youth, and some of a still more remote period. In this ancient cabinet of literary relics I found the certificate of my father's rights as a freeman of the city of New York, — an important and honourable privilege. This document is dated 1765, and signed by John Cruger.

Dinner and Reflections. OCTOBER 9. — I went yesterday to dine at Mr. Blatchford's, at Hell-Gate. The party at dinner consisted of old Mr. J. J. Astor and his train-bearer and prime minister, Mr. Coggeswell; Mr. Jaudon; Ole Bull, the celebrated Norwegian violinist (we used to call it fiddler); and myself. In the evening the party was increased by the addition of Mr. Webster, his brother-in-law, Mr. Page, and Mr. and Mrs. Curtis.

Ole Bull had his two violins, and astonished and pleased us by his wonderful performance. Every note was sounded, from the roaring of a lion to the whisper of a summer's evening breeze; every instrument of music seemed to send forth its peculiar tones.

After an hour or two passed in the billiard-room I retired to bed. When I arose this morning at Mr. Blatchford's, I contemplated the delightful scene: the clumps of fine old trees clothed in the gorgeous foliage of autumn, the lawn still bright and green, the mild, refreshing breeze, the rapid waters of Hell-Gate covered with sailing-vessels and steamboats, — all combined to present a picture of consummate beauty. In this place, so rich in the beauties of art and nature, in the enjoyment of pecuniary independence and happy in his family relations, did the former proprietor commit suicide! Mr. Astor, one of our dinner companions yesterday, presented a painful example of the insufficiency of wealth to prolong the life of man. This old gentleman, with his fifteen millions of dollars, would give it all to have my strength and physical ability; and yet, with this example and that recorded above, I, with a good conscience, and in possession of my bodily faculties, sometimes repine at my lot. He would pay all my debts if I could insure him one year of my health and strength.

OCTOBER 14. — A Whig meeting was held this evening, of about thirty gentlemen, at the Astor House. Great and encouraging were the results. Can a cause fail which is founded upon such principles as ours, and supported by such men? May success be their reward, and their country know how to appreciate their liberality! The first ten men who took pen in hand subscribed $8,100. Of these, six gave $1,000 each, and they have all been giving to the same object every day for months past. I cannot resist the satisfaction of recording their names: George Griswold; Prime, Ward, & King; Grinnell, Minturn, & Co.; John C. Greene; Howland & Aspinwall; Spofford & Tileston. Benjamin L. Swan gave $600, three others $500 each, and many $250; altogether something over $10,000.

OCTOBER 29. — The approaching presidential elec-
The Election. tion engrosses all interest and occupies the minds of
all our citizens. We Whigs believe that the principles
involved in this contest are of the most vital importance. These
principles are well known and openly avowed, whilst our adversaries acknowledge no motive of action but the most malignant and
virulent opposition to our candidates. These are both so strong
in the affections of their political friends, both so distinguished for
talents and public services, and both so clearly and openly identified with the principles of their party, that every description of
rancorous vituperation is resorted to, to influence the minds and
gain the votes of the ignorant and prejudiced.

OCTOBER 30. — The great demonstration of the
Whig Demon- Whigs, which has been in preparation for some time,
stration.
came off to-day. It beggars all description. Nothing
so great, so magnificent, so enthusiastic, was ever before witnessed in New York. The several wards marched in rotation,
with all the mechanical crafts on stages superbly ornamented and
employed in their different occupations, with banners and flags, and
every device which ingenuity and zeal could suggest. I cannot
attempt a description. It will be sufficient for this record of the
event, to say that the procession was more than five miles in
length, and composed of the most respectable men of every profession, trade, and occupation in the city.

The fifteenth ward did me the honour to place me in their *cortège* in an open barouche, with Dr. J. W. Francis, Judge Hammond,
and Mr. Nevins. We left Constitution Hall soon after ten o'clock,
and were detained in Canal street and thereabouts until two, when
we took our place in the line. We then followed on down Greenwich street, around the Bowling Green, up Broadway to Union
place, and down the Bowery, etc. I broke away at Broome street,
on the downward route. After four o'clock, the weather, which
was pleasant in the morning, became raw and uncomfortable, with
gusts of rain and hail; and I was not very well.

This was the greatest affair I was ever concerned in. The houses on the route were decorated with flags, Clay busts, wreaths and festoons of flowers and evergreens; and such a waving of handkerchiefs, and showering of bouquets, and flashing of bright eyes from tens of thousands of animated female countenances, inspired the hearts of all Whigs, sixty-four years old and under, — and all above, for aught I know to the contrary. I came in for a large part of the honours of the day, being cheered and saluted by name, by many of the groups of the assembled multitude of spectators. My house, also, I was informed, was frequently cheered in a manner personally gratifying. We were decorated with flags and evergreens, and had a very handsome display of lady friends to set us off.

November 1. — Our opponents made their appearance this evening in a great night procession, as long

Loco-foco Procession.

as ours on Wednesday, but widely different in the character of its members. Their appearance was low and vulgar, and their banners avowed no political principles. "Destruction to Clay!" "Down with the Coons!" "Polk and Texas!" "No $50,000,000 Bank!" "*Americans shan't rule us!*" (this is a fact), and such-like inscriptions were emblazoned on their standards, and brought into light by the torches which supplied the want of the daylight, in which the Whigs were not ashamed to be seen.

November 8. — Yesterday's news from the West and North has settled the question. The State of New

All Gone.

York has gone for Polk and Dallas by a majority of five or six thousand. This result, which makes them President and Vice-President of the United States, has been brought about by foreign votes, made for the purpose. Mr. Clay is again defeated; the people have rejected their best friend, and repudiated the principles by which alone national prosperity and individual happiness might have been secured. So let it be! We must submit, and have only to pray that the Almighty will avert from the country the

evils which, from present appearances, the people have brought upon themselves, and that the administration may turn out better than some of us now anticipate.

There is a Whig loss in the State since the election of General Harrison in 1840 of about twenty thousand. The slaveholders of the South and the abolitionists of the North have gone equally against us. Free trade and protection have voted for Polk and Dallas. Mr. Clay's talents, public services, and sound principles are too much for this perverse levelling generation. The beauty of his character forms too strong a contrast to their deformity.

The Whigs, at this election, deserted their own candidates almost in a body. Phœnix, of the first congressional district of the city, withdrew publicly, and Hamilton Fish virtually; by which means the Native Americans carried three out of the four congressmen,—Miller, Woodruff, and Campbell (the first and the last, by the bye, as good Whigs as those they succeed). Mr. Folsom (Native American), whom nobody knows, and who has never contributed in any way to the good cause, is elected to the State Senate; that sound Whig and practical American, Hiram Ketcham, was also induced to withdraw. The whole Assembly ticket is elected, and all by the complete coöperation of the Whigs, in the hope that a corresponding support would be given by their opponents to the Clay electoral ticket. It was so, to a certain extent; but the foregoing statement shows that we gave more than we received.

NOVEMBER 13. — I am sick, sick of election returns; ashamed of my countrymen; but I have one bright page for my journal. There is one star in the deep obscurity

All Hail!
Massachusetts.

of our political midnight. Glorious old Massachusetts, the cradle of American liberty, the last refuge of good principles, the faithful among the faithless, has proved herself worthy of her immortal sires. Her election was held on Monday; she gives Clay and Frelinghuysen twenty-five thousand majority; more than the aggregate majorities for Polk and Dallas in New York, Pennsylvania, and Virginia. Governor Briggs is reëlected by an immense majority.

All her congressmen are Whigs with the exception of two or three districts, where the pertinacious abolitionists have prevented a choice. The indomitable old veteran, John Quincy Adams, is re-elected, by an increased majority, against the combination of slave-holders and abolitionists, who stand in awe of his power, and shrink before the light of truth. The Legislature is Whig three or four times over. Mr. Webster's eloquence has not been lost upon his own people, however it may have been contemned in other States, where envy, hatred, and uncharitableness have sought to keep him down.

> " Light of the pilgrims, seen afar,
>   Midst clouds and darkness shining yet !
>   Now, as of old, fair freedom's star,
>   The first to rise, the last to set."

NOVEMBER 15. — The majority in the State of New York for Polk and Dallas, out of nearly half a million of votes, is five thousand and twenty-six. Fourteen or fifteen thousand abolitionists voted for a Mr. Binney, — a man of straw of their own, — and many voted for the successful candidates ; few or none for Clay. If those mischievous men had gone with us, Mr. Clay would have been President. Now the Southern Loco-focos claim a triumph over us as abolitionists ; this is very provoking, but " suffering is the badge of all our tribe." Mr. Clay is defeated by these Northern Ishmaelites, and by naturalized voters, made expressly for the purpose.

Election Returns.

NOVEMBER 20. — The Historical Society celebrated to-day their fortieth anniversary. The members and their guests assembled at five o'clock, at their rooms in the University, whence they walked in procession to the Church of the Messiah, where an address was delivered by Mr. Brodhead, the gentleman who was sent out by the State to collect, from the archives of Europe, annals and records and documents relating to the history of the United States, and especially such as concerned the settle-ment and early history of New York.

Festival of the Historical Society.

At eight o'clock the company, to the number of three hundred gentlemen, sat down to dinner. Among the guests were the venerable ex-President, John Quincy Adams; Mr. Frelinghuysen; Mr. Saltonstall, of Massachusetts; Mr. Reed, of Philadelphia; President Day; President Moore, of Columbia College; delegates from all the historical and literary societies of Massachusetts, Connecticut, and Pennsylvania; several distinguished clergymen of this and other States; judges, etc., in learned profusion in this array of distinguished men. There was a preponderance, of course, of New England men. A better convocation of learning and talents has seldom been seen in New York, nor was there ever more or better speaking. The whole affair went off famously, and the company broke up reluctantly at one o'clock in the morning.

Mr. Gallatin presided during the first hour or two, with Mr. Adams on his right, and General Almonte, the Mexican Minister, on his left. It was a glorious sight to see the two octogenarians, Mr. Gallatin and Mr. Adams, side by side, with heads white as snow and full of knowledge; these two stars who shone together formerly in the fiery heat of opposing politics, shooting hostile flames at each other, now mingling their waning lights to illumine the path of science, and gilding with their declining rays the hours of rational festivity. The vice-presidents, at the head of the table, were Chief Justice Jones and myself; at the lower end, Messrs. Lawrence, Bradish, and Benjamin F. Butler. The stewards (and most attentive ones they were) were P. M. Wetmore, Col. George Gibbs, B. R. Winthrop, John Jay, J. R. Bartlett, T. Harris, H. G. Stebbins, A. H. Bradford, A. M. Cozzens, E. C. Benedict.

NOVEMBER 28. — Flying is dangerous. I never open

Railroad Accidents. a newspaper that does not contain some account of disasters and loss of life on railroads. They do a retail business in human slaughter, whilst the wholesale trade is carried on (especially on the Western waters) by the steamboats.

DECEMBER 5. — I went last evening to a party at Mrs. Charles A. Davis's, where I met many of my travelled countrywomen for the first time since their return. Most of them seem to have escaped the foppery of foreign manners and the bad taste of anti-Americanism. There were the lovely Mrs. Sydney Brooks, Mrs. Robert Ray, Mrs. Crawford, her sister Miss Ward, Miss Phelps, Mrs. Panon, Mrs. and Miss Barclay,—all American foreigners for a short period. Take them together, I do not think New York has any reason to be ashamed of her fair representatives.

DECEMBER 11.—Died in Boston, on Sunday last, aged about fourscore, William Prescott. He was a graduate of Harvard, of the class of 1783. Honoured be his memory, for he was of a race nearly extinct, and which is now seldom reproduced,—a gentleman of the old school. He was thrice illustrious: in his ancestry, for his father was Colonel Prescott, who commanded at Bunker Hill; in himself, for he was distinguished by virtue, talents, and patriotism; and in his posterity, for his son is the accomplished author of " Ferdinand and Isabella."

Death of Judge Prescott.

There is a terrible flare-up between the States of Massachusetts and South Carolina. The former sent to Charleston Mr. Hoar, one of their aged and respectable citizens, to make a friendly issue in the courts of the United States in relation to the tyrannical and uncourteous laws of the latter, by which they arrested and confined in prison free black men, citizens of Massachusetts, employed in their vessels, on their arrival in Charleston. This proceeding gave great umbrage to the doughty sons of the Palmetto State. Governor Hammond charged a big gun, in the form of a message, to the Legislature; and they discharged a volley of imprecations, vituperations, and denunciations against the universal Yankee nation in general, and Mr. Commissioner Hoar in particular,—which missiles, if their power had been equal to the noise they made, would have been sufficient to frighten all the codfish and haddock out of Boston bay. This catastrophe, however, was happily averted. But they sent the ambassador packing. He wisely preferred a sudden retreat to the tender mercy of a furious mob, who were preparing to attack him, and made his exit in his

South Carolina in the Field.

own suit of broadcloth, rather than assume one of tar and feathers, which was in readiness for his equipment. The tempest begins to growl terribly in Mr. Calhoun's teapot.

DECEMBER 14. — Honoured be the State which knows how to do honour to her worthiest citizen! The presidential electors of Kentucky assembled at Frankfort, according to law, and deposited their votes for Henry Clay and Theodore Frelinghuysen. Their consciences are clear of the sin of a participation in the national ingratitude which now soils the escutcheon of America. The high and solemn duty being performed, and the ceremonials properly attended to, the patriotic band of electors proceeded in a body, by the railroad, to Lexington, and thence went on foot in procession, attended by Governor Owsley, ex-Governors Metcalf and Letcher, and all the honest men of the place, escorted by a company of volunteer troops, to Ashland, the residence of the man of whom Kentucky is proud.

Mr. Clay being apprised of their visit, received them on the lawn in front of his house, and from the steps of his door replied to their affectionate address, in terms eloquent and impressive, full of devoted obedience to the voice of the people and prayers for the happiness of a country which has just evinced a melancholy want of appreciation of his eminent abilities and patriotic services. The scene is described by those who witnessed it as one of surpassing interest. America, like other republics, has proved herself ungrateful; but Kentucky takes no share of the disgrace. I would rather be Mr. Clay, with such a vote and such an expression of the favour of my own State, than the President-elect, with the hurrahs of a misguided, mercenary mob, the support of the old incendiary of the Hermitage, and the fruits of successful fraud and corruption.

DECEMBER 20. — Mr. Thomas Ludlow Ogden died on Monday evening, aged seventy-one years; a highly respected citizen, and a lawyer of considerable eminence. He has been an associate of mine in the vestry of Trinity

Church ever since I have been there, and long before that period he was a member, and clerk of the corporation, which office he held, together with that of warden, at the time of his death. Abraham Ogden, Charles Ogden, of New Orleans, and Mrs. Waddington are brothers and sister of the deceased. I attended the funeral this day, at three o'clock, in St. Paul's Church. The pall-bearers were Chief Justice Jones, David S. Kennedy, David S. Jones, A. Tredwell, William Bard, Edward W. Laight, P. G. Stuyvesant, Beverly Robinson.

DECEMBER 27.— The Reverend Mr. Torrey, one of the philanthropic gentlemen who go about meddling with other people's concerns, and creating bad blood between the different sections of the Union, has been tried in Baltimore, and, after an able defence by Reverdy Johnson, convicted and sentenced to an imprisonment in the penitentiary for the term of seven years and three months for the crime of enticing slaves from their master. This is a tolerably hard sentence ; but slaves are property, and stealing is stealing, and the law gives it in black and white.

1845.

THE new year made its appearance clothed in smiles; the weather was fine, and the sun shone brightly during the whole day, and, notwithstanding the muddy condition of the streets, Broadway and the adjacent thoroughfares were thronged with animated pedestrians, whilst vehicles of all descriptions were in active employment. It was summer weather, and I visited for six hours without requiring a cloak or an overcoat. God be thanked for all his mercies! I have witnessed the close of another year, and find myself a year older, certainly, but in no respect worse off or less happy than at its commencement. My faculties are not materially impaired, my health is good, and my affairs in no respect less favourable. I am employed pleasantly and profitably as President of the American Mutual Insurance Company, whose first year's business closes this day. My family are in good health, with the exception of my wife, and she has gained strength of late; so, with a firm trust in Providence, and a determination to make a good and honourable use of the blessings I enjoy, here goes for a new year.

JANUARY 16. — The old *new* Dutch Church, on Nassau, Liberty, and Cedar streets, has not been turned into "a den of thieves," exactly; but its holy uses have departed from it. The government has leased it, and it is converted into *the* post-office; and a splendid one it is. The exterior is not much changed. The clock, once famous as Time's criterion, the rule for courts and schools, churches and banks, by pleading which, in justification, jurors escaped fines, and school-boys flagellation; by whose undisputed authority the bells ceased ringing on Sundays, and protests were legalized, — this ancient chronicle of Time, old as his hour-glass, still performs its hourly and minutely duty, its naked hands unchilled by storm or cold, and strikes as

New Post-office.

hard, but with less malevolent intent, than the practised pugilist.
The gallant cock which surmounts the spire still turns his face to
the enemy, and warns the mariner, the ship-owner, and the under-
writer from which quarter of the compass his danger comes. The
exterior of the building preserves much of its respectable, church-
like appearance ; but the interior has no more resemblance to what
it was when Dr. Livingston's voluminous white wig filled the minds
of the worshipping burgomasters with a holy awe, when the
eloquence of Linn warmed for a brief space their torpid imaginations into momentary activity, or the mild, persuasive voice of
Abeel " almost persuaded them to be Christians," — no more
resemblance, I say, than Gardiner's shop, down Broadway, has to
the Quaker meeting-house.

JANUARY 27. — Dined with Mr. George Curtis. The party was,
Mr. Webster, M. H. Grinnell, Austin Stevens, Charles King, J.
Prescott Hall, R. M. Blatchford, T. Tileston, John Ward, Edward
Curtis, and myself. This is the first time I have met the *great*
senator during his present visit. I was invited to dine with him at
Blatchford's on Friday, and at Draper's on Saturday, but had to
decline both invitations.

FEBRUARY 1. — This beautiful ship sailed for Canton
The " Rain-
bow. "
this morning loaded with American manufactures, — a
strange revolution in trade. The same articles which
we formerly imported from China, and for which nothing but dollars would pay, are now manufactured here at one-third of the cost,
and sent out to pay for teas. The difficulty now is to find sufficient
returns for the American cargoes. We do not send them specie, —
not a dollar. It would be much more likely to come from there.
I went yesterday with Samuel S. Howland on board the " Rainbow," — the finest ship in model, symmetry, and finish that
ever left this port. She appeared to me like a pilot-boat or a
race-horse ; she was so long and slim, and everything about her
so clean and taper. If she does not sail fast there are no fish
in the sea.

Death of a
Patriot.

FEBRUARY 25. — Ah, well-a-day! The race is almost extinct, and modern vocabularies preserve the term only among the obsolete words, of which the present generation have almost forgotten the meaning; but old Ashur Robbins was one. This venerable man, who has been for the last half-century one of the most prominent public men of Rhode Island, died on Sunday last, at his residence in Newport, aged eighty-eight years. He represented the State for fourteen years in the Senate of the United States; was a Whig of the truest principles, and one of the best scholars in the United States. He was appointed postmaster of Newport during the brief administration of General Harrison, and held the office at the time of his death. If Tyler had known how good a man he was, and some one of his satellites had wanted the office, the venerable patriot would not have been left in possession of this small boon of a grateful party.

FEBRUARY 27. — I dined with Mr. Henry A. Coit. The party, besides the host and hostess, consisted of Mr. Horsley Palmer, D. C. Colden, George M. Woolsey, William H. Aspinwall, John Hicks, Theodore de Hon, J. D. P. Ogden, Charles H. Russell, William S. Miller, George Barclay, William S. Wetmore, and myself.

Our Dear
Sister Texas.

MARCH 1. — The great question of the annexation of Texas, which has kept the public mind in an unprecedented state of excitement, and the result of which was doubtful until the last moment, was carried in the Senate, by means the most unconstitutional, on Thursday evening. The party who elected Mr. Polk was determined to carry it through at all hazards, and the foundations of the Republic have been broken up to accomplish the object. The end of all these things is at hand. The Constitution is a dead-letter, the ark of safety is wrecked, the wall of separation which has hitherto restrained the violence of popular rage is broken down, the Goths are in possession of the Capitol, and if the Union can stand the shock it will only be another evidence that Divine Providence takes better care of us than we deserve.

Miss Delia Webster, who was convicted in Kentucky,
Abolition in Kentucky. and sentenced to four years' confinement in the penitentiary for the crime of abducting slaves, has been
pardoned by Governor Owsley, and sent home to her mamma in
Vermont, who probably did not " know she was out." She will
now, it is to be hoped, profit by the lesson she has had to abstain
from meddling in other people's concerns. The sentence was, no
doubt, just ; and, the law being satisfied, it was probably as well that
the executive clemency should be extended to the lady. But her
accomplice, a man named Fairbanks, who was sentenced to fifteen
years' imprisonment, will probably not get off so well. He will be
indulged, a few years at least, in reflecting between four walls
upon the danger of too much zeal in the cause of abolition.

MARCH 4. — St. Polk's day. On this day the new President of
the United States is inaugurated at Washington, and Whittington
was not more astonished when the famous prediction of Bow
Bells, " Turn again, Whittington, Lord Mayor of London ! " was
realized by his investiture with the magisterial ermine, than Mr.
Polk must be in finding himself " King of the Yankee Doodles," as
Cooke, the tragedian, designated our President. Office-hunters,
demagogues, and political trumpeters are now shouting at the top
of their " sweet voices " for a triumph to which each of them claims
the merit of having mainly contributed, and of whom many of
the number will be sadly disappointed when they come to find
that the public swill-pail, capacious as it is, has not room for all
their snouts. As for the Whigs, we have more cause to rejoice
at the retirement of Mr. Tyler than to mourn over the accession of Mr. Polk.

MARCH 5. — The address of the new President,
Inaugural Address. which was made yesterday at noon, in the rain, on the
steps of the great eastern portico of the Capitol, at
his inauguration, was here last night, at eleven o'clock, and is published this morning. It is a plain, sensible document, not very
elegantly written, but apparently honest, and creditable, on the

whole, to its author. He professes as much as Mr. Tyler did when he swore to defend the Constitution and administer the government with justice and impartiality. God grant that he may redeem his pledges with truth and sincerity, as the latter certainly did not !

MARCH 6. — I dined yesterday with a party at Mr. David S. Kennedy's ; the guests were : Mr. Horsley Palmer, Daniel Lord, Jr., William H. Aspinwall, J. D. P. Ogden, John Gihon, Mr. James, William B. Astor, Thomas Dixon, John J. Palmer, Thomas W. Ludlow, and myself.

APRIL 7. — The site of Washington Hall, in Broad-
Relics of
Old Times.   way, between Chambers and Reade streets, was lately sold by the heirs of Mr. John G. Coster to A. T. Stewart, who is preparing to erect on the ground a dry-goods store, spacious and magnificent beyond anything of the kind in the New World, or the Old either, as far as I know. In removing the rubbish which remained after the hall was burned, the corner-stone was brought to light and exhumed this morning, with some formalities, resembling in a degree those of its original deposition. Well do I remember the ceremony of laying this corner-stone on the 4th of July, 1809, when the Federalists were on their high horse, and when I subscribed $250, — which I wish I had now, — and walked in procession to the North Church, where Gulian C. Verplanck (who happened just then to be a Federalist) delivered the oration, and Robert Morris, Jr., father of Robert H. Morris, the late mayor, now an ultra-Democrat, then an out-and-out Federalist, was one of the vice-presidents of the Washington Benevolent Society. These firebrands of that fine old party are now shining lights in the Loco-foco camp, and abuse their old associates who continue to fight under their original colours. How do the very *stones* rise up in judgment against them !

In excavating the cellar of the house to be erected
Another.   by John C. Stevens on part of the ground which he has leased from the college, at the corner of Murray

street and College place, two pieces of cannon were found in perfect preservation. They are supposed to be of the number of
those which were captured on the 23d of August, 1775, from the
king's troops, by "the liberty boys," led by young Alexander
Hamilton, with his collegians. The pieces were buried in the
college grounds, and are now brought to light, as two others were,
a short time since, in the cellar of my father's house in John street.
Overturn, overturn, overturn! is the maxim of New York. The
very bones of our ancestors are not permitted to lie quiet a
quarter of a century, and one generation of men seem studious to
remove all relics of those which preceded them. Pitt's statue no
longer graces Wall street, the old Presbyterian Church has given
place to the stalls of the money-changers, and the Croton river
has washed away all traces of the tea-water pump.

APRIL 11.—The club dined with me yesterday, and
Club Dinner. the day should be marked with a "white stone," for
it was one of great enjoyment. Mr. Webster was with
us, and we all agreed that we had never seen him so agreeable
and entertaining. He was rich in anecdote and story, and his own
early history, and that of his ancestors formed his most delightful
theme. Our dinner and wine were unimpeachable. The following
members of the club were present : Grinnell, Blatchford, George
Curtis, Spofford, Edward Curtis, John Ward, Colt, Hall, Jaudon,
Draper, and Philip Hone ; and, in addition, we had Mr. Webster,
James Monroe, and Charles King.

APRIL 15.—I am sorry that Nathaniel P. Tallmadge has been
removed from the office of Governor of Wisconsin, to which he
was lately appointed by Mr. Tyler, and in which he had hardly
settled himself. The system of proscription is carried to a more
shameful extent now than ever. Some faint hopes were entertained that this new man of ours, having the power to act inde-
pendently, would not follow the infernal policy of indiscriminate
removals from office. But whether the devil puts it into his heart,
and he enjoys this exercise of abused power, or the wolves, who

bay for more carcasses than he can supply, have driven him mad, he turns out all Whigs, Conservatives, and Tyler men, and bestows his favours upon the most profligate of his followers. All the principal actors in the disgraceful rebellion in Rhode Island have been supplied with government places. The Collector of Providence, the United States Marshal, and the District Attorney have been removed from office to make places for leading Dorrites, who would accept a public office now when they may enjoy the privilege of sawing wood or mining coal.

MAY 3. — This splendid packet, the largest merchantman in the United States, is now fitted up and nearly ready for sea. Her accommodations and the magnificence of her cabins exceed anything we have yet seen. Her berths are nearly all taken, and on Wednesday next she is to sail for England. May she prove worthy of her name, and reach " the haven where she would be " with more certainty of success than her illustrious namesake did the haven where he ought to be !

Ship "Henry Clay."

I was one of a highly pleased and exceedingly jolly party who dined yesterday on board this noble ship, on the invitation of her enterprising owners, Grinnell, Minturn, & Co. We poured a full libation to her success, and if complimentary toasts and speeches, hearty cheers and good wishes, will do the ship, her owners, builders, commander, and crew any good, they had them all in honest doses, not measured by homœopathic practitioners. The party consisted of M. H. Grinnell, Henry Grinnell, Robert B. Minturn, Captain Nye, George Curtis, Mr. Delprat, J. W. Webb, Charles King, M. C. Patterson, James A. Hamilton, his son Alexander, Ogden Hoffman, Mr. Vermilyea, Mr. Neil of Ohio, Captain Rogers, George W. Blunt, Mr. Kinney of New Jersey, and myself.

MAY 20. — Richard Caton died yesterday, in Baltimore, aged eighty-three years. He came to this country when twenty-one years of age, and married one of the daughters of Mr. Charles Carroll. Mr. Caton was father of the Marchioness of Wellesley, the Duchess of Leeds, and Lady Stafford ;

The Carroll Family.

and his granddaughter, Miss McTavish, is now engaged to the Hon. Henry Howard, son of the Earl of Carlisle, and brother of the Duchess of Sutherland and Lord Morpeth.

The ladies of this family (natives though they be of Yankee-doodle-dom) seem to possess, in a high degree, the power of capturing the aristocracy of England; and it is said that royalty itself was not insensible to the charms of some of them.

MAY 22.—"In the midst of life, we are in death." There have been two sad and melancholy monitors of the truth of this passage of Scripture. At four o'clock I attended the funeral of Robert C. Cornell, and at six that of Benjamin E. Bremner. Here were two men, with whom I have been during a large portion of my life in habits of almost daily intercourse, both swept off, as it were, in an instant; the smooth, deceitful stream of human life is suddenly disturbed, as if by the casting of a stone, which sinks into the depths of forgetfulness, the waters close over it, and the stream rolls on as before. Poor Bremner! I saw him every day at the office, or in the evening at the Union Club; he was a gentleman amiable in disposition and correct in deportment.

The other case is that of Robert C. Cornell, one of the best men in our city, who has been engaged during his whole life in acts of benevolence, who has been employed in season and out of season in all the prominent charitable institutions of our city, and, unlike most men, never blew the trumpet of his own fame. I have been associated with this good Samaritan more than twenty years in the Bank for Savings, of which he was secretary at its commencement. He never failed to perform his duties with alacrity and fidelity. Since I have been president, his place on my left hand, at the board of trustees, has never been vacant. How he will be missed! I was seated in the office, talking with Mr. George Griswold, on Tuesday, at three o'clock, when we saw Mr. Cornell brought from the office of the Farmer's Loan and Trust Company opposite, of which he was president, and put into a carriage. I ran over and spoke to him; but he replied not, and "word spake he never more." He had been stricken with apoplexy, and died a few minutes after. He was a man of deeds, and not of words; the noblest work of God, — an honest man.

May 23. — The city of New York is so overgrown that we in the upper regions do not know much more about what is passing in the lower, nor the things which are to be seen there, than the inhabitants of Mexico or Grand Cairo. I was informed, by a notice which I saw accidentally in a newspaper, that the Italian Opera Company was to perform on Friday evening, at Castle Garden, scenes from "La Semiramide" and "Le Barbier de Séville." This was the last night of that *suburban* place of amusement; and, lo and behold! when I entered, I found myself on the floor of the most splendid and largest theatre I ever saw, — a place capable of seating comfortably six or eight thousand persons. The pit or area of the pavilion is provided with some hundred small white tables and movable chairs, by which people are enabled to congregate into little squads, and take their ices between the acts. In front of the stage is a beautiful fountain, which plays when the performers do not. The whole of this large area is surmounted by circular benches above and below, from every point of which the view is enchanting. Here, too, is an excellent company of Italians, among whom are Signoras Pico and Majocchi, and Signors Antonigni, Valtotina, and Sanguirico, performing the finest operas of Rossini; and all this, with plenty of fresh air if the weather should be ever warm enough to require it, for the moderate price of fifty cents.

May 24. — The Rev. Alonzo Potter, of Union College, Schenectady, was elected yesterday Bishop of the Diocese of Pennsylvania, in place of the Rev. Henry W. Onderdonk. Dr. Potter is an eminent man, son-in-law of President Mott, a Presbyterian divine. He is, no doubt, a very suitable man for the bishopric; but he must be as much surprised at his sudden elevation in the church as Colonel Polk was at his in the State; but I believe the church has made the best bargain. Dr. Tyng has accepted a call from St. George's Church, in this city, to supply Dr. Milnor's place.

MAY 26.—Prescott Hall drove me out in his carriage to dine with Mr. Blatchford, at Hell-Gate. Our pleasant little party consisted of Mr. Hall; his brother-in-law, Mr. DeWolf; Mr. Jaudon, that fine old English gentleman; Mr. Horsley Palmer; and myself, besides the family. The day was pleasant, the salmon good, and we had a cosey time.

MAY 28. — Gracie King, son of Mr. James G. King, Highwood.   lately married Elizabeth Duer, President Duer's nice daughter. She is seeing company, as a bride, at Highwood, her father-in-law's lovely place in Jersey. My daughter is one of a party of young ladies who are attending the bride, and pass the week at Highwood. I went over with my wife, Emily Foster, and Mrs. Oliver Kane, in Maria DePeyster's carriage, to pay a bridal visit.

JUNE 4. — The ship "Muskingum," a vessel of three Western   hundred and fifty tons, arrived at Liverpool on the 15th Enterprise.   of April, from Cincinnati, Ohio, with a cargo of provisions. This is one of the wonders of "Young America." The place where this ship was built was unknown fifty years ago. She had one thousand seven hundred miles to go before she started on her voyage.

Death of   JUNE 17.—The universal American nation is in General   mourning. Stripes, black as those which border certain Jackson.   resolutions in the archives of the Senate, darken the columns of the newspapers. The flags on vessels' masts, liberty-poles, and public houses are hoisted at half-mast; the conscript fathers of the city, overwhelmed with grief, suspend their labours, and retire, sorrowing, to their respective domiciles; the standard of the Empire Club is shrouded in crape, and the newspaper boys blow their horns and proclaim the news of General Jackson's death. Now, to my thinking, the country had greater cause to mourn on the day of his birth than on that of his decease. This iron-willed man has done more mischief than any man alive. Indomitable in action, he carried the fury of the warrior into the administration of civil affairs, referring all things to personal motives; his iron heel trampled upon the necks of all who stood opposed to his political measures, or dared to gainsay his dogmatical opinions. The undisputed head of a violent, proscriptive party, himself constituting its central power, he did more to break down the republican principles of the government and enslave the minds of the people than all the rulers who went before him; and yet no man ever enjoyed so large a share of that pernicious popular homage called *popularity*. "Old Hickory," "The hero of New Orleans," "The second Washington," "The old General," are the endearing epithets which old women have taught the "lips of infancy to lisp," and sturdy men have gloried in proclaiming at the top of their voices.

Our Mayor, in announcing this event to the Common Council, does not hesitate to call the deceased ex-President "the greatest and best man in the country." *Great* he was in the unbending exercise of his stubborn will, and *good* it may be humbly hoped he has proven himself in the awful Court of Inquiry where his actions are to be judged; but it was somewhat bold in Mr. Havemeyer to use expressions so unqualified. General Jackson is gone, and all good people should pray to be delivered hereafter from the effects of popularity such as followed him.

General Jackson died at his residence, in Nashville, Tennessee, on Sunday, the 8th, at six o'clock P.M., aged seventy-eight years and nearly three months. He was born in the Waxhaw settlement, South Carolina, on the 16th of March, 1767.

JUNE 18.—In the evening I went to a gentlemen's party and supper at Mr. James W. Gerard's fine new mansion in Twentieth street. The party was large. It consisted of the members of the Court of Errors, the Chancellor, Judges of the Supreme Court and of the United States, the Recorder, all the eminent members of the bar, and some of the Hone Club. The host at one end of the table, and Dr. Francis at the other, with sundry bottles of champagne, made considerable noise.

There has been a new organization of the police, by which a general superintendent was to be appointed: a sort of Fouché, with powers less extensive. For this office, the Mayor, Loco-foco as he is, nominated Justice Taylor, a Whig, for the old, obsolete, and very insufficient reason that he, being the best qualified man in the city, ought to have the office without regard to politics. So, also, thought the Aldermen, for a majority of them voted to confirm the nomination. But this spark of reason was soon extinguished by the *patriotic* Board of Assistants, who repudiated the new-born liberality of their brethren, and turned the nominee honestly out of doors. They non-concurred, and yesterday His Honor nominated Justice Matsell, who suited them better. He was confirmed, and the new system goes into operation.

Grace Church, at the corner of Broadway and Rector street, has been sold for $65,000. It is to be converted into stores below, and the upper part into a splendid museum of Chinese curiosities, which is likely to prove a good speculation. Dr. Taylor, the rector, preached the last sermon on Sunday last, in the old edifice. The congregation will occupy a temporary place of worship until their splendid new church, at the upper end of Broadway, is finished. It will be second only to the magnificent Trinity, and will probably be finished about the same time.

June 26. — Yesterday, at twelve o'clock, a party of ladies and gentlemen, to the number of three or four hundred, assembled on board the steamer " New York," which was chartered by Mr. T. W. Ludlow to transport the transported party to one of the most pleasant and well-conducted entertainments I have ever witnessed, at his delightful villa on the banks of the Hudson, near Yonkers, or Philipsburgh. It was a regular New York affair; all the finest married women and the prettiest girls of the city were there, with judges, lawyers, merchants, and a numerous representation of Westchesterites, — all like the celebrated Billy Taylor, " full on mirth and full on glee." Tables were spread in marquees under the trees, where every delicacy was provided to eat and drink; a fine band of music played during the day, and on board the boat during her return to the city. Cotillons, waltzes, and polkas were danced in the house, on the lawn, and on the promenade-deck of the steamer. Several private yachts enlivened the scene on the water; and at half-past seven we reëmbarked and got safely home without accident, and all highly pleased with our entertainment and the hospitalities of our host and hostess.

BOSTON, JULY 7. — I started this morning from *Excursion to Marshfield.* Brooklyn, at a quarter to nine o'clock, on my excursion to Massachusetts, and in exactly three hours and three minutes was at Greenport, — ninety-five miles; fast enough, in all conscience. Greenport is a pretty place in Poconock bay, on the Sound, and must in time, I should think, be a desirable retreat for New Yorkers.

After all this straining of the limbs and nerves of the iron horse we had to stop here for an hour, waiting the arrival of the steamboat to carry us across the Sound. The boat came to New London, and thence up the Thames to Allen's Point, where the Norwich & Worcester Railroad commences; so we came on to Boston at ten o'clock, having lost another hour waiting for a train at Oxford. It has been a hard day's travel, as all railroad cantering is, and I find I have had enough of the Long Island route. But the misfortune I have met with in starting has not tended to put me in the best possible humour. I found on arriving here that I had lost my trunk and dressing-case. I saw them put in the baggage-crate in New York. My only hope is that they were left at Greenport, in which case I have taken measures to have them sent on.

MARSHFIELD (on the broad waters of Cape Cod bay), JULY 8. — Boston was hotter last night — that is, the little room in the Tremont House in which I was baked — than Chabert's parlour in the iron stove where he used to take his recreation at boiling heat. I was glad when nine o'clock came; and, having borrowed a shirt from Mr. Belknap, Judge Warren, Mr. Draper (who came on this morning), and I embarked in the pretty steamboat with a pretty name (the " Mayflower "), and came to Hingham, — a pleasant watering-place, with a large hotel, on the bay. We found Mr. Webster's carriage waiting for us, and soon started for Marshfield, sixteen miles, where we arrived in time to dress for dinner. But, alas! my garments were all borrowed.

Our reception by the noble master of the mansion and his amiable, kind, and ladylike wife was everything that heart could wish. In addition to all his other great qualities, Mr. Webster is the very perfection of a host. At one moment instructive and eloquent, he delights his guests with the charms of his conversation; then, full of life and glee as a boy escaped from school, he sings snatches of songs, tells entertaining stories, and makes bad puns, in which his guests are not behind him.

The house has been lately enlarged and beautified, and is fitted up with great taste. The library, in a splendid new wing, is such a one as might be expected to appertain to Daniel Webster. As for my chamber, which is on the first floor, adjoining the library, to which it gives me access, it is the perfection of sleeping. The table is capital; everything is given at the top of the heart; and while there is no *empressement*, every wish is anticipated. He appears to like his guests; and, for myself, I am bound to him by hoops of iron.

JULY 9. — The journal of this day is as follows: After breakfast Mr. Webster drove Draper and me over his extensive grounds down to the beach, where his boats were ready for a fishing excursion, which is one of his greatest enjoyments. Here was this wonderful man, on whose lips unsurpassed eloquence has so often hung, whose pen has directed the most important negotiations, and whose influence has governed Senates, in a loose coat and trousers, with a most picturesque slouched hat, which a Mexican bandit might have coveted, directing his people, — whose obedience grows out of affection, and who are governed by the force of kindness, —

regulating the apparatus, examining the bait, and helping to hoist the sails and "hold on to the main sheet." So off we went to sea in the good sloop "Comet;" and a tidier, more obedient, smarter little craft is not to be found in Massachusetts bay. We had tolerably good sport for a couple of hours; but the sea was rough, and the vessel uneasy, the effect of which was that I became very sick; but it was some consolation to me that the Lord High Admiral was in the same condition. "I don't wish it made too public, sir," said I; "nor would I have it put in the newspapers; but I am sick! sick!" — "My case exactly," said he; "and I have tried to keep this unusual circumstance a secret; but it won't do, and we must go ashore." So we returned, and our health and cheerfulness returned with us also.

We dined at half-past four, and here was this hero of the slouched hat dressed for dinner, presiding at his table (and a sumptuous meal it was) with the grace and elegance of high breeding, enlivening by his cheerfulness and vivacity the solid hospitality of the feast, and mingling lessons of wisdom with unconsidered effusions of good-humour. Fletcher Webster and Mr. Greenough came down from Boston and joined our party, and two Messrs. Hedge, of Plymouth, were guests at dinner. We had a pleasant game of harmless whist in the evening, and retired at ten o'clock.

JULY 10. — This day was devoted to a journey to Plymouth, under the charge of Judge Warren. The distance by land is about twenty miles; the drive was pleasant, the country of the "old colony" interesting, and Plymouth, with the Pilgrim Rock and all the relics of the forefathers, a fruitful theme, agreeable to them in the recital and to us in the hearing. The two Messrs. Hedge, brothers-in-law of our friend Warren, and his aged mother, one of those bright, intelligent, New England women who are difficult to match, were our entertainers at Plymouth. The venerable lady showed us many interesting remains of Pilgrim days: the chair which was occupied by Lady Otis, as she was called, her grandmother of many generations, when a Pilgrim passenger on board the " Mayflower," in 1620; Governor Winslow's chair; plates brought by the Otis family from Holland; together with most interesting letters from General and Mrs. Washington to Colonel Warren, her husband, and my friend's father; and especially one from John Adams, written the day after the destruction of the tea in Boston harbor, beginning " The die is cast," full of patriotic exultation, fearless of consequences, and confident of success. It was " all for liberty or a world well lost."

Our drive back through Duxbury, Scituate, and other pretty places and towns of the " old colony," with fine weather, agreeable company, and the " squire's " capital horses, are things to be remembered. We returned to Marshfield to dine, after which Farmer Webster showed us his capacious barns, in which many a ton of good Puritan hay is just now being condemned to the *rack;* fields of oats supporting their heavy heads upon slender, but healthy, limbs; cattle combining the advantages of foreign and domestic blood; cows whose sleek sides bear the comfortable signs of milk, butter, and cheese; every vegetable, from the diminutive bean up to the unwieldy pumpkin; while the broad sea lay before him, containing a certain harvest of piscatory enjoyments.

I am no longer dependent upon the wardrobes of my friends; my trunk and writing-case came down to Marshfield this evening. I have not learned where they " slipped out of the slings," nor do I care; I have them, to my great satisfaction.

JULY 11. — A day to mark with a white stone. The High Admiral ordered us out immediately after breakfast. We repaired to the beach, embarked in the " Comet," and put to sea, — Mr. Webster, Draper, and I, with Dr. Perkins, who came here yesterday on a visit with Mrs. Perkins. The wind was favourable, the weather fine, and all things propitious. Casting anchor five or six miles from land, we went to work, and the result of our labour was the capture of twenty-six cod and twenty-two haddock, weighing more than three hundred pounds. I never had such sport and never saw such " spoils," and the sail home in our beautiful yacht was delightful. We returned to a late dinner, of which our fish formed an important part, and the cool wine, taken under the shade of the noble lime-trees in front of the house, to which the agreeable conversation of our noble host gave a zest of the richest character, closed a day to which there was no alloy but the recollection that it was the last we had to spend at Marshfield.

NEW BEDFORD, JULY 12. — Mr. Draper, Judge Warren, and I left Marshfield, at seven o'clock this morning, in Mr. Webster's carriage, and came to Hingham, where we embarked in the " Mayflower," and got to Boston at twelve o'clock, the hottest day of the summer. The good people of Boston, who go beyond their neighbours in all they undertake, have gotten the thermometer up to 100, and are gasping with heat. I determined at once to go to Nahant this evening to sleep, and to remain to-morrow; but my plan was suddenly changed. Mr. Joseph Grinnell came in pursuit of me, and insisted on my going home with him to New Bedford. As this was part of my original plan, I did not require much persuasion; and so, having called and made my excuses to Mr. Otis, whose kind invitation to dinner for to-day was sent and accepted soon after my arrival, and having taken a hasty dinner at the Tremont, I parted from my fellow-traveller, and came away with Grinnell, on the railroad, at four o'clock, and entered my agreeable quarters at his house before tea-time,— only fifty-seven miles.

JULY 19. — It is not quite ten years since the city
Great Fire.   of New York was visited with the dreadful conflagra-
tion which laid the most valuable part of the business portion of the city in ruins, and destroyed property to the amount of $20,000,000. This day will also be marked with lines on the city's calendar not so extensive, but equally black. A fire has occurred, the loss of which is probably $5,000,000; several of the insurance offices are ruined, and all crippled. My office I fear, is in the former category. We have lost between three

and four hundred thousand dollars, which is more than we can pay. This is a hard stroke for me. I was pleasantly situated, with a moderate support for my declining years, and now "Othello's occupation's gone." It is very hard; and a large share of philosophy is required to support it. But the Lord's will be done! I have still much to thank Him for, and trust that He will endue me with resignation to bear up against this and the other misfortunes with which my latter years have been visited.

This fire is not only extensive and destructive, but is marked with circumstances of an extraordinary nature. The great fire of 1835 occurred in the month of December, when the weather was so cold that the firemen could not work, and the water from the engines froze before it reached its destination. This happened about the break of day, in warm, mild weather, with no wind and a plentiful supply of water. The firemen have done their duty nobly, and the civil and military police merit all praise for their exertions. The fire broke out in a repository of saltpetre in New street, — a narrow street, with high houses. There was apparently no danger of its spreading, and the firemen had gotten it under when a dreadful explosion took place. A gasometer, as it is supposed, burst; some say gunpowder, and others a thousand bags of saltpetre; but there are strong doubts whether the latter article can explode with such dreadful effects. Be it as it may, here was the cause of this awful calamity. The stores in Broad street, some of the finest in the city, on one of the broadest streets, were instantly overthrown; the flames were communicated in every direction. Several lives were lost at this moment, of firemen and others, and scarcely a house in Wall street, Broadway, Greenwich street, and the other adjacent streets escaped injury by the breaking of the windows. The people on Staten and Long Islands were roused by what was thought to be an earthquake. Destruction followed in this rich and populous district. All Broad street, with the exception of five or six tenements on each side nearest Wall street, and extending nearly down to the East river, is a heap of undistinguishable ruins; all Beaver street, from William street to the Bowling Green, is destroyed; nearly the whole of New street, Exchange place, and South William street, with their immense quantities of merchandise. Like the fire of 1835, the progress of the flames was so rapid, and its approach so unexpected, that scarcely anything was saved. All, all lies smouldering in ruins. The flames ran up Exchange place to the Waverley House, which is a magnificent ruin; thence all the fine buildings down Broadway to Marketfield street, including Abraham Schermerhorn's hotel, at the corner of Beaver street, are gone. Here it crossed the widest part of Broadway and burned all the houses from Morris street, including Robert Ray's great granite edifice, Brevoort's house, Gardiner Howland's three houses, and all down to Edward Prime's, which is saved.

The number of buildings burned is estimated at nearly three hundred, a large proportion of which were of the most valuable class. They, as well as the goods in the stores, are no doubt insured; but it remains to be seen how far the offices can pay. We are all in confusion at the American. I was at the office until a late hour this evening, cancelling fire and marine policies; for I have very little doubt that the office is bankrupt, and I have advised the insured to cancel ours, and open new policies elsewhere. There is nothing left for me but truth and honesty. There shall be no concealment. My prospects are all blasted in the destruction of this company, but I have nothing for which to condemn myself. The fire insurance was especially my department; there has been no want of diligence or discretion; there never was a list of better policies, taking into view the nature of the risks and the character of the insured. Fortune is against me. I must submit. The Lord's will be done !

JULY 31. — I have received an exceedingly kind letter of condolence, in my misfortunes, from John P. Kennedy, the estimable member of Congress from Baltimore, who is at present at Sharon

Springs, and this morning received a present of grapes, for my wife, from Roswell L. Colt, of Paterson, accompanied by a note full of the kindest and most complimentary expressions. There is balm in this.

ROCKAWAY. — I came down in the five-o'clock evening train to enjoy a couple of days of relief from the care and trouble of my broken Wall-street concern.   The glorious ocean rolls its multitudinous waves upon the monotonous beach as it has for by-gone ages, regardless of the ruined masses of Broad street and Exchange place, and recedes to its unlimited caverns just as it did before the American Mutual Insurance Company was left high and dry on the shores of bankruptcy.

Arrival of the "Great Britain."   AUGUST 11. — The great iron steamer "Great Britain," the leviathan of steam, the monster of the ocean, and unquestionably the largest and most magnificent specimen of naval architecture that ever floated, arrived here yesterday, at three o'clock, in fifteen days from Liverpool, under the command of that fine fellow and successful navigator, Captain Hosken, who has made the "Great Western" proverbial for safety and despatch, and the ocean a macadamized road for her travelling.   The "Great Britain" has been looked for with some anxiety.   A deep interest, accompanied with some doubt, awaited her arrival, arising from her prodigious size, the novelty of her construction (she being propelled by the Archimedean screw, instead of paddles), and the material of which she is constructed, — solid iron plates.   The boast of Archimedes, that his screw might overturn the globe, if he had a place to stand it, does not seem so hyperbolical, after all; and iron is likely to form a better *floating* capital than gold and silver, or even banknotes.

The dimensions of this vessel are as follows : Her total length on deck, 322 feet; her breadth, 50 feet; capacity, 3,000 tons; draught of water, 16 feet; her engines are of 1,000 horse-power. She is, indeed, one of the wonders of this inventive, enterprising, scientific age.   What would our grandsires have thought of crossing the ocean on plates of iron, and shoving vessels ahead by screws !

New York
Enterprise.
In no city of the globe does the recuperative principle exist in so great a degree as in our good city of Gotham.   Throw down our merchants ever so flat, they roll over once, and spring to their feet again.   Knock the stairs from under them, and they will make a ladder of the fragments, and remount.   It is just twenty-four days since the great fire ; the masses of ruins are smoking yet in many places, and flames may be seen escaping from underneath the heaps of incombustible matter, and in the heart of this region of desolation fine stores are being built.   I saw one this morning in South William street, which had reached the eaves; it is built on the site of one destroyed in the fire, the materials of which are too hot to be removed by the naked hands of the workmen.   So in Beaver street, several phœnixes are rising from the ashes, whilst the masons pursue their labour in the midst of the smoke of the buildings which so lately occupied the ground.

SEPTEMBER 1.—The "Great Britain" went to sea on Saturday, with fifty-four passengers ; her departure was quite a gala occasion. She was escorted down the bay by a fleet of fine steam-vessels, bedecked with colours ; and the weather being fine, the Battery and all the piers on her route were filled with spectators, who cheered the "iron monster," and gave her good wishes in abundance.

Died on Tuesday, 26th of August, at the Catholic convent, Georgetown, of which she was an inmate, Virginia, daughter of Major-General Winfield Scott, in the twenty-fourth year of her age, —one of the most accomplished young women of our country. A willing sacrifice to superstition and priestcraft, she became a Roman Catholic, and shut herself up, from her family and friends, in a convent, where she ended her days.   I had a long conference on this painful subject with the General when I was last in Washington.   He was sorely distressed ; but the matter was inevitable, and he was compelled to acquiesce in this most unnatural act of self-will and obstinacy. Her death, in my judgment, should be no cause of mourning to her afflicted friends. It is better she should be in her grave than a living example of self-immolation.

SEPTEMBER 5. — The country has experienced another severe loss. Judge Story, the pride and ornament of the Supreme Court bench, the pupil and follower of the great Chief Justice Marshall, has resigned his seat in that august tribunal. This step, so deeply to be deplored, is caused by the ill-health of the accomplished judge, and it is painful to record, the fact of his indisposition being so serious that there are apprehensions that he will not survive.

Justice Story.

This creates a vacancy to be filled by an administration which will look for no other qualification in the successor whom they shall have to choose than the most unscrupulous devotion to party dictation, undiscriminating approval of all the mischievous measures of the government, and undeniable evidence of having voted and electioneered, and written and spoken, in favour of a President whom nobody thought of four and twenty hours before he was nominated at Baltimore.

The Supreme Court, pure, immaculate, and wise, as it once was, has been falling off ever since the evil day in which Andrew Jackson was installed into the office of President, and now " the sceptre has departed from Israel, and a lawgiver from beneath her feet." Such a man as Webster, or Everett, or Kent, might supply Story's place; but they are not Mr. Polk's kind of men. He has Woodburys, and Walkers, and Duncans, who will suit him better.

SEPTEMBER 12. — The light of the law is extinguished; the worthy disciple and follower of Marshall has, like his great exemplar, descended into the tomb, and has made still wider the chasm which that great man occasioned in the highest tribunal of law and justice in the land. Judge Story died on the evening of Wednesday, September 10, at his residence in Cambridge. He was born in 1780; was appointed

His Death.

an associate justice of the Supreme Court of the United States, by President Madison, in 1811, and was at the time of his death the Dane professor of law in Harvard University. With such an intellect and so great learning, his loss is a national calamity, and he died in the prime and maturity of both ; for he was the junior by seventeen years of his friend and brother in the law, Chancellor Kent, whose precious life may God preserve as one of the ornaments of humanity !

SEPTEMBER 30. — William C. Schermerhorn, son of Mr. Peter Schermerhorn, was married on Wednesday, the 24th, to Anne, daughter of Francis Cottenet, and granddaughter of General Laight.

OCTOBER 18. — The great iron steamer, the " Great Britain," amongst other misadventures on her late voyage, came in contact with some substance, — a rock, perhaps, or sandbank on Nantucket shoals, or, peradventure, a whale. By this accident her propelling apparatus was injured, several of the flanges being carried away. For the purpose of repairing this damage, the immense mass of iron — the burden of the vessel being three thousand tons, and her weight almost equal to that of the Rock of Gibraltar — has been raised by machinery, in the sectional dock at the foot of Pike street, some twenty feet out of the water, and there she lies in perfect safety, with men at work under her bottom. What will John Bull say to Yankee ingenuity and mechanical skill? I am told that the operation could not have been performed in our dear mother-country.

OCTOBER 21. — I heard a pretty good anecdote to-day, which smacks mightily of its Marshfield origin : Mr. George Wood is an eminent counsellor-at-law of this city, at the tip-top of the bar. He is, moreover, of rather a grave deportment, and has a habit of closing his eyes when deep in thought, like the owl. A person called the other day upon Mr. Webster, to engage his services in an important cause, which he agreed to undertake. In the course of his investigations he inquired what counsel was to be opposed to him. "Why," said the litigant, "he is a New York lawyer, with a common-place, every-day name, which I forget." — "What sort of a person is he?" — "Rather a sleepy-looking man." — "Is his name George Wood?" — "That *is* his name." — "Then don't wake him up."

OCTOBER 23. — A leaden pipe was successfully laid on the bed of the East river, to cross the Fulton Ferry, from New York to Brooklyn, for the conveyance of the wires of the magnetic telegraph. The pipe weighs one thousand pounds, all in one piece, without a joint. This is a pretty specimen of mechanical skill, and I see no doubt of its perfect adaptation to the object, except that which arises from the apprehension of danger to the pipe from the anchors of vessels riding in the stream.

OCTOBER 28. — My apprehensions in regard to the submarine pipe in the East river have been realized. The ship "Charles," of Liverpool, in weighing her anchor on Saturday evening, dragged it up, broke the pipe, and of course destroyed the connection. Some other plan must be resorted to.

BOSTON, Nov. 12. — Mr. Blatchford, Mr. Curtis, and I left New York yesterday, at four o'clock P.M., in the steamer "Massachusetts;" were awakened from a short sleep at Stonington, at midnight; came from thence on the Stonington and Boston & Providence railroad, and arrived in Boston at five this morning; two hundred and forty miles in thirteen hours, — a journey which once occupied almost as many days! This is expeditious enough, in all conscience; but a good night's sleep would have been worth more to me than all that is gained by this annihilation of time and space. We have seen Mr. Healy, the artist, and have conferred with him about the portrait of Mr. Webster. He has made a sketch of the *Squire of Marshfield*, with his "slouched hat and fisherman's coat," under the famous "Marshfield tree." He is pleased with the job, and Mr. Webster not displeased with being made its subject.

Excursion to Boston.

Mr. Blatchford and I made two pleasant visits this morning;

the first to Mr. Otis, who is in good health and spirits, and has invited our little party to dine with him to-morrow; the second, to Mr. Prescott, the amiable and accomplished historian of "Ferdinand and Isabella" and "The Conquest of Mexico." Mr. Prescott is engaged in fitting up a fine house in Beacon street, which he bought lately from Augustus Thorndike. He showed us his new library and study, which will be in admirable taste, and a number of curious manuscripts, autographs, and pictures illustrative of his two great works, and collected with that object. I have been busily employed all the morning walking about the city. Boston is improved prodigiously, especially the southern part, where the great railroad depots are situated.

Blatchford, Curtis, and I dined at Mr. Paige's, with all the Websters; Mr. and Mrs. Webster's sister-in-law; Mr. and Mrs. Appleton, his daughter, a nice, little woman; Fletcher Webster, whose wife is Mrs. Paige's sister; Mrs. Joy, another sister; and Mr. Healy, the painter, who is up to the eyes in business, painting portraits. He has just finished Mr. Webster for Lord Ashburton, Mrs. Webster, and Mrs. Paige. I am afraid that he is so much in vogue that the time and price required for our picture may be beyond our patience and money.

We had a merry, pleasant dinner, to which "the Squire" contributed a full quota of anecdote and joke. He was in his boyish mood, which is always agreeable. The folly of a fool is disgusting; that of a wise man, delightful. After dinner we played several games of scientific, solemn, two-shilling whist.

NOVEMBER 13. — We dined with my venerable friend Mr. H. G. Otis, the most perfect gentleman of my acquaintance. Besides our party, and the family of the host, there were Mrs. Harry Otis and her son, a handsome young fellow of about twenty years of age; Mr. Belknap, Mr. Nathan Appleton, and Mr. Truman. Mr. Webster was engaged in a cause in the United States District Court. The dinner and wines, as usual, were excellent, and Mrs. Ritchie charming. I called this morning with Mrs. Webster upon Mr. and

Mrs. Everett, the Paiges, Mrs. Fletcher Webster, and Mrs. Abbott Lawrence.

DECEMBER 8. — John Cotton Smith, the venerable president of the American Bible Society, died at his residence in Sharon, Litchfield County, State of Connecticut, on the 7th of December, in the eighty-first year of his age. He was a member of Congress in 1800, since which he has been Governor of Connecticut, member of the State Legislature, and Judge of the Supreme Court.

DECEMBER 12. — The faint hopes of the lovers of peace that the danger of a serious collision with Great Britain about the miserable Oregon question, arising out of the President's intemperate message, might be averted by the patriotism and discretion of the Senate, are greatly diminished by the announcement of the standing committees which have been elected, as they formerly were, by a vote of the Senate. There is a small majority of Loco-focos in that body ; but some reliance was placed upon the moderation of a portion of their number. But, alas ! party discipline is stronger than judgment, and Mr. Polk must carry his object. Already had Charles J. Ingersoll, of Pennsylvania, been placed at the head of the committee of foreign relations in the House of Representatives, a committee which in the present crisis has the destiny of the nation in its hands, and now Mr. Allen, of Ohio, is elected to the same responsible situation in the Senate. Two more rabid, uncompromising demagogues are not to be found between Nova Scotia and California, — men who will not hesitate to plunge the country into a disastrous war to promote their personal and political views, who would see every warehouse and manufactory levelled with the ground rather than Henry Clay should be President, and every ship sunk at the wharves if thereby their chance of being great men with the populace might be secured.

Oregon Question.

Our sister city of the Bay State has been without a chief magistrate for some time past, owing to a triangular state of parties, Whigs, Native Americans, and Loco-focos, by which no candidate could get the requisite majority of all the votes. They have come together at last, the Natives having discovered that they and the Whigs were of the same family ; and they have now elected Josiah Quincy, Jr., son of the late president of Harvard University, himself formerly the efficient and able mayor. The new mayor glories in the blood of the Revolution which runs in his veins, and the Whig party glories in him as one of its ablest disciples and firmest supporters.

1846.

THE new year commences under circumstances of greater general prosperity than the last; the great fire of the 19th of July was the only serious disaster which occurred in its progress; in other respects the blessings of a beneficent Providence have, as heretofore, been extended in a measure more abundant than our merits. We, of New York, have come in for a full share. The bright star of hope, too, would shine on the future if the madness of the people did not interpose this pestiferous cloud of war to intercept its rays. Jealousy of rival interests and impatience of the prosperity arising from commercial enterprise have prompted the men of the West to pursue a course ruinous to us of the seaboard. They have gotten Texas, through the instrumentality of their accidentally picked-up President; and now they must have Oregon, — the whole, they won't abate a rood, — and California too, and Cuba and Mexico; and, finally, the whole North American continent; and, moreover, they must have war with Great Britain, with or without a cause. If she troubles the water above or below us, it is all the same thing; she must not drink out of the same stream.

JANUARY 7. — I dined yesterday with Mr. Peter G. Stuyvesant, in his splendid new house in the Second avenue, near St. Mark's Church. Our party consisted, besides the host and hostess, of David B. Ogden, John A. Stevens, Herman Thorn, Hamilton Fish, Henry Barclay, John T. Brigham, George Laurie, John C. Hamilton, Mr. Kean, and myself.

SATURDAY, JAN. 31. — We had a pleasant dinner-party, consisting of Mr. Herman Thorn, Augustus Thorndike, James Thomson, William B. Astor, J. D. P. Ogden, Sidney Brooks, P. G. Stuyvesant, J. C. Delprat, Philip S. Van Rensselaer, George Curtis, and Charles H. Russell.

FEBRUARY 5. — The new church at the head of
Grace Church. Broadway is nearly finished and ready for consecration.

The pews were sold last week, and brought extravagant prices, some $1,200 to $1,400, with a pew-rent on the estimated value of eight per cent. ; so that the word of God, as it came down to us from fishermen and mechanics, will cost the quality who worship in this splendid temple about three dollars every Sunday. This may have a good effect ; for many of them, though rich, know how to calculate, and if they do not go regularly to church they will not get the worth of their money.

This is to be the fashionable church, and already its aisles are filled (especially on Sundays after the morning services in other churches) with gay parties of ladies in feathers and *mousseline-de-laine* dresses, and dandies with moustaches and high-heeled boots ; the lofty arches resound with astute criticisms upon *Gothic architecture* from fair ladies who have had the advantage of foreign travel, and scientific remarks upon *acoustics* from elderly millionaires who do not hear quite as well as formerly.

FEBRUARY 14. — I dined with Mr. William B. Astor, in his magnificent house, Lafayette place. The party consisted, besides Mr. and Mrs. and Miss Astor, of the following guests : David S. Kennedy, James D. P. Ogden, Herman Thorn, John W. Schmidt, Robert B. Minturn, Thomas W. Ludlow, Thomas Oliver, Gardiner G. Howland, Samuel S. Howland, John C. Hamilton, Gabriel Mead, and Philip Hone.

FEBRUARY 16. — Mr. Southard declines to accept the
Trinity call as assistant minister of Trinity Church. I regret
Church. it, but did not hope for a different result. His acceptance would have had a twofold favourable operation. We should have had an excellent young minister, good now, and of an age and disposition for improvement. We should also have escaped another, who will (in case of his being chosen by party management, for that is to be found even in the holy places of religion) give great dissatisfaction to the moderate Episcopalians, who prefer the word

of God preached in the spirit of peace and good-will, to the establishment of an unessential dogma, and who wish the Scriptures taught in the spirit in which they were written. The rejection of this offer is a great sacrifice on the part of Mr. Southard, which cannot fail to endear him to his congregation. The place he refuses is in present value one of the most lucrative and honourable of the church in the United States; and for such a man as he, so young, so eloquent, and so accomplished in his holy profession, an almost certain reversion (if he lives) of the dignity of bishop of the diocese. All this he resigns to continue the charge of his little, cottage-like Calvary Church, and some $1,500 or $1,600 a year. If he had their hearts before, he must have them now, body, soul, and all.

FEBRUARY 17.—I dined to-day with Mr. and Mrs. William H. Aspinwall, in their new house, University place, one of the palaces which have been lately erected in this part of the city. A more beautiful and commodious mansion, or in better taste in every particular, I have never seen. This gentleman is one of the " merchant princes " of New York; long may he enjoy his prosperity! He deserves it. He is an upright and honourable merchant, a liberal and public-spirited citizen, and a hospitable and right-minded gentleman. Our party consisted, besides the host and hostess, of the following: Mr. and Mrs. James Brown, Mr. and Mrs. Thomas W. Ludlow, Mr. and Mrs. Charles A. Davis, Mr. Henry Cary, Mr. and Mrs. Constant, Mr. and Mrs. William B. Astor, Mrs. Henry Coit, G. G. Howland, and myself.

FEBRUARY 20. — The arrival of the steamer " Cambria " has been looked for with great anxiety, from the important bearing of the news she brings upon the great question of peace or war. Expresses were sent on by the newspaper establishments to anticipate the news at Halifax and bring it on before her arrival in Boston. She arrived at Halifax on Tuesday morning. The express started immediately, and would have accomplished its enterprising object had it not encountered the great snow-storm. As it was, we had the news here in New York yesterday at noon; a rival express of the " Herald " being an hour or two ahead of the Nova Scotia racers. The distance from Boston, two hundred and forty miles, was travelled by railroad and steamboat in the astonishingly short time of *seven hours and five minutes*. What a change from the times when the mail stage left New York for Boston *once a fortnight*, and consumed a week in going to Philadelphia !

The news by the " Cambria " is, indeed, very important, and things wear a more smiling aspect. Our cousin, John Bull, is particularly amiable. Parliament convened on the 22d of January, the Queen's speech (which the little lady delivered in person) containing no bitterness toward this country in relation to the Oregon question. I am afraid Mr. Polk will be affronted at the fact of her not being angry at his threats. On the contrary, she makes light of the whole matter. Sir Robert Peel is not apprehensive of a war, but seems disposed to keep on good terms with us, if possible.

FEBRUARY 24. — The Racket Court was opened to-day at noon by a *déjeuner à la fourchette*, — a grand entertainment of music, dancing, eating, and drinking, at which were present the members of the club, with those belonging to the Union and other kindred associations, each gentleman being provided with four ladies' tickets. Soon after twelve o'clock every part of this beautiful edifice — the dining saloon, reception, reading, and billiard rooms — was crowded with the most genteel people in town. The immense Racket Court appeared, from the upper galleries, like a garden of moving flowers, and a band of thirty musicians left no room to doubt that the place was a *Racket Court.*

FEBRUARY 25. — I begin to think that there is no
Old Age. such thing as old age ; that the ability to perform the
tasks and duties of the intellect is as perfect at fourscore as fifty ; something unquestionably depends upon good health and physical strength, but much more upon the habits contracted in early life. Industry, application, and perseverance, whilst they

train up the mind to the performance of nature's miracles, serve also to establish the strength, vigour, and activity of the body, which are such important adjuncts in the exercise of the powers of the mind ; but as for *old age*, it is a term convertible and indefinite. Some men are older at fifty than others at fourscore ; not in wisdom or learning, but in the failure of the scanty stock of those commodities with which they began the business of life.

There is Chancellor Kent, for instance, an octogenarian, preparing a new edition of his Commentaries, — a work without a knowledge of which no law education is complete, — reading with ardour, and criticising with taste, all the new books of celebrity and merit, his mind being deeply laid with a substratum of classical knowledge and the literature of the former ages, active and ardent in body and mind as he was twenty years ago, when the ermine of judicial equity fell from his shoulders, and an absurd law of the State pronounced this ripe scholar and accomplished lawyer superannuated !

And Albert Gallatin, too, who is several years older than Mr. Kent, in the full possession of his mental faculties, has been writing a pamphlet on the Oregon question ; the best, the cleanest, and the soundest which has been presented to the American people on this exciting subject. Pure and vigorous in style, it betrays no marks of age ; sound and convincing in argument, the experience of a long life is brought in aid of inherent talents and literary accomplishments. This book is as well written (and probably in better temper) than Mr. Gallatin would have written it at forty years of age.

MARCH 3. — We drive the aborigines of our country
Civilization. away from the places of their birth, from the altars of their " great spirit," and the tombs of their ancestors, to make room for civilization (another name for land piracy) ; and the records of every day present the disgusting accounts of personal conflicts among civilized " pale-faces," which might cause a Pawnee or a Comanche to blush. One of these pleasant encounters, so characteristic of " Southern chivalry," occurred on the morning of last Wednesday, at Richmond, Virginia, between John Hampden

Pleasants, late editor of the " Richmond Whig," and more recently of the " Richmond Star," a man fifty-five years of age, with a wife and children, and Thomas Ritchie, Jr., a twenty-five-year-old sprig of the " chivalry," son of the celebrated Loco-foco oracle of Virginia, and one of the editors of the " Enquirer." These white savages had been exercising the " liberty of the press " and edifying their readers by abusing each other, when one of them (probably finding the truth come rather hard) resorted to the gentlemanly mode in vogue at the South to justify himself and put his adversary in the wrong by cutting his throat (an effectual method, certainly). A challenge was given, and the duel took place as above mentioned. The plan of warfare was arranged by seconds, — honourable men, no doubt, members of a Christian community who wear pantaloons instead of breech-clouts, and carry walking-canes, not tomahawks. Disgraceful and shocking as it may appear, the combatants were permitted to go into the combat with all kinds of weapons, — pistols, rifles, broadswords and broadaxes, tomahawks and bowie-knives. They were placed at thirty paces apart, and at it they went, blazing away first with fire-arms, and then rushing at each other, hacking and slashing in slaughter-house fashion. The account relates, pleasantly enough, how at such a cut one lost three fingers, at the next the other had his mouth extended to the ear ; how the abdomen of this *civilized cavalier* was laid open, and how the thigh of that received a deep incision. Finally the dispute was settled in favour of Mr. Ritchie. The truth was made manifest and the argument decided by the removal of Mr. Pleasants from the field of battle " with twenty trenched gashes on his head, the least a death to nature," and his subsequent death. Who dares dispute the chivalry of the paladins of Virginia, or the efficacy of the " code of honour " ?

MARCH 10. — The corner-stone of the new Calvary Church, at the corner of 21st street, was laid yesterday afternoon with appropriate religious ceremonies. The Bishop laid the stone. The edifice is erected by the congregation under the charge of the talented and popular young divine, Mr. Southard.

MARCH 25.—Another melancholy and destructive marine disaster is to be added to the list. The beautiful packet-ship "Henry Clay," belonging to Grinnell, Minturn, & Co., lies a wreck on the fatal Squan beach, about a mile from the spot where the "John Minturn" was lost. She went ashore in a violent gale, last night, at twelve o'clock. This will make Wall street groan. The ship was one of the largest and most costly class, and at this season of the year it is probable her cargo is very valuable. The particulars have not come up from the beach; but from the accounts of the mate, who took the railroad at New Brunswick and arrived here this evening, there is strong hope that of the passengers and crew, consisting of three hundred persons, a large proportion will have been saved by means of a hawser which was carried to the shore. A boat, however, was known to have been swamped in the surf, and six persons drowned. This noble ship (with a great, but unlucky, name) sailed on her first voyage last May. I dined on board on the 3d of that month, with a large jovial party, the particulars of which are given in this journal; and now all the splendid decorations of her cabin, so much admired at that time, and all the perfect examples of naval architecture then exhibited, are left to rot in the sands of Squan beach. Why is it that so many vessels are lost thereabouts? When will the ship-masters learn that there is land there? And why is not the lead more frequently used? Captain Nye is an experienced seaman. But the only way to remedy the evil in these cases is to say to every one of them, without discrimination, "Never more be officer of mine."

APRIL 9.—Man is the only animal that man hates. Other species may excite terror, fear, disdain; but this darkest and deadliest passion of the human mind is only brought into action against such as, like himself, are made in the image of his Creator. The trial of Thomas Ritchie, Jr., for killing John H. Pleasants, in that savage, barbarous duel, has resulted in his acquittal, without a moment's hesitation, by the jury. The account of the verdict closes with the very complimentary and consolatory remark that "he has borne himself under the whole trial, down to the last scene of the eventful, yet painful, drama, with the equanimity which became a man."

APRIL 14. — The "Henry Clay" came up to the city yesterday from her uncomfortable berth on Squan beach. The result of this disaster is a proud testimony to the strength and construction of the New York commercial marine. This noble vessel has been lying for the last twenty days, broadside to the shore, on a stormy beach, the destroyer of many a tall merchantman, and the grave of many a hardy seaman. Everything which has been stranded there during the late gales has gone to pieces except this fine ship, which, like him from whom she is named, strong and sound in materials, honestly and skilfully put together, though beaten, is not broken, and will soon be ready for a new voyage.

APRIL 16. — I went last evening to a pleasant party at Mr. Harvey's, given to show off certain Boston lions ; and fine animals they are : Messrs. George Ticknor, William H. Prescott, and Charles Sumner. The amiable and accomplished historian of " Ferdinand and Isabella " is here to consult an oculist about his eyes, which trouble him again. I fear he will not live to add many more leaves to the undying wreaths of his literary fame.

APRIL 16. — This is the commencement of the twenty-fourth volume of this diary. The last is a record of one year of my life. It has been a year of trouble, and the care and anxiety attending the discharge of my several duties have interfered with the regular diurnal posting up of my journal ; nay, the same causes have occasionally made me hesitate about going on with this task, heretofore so pleasant. But I do persevere, and the beginning of this new volume is an earnest that my determination at this moment is not to abandon it. It will probably be less interesting ; but I must have a safety-valve for my imagination. I must write, even if I do not write well.

APRIL 17. — The ship " Rainbow," belonging to Howland & Aspinwall, arrived to-day, in seventy-five days from Canton. This beautiful vessel, a perfect model of marine architecture, brilliant and bright as the bow of Hope, the name of which she bears, has made two complete voyages to and from Canton in the space of fourteen months, just about the time formerly consumed in one voyage. Everything goes fast now-a-days; the winds, even, begin to improve upon the speed which they have hitherto maintained; everything goes ahead but good manners and sound principles, and they are in a fair way to be driven from the track.

APRIL 25. — Healy's picture of Mr. Webster came on yesterday from Washington, where it was painted for the Hone Club. This " counterfeit presentment " of our honorary member, the distinguished Massachusetts senator, is a great picture, — the best by far that has been done of him. It will cost, including the frame, $550, to be paid for by the fifteen members of the club. The picture is to remain in my possession until a new president is appointed, and is to go at my decease to the oldest surviving member. Mr. Healy is an artist sent out to the United States by the King of France to take the portraits, for his gallery, of some of our eminent statesmen. He has been very successful; but in none more than in this, which does not go into royal hands, but into the hands of a set of royal fellows, and when Louis Philippe comes to New York, Philip Hone will show him as good a picture as any in his American gallery. The great original and Mrs. Webster arrived here last evening. He is on his route eastward. He is in excellent spirits, pleased with the state of things at Washington, and not a bit the worse for his contaminating collision with the Pennsylvania calumniator.

Mr. Webster's Portrait.

MAY 7. — Affairs in this quarter wear an alarming aspect. If the government intended by its measures to bring disaster and defeat upon the insufficient forces sent into that unhappy country, and thereby make popular the war which it is preparing to wage against Mexico, it is likely that it

Mexico.

may succeed; but the people will have an awful account to settle with it. A war simultaneously with England and Mexico for Oregon and Texas,—neither of which is worth the blood of a single American soldier, — and without a force adequate to carry out the least of those enterprises, would be pushing the forbearance of the people to a dangerous length. But we have reason to know that the tyranny of party discipline is more absolute in this country than the mandate of the Czar of Moscow, or the will of the Khan of Tartary.

General Ampudia has cut off the force of two thousand men under our General Taylor, who had gotten where he ought not to be, and some of our fine fellows have been captured and killed. In the number of the former is Colonel Cross; and Lieutenant Porter (a son of the late gallant commodore) and three men were killed, while on a foraging party, by a body of Mexican ranchers. In the mean time General Worth comes away with many of his brother officers, glad, no doubt, to escape from the disgrace which is likely to attend upon ill-concerted measures.

May 9. — Worth is ordered back to Mexico. It is *Mexico again.* difficult to judge of these matters, but it seems to me he ought not to have come away just at this time. Mr. Polk and his party have accomplished their object: the war with Mexico is fairly commenced. The President (in violation of the Constitution, which gives to Congress the exclusive power to declare war) announces formally that a state of war exists, calls for volunteers and money, which Congress unhesitatingly grants; and if any old-fashioned legislator presumes to doubt the authority of Pope Polk, or questions the infallibility of his bull, he is stigmatized by some of the ruffians of the West as an enemy to his country, in league with the Mexicans. These charges he must submit to, or, by making a suitable retort, expose himself to the necessity of fighting himself out of his difficulty, or leaving a vacant seat to be filled by some more subservient representative of the magnanimous *American people.*

This war has commenced most disastrously, as might have been expected from the scanty force sent into the disputed territory. My suggestion of Thursday appears uncharitable ; but it really looks as if this result was anticipated, and the American blood shed was to excite American feelings, and to make the war popular. It was so in the last war. The disgraceful defeat and capture of Hull at Detroit was the cement which bound together friends of war and friends of peace into a united band of friends of national honour. But it looks now as if this experiment were to cost too much. Extras were published to-day, by all the papers, giving further particulars received from New Orleans of the dangerous position of General Taylor's little army on the Rio Grande. He is cut off by Arista from his resources at Point Isabel, at the mouth of the river, and, although within cannon-shot of Metamoras, on the opposite side of the river, he cannot send men to attack it. These disasters will raise the blood of the American people to the war point, and cause them to cease inquiring, What is this war about? What compensation is to be had for the blood shed and the treasures squandered? and, How will the national character be redeemed which we have staked on this dreadful issue? They will thus be compelled to support a cause which their conscience condemns and their judgment disapproves.

Mr. Polk's War.

MAY 12. — The President's message, announcing a state of war with Mexico, was sent to Congress yesterday, who forthwith granted him power to call out fifty thousand volunteers, and appropriated ten millions of dollars as a small outfit for his military operations. This is a horrible state of things. But a little philosophy can extract grains of comfort even from this. The tariff cannot be touched whilst such expenditures are incurred, nor will the sub-treasury and specie scheme be carried into effect with such a war impending.

MAY 19. — We are all agog with the news of a great victory gained over the Mexicans on the great river. General Taylor, having left his camp with a force of twelve or fifteen hundred men, to open communication with his supplies at Point Isabel, at the mouth of the river, the Americans, under command of Major Ringgold, were attacked. This brought on a general engagement, and resulted in the defeat of the enemy, with a loss, it is said, of seven hundred men, our loss being inconsiderable. This account is probably exaggerated, for vain-boasting is unfortunately the vice of our country; every officer is a hero, every raw recruit equal in prowess to an ancient Roman legionary, and in discipline to one of the *old guard* of Napoleon, and every skirmish is a battle of Waterloo. But there has been a fight, and probably a victory, and we are bound to rejoice.

MAY 21. — This day being the Feast of the Ascension, agreeably to the notice given and the arrangements made, the new Trinity Church, the pride of Episcopalians and the glory of our city, was consecrated to the service of Almighty God. I was one of the committee of arrangements, and have been for the last two or three weeks most sedulously employed every day in the discharge of the duties of this office. The clergy, the rectors, wardens, and vestrymen of the several Episcopalian churches, the members of the Theological Seminary, the present and former mayors, the scholars of Trinity School, and invited guests, assembled at ten o'clock, at Mr. Bunker's, in Broadway, and marched in procession to the church. At eleven o'clock the grand and solemn assemblage, preceded by Right Rev. Bishop McCoskry, who officiated as bishop of the diocese during the suspension of Bishop Onderdonk, entered during the impressive chanting of one hundred and fifty clergymen, in white surplices and scarfs, followed by a most dignified and respectable body of laymen. The consecration service was performed by the Bishop, assisted by a number of prominent ministers; and the splendid vaultings of the solemn temple resounded with the notes of the grand organ and with the sounds of praise and adoration from the voices of the devout assemblage.

MAY 23. — The club dined with me to-day, on the
Club Dinner.   occasion of the inauguration of Healy's fine portrait of
Mr. Webster, belonging to the club, which has been
hung (the picture, I mean) in the dining-room.   Several gentlemen brought each a bottle of his best wine, and such a drink
would throw the nectar of the gods into the shade.   Hebe would
have emptied the contents of her goblet (as Mrs. Delavan did her
medicine) into the gutter, and Bacchus would have turned water-
drinker rather than stand the comparison.

I made a speech about the picture, the illustrious original, the
great Harrison cabinet, and the glorious Congress of 1842, which
I closed by reading the concluding remarks of Mr. Webster in his
speech made in the Senate on the 6th and 7th of April last.   We
drank his health with three times three.   The members of the club
present were M. H. Grinnell, George Curtis, Simeon Draper, R. M.
Blatchford, John Ward, T. Tileston, Prescott Hall, Dr. Francis,
P. Spofford, and J. W. Webb.   Absent were Bowen, Edward Curtis,
Colt, and Jaudon, whose places were filled in part by Messrs. Russell, Blatchford, Jr., and my old acquaintance, Mr. Van Wart.

JUNE 15. —The Oregon treaty was signed this day, at
The Treaty.   three o'clock, for approval and confirmation to-morrow,
where it will, of course, pass by the same vote at least
as that which advised its ratification.   It was a pleasant circumstance, and it makes an interesting item in my journal, that I should
have dined with the British Minister on the day on which this joyful event occurred, — an event which restores the prosperity of
the nation, sets commerce again upon its legs, makes the hus-
bandman's corn grow higher and his grass more green, and would
equally rejoice the manufacturers, if they would let this unhappy
tariff alone.   Mr. Pakenham's dinner was a beautiful affair; the
party consisted of only seven, — he and Mr. Ponsonby, his secretary, Messrs. Webster, Curtis, Ashman, Colt, and myself.   The
service, all but the plates, was of silver which he brought from
Mexico.   The dinner was excellent; I never partook of a better;

good wine, good taste, and good manners. We went at seven, and came away at ten o'clock.

JUNE 24.—I dined yesterday as the guest of Prescott Hall, with the Yacht Club, at Hoboken. They have a club-house,—a handsome Gothic cottage,— erected for the use of the club in a pleasant grove in the Elysian Fields, by that prince of good fellows, John C. Stevens, who makes the punch, superintends the cooking, and presides at the table, under the appropriate title of "Commodore." A choice company of forty-three gentlemen sat down to an excellent dinner of turtle and other good things, with capital punch and plenty of good wine. The Commodore, after some remarks personally complimentary, proposed me as a member of the club, and, the probationary term being dispensed with, I was admitted by acclamation. In acknowledgment of this compliment I gave the following toast, which was received with the most marked approbation: "The Yacht Club: river gods who ride upon the waves, and sip their nectar in the Elysian Fields."

Yacht Club.

JULY 6.—The iniquity is consummated. The bill to break down the tariff of 1842 passed the House of Representatives on Friday afternoon. The independence of the nation is now an idle boast. American industry is sacrificed to party power, and honest labour doomed to lose its just reward. This nefarious act was consummated by a vote of 114 to 95, and there seems to be little doubt that it will pass the Senate by a similar party vote.

The Tariff Bill.

JULY 17.—The regatta of the Yacht Club came off yesterday. It was a grand display, for which great preparations had been made, and great expectations raised. Twelve schooners and two sloops were entered for the race, viz.: Schooners, "Lancet" (Mr. Rollins), "Gimcrack" (Mr. Stevens), "Coquille" (Mr. Jay), "Minna" (Mr. Coles), "Brenda" (Mr. Sears), "Spray" (Mr. Wilkes), "Sibyl" (Mr. Miller), "Cygnet" (Mr. Suydam), "Pet" (Mr. Parsons),

Regatta.

" Northern Light " (Mr. Winchester), " Siren " (Mr. Miller), " Coquette " (Mr. Perkins). Sloops, " Newburgh " (Mr. Robinson) and " Mist " (Mr. Depau).

The prize, a superb silver goblet, was won by the sloop " Mist," belonging to Mr. Lewis Depau. The steamer " New York " was provided for the members of the club and their guests, of whom a large party went down the bay, and returned with the yachts.

SPRINGFIELD, JULY 30. — " Polk, Dallas, and the tariff of 1842," — such was the inscription on the banners used in Pennsylvania to effect the election of Mr. Polk ; such was the subterfuge by which alone the vote of that State could have been secured for this faithless, corrupt administration ; and now the tariff of 1842 is destroyed, the industry of the country laid at the feet of foreign competition, and national prosperity sacrificed to party discipline. This nefarious act was consummated on Tuesday, the 28th of July (let the day stand accursed in the calendar !), recommended and enforced by this same James K. Polk, and carried by the casting vote in the Senate of this same George M. Dallas. Long may their names be recorded on the same page with those scourges of mankind, war, pestilence, and famine, and the measure they have accomplished be included in the category of cholera, small-pox, and yellow fever !

MONDAY, AUGUST 3. — The President signed the tariff bill on Friday, and on Saturday sent in his veto upon the bill making appropriation for the improvement of rivers and harbours. Thus is the country equally cursed by what this man does, and what he refuses to do. Next comes direct taxation, to carry on the Mexican war. This is worse than Egyptian bondage : they take from us the straw, and then scourge us for not *making bricks.*

Executive Execution.

AUGUST 5. — I went out yesterday to dine with Mr. Thomas W. Ludlow, at his beautiful cottage on the banks of the Hudson river, below Yonkers. Our party at dinner consisted of Mr. and Mrs. James A. Hamilton, Mr. and Mrs. George Schuyler, Mr. and Mrs.

Moses H. Grinnell, Mrs. Boggs, Mrs. Storrow, Mr. Bowdoin, Mr. Alexander Hamilton, Mr. Lewis Morris, Mr. Stewart Brown.

AUGUST 12. — Congress adjourned on Monday night,
Adjournment
of Congress. after a session of nearly eight months; the most corrupt, profligate, and disastrous the United States have ever known. Pliant and subservient to a wicked administration, the Constitution has been violated, the industry and enterprise of the people have been sacrificed to foreign influences, the currency disturbed, commerce deprived of its customary facilities, the country plunged into an unjust, unnecessary, and expensive war, and national honour, honesty, and good faith made the sport of party dictation and executive power.

The pestilence is stayed for a brief period; but its victims lie unburied in the sight of the survivors, or linger on paralyzed and mutilated. The storm is abated; but its ravages will long be seen in the shattered ruins of domestic industry. The dark clouds which have overshadowed the land, late so happy and prosperous, are dispersed; but no star of hope is left to cheer the prospects of the future.

In the midst of this moral and political desolation Providence has not abandoned us to the extremity of fate which we have so well deserved. The glorious Whig phalanx in the Senate, erect as the cedars of Libanus, true as the tables of stone, and firm as the sacred mountain on which their holy precepts were promulgated, have succeeded, by the aid of a portion of their political opponents whose immediate sectional interests, happily for the cause of humanity and religion, were on this occasion identical with theirs, in averting one of the calamities which threatened the country. We are at peace with England, — thanks to Webster and Calhoun, Evans and Benton, Crittenden and Heywood, and the noble host who united to save their country from a war, " the cost of which," to both countries, as Sir Robert Peel says, " every day, every hour, would have been more than the whole value of the subject in controversy."

AUGUST 13.—I passed a short time yesterday at
A Tall Trio. the Astor House, with three pretty considerable men:
Daniel Webster, of Massachusetts; John J. Crittenden,
of Kentucky; and George Evans, of Maine. If three others equal
to them can be collected together in this country, then we are
richer than I thought. Three more such men would save our
political Sodom and Gomorrah, —great, not only here; I doubt if
any political combination could be made in Europe superior to it.
Webster, Crittenden, Evans; Polk, Dallas, Walker, —imagine
these men to have changed positions during the year. I dare not
think of it. Peace, happiness, prosperity, on one side; war, embarrassment, despair, on the other. God help us!

SEPTEMBER 10. — Mr. Stewart's splendid edifice,
Extravagance. erected on the site of Washington Hall, in Broadway,
between Chambers and Reade streets, is nearly finished, and his stock of dry goods will be exhibited on the
shelves in a few days. There is nothing in Paris or London
to compare with this dry-goods palace. My attention was attracted, in passing this morning, to a most extraordinary, and I
think useless, piece of extravagance. Several of the windows on
the first floor, nearly level with the street, are formed of plate-
glass, six feet by eleven, which must have cost four or five
hundred dollars each, and may be shivered by a boy's marble
or a snow-ball as effectually as by a four-pound shot; and I
am greatly mistaken if there are not persons (one is enough)
in this heterogeneous mass of population influenced by jealousy,
malice, or other instigation of the devil, bad enough to do such
a deed of mischief.

SEPTEMBER 19.— Died on Thursday last, Mr. James Swords,
aged eighty-two years, the surviving partner of Thomas and James
Swords, the oldest booksellers, publishers, and stationers in New
York. They published the first monthly magazine. The first
article of my writing which came up in the dignity of types
astonished the world in the pages of this periodical.

Magnetic
Telegraph.

SEPTEMBER 26. — Strange and wonderful discovery, which has made the " swift-winged lightning " man's messenger, annihilated all space, and tied the two ends of a continent in a knot! The whole extent of this newly discovered phenomenon was never made so apparent to me as on the day of the meeting of the convention ; during the hour of adjournment to dinner a message was sent by the telegraph to Mr. Fillmore, at Buffalo. The answer came immediately, that " Mr. Fillmore was not in his office, and could not be found." Soon after, another communication was received, authorizing the withdrawal of his name, and expressing his satisfaction at Mr. Young's nomination. This was handed to me on my taking the chair, and had travelled four hundred and seventy miles during our short recess of an hour.

Compliment.

OCTOBER 19. — I heard to-day, for the first time, of a compliment which has been made to me, which touched my feelings very sensibly, and for which I cannot be sufficiently grateful. Twenty gentlemen of New York sent out $500 to Italy to procure my bust, which was begun by Clevenger, and finished, I believe, by Powers. It has arrived, and has been presented to the Clinton Hall Association, where it is intended to be placed in the lecture-room. This most acceptable manifestation of the regard of my fellow-citizens is rendered more grateful to my feelings by its location in the hall of an institution with which it has been my pride to have been identified since its creation, and of which I have been for so many years the presiding officer. I do not pretend that I am not susceptible to flattery, perhaps vain ; but there was a delicacy about this matter, in the keeping of it so profound a secret, and in the kind expressions of personal regard which accompanied the act, that I shall not very soon forget.

OCTOBER 26. — My old friend, Mr. Abraham Ogden, president of the Orient Insurance Company, has sunk at last under the effects of a long and painful indisposition. He died on Saturday, in his seventy-second year.   He was a gentleman of the old school; honest, intelligent, and amiable; an affectionate husband and father, an upright merchant, a true friend, and a valuable citizen.   These are the qualities which ornament human nature during a man's lifetime, and after death endear his memory to his friends; but, unfortunately, they do not always lead to wealth nor personal popularity.

The Slave Case.

OCTOBER 27. — I witnessed this morning, from the steps of Clinton Hall, a scene which is calculated to cause alarm as to future collisions between the citizens of this country, — a trifling incident in the appalling drama which we shall be called to witness, and perhaps bear a part in, during the course of not many years.   A negro boy, named George Kirk, a slave from Georgia, secreted himself in a vessel commanded by Captain Buckley, and was brought to New York.   Here he was arrested and confined, at the instance of the captain, who is subjected to severe penalties for the abduction of the slave.   The claim of the master to have the fugitive sent back to Georgia was tried before Judge Edwards; N. B. Blunt appearing for the captain, and Mr. John Jay and J. L. White for the slave.

The judge's decision set the boy free, for want of evidence to prove his identity; and such a mob, of all colours, from dirty white to shining black, came rushing down Nassau and into Beekman street as made peaceable people shrink into places of security.   Such shouting and jostling, such peals of negro triumph, such uncovering of woolly heads in raising the greasy hats to give effect to the loud huzzas of the sons of Africa, seemed almost to " fright the neighbourhood from its propriety."   A carriage was brought to convey the hero of the day from his place of concealment, but it went away without him.   This is all very pretty; but how will it end?   How long will the North and the South remain a united people?   Different interests must provoke unkind feelings, and charity, patriotism, and mutual forbearance on the part of reasonable men on both sides will prove ere long insufficient to preserve the bonds of national brotherhood.

Since writing the above, I am informed that a process has been issued by the Mayor, on the application of an agent of the master, and the boy, found secreted in a box in which he was being conveyed by his friends from the place of his concealment, was taken back by the officers and reincarcerated in his old quarters in the Tombs; so the whole business, with its attendant excitement, must be gone over again.

NOVEMBER 11.—Died in Washington, yesterday, Commodore John B. Nicholson, of the United States navy, in the sixty-third year of his age. Captain Jack, as his friends called him, with whom he was always a favourite, entered the navy as a midshipman, in 1805, on board the brig " Hornet," then under the command of my old friend, the late Captain Chauncey. He fought as lieutenant at the capture of the " Macedonian," and was first lieutenant of the " Peacock " in her brilliant engagement with " L'Epervier," which vessel he brought into port a prize. He has held important and honourable appointments. He was commander of the Mediterranean squadron, and more recently has been stationed at the navy yard at Charlestown, near Boston, where he exercised a liberal hospitality, alike creditable to the service and himself, of which I have been the recipient. Adieu, thou good fellow and honest sailor! How often have thy legs and mine been placed under the same mahogany!

NOVEMBER 24.—The honourable John Quincy Adams was stricken by paralysis on Thursday last, whilst walking from his son's house in Boston. The last accounts state that he had partially recovered, his consciousness having returned and his speech being restored. Hopes are even expressed that he may be able to go on to his family, who are in Washington, and resume his seat in the House of Representatives. This is " a consummation devoutly to be wished." The country cannot afford to lose such a man. With all his eccentricities, prejudices, and want of tact, we have not his equal in this country for the most minute information on all subjects, technical, statistical, artistical, historical, and diplomatical. No man knows so much, nor so accurately. He has probed deeply into the arcana of all the sciences, understands and can explain all subjects, from the solar system down to the construction of a tooth-pick. He has the Holy Scriptures at his fingers' ends, knows every line of Shakespeare, can recite Homer in the original Greek; could name, if he had a mind to do it, the author of "Junius," and knows all about Jack the Giant Killer. He speaks on all subjects, overthrows his opponents, and bothers his friends; and, in short, does more work than any day-labourer, and this, too, under some physical disabilities. He is so nervous that his pen has to be tied to his fingers. This prodigious amount of labour is accomplished by early rising, exact method, and the most untiring industry.

But Mr. Adams cannot last forever. He is eighty years of age, and it is greatly to be feared that the warning voice has come to him in this recent visitation. What a pity it is that on his decease he cannot leave his knowledge behind him; it would, indeed, be a rich inheritance.

November 25. — Accounts from Washington, received last night by telegraph, state that General Scott left the city yesterday to take the command of the army in Mexico, and to conduct a meditated attack upon Tampico. If he has a chance, he will sustain his high character for personal bravery and military talents, and his " hasty plate of soup " may possibly be overlooked, by the severe critics who constitute the " American people," in the glory of a successful Mexican campaign. Worth has completely recovered from the effect of one bad step; and I trust that Winfield Scott will prove that he is not the man to be laid aside, and all his former services forgotten, for one or two ill-judged expressions in the course of a correspondence in which he displayed more *truth* than tact.

NOVEMBER 26. — This is a day set apart by the authorities of the State, and the regulations of the Episcopal Church, to be observed as a day of thanksgiving to Almighty God for the blessings we enjoy as a community, and as individuals for our share of the bounties of Divine Providence. It is an interesting occasion. The incense of adoration, praise, and thanksgiving ascend from the altars of sixteen of the States forming this Union; a simultaneous abstinence from their usual occupations is observed, with more or less of the sincerity of devotion, by millions of rational and responsible creatures; the Author of all good is acknowledged, at least in form, in every place of worship, from the solemn, magnificent cathedral, down to the modest, unassuming village church, whose devotion swells not into notes so loud and sonorous, but proceeds from hearts equally sincere.

Thanksgiving Day.

I went with my family to St. John's, where our good Doctor Wainwright gave us an excellent Thanksgiving sermon. He enumerated the great national blessings we enjoy, of civil and religious liberty, the abundance of all things necessary for the subsistence and comfort of man, our exemption from internal commotions, and our preservation from pestilence and other evils. He also deprecated the war in which we are engaged, and the consequent shedding of the blood of the brave men who are engaged in it, and urged that our prayers, as patriots, for the success of our arms should be accompanied by supplications for a return of peace. This is all very well; the reverend gentleman could say no more. But it occurred to me that, next to the favour of the God of peace, to avert this calamity, the exertions of all good men and sincere Christians should be employed to remove from office the men who have brought upon us this unjust and unrighteous war, — this war of usurpation and aggression, unsanctioned by the Constitution and at variance with the moral sense of the people.

NOVEMBER 30. — My venerable friend, Chancellor Kent, who has for a long time declined dinner invitations, honoured us by becoming one of our guests on Saturday, and another equally venerable octogenarian, Judge Spencer, graced my board. It was a bright day of joyous hilarity and intellectual enjoyment, as it could not fail to be with the following party: Judge Spencer, Chancellor Kent, David B. Ogden, George Curtis, Luther Bradish, Rev. Dr. Wainwright, Henry Brevoort, J. Prescott Hall, R. M. Blatchford, Charles H. Russell. The Chancellor was very agreeable until news was brought of his son's arrival, when he started off with his usual rapidity, and was seen no more.

DECEMBER 15. — The *better sort* have been regaled, *Wedding Festivities.* of late, by a grand wedding. Mr. John J. Astor, son of Mr. William B. Astor, and grandson of Mr. John Jacob Astor, married Miss Augusta Gibbes, daughter of Mr. Thomas L. Gibbes.

The wedding was attended, at the house of her father, by all the fashionable people of the city. Last evening my daughter and son went to a grand party at Mr. Astor's, and I also was tempted to mix once more in the splendid crowd of charming women, pretty girls, and well-dressed beaux. The spacious mansion in Lafayette place was open from cellar to garret, blazing with a thousand lights. The crowd was excessive; the ladies (such part of their exquisite forms as could be distinguished in the *mêlée*) elegantly and tastefully attired, with a display of rich jewelry enough to pay one day's expense of the Mexican war.

1847.

JANUARY 1. — The old year 1846 is gone, despatched and not to be recalled. The good we have left undone, which we might have done, is carried to the debit side of our account, arranged in broad standing characters alongside of the lines of commission which are fairly chargeable to the account of delinquency.

The last year was a wretched one in regard to the political condition of the country. If, instead of this most lame and impotent administration, Mr. Clay had been elected President instead of Mr. Polk (which was certainly the voice of the American people), we should have been, as a nation, prosperous beyond all former example, with no annexation of strangers' land to promote party views, no wars to drain the best blood of the country for an issue which can never redound to our honour, nor pay in any proportion for the loss of blood, treasure, and reputation which it will have cost. The enterprise of the people checked, honest industry paralyzed, and national pride humiliated; James K. Polk President of the United States, — can such things be?

JANUARY 2. — New Year's presents have abounded

The Bust.   this year. This is the Parisian mode of celebrating *le jour de l'an,* and we are getting into it very fast. Some of the houses where I visited yesterday presented the appearance of bazaars, where rich presents were displayed, from the costly cashmere shawls and silver tankard to the toy watch and child's rattle. I, too, have received marks of kindness; but that which forms the subject of the following letter is the most acceptable of all : —

NEW YORK, 31st December, 1846.

PHILIP HONE, ESQ. : —

MY DEAR SIR, — To your inquiry asking who sent your bust, by Clevenger, to be placed in the rooms of the Mercantile Library Association, I reply by attaching hereto the names of the persons: James Brown, Walter R. Jones, Samuel Jaudon, John Ward, G. G. Howland, Jonathan Goodhue, M. H. Grinnell, Samuel S. Howland, John A. Stevens, Robert B. Minturn, William H. Aspinwall, Henry Grinnell, Edward Prime, Robert Ray, George Curtis, Charles H. Russell, Spofford & Tileston, John Haggerty, R. M. Blatchford, Thomas W. Ludlow, J. Prescott Hall, William B. Astor, James G. King.

High and constant as are the respect and attachment of all these friends to you personally, they had a higher and more abiding motive in this act. They knew that your long career of uprightness as a member of the mercantile community had been crowned in the decline of life by your having voluntarily, and from the highest considerations of honour and good faith, assumed obligations in behalf of some relatives, and by your having been obliged to sacrifice a large portion of your property, by sales in adverse times, to meet those obligations with your wonted punctuality. To mark this signal instance of self-denial and integrity some of your fellow-merchants and friends felt that an appropriate testimonial was due, and that no more fitting opportunity could have occurred than the accidental meeting with this bust by so distinguished an American artist as Clevenger, and that no more suitable place for depositing it could have been selected than that where the well-known features of their old friend and president will derive an additional value in the eyes of the commercial clerks, from the example which you have set to them, *the future merchants of New York*, and from this acknowledgment of it, which we have thus endeavoured to render perpetual.

I remain, etc.,

JAMES G. KING.

JANUARY 20. — Peter R. Livingston died yesterday, at his residence, Rhinebeck, aged eighty-one years. He was originally a Democrat of great powers, and played an important part in wresting the political administration of the State from the hands of the Federalists; an eloquent declaimer at public meetings; a demagogue of the highest class. Few could oppose him with success. As in religion, so it is in politics: the first-fruits of men's lives are given to the propagation and support of disorganizing principles, and when they become old they turn to better principles, and exert themselves to eradicate the seed which they assisted in sowing. Mr. Livingston, at the close of his life, was a leading Whig, and even when broken down by physical infirmity, the bright light of early eloquence broke occasionally through the shadows of superannuated debility. In early life he went out with his relative, Chancellor Livingston, as Secretary of the Legation, to France, where the excesses of that capital left him a trembling martyr to dissipation for the remainder of his life. Thus, with bodily powers broken down, but unimpaired powers of mind, he lingered out his life to fourscore years. He has held many important offices under Democratic administrations, — State senator and member of the Council of Appointment, elector of President, member of Congress, etc. I have played many a game of whist with him, and whilst his tremulous hand was incapable of dealing the cards, he never failed to make the most of them.

Mrs. Ray's Party. JANUARY 28. — My children called to take Mr. Russell and me from Mr. Spofford's dinner to a party at Mrs. Robert Ray's, away up at the corner of 28th street and the Ninth avenue. The house is one of those palaces which have lately sprung up in places where a few years since cattle grazed, and orchards dropped their ripened fruits. This magnificent abode of costly luxury, now the *town* residence of my good friend Mr. Ray, stands on the very spot where his father's garden, away *out of town*, flourished long since my hair turned gray. This was *the* party of the season. Every luxury was supplied in abundance, and with good taste, to all the elegant women and fashionable gentlemen about town; every room was filled, and even I (somewhat antiquated, and not much given of late to party-going) partook largely of the general enjoyment of Mr. and Mrs. Ray's first party in their new house in *Fitz-ray place.*

State of Society. JANUARY 29. — Our good city of New York has already arrived at the state of society to be found in the large cities of Europe; overburdened with population, and where the two extremes of costly luxury in living, expensive establishments, and improvident waste are presented in daily and hourly contrast with squalid misery and hopeless destitution. This state of things has been hastened in our case by the constant stream of European paupers arriving upon the shores of this land of promise. Alas! how often does it prove to the deluded emigrant a land of broken promise and blasted hope! If we had none but our own poor to take care of, we should get along tolerably well; we could find employment for them, and individual charity, aiding the public institutions, might save us from the sights of woe with which we are assailed in the streets, and the pressing applications which beset us in the retirement of our own houses. Nineteen out of twenty of these mendicants are foreigners cast upon our shores, indigent and helpless, having expended the last shilling in paying their passage-money, deceived by the misrepresentations of unscrupulous agents, and left to starve amongst strangers, who, finding it impossible to extend relief to all, are deterred from assisting any. These reflections upon the extremes of lavish expenditure and absolute destitution are forced upon me by my own recent experience. I partook yesterday of a most expensive dinner, where every article of costly food which the market affords was spread before the guests, and fine wines drunk in abundance, some of which might command eight or ten dollars a bottle; and from this scene of expensive hospitality I was conveyed to another more splendid and expensive entertainment, where the sparkling of diamonds, the reflection of splendid mirrors, the lustre of silks and satins, and the rich gilding of tasteful furniture were flashed, by the aid of innumerable lights, upon the dazzled eyes of a thousand guests. Now this is all right enough; in both these cases our entertainers could well afford the expense which attended the display of their hospitality, nor is it within the scope of the most remote probability that the money of any others than themselves can be involved in the outlay of their entertainments.

It may be painful to reflect how far the cost of a single bottle of Mr. Spofford's wine or one of Mr. Ray's *pâtés de foie gras* might contribute to alleviate the distress of those miserable objects who stretch out the attenuated arms of wasted poverty, or display the haggard countenance of infantile deprivation, or the tattered habiliments incapable of resisting the inclemency of the winter's cold. These gentlemen are liberal and charitable, and no doubt do their part in almsgiving; but they have other duties to perform. The city demands that their riches shall contribute to maintain its character for hospitality, and they can no more avert the evils which are inevitable in such a state of society as exists in our city than they can arrest the pestilence, present a barrier to the ravages of the flood, or extinguish the destroying flame. The accounts of the sufferings of the poor wretches who were brought up from the ship "Garrick" make me feel almost guilty in my participation in the luxuries of yesterday's entertainment; we are told that twelve of the number died on the passage, and several since the vessel went ashore, and those who were landed here are perfectly destitute, — no clothes, no friends, no object in view. They fled from starvation at home to starve here, or be relieved by public or individual charity. I may philosophize on this subject forever, and feel a little bad about it sometimes; but, after all, I am inclined to think that whenever Mr. Spofford or Mr. Ray invites me again I shall go.

This nutritious grain, food for man and fodder for
Indian Corn.   every edible animal, is the great social momentum of
the present day. The quantity raised in this country is so great as to be with difficulty expressed by figures; and now that famine presents its horrid features to the distressed poor of Europe, we supply them with excellent food, after having taught them how to eat it and to like it as we do.

I witnessed on Thursday one of the triumphs of this great American staple production. A procession of twenty or thirty carts, the forward one being drawn by six white horses and decorated with flags, proceeded up Broadway to the *grunting* of martial music, each cart loaded with four or five enormous dead hogs; the whole number was 106 hogs, weighing 40,262 pounds, an average of 380 pounds. These overgrown animals were raised by five farmers of Burlington county, New Jersey, and sold to a pork-dealer here. They were nearly uniform in size, with short duck legs, like Grant Thorburn's; little, twinkling eyes peeping out between two mountains of fat, like pins upon a pin-cushion; and hams as round as a full moon and luscious as a turtle's calipash. There was *Indian corn* written in legible characters upon their jolly features, and shining on their swelling sides; dead though they were, they had, out of benevolence to mankind, laid down their characters as swine to assume that of pork; every spare-rib and every link of sausage, as well as the more important parts of these children of Ham, will sing the praises of *Indian corn.*

FEBRUARY 3. — Dr. Johnson says somewhere, "Who that ever asks succour from Bacchus was able to preserve himself from being enslaved by his auxiliary?"

A Dangerous Auxiliary.

I am reminded of a case in point, but not attended with the bad consequences imagined by the great moral essayist. Dining many years ago with my lamented friend, Commodore Chauncey, at the navy yard, I remarked to the distinguished statesman, Mr. Webster, who graced our party, "My dear sir, I observe that you are not altogether indifferent to the virtues of a glass of good wine." — "By no means," he replied, "and I will tell you how it came about. When I began to practise law in Massachusetts I was honoured by the notice and friendship of Christopher Gore, who frequently invited me to his house. On one occasion, seeing me look pale and feeble, from the effects of study and hard work, he kindly inquired how I lived. I told him I fared rather poorly at my humble lodgings, in the house of Mrs. So and So; that I ate corned beef and cabbage and drank water. 'That will not do,' said Mr. Gore; 'you must drink a glass of good wine occasionally, and eat an apple after dinner to promote digestion.' — 'But,' said I, 'I cannot afford to drink wine.' — 'I will take care of that,' said my liberal friend; and from that time I received occasional presents of fine old wine from his well-supplied garret. Well, sir, it did me great good. I recovered my health, and was enabled to pursue my studies and perform my task with renewed ardour. But, alas! like a beleaguered city which is compelled to call in the aid of auxiliary forces, I repulsed the enemy; but, the auxiliaries having established themselves in the citadel, I have never been able to dispossess them."

FEBRUARY 8.—Died yesterday, Mr. James Roosevelt, in the eighty-eighth year of his age; a highly respectable gentleman of the old school, son of Isaac Roosevelt, the first president of the first bank in New York, at a time when the president and directors of a bank were other sort of people from those of the present day. Proud and aristocratical, they were the only nobility we had (now we have none); powerful in the controlling influence they possessed over the commercial operations of the city, men could not stand straight in their presence; and woe to them who bowed not down to the representatives of a few bags of gold and silver, the potential dispensers of bank favours. Chancellor Kent told me last evening that he and Mr. Roosevelt were in college together, and both studied law in Judge Benson's office.

FEBRUARY 12.—There is a great movement in behalf of the suffering people of Ireland. A meeting preliminary to more important movements was held this day in Prime's building, in Wall street, which was well attended by the right sort of folks. Mr. Van Schaick presided; nine thousand dollars were subscribed by those present, and measures were taken to collect the fund required to freight a vessel with a cargo of bread-stuffs and other provisions and send her to Cork or some other port in Ireland. A call was made on the clergy to receive contributions in the several churches, and notice given of a general meeting to be held on Monday evening at the Tabernacle. This is a good feeling and prompt action on this interesting subject.

In connection with the above remarks I must record a circumstance which occurred yesterday at the club dinner at Ward's, honourable to the parties concerned. Mr. Wetmore stated that he had lost to Mr. Grinnell a bet of two dinners for the company; that the illness of his wife prevented him from giving these dinners at his own house, and proposed, instead thereof (if Grinnell and the company approved), to commute the claim by handing over to me the sum of three hundred and sixty dollars, which was estimated to cover the expense of two such entertainments, with fine wines; this sum to be appropriated, in such a way as I might judge best, for the relief of the suffering Irish. This liberal offer was, of course, agreed to, and I received this morning Mr. Wetmore's check for the amount, which I handed to the relief committee. Hereby we dispense with two sumptuous dinners (for which it is doubtful if any of us would have been the better), and the means are furnished to add fifty barrels of wheat flour, or the value in other provisions, to the contributions of our citizens for saving hundreds of our suffering brethren in Ireland from starvation. I must add that the generous donor of this gift stipulated that this should be independent of any donation he might think proper to make otherwise for the same object, and on my calling this morning at the office of the committee I found his name as a subscriber for five hundred dollars. Mr. Wetmore is a very rich man, and liberal in proportion to his means. May the God of mercy and goodness prosper his riches, and continue his ability and inclination to make a good use of them!

FEBRUARY 16. — There was a great meeting last evening at the Tabernacle, for the relief of the famished Irish, called by the committee. Myndert Van Schaick presided, with a host of vice-presidents, of which I was one. Speeches were made by the Rev. Dr. Wainwright, Rev. Mr. Adams, George Griffin, Charles King, and Barnabas Bates. The large building was filled with a respectable male audience, and an exceedingly good feeling was evinced.

In the House of Representatives, yesterday, the question was taken on the long-contested amendment introduced by Mr. Wilmot to the bill granting three millions of dollars to our warlike President for the purpose of carrying on the war in a snug way. This amendment, which prohibited the introduction of slavery into the newly acquired Territories, was carried by a vote of one hundred and fifteen to one hundred and five. It is an important measure, which may alter the whole organization of political parties in the country, and defeat the great objects of the annexation of Texas and its consequence, the unrighteous war with Mexico.

John Quincy Adams.
An interesting occurrence took place on Saturday in the House of Representatives ; the venerable member from Massachusetts, ex-President Adams, made his first appearance in the House since his dangerous attack of paralysis, and resumed his accustomed seat, which was courteously surrendered to him by its temporary occupant, Mr. Johnson. On his welcome advent the members all arose. He was addressed by the Speaker, and replied with deep sensibility. At the moment of his entrance, the member who was addressing the House, Mr. Kent, suspended his remarks, and, on resuming, alluded to the interesting event which had caused their interruption. This was a proud homage to exalted talents, devoted patriotism, and long and faithful public services. He has, in the course of his legislative career, crossed the path of many of those who now joined in this honourable demonstration, — a circumstance most honourable, equally creditable to the donors and grateful to the recipient, and which is well calculated to soften the rays of the intellectual sun which there is reason to fear is about setting.

Washington's Birthday.
FEBRUARY 22. — This is the anniversary of the birth of him whose name is indissolubly connected with the glory of our republic. " First in war, first in peace, and first in the hearts of his countrymen," his name will grace the brightest page of history as an example of disinterested patriotism, unstained honour, and wise conduct.

A small detachment of citizen soldiers, calling themselves veterans, are at this moment passing my window, clad in the old, quaint uniform of the Continentals, — long blue coats, faced and turned up with buff, with three-cornered cocked hats and long boots; not by any means a graceful costume, but interesting, as it brings to recollection the days of the man honoured by his countrymen and chosen by his Maker as the leader of the people. What would this man have said, were he still among us, at the degradation of his countrymen in permitting a chief ruler, the accidental choice of a reckless faction, to exercise a power equally arbitrary and unconstitutional; and by usurping the people's rights, and the sovereignty of the States delegated to their representatives in Congress, to involve the nation in an unjust and inglorious war of aggression upon a neighbouring republic, which, if it had strength equal to its sense of wrong, would send back our forces dishonoured and discomfited. The blood of many a brave and gallant American will be shed in this contest; consecrated, it is true, by personal bravery, but unhallowed by the consolation of lamenting friends and fellow-citizens, that the cause in which they fell was just.

Shade of the great and good Washington, look down upon thy beloved country, and warn us of the bad effects of corrupt and unrighteous councils !

FEBRUARY 25. — Immense shipments of bread-stuffs are made from every port in the United States; freights are enormously high, — eight to nine shillings for a barrel of flour. The Liverpool packets, which have been lately built of increased tonnage, as if in anticipation of the present demand, are making unprecedented profits. The new packet-ship "Constitution," belonging to Woodhull & Minturn's line, sailed yesterday for Liverpool, with the following enormous cargo of bread-stuffs: Ten thousand bushels of wheat, twenty-five thousand bushels of Indian corn, two thousand seven hundred barrels of corn-meal, one hundred and sixty boxes of soda biscuit, four thousand barrels of flour; besides which she has six hundred and sixty-one bales of cotton, forty-two boxes of clocks, and nineteen barrels of beeswax. The bread-stuffs are equal to sixty-eight thousand bushels; these will stop the croaking of many an empty stomach.

MARCH 1.—The subscriptions for the relief of the
Collections for Ireland. Irish are kept up with undiminished spirit. The Relief
Committee have received upwards of $50,000. Collections were made yesterday in several of the churches: the amount given in St. John's Church was $556; Grace Church collected the previous Sunday $1,800. The Catholic churches have given nobly, and every denomination of Christians has assisted liberally in the good work: Episcopalians, Presbyterians, Methodists, Baptists, and Romanists are all united as one congregation in the brotherhood of charity.

MARCH 4.—The twenty-ninth Congress ceased to
Congress Adjourned. exist last night. It should be a cause of rejoicing; for never was a nation cursed with such a body of representatives. "Their works will follow them," bad as they were. But how do we know that, in the present downward tendency of public affairs, the next Congress may not be equally bad? The House of Representatives had still their Winthrop, Adams, Ashmun, Mosely, Grinnell, etc., some of whom are reëlected to the next Congress. But the great falling off will be in the Senate. Evans, Archer, Berrien, and several others of the staunchest Whigs and ablest senators, close their labours in that body with the close of the session; some have been reëlected, but a large proportion must make way for such as their Loco-foco legislatures may think proper to send. The House may possibly be Whig, but the Senate is irrevocably Loco-foco.

The three-million bill passed, without Wilmot's proviso prohibiting the introduction of slavery in newly acquired Territories. This proviso prevailed at first in the House of Representatives; but, by the force of party drill, a majority was found against it at the last moment, and this large appropriation is given to Mr. Polk with which to do what he pleases. Charles J. Ingersoll would have Mr. Webster impeached for some paltry sum of $1,000, unaccounted for or misapplied, if that great man had not possessed proofs of the utter falsity of the base insinuation. Now this tool of party votes

to cast three millions into the pool of executive corruption. And
now let us see the compensation for this foul act. Polk nominated
this man on the last day of the session as Minister to France.
The nomination was rejected by the Senate, although a majority of
that body are the political associates of the nominee ; immediately
after which the name of Richard Rush, of Pennsylvania, was sent in
and confirmed. Mr. Rush was Minister to England when I was
first there, in 1821, and I have always been grateful for his kind
attentions during my stay in London. He is not a man of much
force, but much better than we usually get in these times of national
degradation. The escape of the country from the disgrace of
Ingersoll's appointment might reconcile us to a less respectable
Minister than Mr. Rush.

MARCH 9.— Dined with Judge David S. Jones. The
Dinner-parties. party consisted of the following gentlemen, and the
dinner was pleasant : Moses H. Grinnell, Henry Par-
ish, Charles A. Clinton, John A. King, Paul Spofford, William B.
Astor, William Douglass, Henry Brevoort, Clement C. Moore, Mr.
Finlay, Robert Ray, Thomas Tileston, J. Prescott Hall, and P. H.

MARCH 12.— I dined at Mr. Astor's, with the following party,
besides the host and hostess : Mr. and Mrs. Gibbes, Mr. and Mrs.
John J. Astor, Mr. and Mrs. Bristed. The two last-named ladies
were Miss Augusta Gibbes and Miss Laura Brevoort ; their husbands
are grandchildren of old Mr. Astor, as are Miss Astor and Mr.
Walter Langdon, who were also at the dinner. Besides these, there
were Mr. and Mrs. Thomas W. Ludlow, Mr. Charles E. Davis, Mr.
Truman, Mr. K. Armstrong, Judge David S. Jones, Mr. Cogs-
well, and myself.

MARCH 31.—The news from Mexico, which has
Mexico. been anxiously expected for the last two or three days,
was brought to-day by express from Washington. The
rumours of a great battle in Mexico between General Taylor and
Santa Anna have taken the form of authenticity. The conflict
which was foreshadowed was realized, and a bloody battle fought

by the Mexicans and their invaders on the 22d and 23d of February, at a place called *Buena Vista*, six miles west of Saltillo, the result of which extricates the American forces under General Taylor from a position of great danger. Five thousand of our troops were surrounded by fifteen thousand Mexicans, and with this disparity of force Taylor gave battle. The action was desperate. The Americans, as usual, fought with the utmost bravery, and the contest was well sustained by the enemy. The carnage was tremendous : four thousand Mexicans are killed and wounded, by our accounts ; but it is painful to relate that the blood of seven hundred to a thousand Americans was offered up to the Moloch of war and unjust aggressive hostility, of whom sixty-three were officers, — gallant, noble fellows who fought for their country, reckless of life and regardless of the merits of the controversy. As old Caspar says, " But 'twas a glorious victory." Who shall comfort the afflicted parents, wives, children, and friends of the brave men who have thus "sacrificed their lives to honour"? Who shall be the first to convey the melancholy tidings of his son's death to Mr. Clay, whose whole life has been employed in the service of an ungrateful people? They are willing he should work for them, negotiate for them, and sacrifice his time, talents, and property in their service, and send his sons to fight their battles and die in their cause ; but most ungratefully refuse his just reward, and bestow their favour upon one who went to bed one night a man no bigger than a million of other men in the country, and rose the next day President of the United States. One must be struck with the disparity of loss, in all the actions of the present war, between the officers and privates. In the wars of Europe, where war is brought to a system and practised as a science, and where the men are formed into machines to carry on the trade, their officers have only to set them in motion and keep them to their work ; and only in extreme cases is it necessary for the commanders of divisions, brigades, and regiments to put their lives in jeopardy. The loss of one general or colonel has a greater influence upon the fate of a battle than that of a hundred men. Napoleon risked his life at the bridge of Lodi because the emergency of the occasion required the example; but he knew the value of his life, and refrained from exposing the property of France. We have a different kind of warfare to wage. The troops now engaged in Mexico are principally raw recruits, undisciplined and unpractised, — brave enough in battle, but governed by impulse; they require constantly the example of their officers to lead them on, and this example is never withheld. The officers are a set of the most chivalrous, daring fellows in the world. Most of them of good families, they fight for glory, and, knowing the risk attendant upon its acquirement, never hesitate to encounter it.

We had a pleasant dinner-party to-day, given in honour of the accomplished author of " Ferdinand and Isabella " and the " Conquest of Peru." My round table was graced by the presence of the following guests: William H. Prescott, Rev. Dr. Wainwright, Jonathan Meredith, Governor Seward, Francis Granger, Henry Brevoort, Clement C. Moore, J. Prescott Hall, James W. Webb, and Ogden Hoffman. I gave this toast in compliment to the principal guest: " Mexico and Peru : we have conquered the one, and intend soon to *turn over a new leaf* with the other."

The first edition of the " Conquest of Peru," consisting of seven thousand five hundred copies, has been purchased, at one dollar a set, by the Harpers. Mr. Prescott reserves the copyright, and will, of course, receive all the profits of future editions. He told me that his works have thus far produced him $8,000. He finds book-making a good trade ; but few such books as his are made.

April 17. — There is a pleasant account in the papers of a fishing party of the tallest kind, which " came off " on Tuesday last, at Southampton, Long Island ; a school of whales made their appearance in the bay on Monday afternoon, which proved to be a most unfortunate visit (for the whales, I mean). As soon as they were descried, several boats, manned by the hardy and intrepid whalemen who inhabit that sea-girt region, went in pursuit, and, in full view of the delighted and excited non-combatants on shore, attacked, conquered, and landed four whales of the largest kind, from which they will obtain from thirty to sixty barrels of oil each.

APRIL 27. — Mr. Webster has left Washington, and gone to the South, where he seems to be gaining "golden opinions." We already hear of his arrival at Richmond, and his being received by crowds prepared to escort him to his lodgings; of a public dinner being provided for him, and every demonstration of respect during his brief sojourn in the capital of Virginia. Similar greetings are prepared on the line of his route. They have heard of Mr. Webster, but have not seen him; and if he relaxes his iron brow, and condescends to open out himself to their inspection, and show them that his proud name was not misapplied, the Southerners may be made to acknowledge that even the East may produce great men. It looks as if the Massachusetts senator was looking out for votes. I wish he may get enough to make him President; but I fear he will find the *Taylor's measures* more to the people's liking than the more experienced culture of the Marshfield farmer.

MAY 1. — The great day of domestic locomotion is, happily for the sufferers, bright and clear. Spring carts are in great request; straw beds are cast into the streets; pots, pans, and kettles are seeking a new sphere of usefulness; women scold, children cry, and the head of the family begins to find that his notions of personal importance are of little consideration in the turmoil of May day.

MAY 3. — The Tallahassee "Sentinel" of 20th of
Prince Murat. April announces in the following terms the death of a scion of the Bonaparte stock, who has resided in this country, a naturalized American, for many years: " Prince Charles Napoleon Achille Murat expired at his residence in Jefferson County, Florida, on Thursday last, the 15th inst. He was the son of Joachim and Caroline Bonaparte Murat, King and Queen of

Naples; the former the celebrated marshal of Napoleon, the mirror
of chivalry and valour; the other, a sister of the immortal emperor.
After the expulsion of his family from Italy, Prince Murat resided
in Austria until 1821, when he removed to this country. He has
spent most of his days in Florida, in all the quiet and retirement of
a country gentleman." He was borne to the grave in this city, on
Saturday, attended by his Masonic brethren of Jackson Lodge, and
by a concourse of citizens. Minute-guns were fired during the
moving of the procession, and he was interred with all the solemn
ceremonies of the Masonic order.

MAY 7. — This was a day of rejoicing, ordered by the
city authorities to celebrate the victories of our armies
in Mexico. There was a grand military display, sal-
vos of one hundred guns, a general display of flags from all the
vessels in the harbour, and from every public edifice in the city
which had the bunting to show. In the evening occurred an illu-
mination of all conspicuous houses; the City Hall and other public
buildings, hotels, and club-houses were lighted up, and transparencies exhibited, in which Scott and Taylor, Worth and Wool, were
blazoned forth by " inch of candle; " and Palo Alto, Resaca de los
Palmos, Monterey, Buena Vista, and la Vera Cruz were as familiar
to the tongues of old age and infancy, male and female, gentlefolk
and common folk, as the places where they were born.

I went with my daughters and Mr. William Hoppin to see the
show. The crowd in the streets was great beyond description.
Broadway, for its whole length, was a solid mass, and in the Park
it looked as if humanity was piled three or four deep. We went
along with the tide (for returning was impracticable) as far as
St. Paul's Church, and thence up Chatham street and the Bowery,
home, where we arrived tired and bruised, but gratified with what
we had seen; and not much the worse for wear, for, although the
crowd was so great, it was a good-natured crowd, — a little scream-
ing, some swearing, but more laughing, and no accidents that I
have heard of.

MAY 10. — Scarcely had the last inch of candle shed its rays, and the last charge of powder sounded the harmless blast of rejoicing for battles fought and gained by the Americans in Mexico; scarcely had the bells ceased to toll and the drooping flags been hauled down from the mast, which have been the sounds and symbols of mourning for American blood shed in acquiring these victories, — than we are called upon to record another triumph of the invading army.

General Scott achieved a decisive victory over the Mexican forces under Santa Anna, on the 18th of April. It was a hard-fought battle; the loss of the Mexicans was immense. They fight bravely and die hard; they are beaten again and again, and will not stay beaten. This battle was fought in the mountains and amongst the *chaparrals*. The rout was complete; besides the dreadful loss in killed, our army took six thousand prisoners, including two generals, with ten or twelve other officers of high importance, who were all sent to report themselves to our commandant at la Vera Cruz, and thence, by their own choice, are to come to the United States. The commander-in-chief, General Santa Anna, had a narrow escape. By cutting loose one of the mules from his travelling-carriage and mounting her, he got clear into the mountains, leaving his equipage in the hands of the victor (to whom, as we have it from high authority, " belong the spoils "), with his rich service of plate for General Scott's use, and his wooden leg, which I pray the latter may never have occasion to use.

But now comes the dark side of the picture. More precious blood has been shed. General Shields, one of the bravest of the brave, was desperately, probably mortally, wounded. The names of the killed and wounded are not given, nor is there as yet any official account. If matters continue at this rate the Mexicans will be exterminated, our own precious blood will be shed in the achievement, and the nation will gain nothing by the conquest. While these victories are gained on the land, the seaports in the bay are falling one after another into the hands of the navy, from whom the army has received the most efficient help and harmonious coöperation since the fall of la Vera Cruz and its formidable defences.   Alvarado has been captured, and this morning we have accounts of the Port of Tuspan, sixty or seventy miles north from la Vera Cruz, having been taken by the squadron under command of Commodore Perry.   Among the names mentioned of the wounded, incidentally, in the vague accounts of this battle, I perceive that of Lieutenant McLane, whom I take to be the son of my friend, Louis McLane, of Baltimore, late Minister to England.   It will turn out, I think, that this has been the most disastrous battle for the Mexicans.   Poor creatures ! they are paying severely for the unpardonable sin of rejecting the modest, unassuming plenipotentiary, Mr. John Slidell.   I rejoice that my friend Scott has brought himself up so finely ; this battle adds a broad leaf to the laurel wreath which he gained at la Vera Cruz.

Webster at the South.

Mr. and Mrs. Webster were at Charleston, S. C., on the 29th ult., on which day he partook of a public dinner, the invitation to which was signed by sixty-two names, comprising all the chivalry of Carolina.   The affair was gotten up in good taste, and marked with the best sort of feeling, in the preparatory meeting and the Mayor of Charleston presided.   The resolutions were proposed, and a highly complimentary speech made, by Colonel Hayne, in the struggle with whom Mr. Webster, in the celebrated debate in the Senate on Foote's resolutions, acquired his brightest laurels, and gained a proud victory over an opponent of his prowess

Club Dinner.

MAY 13. — The Hone Club dined with J. Prescott Hall.   The attendance, owing to absence from town, sickness, and death in families, was unusually small, consisting of the following members : Hall, John Ward, Grinnell, George Curtis, Paul Spofford, Draper, Bowen, and myself ; in addition to whom were Judge Nelson, of the Supreme Court of the United States ; Judge Betts, United States District Court ; Judges Beardsley and Jewett, Supreme Court of the State ; and Mr. Charles King.

MAY 14. — We had a pleasant party at supper, consisting of Mr. and Mrs. DePeyster, Mr. and Mrs. Foster, Mr. and Mrs. John Hone, Mr. and Mrs. Van Schaick, Mrs. Oddie and Alida, Mr. and Mrs. Isaac Hone, Dr. Matthews, his two daughters and son; Mr. Anthon, his daughters; William and Hamilton Hoppin, Mr. William Wood and Miss Wood, William Ashurst, Mr. Muller, and Mr. Francis Dorr.

MAY 26. — I received yesterday a circular letter Chicago Convention. from the Hon. William A. Mosely, chairman of the corresponding committee of Buffalo, an estimable Whig member of Congress, inviting me to attend a great convention to be held at Chicago, Illinois, on the 5th of July. The object of this convention is to put forward the claims upon the government of the enterprising citizens of the great western lake country, and consequently to rebuke the contumelious treatment they have received from the person who has, accidentally, obtained the power to defeat the wise and *constitutional* measures adoped by the people's representatives. I have replied to Mr. Mosely's letter, accepting the invitation of the committee, and promising to be at Chicago on the 5th of July, my health permitting. This fits in well. I have been making arrangements to go early next month to Lake Michigan, Green Bay, and Chicago; and here is an additional inducement.

MAY 31. — Among the liberal donations for the relief of the famished Irish which have passed through the hands of the committee was one received last week, of $5,000, from Messrs. Corcoran and Riggs, of Washington. These gentlemen have made a princely fortune by taking the whole of the last government six-per-cent. loan, and have thus, with becoming liberality, contributed of their abundance to this good object. The capture of la Vera Cruz and the battle of Buena Vista furnished the means of sending a thousand barrels of corn to Ireland; and Scott and Taylor, whilst employed in knocking out the brains of Mexicans, were unconsciously the instruments of saving the lives of Irishmen.

New York Harbour.

JUNE 1.— The glorious harbour of New York presented to-day an animated picture. Vessels of every description, from the largest-class frigate to the little, fairy skiff, with magnificent steamers, carrying out, to its utmost extent, the American go-ahead principle, and noble merchantmen loaded down with the staff of life for hungry Europe, waiting for a wind to hoist sail and away. Several causes operated to increase the usual animation of this great aquatic theatre. The new steamer "Washington," the first government mail vessel intended for England and the continent, went to sea. She takes out Mr. Hobbie, an agent of the general post-office department, who goes to establish an international system of postage with the European governments.

A great steamboat race came off between the "Cornelius Vanderbilt," which bears the name of her enterprising proprietor, and the "Oregon," Captain Law. They went to Croton Point and returned, seventy-five miles, in three hours and fifteen minutes, — a rate of speed which would carry a vessel to Liverpool in five or six days. The "Oregon" gained the race, and Captain Vanderbilt was beaten for once. The annual regatta of the Yacht Club was to have taken place, but there was not wind enough to start the boats. I intended to have gone down with my daughter in the steamer "Eureka," which was provided by the club to accompany the yachts, with the members. The affair was postponed until to-morrow. Among the other incidents of the day interesting to the spectators on the Battery was the arrival of the "Southerner" from Charleston, with Mr. Webster and other distinguished passengers.

Journey to the West.

HARRISBURG, JUNE 10.— We left Philadelphia at seven o'clock, and came to this place, one hundred and six miles by railroad, at three o'clock. The weather is warm, but a fine breeze made the ride delightful. The road passes through one of the most fertile and best-cultivated districts in the United States; but there is not a pretty town on the route, and none of any note but Lancaster; nor is Harrisburg, though dignified by the name of the capital of the great State of Pennsylvania, anything more than a miserable collection of lawyers' offices and barber-shops. There is not a handsome edifice in the place, that we could find, with the exception of the State-House and public offices, which are in good style, but constructed of the everlasting red brick and white marble. The town is beautifully situated on an eminence overlooking the Susquehanna, which is here a fine stream, and deserves something better than this loafer-looking city to grace its banks. We have determined, as a choice of evils, to go to-morrow to Pittsburg by the canal, although we shall be three nights on the voyage, in preference to one hundred and fifty miles of stage travelling by Chambersburg, on dusty roads in this warm weather.

JUNE 11.—At three o'clock we embarked in the *Pennsylvania Canal.* canal-boat "Delaware," Captain Kellar, on a canal voyage of more than two hundred miles. The weather is pleasant, and we have an agreeable set of passengers; not too many. The day does very well, but the sleeping is tolerably uncomfortable (there is not much of *that*, however). The delay on this, the first day of our long voyage, is rather discouraging; there has been a breach in the canal, which has caused an accumulation of loaded boats; but the scenery is splendid. Just at the sun-setting (a more glorious one I never saw) we came to the junction of the Susquehanna and Juniata rivers, fifteen miles from Harrisburg, where the boat crosses the dam, the tow-path being conveyed across on a long bridge of light and delicate construction, on piers of massive and solid masonry. At the mouth of the Juniata is a handsome mansion and fine estate of four hundred acres, called Duncan's Island, belonging to a lady of that name, whose character seems to be worthy of such a position. Here we leave the Susquehanna, and follow the course of the Juniata,—a beautiful stream, abounding in romantic and picturesque scenery.

EN ROUTE, JUNE 12.—The breach in the canal caused us to stop several hours during the night, and this morning, at sunrise, the "Commet," a huge coal-boat, had the bad manners to get stuck across the canal (what better could be expected from a fellow who spells Comet with two m's?). Here I witnessed a gallant exploit of our captain, — the *raising a swell*, which is thus performed : he puts six horses on the tow-lines, backs the boat, and then, dashing on with the fury of the horses in the hippodrome, raises a swell like the waves at Rockaway. The first onset removed the " *Commet* " a little from her orbit, and the second carried us triumphantly through the obstacle. The sight of this spirited display of canal tactics compensated for the delay. We sat down to breakfast and went on our way rejoicing.

CANAL, JUNE 13. — This canal-travelling is pleasant enough in the daytime, but the sleeping is awful. There are two cabins, in which the men-folk and the women-folk are separated by a red curtain. In the former apartment the sleepers are packed away on narrow shelves, fastened to the sides of the boat, like dead pigs in a Cincinnati pork warehouse. We go to bed at nine o'clock, and rise when we are told in the morning ; for the bedsteads are formed of the seats and the tables. " A couch by night, a chest of drawers by day ! " If I should ever be so happy as to sleep in my own bed again, my comfort will be enhanced by the remembrance of my present limited, hard, sheetless dormitory.

JUNE 14. — An extra car brought us from Holidaysburg, at six o'clock this morning, to take the Portage railroad across the Alleghany mountains to Johnstown,—thirty-six miles,—which is effected by ten inclined planes, five ascending and five descending, similar to those on the Delaware and Hudson railroad. It is somewhat exciting, but nothing when we get used to it. The scenery of these mountains is astonishingly grand, wild beyond description ; and would have been gratifying but for the hard rain and extreme cold, which compelled us to keep the windows closed. The delay of the early part of this tedious voyage still follows us. Being an extra train, nothing was ready ; locomotives were to be sent for, and horses not to be had. We have lost already three days since we left Philadelphia, and while writing, the new boat, the " Louisiana," lies at the dock at Johnstown, waiting for the passengers who were a day behind us. Six o'clock. The cars are in; an influx of passengers, of not so good a description as the original set, have come on board, with a fair quantity of crying children and vulgar mothers, and we are off once more.

June 15. — Our canal voyage has been pleasant, on the whole, though tedious, and longer than it should have been by a day and a night at least, owing to delays on the first night, which we could not recover during the voyage. But we arrived at "the Birmingham of America" at eleven o'clock this evening. I regretted the necessity of entering the city at night; but its appearance was quite a novelty: bright flames issuing from foundries, glass and gas works, and rolling-mills, steam-engines puffing like broken-winded horses, and heavy clouds of smoke making the night's darkness darker, gave us a grand *entrée* to Pittsburg, where we are sumptuously lodged at the Monongahela House.

June 16. — This is one of the most active, business-like places I have ever seen, with every appearance of present prosperity and future greatness; manufactures of iron, glass, and machinery are carried on extensively and under great advantages; iron abounds in every valley, and bituminous coal of the best quality comes cantering down from the surrounding mountains, and is delivered by contract at four and a half cents per bushel, or about $1.20 the long ton. A place so situated, with such natural advantages, must rise to greatness. I have seen nothing like it in Pennsylvania.

At Pittsburg.

June 20. — The voyage down the Ohio — four hundred and ninety-six miles — has been exceedingly pleasant. We had a fine boat, excellent fare, comfortable staterooms, and good company, and arrived here this morning in time to dress and attend divine worship at Christ Church, — an Episcopal congregation. Cincinnati is a noble city, as I expected, of seventy-five thousand inhabitants, with splendid private dwellings and every appearance of prosperity.

At Cincinnati.

At Lex-
ington.

JUNE 24. — Mr. Clay sent us last evening a note, inviting us to breakfast. Mr. Crittenden, Margaret, and I went out this morning to Ashland. A more delightful visit cannot be imagined; I shall ever remember it as one of the bright spots in my life. Our illustrious host received us with the utmost kindness. He looks well, and talks, as usual, "like a book." Recent events have cast a shade of melancholy over his expressive countenance, without diminishing the warmth of his friendly feelings, but rather adding an interest to their expression. He talked much to me about his son. He was baptized on Sunday, preparatory to his joining the Episcopal Church. After breakfast (such a breakfast as could only be found in such a mansion and such a country) he took us around his grounds. I never saw so fine a farm; his crops of wheat, Indian corn, and hemp are in the highest degree of perfection, his trees (nearly all of which were planted by himself) magnificent, and the stock do credit to the pastures on which they are reared. Why should such a man, so situated, desire to succeed in public office a man like James K. Polk?

Mr. Clay.

After spending three or four hours in this pleasant manner, Mr. Clay brought us to town, and drove me in his carriage about the environs, to see the public edifices, private dwellings, and beautiful adjacent country. We then parted (never perhaps to meet again). Long life and honour to Henry Clay! I am as deeply impressed with his hospitality in private as I ever have been with his talents and patriotism in public life. How have I been gratified with this fortunate visit, which brought my daughter and me in friendly communion with two such men as Henry Clay and John J. Crittenden, not forgetting that prince of good fellows, Governor Letcher.

At Louisville.

JUNE 25. — We came from Frankfort — fifty-four miles — by the stage. The day has been very hot, and we had a heavy load of passengers, among whom was

General Shelby, son of the celebrated governor of that name, whose acquaintance I made at Lexington. We stopped to dine at Shelbyville, — a pretty town twenty-two miles from Frankfort. The road is good, and the country through which it passes, like the whole of western Kentucky, beautiful; fine farms, highly cultivated with heavy crops of Indian corn, hemp, and wheat; rich valleys, "standing so thick with corn that they do laugh and sing;" and forests in which the handiwork of nature has left nothing for the improvement of art. These are the bright pictures of this fine country; I have seen nothing to mar them either in the State or its inhabitants. We are lodged in the Galt House, under the charge of its gentlemanly proprietor, Major Throckmorton, the acknowledged prince of landlords.

At the last lock, the new passengers all went ashore to see Porter, the Kentucky giant. He keeps a large hotel, and makes a good living out of the curiosity of travellers who stop to drink with him. The captain introduced me to the *great man*. He said he had heard of me in New York, talked with me (the only one of fifty men present), and wished me a pleasant voyage and safe return. This mighty piece of humanity is seven feet eight inches in height, thirty-five years of age. I stood at his side; he stretched out his arm at right angles with his body, and it was six inches above my head. He is not so fine a looking man as when I saw him in New York, and complains of bad health. I fear that this last of the *race* of giants will have run his earthly *race* ere long. These people persist in calling me *Colonel*, notwithstanding I tell them that I am plain *Mister*. Well, I would rather have the people's commission than that of President Polk, or Governor Young.

JUNE 29.—I was called out of my berth by my request to the clerk, at two o'clock this morning, to witness the union of the "Queen of the West" with "The Father of Rivers." This interesting ceremony takes place at a settlement called Cairo, on the extreme southerly point of the State of Illinois. The moon being obscured, and my sight, from being suddenly called up, not very clear, I could only judge of the situation of the place, but saw enough of it to satisfy me that it was not *Grand Cairo*. We have now followed the course of the Ohio from its commencement at Pittsburg, where the confluence of the Alleghany an 1 Monongahela forms its origin, one hundred miles, to the spot where it becomes lost in the Mississippi. The river is rising, there is plenty of turbid yellow water, and no more danger of getting aground.

JUNE 30. — We came to this great city (for such it At St. Louis. truly is) at six o'clock in the evening of this lovely 30th of June, three weeks since our departure from New York, and put up at the Planters' House, — one of those great hotels which astonish us in the great West. After tea, according to my practice, I started to perambulate the busy haunts of this Western Babylon. I walked the whole extent of the front on the river, called (as is usual in the Western cities) the levee, and my astonishment at the scene there represented is greater than I can describe. Fifty large steamboats, at least, lie head on, taking in and discharging their cargoes ; some constantly arriving from New Orleans and other ports on the Mississippi ; Cincinnati, Louisville, etc., on the Ohio ; from the great Missouri and its tributaries ; the Illinois river, where we are bound, and the whole Western and Southern waters, which make this place their mart ; whilst others are departing, full of passengers, and deeply laden with the multifarious products of this remarkable region. The whole of the levee is covered, as far as the eye can see, with merchandise landed or to be shipped ; thousands of barrels of flour and bags of corn, hogsheads of tobacco, and immense piles of lead (one of the great staples), whilst foreign merchandise and the products of the lower country are carried away to be lodged in the stores which form the front of the city. My walk led me through the Corlears' hook and ship yards of St. Louis ; among boatmen, draymen, and labourers, white and black ; French, Irish, and German, drinking, singing, and lounging on benches. This was an excursion which few travellers would undertake, especially after dark; but I like it, and, as the man said who went to be married, when asked by the priest, "Wilt thou take this woman to be thy wedded wife?" I answer, "Sartainly; I came for that."

JULY 1. — We left St. Louis with infinite regret, at five o'clock this afternoon, on board the steamer "Domain," for Peoria and Peru, on the way to Chicago. I have more to say about St. Louis than I can find time for. We have met with here (as we have in our whole progress) the most distinguished attentions. Many gentlemen have called upon me with offers of services which our short sojourn prevents us from accepting. Colonel Benton, the Missouri senator, the great gun of the great West, called with his niece, Miss Brant (the daughter of Colonel Brant, who has one of the finest establishments in the city), and took us in his carriage to see everything worthy of note in the city and its environs, — the churches (which are very numerous), the convents, the college, and arsenal, and market-places, and a number of beautiful country-seats.

JULY 4. — Chicago is truly the wonder of the West-
At Chicago. ern world. It was ceded to the Americans by the Winnebagoes after General Scott's treaty in February, 1831, and now it is a large town, beautifully situated at the head of Lake Michigan, a transcendently beautiful Mediterranean sea, with streets laid out at right angles, streets of stores, and fleets of vessels; cottages for people of taste, brick houses for people of wealth, hotels for travelling people, and churches for good people.

JULY 8. — We arrived soon after daylight at Mil-
At
Milwaukee. waukee, where we remained until ten o'clock. Here is another wonder of the Western world, — an Aladdin's palace on a large scale, raised in a night, but likely to be of longer duration. The town is well situated, in the State of Wisconsin, ninety-five miles below Chicago, with a fine harbour; streets of business filled with wagons, some conveying the merchandise of New York into the interior of the State, and others bringing in *new country* produce, and taking out *old country* immigrants; churches,

printing-offices, markets, and milliners, — and all these in a place where twelve years ago there were just three log-shanties.

At Fond-du-
Lac.JULY 10. — My business at Sheybogan being accomplished, Margaret and I started this morning, at seven o'clock, in an open wagon, with a good pair of horses and a handy boy to drive, on this journey of forty-four miles. But such a journey I never suffered; the road until the last seven or eight miles lies through a dense forest, generally beech and maple, with now and then a clearance, with the trees still burning; a log-cabin, with swarms of children; pigs; a cow, perhaps; and a pot boiling upon the cross-sticks. Every mile we meet a family of German emigrants, with their goods and chattels stowed away in a huge ox-wagon, with legs of all sizes projecting, from those of the mother, of the size and form of a horse-block, to the pipe-stems of the latest pledge of connubial industry. The road, with the exception of the first six miles to the new and thriving settlement at the falls of the beautiful Sheybogan river, and the last six on the prairies of Fond-du-Lac, is abominable; stumps and roots alternate with stones so thickly sown that there is no room for the wheels to pass between them; and occasionally, that art should come in to dispute with nature the credit of the construction of this *via infernale*, a bridge formed of rough logs, of all sizes and forms, is thrown over a deep swamp of black mud. Thus we came plunging into holes, and brought up by stumps, at the rate of two miles an hour, in the hottest day there has been this summer. Besides all this, we have the delightful prospect of returning by this road on Monday. Governor Tallmadge, who, with his daughter, has been a fellow-sufferer in another wagon, kindly insisted upon our becoming his guests at his log-cabin three miles from Fond-du-Lac, and here we hope (if the mosquitoes will let us) to sleep away the fatigue and soreness of our hard day's journey.

On Lake
Huron.JULY 17. — Our misfortunes are not yet ended. We were dining at the St. Marie's Hotel, when news was brought that the steamboat, with all our baggage on board, had started fifteen minutes before her time. We rushed down to the wharf and made signals to her. To our great joy she laid by; we put off in a small boat, were nearly run down, were hauled on board at the risk of our lives, and thus ends the adventures of Sault Ste. Marie. We are now on Lake Huron, steaming down to Detroit, almost home, — only about twelve hundred miles to go.

JULY 19. — Detroit is a busy, active city of twelve or fifteen thousand inhabitants, with wide streets, handsome shops, and plenty of fine churches.

On Lake Erie.

JULY 20. — A fine day, but very hot. At five o'clock this morning we came to Cleveland, in the State of Ohio, about half-way between Detroit and Buffalo. This is a pretty town, with a good show of business, many fine private buildings, displaying a great deal of taste and neatness.

At Buffalo.

JULY 21. — I find it exceedingly difficult to call to my recollection the city of Buffalo as I formerly knew it. Rows of warehouses occupy ground which was then vacant, and corn-fields and gardens have made way for streets of brick houses. The basin and harbour are so obstructed with steamboats and lake crafts that hours are consumed in the ingress and egress.

Niagara.

JULY 23. — I went to bed at the Falls last night at an early hour, fatigued with my day's exercise, and labouring under an indisposition of several days' standing, which made me less able to stand the fatigue. After a restless night I arose this morning very early, and while sitting at my window, from which I had a fine view of the rapids on the American side, the morning sun arose clear, bright, and glorious, lighting up the agitated waters, which, foaming and tossing about in fantastic forms, rushed with the speed and fury of a wild horse on the prairies to the awful brink of its grand descent into the whirlpool below. It seemed like a sea of melted silver casting out myriads of sparkling jewels to meet the sunbeams' early embraces; languid and faint, I gazed with awe and admiration, and felt how insignificant an object I was in this glorious pageant of Divine power.

JULY 25. — On my arrival at Buffalo I found a letter from my friend Mr. Granger, of Canandaigua, inviting us, in the kindest and most pressing manner, to pass a day or two at his noble mansion. This chimed in so well with our arrangements, and the promise it held out of an agreeable resting-place, induced us to accept the invitation without hesitation, and I wrote to that effect previous to our hasty visit to Niagara.

Canandaigua.

Canandaigua is widely different from the youthful towns of the West, where the people do not find time to live as they might; taste is troublesome, and comfort costs time; eating dinner interferes with some go-ahead operations, and shutting the door requires the use of hinges and locks. Here, from the princely residence of Mr. Grieg to the house of the industrious mechanic, many of those items are seen which collectively, according to their several conditions, make up the enjoyments of life. We had Mr. Mark H. Sibley at dinner yesterday, and Mr. and Mrs. Grieg on their return from Rochester passed the evening with us, and Mr. Wood, the antiquarian and philanthropist, came after dinner. I am very sick. My friend Granger's hospitality is thrown away.

JULY 12. — We have been from home seven weeks, travelled, according to my account, three thousand nine hundred and sixty-seven miles; seen everything for the first time, met with many distinguished persons, and received everywhere marks of kindness and respect, ever to be gratefully remembered. We have accomplished everything we undertook, by the plan laid down, and all has gone well, excepting my indisposition, under which I have laboured for the last three or four weeks. I have not permitted it to interrupt my travelling, but I return not half the man I went forth.

At Home.

July 31. — Accidents, disastrous and generally fatal, are of almost daily occurrence in this country of rapid progress and reckless management. There may be a hope that these evils may be remedied in part by greater prudence, resulting from more experience in the use of that dreadful agent, steam, and the machinery used in its operations; but the accidents occasioned by racing call for the remedies of strong laws, rigidly enforced, and public opinion undeviatingly directed.

Conquest
of Peru.

August 4. — I found on my table, on my return from the West, a copy of Mr. Prescott's new work, "The Conquest of Peru," — a presentation copy from the accomplished and amiable author. I anticipate a treat in reading it. "I roll it like a sweet morsel under my tongue," and shall reserve the gratification until I get to Rockaway, where, from the preparations going on around me, we are destined to be very soon. Prescott has established his claim to rank as *the* historian of the United States; and good taste and discriminating criticism, now and in all future time, will not hesitate to assign him an exalted place among the most distinguished historians of Europe of former or contemporaneous times.

Rockaway, Aug. 6. — Sick and sorrowful, I am trying a new experiment. Rockaway air and bathing may do that for me which the Franciscan treatment has failed to accomplish. It may enable my stomach to retain some food, and restore in some degree my exhausted strength. Rockaway has not failed hitherto. I will grapple with the enemy; but, alas! I have no *stomach* for the contest.

Death of Mr.
Stuyvesant.

August 18. — The papers brought down from the city contain the intelligence, received by the magnetic telegraph, of the death of Mr. Peter G. Stuyvesant, which occurred on Monday last at Niagara. Mr. Stuyvesant was a grandson of Governor Stuyvesant, and inherited a large share of his immense estate. He has no children. The particulars of his will are as follows: To Hamilton Fish, Gerard Stuyvesant, and the son of Mr. Rutherford, who married his ward, Miss Chanler, half a million each, the boy to take the testator's name. To his widow, $12,000 a year, with the house and furniture; the residue of the estate to be divided among his other nephews and nieces, which is estimated to produce $100,000 each. How much this gentleman's son lost by never having been born !

SEPTEMBER 13.—A beautiful piece of statuary, the work of Hiram Powers, the celebrated American sculptor at Rome, is now being exhibited at the National Academy, and attracts crowds of visitors from morning to night. And so it ought, for it is admirable. I have no rule by which to estimate the merit, or appreciate the faultless beauty, of this statue which could guide me in placing it below the Venus de Medici. I have no personal acquaintance with Powers, nor had I with Praxiteles; but I am not willing to undervalue my countryman because he was not born so soon as the other gentleman of the chisel. I certainly never saw anything more lovely.

The Greek Slave.

SEPTEMBER 14.—The anxiety which has prevailed for several days past to learn the progress of this glorious, but dreadful, war is at length gratified, if gratification it can be called to read accounts of the fiercest battles and shedding of blood which have ever occurred on this continent.

Battle of Mexico.

General Scott has gained a great victory under the walls of Mexico. The modern Cortez wades through Mexican blood to conquer again the ancient city and subjugate anew the unhappy descendants of the Montezumas. He has gained a great victory, but with the loss of a thousand of his own army, poorly compensated for by that of five thousand of the enemy. He attacked the Mexicans under Santa Anna, who were strongly entrenched and well provided with artillery and ammunition, and whose numbers are stated at from twenty to thirty-two thousand, with a force of seven thousand, and drove them in with horrid slaughter. This battle was fought on the 19th and 20th of August, during an uninterrupted and drenching rain. The details are sickening. Scott and

Worth have added new, but blood-stained, laurels to their already over-burdened brows. Their brothers in arms have well sustained their former reputation, and the men fought like tigers ; but of their number enough have been killed and wounded to satisfy the most unreasonable admirers of this unrighteous war. The names of the officers whose blood now stains the approaches to the city, the object of our cupidity and rapacity, are published in detail, and I distinguish many whose fate will cause silent tears to fall from the eyes of loving mothers and loud curses from philanthropists and patriots.

SEPTEMBER 25. — The venerable, amiable old man could not make out his century. The pale light of the lamp went out, the worn-out machinery ceased to move, the attenuated cord no longer retained its hold, and the old man of ninety-five years left this day the generation of men, amongst whom age had made him a stranger. A man in the prime of life at the Declaration of Independence, he fought the battles of his country, and exchanging, at the termination of the glorious struggle, his continental uniform for the habiliments of a life of peace, witnessed the rise and progress of New York from a handful to an armful ; from a little clump of ill-built tenements of which Wall and Broad streets were the limits, to the magnificent capital of the Empire State ; from twenty thousand to four hundred thousand inhabitants.

Death of Major Popham.

SEPTEMBER 28. — It is to be hoped that the senseless clamour of ignorant fools in Congress, who have been placed by constituents as ignorant as themselves in a situation where folly becomes dangerous, and ignorance is supported by power, will now cease to be employed against the noble institution, the military academy of West Point. The utility of this establishment has been proved to the full extent of the favourable predictions of its friends, and the utter overthrow of the disparaging prognostications of its enemies. The students of West Point have been foremost in the career of glory in the Mexican war, in

West Point.

the front of the battle, reckless of danger, adding to the most chivalric bravery the benefit of military science acquired at this excellent national school. These lads, in gathering a rich harvest of renown for themselves, have effectually succeeded in rescuing the fountain, from which their science and practice were derived, from the poisonous effusion of the malice and prejudice of the Allens and others, worthy representatives in Congress of an ignorant and prejudiced constituency. Among our New York boys, whom West Point has sent out as samples to the wars, are Hamilton (John C. Hamilton's son), Graham (son of J. Lorimer Graham), Herman Thorn's son, all of whom were wounded in the battles of Mexico; Chandler, son of General Chandler, and Clay, whose testimony was sealed with their life's blood; all have done their duty, and the nation may be proud of the seminary in which they were taught.

OCTOBER 8. — How the cavernous eyes of Webster must have looked out from under the heavy archway of his expansive brows, when, in his late speech at Springfield, in which he laid open with a bold hand the secret springs and corrupt motives which produced the Mexican war, he used, with satirical bitterness, the following expression. Speaking of the mysterious policy of Mr. Polk, in furnishing to Santa Anna a safe-conduct from Cuba, his place of exile, to his Government of Mexico, the Massachusetts senator remarked, " That the President must be gratified to know that in the subsequent battles, which have cost so much blood and treasure, the commanding general on both sides was of his own choosing."

OCTOBER 18. — The meeting of the convention has

Episcopal Convention. filled the city with Episcopal clergymen, and our pulpits with able preachers, very much, I dare say, to the relief of the regular officiators, whose new sermons (if they have any) may be laid aside for future use. I heard, with great pleasure, two bishops yesterday, — Bishop McCoskry, of Michigan, preached, in the morning, in Trinity, and Bishop Jones, in the evening, in the Church of the Ascension, to crowded congregations.

One may know these reverend visitors in the streets by their good-looking, complacent, self-satisfied countenances, well-brushed black coats and white neck-cloths, and gentlemanly, dignified deportment. Some of them may be seen with neat little wives hanging on their arms, well dressed, each with a little satin bonnet, a little inclining to be gay; and many a wistful glance is cast at Beck's, and Seaman & Muir's, and Rogers' windows, and at Stewart's palace of haberdashery, with a suppressed sigh of regret that the doctor's stipend is so small. It may be a subject of doubt whether this autumnal visit to New York will make these worthy folk feel better during the winter.

OCTOBER 22. — I dined yesterday with Mr. Bradish, the first dinner-party at which I have been since my return from the West. The temptation was too great to be resisted, and I went. Weak as I am, I enjoyed myself exceedingly. Our party consisted of Mr. and Mrs. Bradish and Miss Hart; Bishop Potter, of Pennsylvania; Rev. Dr. Taylor, Grace Church; Professor Agassiz, lately of France, who has been appointed Professor of Natural History on the Lawrence foundation of Harvard College; Mr. Joseph R. Ingersoll, Philadelphia; Colonel Memminger, Charleston, S.C.; Mr. Hamilton Fish, John A. King, Samuel B. Ruggles, H. Van Rensselaer, John C. Hamilton, and myself.

OCTOBER 25. — I am sixty-seven years of age. My
My Birthday. mind, thanks to my Heavenly Father, is unimpaired, as
I am still encouraged to hope; but I am weak in body, and labouring still under the effects of the protracted illness which I brought home with me last summer from the West. My flesh has departed, but my spirit remains; my knees tremble, but my heart is stout; as I said, the other day, in a letter to Mr. Wood, of Canandaigua, who inquired kindly about my health, "I am weak as the argument of an unfeed lawyer, thin as the fourth day's soup of a shin of beef, and cross as a disappointed barnburner." I think, however, I shall get up again; but, if it shall be otherwise ordered by my Divine Master, I trust I shall have resignation, faith,

and hope to enable me to say, in sincerity of heart and fulness of conviction, " Thy will be done."

Capture of
Mexico. General Scott entered Mexico on the 14th of September, after a series of battles, in which the greatest gallantry was displayed by the Americans, and in which the commander and his officers covered themselves with glory ; but the conquest was obtained at an awful expense of American blood. These victories and the occupations of the city cost three thousand men, killed and wounded, leaving six or seven thousand men to sustain themselves in a conquered city of two hundred thousand exasperated, desperate Mexicans.

The particulars of the bloody engagements which preceded the capture of Mexico, the resignation of General Santa Anna, the astonishing achievements of Scott, Worth, Quitman, Persifor Smith, Pillow, Twiggs, and the whole band of heroes, are all recorded in a paper of Saturday, which I have preserved. Scott's march to Mexico with his handful of men, through an unknown country filled with infuriated bands of armed guerillas, and the occupation of the city by the American forces, is an event equal to the most brilliant recorded in history. But, alas ! how dearly has this glory been purchased ! The list of killed and wounded is also contained in this paper. The best blood in the country has been shed. Worth lost eighteen hundred men. Thorn's gallant son has been wounded again ; severely this time. Thomas Morris's young son was killed ; Major Twiggs fell gallantly fighting ; but the melancholy record would occupy too much space in my journal. National glory is attained at the expense of individual distress ; the tears of the survivors may not blot out the record, but it will be sadly defaced. Colonel McIntosh and Col. Martin Scott, two of Worth's brigade, were killed in the sanguinary charge of the 8th ; the former died of his wounds on the 24th. Bravest among the brave, the loss of such men cannot be compensated by the conquest of the whole country we are fighting for. Cannot Polk, and Buchanan, and Marcy be prevailed upon to go and take a hand in the beautiful game they are making others play?

OCTOBER 29. — In the list of noble young fellows whose gallant conduct, indomitable bravery, and military accomplishments in the Mexican war redound to the glory of West Point, their military alma-mater, there are several New York boys, sons of our friends and associates, who, if they ever get back, will come to their homes covered with glory, jewels in our city's treasury, the pride of their parents and the children of the Republic. These are the fruits of a West Point education. Shame on the malignant demagogues who have laboured to overthrow such an institution ! The following are foremost in the list of young heroes, whom we claim as our own : —

New York Boys.

Schuyler Hamilton, son of John C. Hamilton, grandson of General Schuyler and Alexander Hamilton, is an aide of General Scott. With such blood in his veins, and such a name, he could not fail to acquit himself with honour. Nobly has he sustained them. He was badly wounded in a dangerous reconnaissance, and was rescued by Lieutenant Graham, son of Mr. S. Lorimer Graham, another of our boys who has signalized himself.

Lieutenant Thorn, son of Col. Herman Thorn, brave as the bravest, is aide to Colonel Garland. Twice he has been wounded, and was always found in the thickest of the fight.

Lieutenant Alfred Gibbs, of the Rifles, was wounded in the desperate affair of the 8th of September, at the storming of Molino-del-Rey. Ordered to the hospital, he refused to go, but was carried on the back of a soldier, and entered the city in the midst of the conquering army. This officer, son of Col. George Gibbs and grandson of Oliver Wolcott, is the author of several very interesting letters which have been published on the subject of the Mexican war.

Lieutenant Morris, the gallant son of Thomas Morris, and grandson of Robert Morris, the great financier of the Revolution, and friend of Washington, equally brave, was less fortunate than his

young associates in arms.   He, too, was wounded in the attack on
" Kings-Mill," on the 8th of September.   He was shot in the leg,
from which wound a hemorrhage ensued, and he died on the 13th,
without entering " the halls of Montezuma."   Alas ! will his gallant
deeds and death of glory assuage the grief of his parents, or dry
the tears of his sisters?   These are the trophies of West Point !
Shall it not be supported?

NOVEMBER 4. — Henry Wheaton, formerly of this city, who has
been American minister in foreign courts for the last twenty years,
has, since his recent return, been appointed lecturer on Civil Law
and the Law of Nations in Harvard University.

I dined on Tuesday with Mr. Stebbins, one of the nabobs of the
Fifth avenue.   He is a partner of Mr. Jaudon, lives in an elegant
house, and gives good dinners.   The following was the party,
besides the host, the hostess, and Miss Stebbins: Moses H. Grinnell, Simeon Draper, Francis Griffin, Mr. Anderson, Mr. De
Launay, John Schermerhorn, Moses B. Taylor, Mr. Jaudon, Mr.
Brigham, R. M. Blatchford, George Curtis, and myself.

NOVEMBER 8. — I have refrained of late from keeping a record
of railroad and steamboat accidents.   I never take up a paper that
does not contain accounts of loss of life, dreadful mutilation of
limbs, and destruction of property, with which these reckless,
dangerous, murderous modes of locomotion are attended.   The
detail of loss of life by boiler-bursting, collisions, and snakesheads
is as regular a concomitant of the breakfast-table as black tea and
smoked beef.

NOVEMBER 13. — Grinnell, Minturn, & Co. are
building a fine packet of one thousand two hundred
tons, to go on their Liverpool line.   I am delighted to
learn that she is to bear the honoured name of " Winfield Scott,"
— a compliment creditable to her respected owner as it is well-
merited by the commander-in-chief of the American army.

This noble ship will bear on her bows the name and image of
a man whom the history of our country will place on its highest

and brightest page ; a merited distinction, of which party spirit, ignorance, and jealousy have in vain conspired to deprive him. A soldier accomplished in the art, and chivalric in the practice of war, the echoes of our country have rung with the name of Zachary Taylor. He · well deserves his laurels ; but I say that Winfield Scott is " a better " as well as " an older soldier." The laurels that budded upon the warrior's youthful brow at Chippewa have preserved their freshness at all times and under every climate. Untarnished by the chilling blasts of the northern lakes, or the scorching rays of southern suns, they assimilate with equal grace and appropriateness with the gray hairs of mature age. At all times, " in season and out of season," in the negotiations of peace as in the strife of war, in the closet as in the field, General Scott has stood ready to serve his country, to do all that was required of him, and to do it well, — a man of letters and a gentleman in the best sense of the term ; prone to vanity there is no denying, but having much to be vain of. He does not write as well as he fights ; but he seems to value the triumphs of the pen more than those of the sword, and thus, in seeking to gain advantage by the former weapon, he has on some occasions committed himself to opponents less able, but more artful, than himself, and the fox has seen with satisfaction the lion encompass himself in the toils which he could not have cast over him ; so it was in his late correspondence with the war department. He was right in principle, just in feeling, correct in judgment ; but, unfortunately, deficient in taste. He aimed to out-write his adversaries, and made his pen so sharp that it bespattered the ink back on himself. But all is right now. The people have had their laugh at the " hasty plate of soup ;" but the masterly capture of la Vera Cruz, the triumphal march, with forces greatly inferior to those of his enemy, over a hostile and till then unknown country of three hundred miles, and the gallant achievements which resulted in the conquest of the Mexican capital by the modern Cortez, will entitle him to the proud appellation of " Marshal Turenne," when the cause of Christopher

Hughes's invidious application of the term shall have been forgotten, or perhaps remembered with regret only by its witty author.

Chancellor
Kent.

NOVEMBER 15. — "No more study for me," said this great and good man the other day; and I fear the bright light of his intellect is very soon to be removed from the sphere which it has irradiated. I was so unwell yesterday that I remained at home until evening, when I went to pay my accustomed visit to Union place. The accounts are unfavourable, the lamp burns dimly, the sun is nearly set.

Thanksgiving.

NOVEMBER 25. — On this day the incense of prayer and thanksgiving ascends from the altars of twenty-one of these United States, and the District of Columbia in addition, to the Almighty Giver of all good things, for the blessings, national and individual, which we enjoy. This simultaneous action of so many States presents an interesting spectacle to the minds of reflecting men, — a nation on its knees, confessing its obligations and acknowledging its dependence upon Divine goodness and mercy. No matter what proportion of the mass may be insincere, or what may have been the motives of a part of the rulers who appointed this religious festival; it is a good and wise measure, beautiful and interesting, and derives efficacy from the sanction of the civil authority. The people are placed in the right track; it is their own fault, and they are answerable, if they do not walk in it. No nation ever had more causes for thanksgiving. Besides the innumerable positive blessings of our position, our exception from two of the great calamities of human life, pestilence and famine, is a prominent cause of gratitude; if the third, the sword, cannot be added, we have ourselves alone to thank for it.

Meeting of
Congress.

DECEMBER 7. — The Thirtieth Congress met yesterday. The state of parties is so close that the members themselves were ignorant of their own strength, so that the wish to be in time was unexampled. The whole Western world, from Lake Superior to the Rio Grande (Mr. Polk says that is the boundary); from the turbid waters of the upper Missouri (nay, from the mouth of the Columbia) to the engulfment of the St. Johns, sent their three hundred representatives to the common centre. Hotels and boarding-houses were filled as by a mighty rushing stream, and black waiters grinned at the prospect of undeserved quarter-dollars. Two hundred and twenty members of the House of Representatives answered to their names on the call of the roll at twelve o'clock, and were sworn in by Mr. French, clerk of the last Congress.

Robert C. Winthrop, of Massachusetts, a fine fellow and a true Whig, was elected Speaker, on the third ballot, by a majority of one vote. The rival candidates for the clerkship (which seems to be a more exciting bone of contention even than Speaker) are French, the old clerk of the Loco-focos, and Campbell, Whig. The House adjourned without filling this office. The President's message was not sent in.

DECEMBER 13.—The bright light which illumined the paths of science and literature, cleared away the intricacies of legal jurisprudence and shed a benign lustre upon the relations of social life, was extinguished at half-past eight o'clock in the evening of Sunday, the 12th of December, 1847.

Death of James Kent.

Chancellor Kent is no more; his useful and brilliant career, which was extended in blessing to mankind to the protracted term of fourscore and four years, has come to a tranquil and peaceful termination. Dr. Francis called, about five o'clock, to inform me of his approaching dissolution. I went immediately to his residence, and formed one of the mourning group which surrounded the couch of the great and good man, and watched with painful solicitude the heaving of his last breath. I did not witness the closing scene, having returned home a short time before it took place. His death was such as every one must have desired who loved him (and all who knew him did, and none more than myself). He lay on the sofa in the library, the apartment where he laboured, studied, and wrote, and where he most enjoyed the pleasure of social intercourse with his family and friends.   How different was the scene from that which I have been accustomed to witness in this place !   The hand which formerly grasped mine laid cold and nerveless at his side; the lips, from which lessons of wisdom, interspersed with remarks of childlike simplicity, were wont to proceed, uttered no sounds; the eyes closed upon all surrounding objects, the beloved octogenarian breathing fainter and fainter, surrendered his pure spirit, unconscious of its departure.

Chancellor Kent was born on the 31st of July, 1763.   I never knew a man whom I loved and venerated more entirely.   Whilst I sat at his side I was led to reflect on the transition which I had witnessed in the course of a few minutes; the two extremes of human life were present to me.   When Dr. Francis called it rained very hard, and I sent for a carriage; before it came I went over to Mr. Russell's, to see my grandchildren, and there they were, in my arms, full of life and spirits, unconscious of anything but present enjoyment: two sparkling dew-drops, glittering in the morning sunbeams; two blossoms just expanding from the buds, and beginning to emit their early fragrance.   In a brief space of time I was called to witness the extinguishment of a lamp which had enlightened mankind for nearly a century, and to mark the withered fruit falling from the sapless bough.   "So passes man's life away, and he is gone."   Happy should we be, if at the close of such a life we might have a reasonable assurance of such a death !

DECEMBER 15.—The remains of James Kent, the man whom all men delighted to honour, were interred this afternoon, in the cemetery on the Second avenue.   The funeral procession, which embraced the members of the Bar in a body, the Common Council, with their staves of office, and countless hundreds of the most respectable citizens, proceeded to Calvary Church, where a part of the funeral service was read by the reverend pastor, Mr. Southard.   Thence the sacred ashes were conveyed to the vault of the deceased, and the final ceremonies performed.   The pall-bearers were: Chief Justice Jones, Mr. John Duer, David S. Jones, Sylvanus Miller, George Griffin, Thomas Morris, Judge Oakley, and myself.

Every demonstration of public respect has been paid to the memory of this excellent man. The Common Council met on the call of the Mayor, and passed suitable resolutions, among which was one to procure his portrait. The city standard and flags on public edifices and shipping were displayed at half-mast, the courts were all suspended, and all the obituary notices in the newspapers are highly eulogistic. The proceedings of a meeting of the New York Bar held yesterday, at which Chief Justice Jones presided, were exceedingly impressive. It seems to have been an expression of the most fervent feeling, an offering of personal affection rather than a public demonstration; and this sentiment prevailed throughout the whole proceedings. Speeches were made by Ogden Hoffman, Benjamin F. Butler, Daniel Lord, and Hugh Maxwell; eloquent, of course, proceeding from such lips, but rendered peculiarly interesting by the prevalence of the sentiment above alluded to. I have preserved the public report of these speeches as among the most beautiful specimens of funeral eloquence I have ever met with.

DECEMBER 17.—Another old friend is gone. Peter A. Mesier died suddenly, on Wednesday night, in the seventy-fifth year of his age. I attended the funeral as a pall-bearer this afternoon, from his house, No. 51 Dey street, next door to the one in which I was married, more than forty-six years ago. The funeral ceremony was performed in Trinity Church. The following were the pall-bearers: Gen. Edward W. Laight, Jonathan Goodhue, James Lee, Gen. Augustus Fleming, L. C. Hamersley, Garrit Storm, Joseph Tucker, and myself.

DECEMBER 22.—The New England Society celebrated their anniversary yesterday, by a gathering at the Tabernacle, at two o'clock, and the usual dinner at a later hour. I attended the first, and not the second, having no regular call nor complimentary invitation; and well it was for me, for the confinement to one position for nearly three hours in the Tabernacle was almost insupportable in my feeble state, and I was placed in so conspicuous a situation, directly in the eye of my friend, the orator, with Mrs. Webster, Mrs. Hall, and Mrs. Cutting directly behind, and in gossiping communion with me, that I could not make my escape. Had it been otherwise, and I had been wise enough to secure a retreat, the oration, beautiful as it was, could not have detained me. Prescott Hall was the orator. His address, bating its being a little too statistical and too long by half an hour (two hours and ten minutes), contained some splendid passages, especially a glowing and most eloquent peroration, and was read with the grace which was to be expected from J. Prescott Hall.

What strange changes have of late come over the spirit of the times! One of the standing toasts at the New England dinner was "Pius IX., Pope of Rome;" and Bishop Hughes, an invited guest, occupied the seat of honour on the right of the President, and made a speech, in which he could not avoid expressing his astonishment at finding himself in such companionship; and well might he be astonished. The sons of the Pilgrims toasting the old lady, whom their fathers complimented with the titles of "whore of Babylon," "red harlot," and such-like tender and loving appellatives! What would the Carvers and the Bradfords, the Winslows and the Winthrops, say, if they could rise from their ancient places in the "old colony," and witness their descendants toasting the Pope, for whom no better place could formerly be found in their celebration of the "Gunpowder Plot" than as one of the respectable trio of Pope, Pretender, and Devil! All Hail, a return of the days of bulls, dispensations, indulgences, and excommunications! New England toasts the Pope.

December 28. — The line of English mail steamers is to be divided, and one-half are to come to this port alternately with the Boston line. For this purpose the "Hibernia" arrived here from

Boston this morning, to take her place, and sail hence on Saturday. A meeting of merchants was held to-day at the Exchange, at which Mr. George Griswold presided, with James Brown, Anson G. Phelps, Jonathan Goodhue, Robert B. Minturn, and William Whitlock as vice-presidents, for the purpose of giving a welcome to Captain Ryrie, the commander of the " Hibernia."

1848.

ON the first day of January, one thousand eight hundred and forty-eight, with the opening of a new year, I am permitted to open a new volume of my humble annals. I pray that the gloomy aspect of things out of doors, the thick, foggy air overhead, and the muddy ways underfoot, may not be prophetic of national or individual calamity; but that bright skies and genial sunshine may soon dispel the clouds of the moral, as it soon will those of the natural, atmosphere.

The year which has just passed away, and is laid by on the shelf of time, like a cast-off garment to feed the moth of tradition, has been productive of events of startling moment and fearful importance, here and elsewhere. Our country is engaged in a most unrighteous war, waged from motives corrupt and sinister, with a neighbouring Republic, — a war in which the gallant achievements of our officers and men have shone conspicuously, but in which the blood of our countrymen has enriched the fields of Mexico, and in which untold millions of the nation's treasure has been expended, and is yet to be expended, in fighting the battles of a bastard branch which in an evil hour was admitted into the American family. Individual prosperity has increased in this part of the Union; men have grown rich in supplying the wants of the starving population of Ireland; palaces have been erected out of the freights of nine shillings sterling for flour; and the extravagance and love of show, to which our people are prone, has had ample scope in the successful mercantile operations of the year. These bright days, however, have in a measure passed away, and there is some danger that some among us may wish during the year 1848 that they had not spent so much money in 1847.

In Europe the leading events have been the dreadful state of famine and destitution, crime and discontent, in Ireland ; a civil war in the cantons of Switzerland, waged against Jesuitical influence ; a new Pope, who is trying very hard to introduce salutary reforms in the government of the Papal See, and striving to make his subjects happy. In our own country a change has taken place in the state of parties. The Whigs have recovered their ascendency in the public councils ; there is a Whig Speaker and a small majority of Whigs. in the House of Representatives ; the Governor, and other State officers, with a large majority of both Houses of the Legislature, are Whigs, as are also the Mayor and both branches of the Common Council of the city ; so, if things go wrong, we must take the blame.

As for myself, for the last six months I have been struggling against the effects of indisposition contracted during my Western tour, which has taken away my strength, and reduced my flesh by the amount of forty pounds. Of this disease I am not relieved, but am better. I have borne up well under the affliction, and have hopes that, with the blessing of God, I may yet overcome it. But, let the event be what it may, I hope to be willing to leave the issue in the hands of the Almighty Author of my existence, and to say, with hope and confidence, and with a grateful acknowledgment of the blessings heretofore derived from that beneficent source, " Thy will be done." My affairs, to say the best of them, are not improved since last year, nor are they worse. I am deeply in debt ; but I have the means to pay all, and have thus far met every engagement with undeviating punctuality. Let those who are better off say as much.

JANUARY 12.— I am feeble, and scarcely able to go abroad ; but I am not permitted to stay at home. The warm fire of my domestic hearth burns not for me. I attended yesterday, at five o'clock, a meeting of the Trustees of Columbia College, and in the evening presided at the annual meeting of the Mercantile Library. This duty, always gratifying to me, was peculiarly so on this occasion, from the kind expression of feeling with which I was greeted.

General
Scott.

JANUARY 13. — It appears to be a "fixed fact" that the great captain, General Scott, has been recalled from his command in Mexico. The ostensible object of this disastrous measure is probably to give the general an opportunity to make good the charges on which the arrest of Generals Worth and Pillow and Colonel Duncan was ordered (as I think in an evil hour). These officers are also ordered home, to meet the court-martial which must be called to investigate the charges. But it is more likely that the administration is glad of an excuse for preventing a further accumulation of laurels on the brow of the able and gallant commander-in-chief, for his glory forms a contrast rather unfavourable to their claims upon the people's favour. They hate him, and are glad to get rid of him. What a pity that he should, by his own hasty act, have furnished them the means of carrying out their hostility!

General Scott has a claim ten times stronger upon the gratitude and favour of the American people for services rendered to the country than General Taylor; and yet the latter chieftain, by the exercise of more discretion, and manners more popular, would beat the hero of Chippewa, of Vera Cruz and Mexico, ten to one, in a contest for the Presidency. Thus it is in this "land of freedom;" and such things prove the truth of the maxim that "republics are ungrateful." The Duke of Wellington, with no better claims upon his country's liberality than our Scott, bends under the weight of merited rewards; jewelled stars and heraldic orders cover his breast; accumulating titles are emblazoned upon his escutcheon, and domains and other substantial endowments attest a sense of the value of his services; whilst our ripe and accomplished soldier (of whom I am informed that the "great Duke" has lately said, the campaign which commenced with the taking of Vera Cruz and terminated with the military occupation of the Mexican capital, was one of the most splendid achievements of modern warfare) is recalled to be laid upon the shelf, and obtain his diurnal "plate of soup" from the inadequate pittance of a government bureau.

FEBRUARY 8. — I dined to-day with Mr. Blatchford, at the Astor House, where his family is boarding during the winter season. The dinner (as is always the case at that house) was excellent. The controversy on the Clay and Taylor question waxes somewhat warm. In that company I was almost alone for Clay, and had to contend with Webb, Hall, and Grinnell, with occasionally a side-cut from George Curtis; but they know no more about public opinion in New York than they do of the secrets of the Grand Seignior's seraglio. In reply to Colonel Webb, I read the letter which I had just written to Charles King; and, on the whole, sustained myself tolerably well against the professed friends, but secret enemies, of Henry Clay. Our party consisted of R. M. Blatchford, J. P. Hall, John Ward, Paul Spofford, T. Tileston, M. H. Grinnell, Daniel Fearing, J. W. Webb, R. L. Colt, George Curtis, C. H. Russell, M. Morgan, Stebbins, and myself; and that noble Whig and fine fellow, George Evans, of Maine, whose loss in the Senate all good men deplore.

FEBRUARY 15. — Died on Saturday, the 12th, at his residence, Kattskill, Thomas Cole. The death of this eminent artist, in the prime of life and the meridian of his fame as a landscape painter, is a loss to the arts and a severe affliction to his friends, for both suffer equally from the melancholy deprivation. I knew poor Cole from the first day he came here from Philadelphia, — a fine young fellow, full of undying ardour in the pursuit of knowledge, a lover of nature, with a conscious ability for the portraiture of her features. Modest and unassuming, he was unacquainted with the artistical quality of humbug, and, alas! he was not then the fashion. If genius did not sometimes overcome discouragement, here was a case in which it might have despaired. When Cole came to New York he brought with him two pictures, original views of the *Kaaters Kill* or Kattskill mountains, and the *Still-Lake* which forms its head-waters, with all the beautiful scenery of that romantic region, taken on the spot. Days were devoted to rambling, sketching, and the results successfully transferred to the canvas: the glowing impressions of a warm imagination, the rich fruits of an artist's study, the children of prolific genius; and these pictures, the labour of many weary days, taken faithfully and with talent from one of the most beautiful repositories of nature's riches, the artist offered for sale repeatedly, in Philadelphia, for ten dollars each, without finding a purchaser; for he was not then the fashion. These pictures are now mine; they adorn the wall of my back parlour.

Cole came here, poor, friendless, and, worse than all, modest. He was fortunate enough, however, to attract the notice of Colonel Trumbull and William Dunlap, two artists, now both deceased, whose favourable opinion was of great value, and was freely bestowed. They bought, each of them, one of the pictures in question for $25. I was so much pleased with them that I succeeded in getting the two for $125, and now that my friend, whose recent death is so deeply deplored, has emerged from the clouds of neglect and shone out in all the brightness of fashionable popularity, it is not an extravagant surmise that some of the Philadelphia *dilettanti*, who could not formerly discover $10 worth of merit in these early productions of the artist, would now be glad to buy, at a cost of $600 or $800, two of the works of his pencil, of no greater merit than mine. The late Mr. Samuel Ward gave him $2,500 for a series of four beautiful pictures, called "The Guardian Angel," and the late Mr. Luman Reed, a price nearly equal for another series of four, which he styled the "March of Empire." Poor Cole! He struggled against every discouragement to reach the top of the hill, but was not long permitted to enjoy his elevated station.

FEBRUARY 24. — Poor Mr. Webster! My heart bleeds
Mr. Webster. for him. A few weeks ago his only daughter, Mrs.
Appleton, died of consumption, suddenly contracted and fatally hasty in its progress; and now, himself in feeble health, he has just received the news of his son Edward's death in Mexico, where he commanded a company in a regiment of Massachusetts Volunteers. He died of one of those diseases of the climate which

there is reason to fear will be the passport to a stranger's grave for many a young American. I passed a few happy days, the summer before last, at Marshfield, with these two young persons, whose premature deaths will wring their parents' hearts, and bring a sympathizing tear into the eye of many a friend. Edward Webster had a strong desire for military distinction, and would probably have made a distinguished officer. He was taken ill last summer, obtained leave of absence, and came home ; whence he returned to Mexico, restored to health, as he believed, but only to add another victim to a destroying climate.

Death of
Mr. Adams.

John Quincy Adams is no more. Full of age and honours, the termination of his eventful career accorded with the character of its progress. He died, as he must have wished to die, breathing his last in the capitol, stricken down by the angel of death on the field of his civil glory, — employed in the service of the people, in the people's Senate house, standing by the Constitution at the side of its altar, and administering in the temple of liberty the rites which he had assisted in establishing.

At twenty minutes past one o'clock, on Monday, the 21st, Mr. Adams, being in his seat in the House of Representatives (from which he was never absent during its session), attempted to rise (as was supposed, to speak), but sank back upon his seat and fell upon his side. Those nearest caught him in their arms. Mr. Grinnell bathed his temples with ice-water, when he rallied for an instant. The House immediately adjourned, in the utmost consternation, as did the Senate, when informed of the melancholy event. His last words were characterized by that concise eloquence for which he was remarkable : " *This is the last of earth ; I am content.*" Dr. Fries of Ohio, a member, raised him in his arms and bore him to the Speaker's room, where he lay, with occasional indications of consciousness, until last evening, a few minutes before seven o'clock, when he breathed his last. The intelligence of his death came to Albany by the telegraph.

Thus has " a great man fallen in Israel," — in many respects the most wonderful man of the age ; certainly the greatest in the United States, — perfect in knowledge, but deficient in practical results. As a statesman, he was pure and incorruptible, but too irascible to lead men's judgment.   They admired him, and all voices were hushed when he arose to speak, because they were sure of being instructed by the words he was about to utter; but he made no converts to his opinions, and when President his desire to avoid party influence lost him all the favour of all parties.   In matters of history, tradition, statistics, authorities, and practice he was the oracle of the House, of which he was at the time of his decease a member.   With an unfailing memory, rendered stronger by cultivation, he was never mistaken ; none disputed his authority.   Every circumstance of his long life was " penned down " at the moment of its occurrence ; every written communication, even to the minute of a dinner invitation, was carefully preserved, and nothing passed uncopied from his pen.   He " talked like a book " on all subjects. Equal to the highest, the planetary system was not above his grasp. Familiar with the lowest, he could explain the mysteries of a mousetrap.

I listened once, at my own table, with a delight which I shall never forget, to his dissertation on the writings of Shakespeare, and an analysis of the character of Hamlet,— the most beautiful creation (he called it) of the human imagination.   At my request he afterward sent me a synopsis of the latter part of this delightful conversation ; a paper which has always been a treasure to me, and which will be more precious now that its illustrious author is no more.   I listened once, with Mr. Webster, for an hour, at Mr. Adams's breakfast-table in Washington, to a disquisition on the subject of *dancing girls ;* from those who danced before the ark and the daughter of Jairus, whose premature appearance caused so melancholy a termination to her graceful movements in the dance, through the fascinating exhibition of the odalisques of the harem down to the present times of Fanny Ellsler and Taliogni.   He was ignorant on no subject, and could enlighten and instruct on all ; he loved to talk, and was pleased with good listeners. Vain, no doubt, and not entirely free from prejudices, but preserving his mental faculties to the last. His sudden death, even at the advanced age of eighty years, to which he arrived in July last, will be acutely felt and deeply deplored by those who have habitually enjoyed the refreshing streams which flowed from the copious fountains of his diversified knowledge.

Mr. Adams's name will be recorded on the brightest page of American history, as statesman, diplomatist, philosopher, orator, author, and, above all, Christian. The events of his life may be thus briefly enumerated : John Quincy Adams was born in 1767. In 1781 he was private secretary to Francis Dana, minister to Russia. In 1794 he was appointed, by Washington, Minister to the Netherlands. In 1803 he was senator in Congress from Massachusetts. He resigned in 1808, and the next year was sent by Madison as Minister to Russia, where he remained, until, with Henry Clay, James A. Bayard, and Albert Gallatin, he negotiated the treaty of Ghent in 1814, and was sent as Minister to England. He was recalled in 1817 to take the place of Secretary of State under Mr. Monroe. He succeeded Mr. Monroe as President of the United States in 1825. In 1829, having completed his term, he retired, for the first time in thirty-six years, to private life. In 1831 he was returned to Congress from his native district, which he continued to represent uninterruptedly to the day of his death.

FEBRUARY 29.—The subscribers, members of the Racket-Court, gave a ball and supper this evening to the ladies, and there has been nothing more *recherché*, nothing better arranged, and nothing attended with more complete success, since the last leap-year. I attended during the whole evening, first with Mrs. Fearing, my wife, and daughter, to see the preparations, and afterward in attendance upon Miss Sarah Duer and my wife. There were about three hundred subscribers, at $10 each, and the whole money was expended. The Racket Court,

The Racket-Court.

one hundred and twenty feet by forty, was converted into a danc-
ing-saloon, fitted up and ornamented in the most perfect taste, in
the form of a tent, with three thousand six hundred yards of
muslin, divided into diamonds by strips of gold galloon, and interspersed with artificial flowers. The orchestra, with thirty-five performers, was placed on the north side; the supper-table was laid
out in the bowling-alley, where the most ample provision was made
for the epicures and lookers-on. Pretty girls, with pink dresses,
were attended by beaux with black mustaches and white vests.
All the other rooms in this spacious edifice were decorated and
laid open for the pleased and happy company; the gallery, which
looked down upon the dancers, was filled with charming girls and
agreeable cavaliers, forming, on this occasion at least, from their
relative situation, the *upper crust* of society. The affair went off
splendidly, and hundreds of worthy people, employed in the
getting-up, have been made to rejoice in what is called, by some
fastidious persons, the extravagance of fashionable life. There was
a large committee of arrangements, and the *fête* was sanctioned by
a committee of ladies, styled lady-patronesses, of which my wife
was one. This dignified body, who did little to earn their honours,
consisted of the following: Mrs. Philip Hone, Mrs. D. C. Colden,
Mrs. George Barclay, Mrs. A. le Barbier, Mrs. Robert Emmet,
Mrs. H. C. de Rham, Mrs. John A. Stevens, Mrs. J. W. Schmidt,
Mrs. Henry Parish, Mrs. J. Prescott Hall.

MARCH 7. — This was the day appointed for the
arrival of Mr. Clay from Philadelphia, on a visit to
New York, as the guest of the Mayor and the Corporation. The new steamer, "Cornelius Vanderbilt," which was
gratuitously furnished by her owner and namesake, left town at
nine o'clock, with the committee and members of the Common
Council and a large company of invited guests, which latter honour
I was compelled to decline. But I accompanied the Mayor to
Castle Garden, which was filled on our arrival with a mass of men,
equal in numbers and general good appearance to the multitude

which assembled in the same place, on the recent occasion of the great Clay Whig meeting. The boat arrived precisely at the appointed time, and Mr. Clay and his *cortège* mounted the stage at two o'clock. Alderman Franklin, chairman of the joint committee of arrangements, then surrendered the illustrious visitor to the Mayor, who gave him a warm reception and hearty welcome, to which Mr. Clay replied, in one of the most touching and best-imagined little speeches I ever heard him make.

At the close of his speech he adverted to the painful and impressive contrast presented by the rejoicing, the shouting, the excitement of which he was the honoured object, and the mournful obsequies of the next day, in which our citizens were preparing to do honour to the remains of the truly great man who had just finished a long life of public services in highly honourable stations. Here now were assembled, in one place, the three principal negotiators of the treaty of Ghent (the other two, Messrs. Bayard and Russell being no longer living). Of these three the venerable Albert Gallatin is one of our fellow-citizens, honoured in old age. Henry Clay was addressing us, and the mortal remains of the third we were to speed, the next day, on its mournful transit to the tomb of his fathers.

MARCH 8. — The day of joyful gratulation and loud shouting is passed ; the recipient of the people's honours is left to undergo the pains of oppressive hospitality ; and, instead of songs of triumph for a great man living, our city has sent up the mournful dirge for a great man departed. The body of John Quincy Adams arrived at the Battery, from Philadelphia, at three o'clock, where it was received by a splendid military escort, and accompanied by a civil procession, consisting of eighteen pall-bearers, of which number I was one. The Mayor and Corporation, the committee of the House of Representatives appointed to accompany the body, the members of the Massachusetts delegation, the precious relics of the Cincinnati, — everybody was in the procession who ought to have been there, and everything was done which the occasion required. The streets on the line of march were filled to the edge of the sidewalks with the greatest body of men and women ever assembled in the city. Unlike the heterogeneous mass of excited spectators which covered the same ground yesterday, these were well-behaved, well-dressed people, of grave deportment and orderly behaviour; the streets were relieved from the annoyance of omnibuses and other vehicles; the police succeeded in preserving order, with the exception of an occasional outbreak in the immediate vicinity of the carriages in which Mr. Clay and General Gaines rode. The pall-bearers were nearly as follows: Luther Bradish, David S. Jones, Samuel Gilford, Stephen Allen, William B. Crosby, Stephen Whitney, Egbert Benson, Edward Laight, Richard S. Williams, Gulian C. Verplanck, A. Van Nest, Gideon Ostrander, Clement C. Moore, J. M. Bradhurst, George Tappan, Anthony Lamb, Samuel B. Warner, Philip Hone.

MARCH 11. — Mr. Clay survives; but such a time no man ever had. This was the day set apart for his reception of the ladies. Tens of thousands of females, with a careful exclusion of the grosser sex, were presented, for each of whom he had a word of gallantry. They all pressed his hands; many kissed him; and one hand, "more lucky than the rest," prompted by a spirit of Amazonian hardiness and armed with "the glittering forfex," which, like the adventurous baron who despoiled the lovely Belinda of her cherished tresses, she had brought for the nefarious purpose, did actually commit a new "Rape of the Lock."

MARCH 13. — Mr. Clay went yesterday, with the Mayor, to St. Bartholomew's Church. Here, again, was one of those scenes which mark the movements of this popular man. A long time before his arrival at the church, the vestibule and the walks in front were filled with an expectant mass of people, who received him uncovered, and on his entering the church, the aisles and every part of which were crowded, the congregation arose. If their worship of God was ardent and sincere as that of man, some good may result

from this Sunday manifestation.   On his leaving the church, with
Mrs. Brady on his arm, and when the carriage drove off, these
marks of homage were repeated.

Peace with Mexico. The treaty negotiated by an unauthorized agent, with an unacknowledged government, submitted by an accidental President to a dissatisfied Senate, has, not-withstanding these objections in form, been confirmed in substance by the decided vote of thirty-nine to thirteen, and will be forwarded immediately to Mexico, approved by President Polk.   Parties have not divided on this question by political boundaries, as on others. Cass and Crittenden voted for, and Benton and Webster against, it. The war, originated in the vilest cabal that ever was set on foot by corrupt demagogues, has been conducted, so far as the government was concerned, with the most reckless extravagance, and owes now a reluctant confirmation to the strong desire of a majority of the Senate to get rid of a present evil, and avoid the future disastrous consequences of a protracted war.   For these laudable objects the Whigs voted for the confirmation of the rickety treaty, and the administration party to save their rickety cabinet from further dis-grace. Mr. Trist, a clerk in one of the departments at Washington, after his recall from a special job committed to his care, makes a treaty " upon his own hook."   Mr. Polk, elected President nobody knows how, submits it to the Senate to get himself out of a scrape, aud they agree to it for fear of something worse.

MARCH 24. — Dined with Mr. Tileston ; a sort of a club dinner, as in former times, ten members being present. The party con-sisted of George Curtis, John Ward, J. Prescott Hall, Paul Spofford, Simeon Draper, James W. Webb, Moses H. Grinnell, Samuel Jaudon, Thomas Tileston, and myself, of the club ; invited guests : Henry A. Coit, S. Knapp, D. S. Jones, Charles H. Russell, Daniel Fearing, Mr. DeWolf, Henry Cary.

Death of Mr. Astor. MARCH 29. — John Jacob Astor died this morning, at nine o'clock, in the eighty-fifth year of his age ; sensible to the last, but the material of life exhausted, the machinery worn out, the lamp extinguished for want of oil. Bowed down with bodily infirmity for a long time, he has gone at last, and left reluctantly his unbounded wealth. His property is estimated at $20,000,000, some judicious persons say $30,000,000 ; but, at any rate, he was the richest man in the United States in productive and available property ; and this immense, gigantic fortune was the fruit of his own labor, unerring sagacity, and far-seeing penetration. He came to this country at twenty years of age ; penniless, friendless, without inheritance, without education, and having no example before him of the art of money-making, but with a determination to be rich, and ability to carry it into effect. His capital consisted of a few trifling musical instruments, which he got from his brother, George Astor, in London, a dealer in music. He sold his flutes, and set up a small retail shop of German toys, but soon emerged from obscurity, and became a great and successful merchant. The fur trade was the philosopher's stone of this modern Crœsus ; beaver-skins and musk-rats furnished the oil for the supply of Aladdin's lamp. His traffic was the shipment of furs to China, where they brought immense prices, for he monopolized the business ; and the return cargoes of teas, silks, and rich productions of China brought further large profits ; for here, too, he had very little competition at the time of which I am speaking. My brother and I found in Mr. Astor a valuable customer. We sold many of his cargoes, and had no reason to complain of a want of liberality or confidence. All he touched turned to gold, and it seemed as if fortune delighted in erecting him a monument of her unerring potency.

APRIL 1.—The funeral took place this afternoon, from the house of Mr. William B. Astor, in Lafayette place. The following were the pall-bearers, ten in number: David B. Ogden, Judge Oakley, Washington Irving, Ramsay Crookes, Isaac Bell, Sylvanus Miller, James G. King, James Gallatin, Jacob B. Taylor, and myself.

SATURDAY, APRIL 15. — The " Milwaukee Sentinel " contains the following article,—a most wonderful illustration of the magical performance of the lightning post, the last miracle of the scientific triumphs of the present age : "At nine o'clock yesterday morning we had, by telegraph, the news and markets from New York, distant some *fourteen hundred miles*, up to three o'clock of the *preceding* afternoon ! This is, indeed, a startling fact, and may well make us pause and wonder at the agency which has brought it about." I was once nine days on my voyage from New York to Albany.

The Stuyve-
sant Pear-tree.

MAY 1. — I have seldom witnessed a more interesting sight than that of the old pear-tree on Third avenue, now in the full exuberance of its spring garb of blossoms. It is now two hundred and one years old, having been planted by Governor Stuyvesant in his garden, which embraced all this populous part of the city, on his arrival from Holland. In laying out the streets and avenues, this relic of antiquity came at the corner of two wide thoroughfares, where it is protected ; its wide, dark trunk standing strong and stout, and its branches spreading out in fantastic forms, and new blossoms vouching, on the return of spring, for the vitality of the ancient child of the former garden, of which it is the sole memorial. It is now in full blossom. Having expressed my admiration of the time-honoured tree, at Mr. Fish's dinner, among the Stuyvesants, the Fishes, and the Winthrops, they very politely had some of the blossoms gathered and sent to me, which I intend to preserve as a specimen of long-lived vegetation, and a floral reminiscence of the Stuyvesant dynasty.

Hail to the
Chief!

MAY 25. — I have been glorifying all day, and returned fatigued and hungry. General Scott's reception has been splendid and enthusiastic. The arrangements of the Corporation were excellent, and everything well conducted ; the people seemed willing to carry their hero upon their shoulders, notwithstanding his pretty considerable bulk, and the additional weight of his laurels. The sword had erased the errors of the pen, and the "hasty plate of soup" was forgotten in the shouts of " battles won," and conquests secured.

MAY 26. — I dined with a large party at Moses H. Grinnell's, in his magnificent mansion in Fourteenth street. It was a dinner given to the directors of the Phœnix Bank, the result of a wager lost to Mr. Fearing. All the delicacies of the present prolific season, — turtle, salmon, peas, asparagus, terrapins, strawberries, — all that could tempt the epicure or satisfy the gourmand, were spread before the guests, and wine such as Hebe ne'er poured out for the gods made every man wish "his neck was a mile long." The party consisted of James W. Otis, Daniel B. Fearing, Mr. Corse, Paul Spofford, Garrit Storm, P. Hone, Thomas Tileston, Henry Cary, Mr. Henry, N. G. Ogden, William E. Laight, Charles H. Marshall, Washington Irving, D. Mills, and Mr. Stebbins.

JUNE 7. — The Whig Convention met this morning, at the Chinese Hall, Philadelphia. Great excitement prevails. The friends of General Taylor and of Mr. Clay are equally raised to "fever heat." The former have nominated, out of doors, their candidate to run with or without the sanction of a nomination, and many of the latter have expressed a determination to support no other but theirs. As for myself, I am as much of a Clay man as the best of them ; but if General Taylor gets the nomination (of which there seems to be a strong probability), I will support him to the best of my power. Mr. Clay deserves the nomination ; but there is a question beyond his success and the gratification of our predilections. Shall General Cass be the President? Never, if I can prevent it. His principles are more dangerous than those of any other man who has been named by his party as their candidate. He is an embodiment of political humbug and demagogism, administering to the worst part of the community. He made a fool of himself, when minister to France, by writing a book of gossip about the king and court, and since his return has courted the populace by declaring war pretty much against all "princes, potentates, and powers." The annexation of Texas and the war of Mexico received his hearty support, and he now threatens to subjugate the whole of the American continent.

Whether he would as chief magistrate carry out these threats may be doubtful; but, demagogue or destroyer, Oliver Cromwell or Charles of Sweden, I want none of him. "I intend," said a good, stiff Loco-foco, "to give General Cass my unqualified support." — "And if he succeeds," replied his Whig interlocutor, "you will have an *unqualified* President."

JUNE 10. — The Whig Convention, in Philadelphia, completed their important business yesterday, by the nomination of Zachary Taylor, of Louisiana, for President, and Millard Fillmore for Vice-President. I am disappointed, but I am satisfied. The Clay Whigs generally are not so easily satisfied; they are exasperated, and swear all sorts of opposition to the nomination. They will go for the Barnburners; they will get up an opposition candidate; they will support Cass, — an ebullition of rage which will lead them farther than they wish to go. Hereafter I am for Taylor and Fillmore. The last was a judicious selection. New York is the great Clay State, and Mr. Fillmore being a Clay man, it will serve to reconcile the party in a good measure. Some will undoubtedly remain refractory; but we shall gain as many from the Loco-focos. Hurrah, therefore, for Taylor and Fillmore!

SEPTEMBER 29. — The Clay Whigs are falling into the Taylor ranks, reluctantly in some instances, and with a bad grace. Mr. Greeley, editor of the "Tribune," who sets himself up as the oracle of the party, has concluded at last, after deep deliberation, and at the expense of many wry faces, to swallow the dose, and hoists, in his paper of this day, the Taylor and Fillmore flag, but thinks proper to make an apology for his course. He only prefers Taylor to Cass, and damns the former with faint praise. This is in abominably bad taste, as well as impolitic in the last degree. But the object is clear enough; if General Taylor is elected, and makes a good *Whig* President (of which I have the fullest confidence), Mr. Greeley can say, "I supported him; look at my paper, where his name appears in large capitals;" but if he is defeated, or, like John Tyler, proves a traitor to the party which elects him, the same adroit editor will refer to the same paper to prove that he was not his choice.

Death of
Mr. Otis.

OCTOBER 28. — The telegraph brings the melancholy, but not unexpected, intelligence of the death of Harrison Gray Otis, of Boston. The brilliant and useful career of this most estimable man was brought to a close this morning, at two o'clock. He completed his eighty-third year about three weeks since, and has gone to the grave full of years, loaded with honours, and rich in the affections of his friends and fellow-citizens. Mr. Otis was one of a class almost extinct, — a gentleman, in the full extent of the term; of shining talents and the most polished manners. He has held many important public stations; as a senator from Massachusetts in the Senate of the United States, his eloquence shone with a lustre the rays of which have been transmitted to his illustrious successors. As the Mayor of Boston, his legal knowledge, sound judgment, and dignified deportment imparted strength and grace to the magistracy. Descended from a family and inheriting a name sacred in the annals of the Revolution, he was a Federalist in the best days of that glorious and abused party; a Whig then, and a Whig ever since. His intellect was unimpaired to the last hour of his life, and it is remarkable that a few weeks since, whilst suffering under the pains of a hopeless disease, and sinking beneath the weight of fourscore and three years, he wrote and published a long letter urging his fellow-citizens of Massachusetts to the support of the Whig nominees for the offices of President and Vice-President. This paper is marked by all the strength of argument and brilliancy of style which characterized the productions of his middle age. I have again to lament, in the decease of Mr. Otis, the loss of another dearly-valued friend, whose uniform kindness and hospitality always constituted one of the greatest enjoyments of my visits to Boston.

NOVEMBER 7. — This is the day of the great election to decide not only whether General Cass or General Taylor is to be President for the four ensuing years, but whether the policy and principles of the government, as established by the great fathers of the Republic and confirmed by the Revolution, and the adoption of the Federal Constitution, shall be restored to their first purity; or those of the present administration, which we Whigs hold to be subversive of the prosperity of the country and the happiness of the people, shall be continued with renewed energy and less scrupulously, under the man who has "played most foully" for the prize he seeks to obtain.

Le Jour D'Austerlitz.

The glorious sun rose this morning in a clear sky and sharp atmosphere, as if to give the light of heaven to the simultaneous action of a whole population. It is a grand and interesting subject of reflection, that millions of men in this widely extended country are resorting on the same day to their respective polls, to decide by casting in, each of them, a little slip of paper, the choice of their rulers to control the action of the government for the weal or the woe of the people. The sun which rose this morning will, at its setting, see the momentous question settled, and that which rises to-morrow will scarcely find a vestige of the great struggle. Men will resume their accustomed pursuits, labours, occupations, pleasures, and strivings; and women will buy new bonnets, and walk in Broadway with them, as if nothing had happened. The hurrahs will have subsided, the guns will be silenced, the flags lowered from their staffs, a few broken heads plastered up, and many of us will think we had better have minded our business. The elections being held on the same day throughout the Union is a wise precaution to prevent intrigue, corrupt management, and improper interference with the people's prerogative. Here in New York "the work goes bravely on."

NOVEMBER 8. — The sun of Buena Vista set last night upon the most decided victory ever achieved in this city by the Whig forces, — a perfect rout;

The Battle.

everything is gained.   The Taylor electoral ticket has a plurality over Cass of 9,805, and a majority over Cass and Van Buren united of 4,706.   Hamilton Fish is Governor of New York.

Gold and Cholera.   DECEMBER 16. — Now that the election is over, and General Taylor President past peradventure, California gold and the cholera are the exciting topics of the day.   These two diseases are equally infectious; both interfere with the honest pursuits of industry, and, though the former does not so immediately affect the health and endanger the lives of its subjects, its injurious effects may be of longer continuance.

Our newly acquired territory of California, having passed from the hands of Spaniards and Indians into those of the enterprising Yankees, who run faster, fly higher, and dig deeper than any people under the sun, has now developed its riches.   The region of country watered by the river Sacramento is found to abound in pure gold ; the shining tempter of mankind is found in the land and crevices of the rocks, and all the world have become diggers and delvers.   The towns are deserted by all but the women ; business is neglected ; houses stand empty ; vessels are laid up for want of hands ; the necessaries of life cannot be obtained, and the people are starving, with their pockets full of gold.   The most extravagant stories are told of the prices of the ordinary articles in use in this new business ; pick-axes, spades, and hammers are literally "worth their weight in gold," which latter commodity has fallen in value from $18 to $10 per ounce, whilst the products of the neglected earth are producing a "golden harvest." Some of the gold has reached our part of the world, and has been assayed at the mint ; and it is found, in fact, that "it *is* all gold that glitters."   The papers are filled with advertisements and enticements . to adventurers, and California takes up all the commerce of the seaport.

1849.

JANUARY 20. — I was at a very delightful little dinner-party at Mr. Frederic DePeyster's, which I enjoyed exceedingly. I am not so old nor time-worn as not to be able to appreciate and enjoy the refined pleasures of female society, as I found it to-day. The party consisted of Mr. and Mrs. DePeyster, Mr. and Mrs. Philip Van Rensselaer (the lovely and beautiful Mary Tallmadge of other times), Mr. and Mrs. Vail, Isaac and Eliza Hone, Miss Sedgwick, and myself, to say nothing of the men (who were not by any means deficient in good sense and agreeable qualities). I take it to be a very difficult task to select from the female society of New York five finer women than those who graced the table on this pleasant occasion.

JANUARY 26. — The California fever is increasing in violence; thousands are going, among whom are many young men of our best families; the papers are filled with advertisements of vessels for Chagres and San Francisco. Tailors, hatters, grocers, provision merchants, hardware men, and others are employed night and day in fitting out the adventurers. John Bull, too, is getting as crazy as Brother Jonathan on this exciting subject.

FEBRUARY 3. — I was a guest at a splendid dinner to-day in Mr. John C. Stevens's palace, College place. The house is, indeed, a palace. The Palais Bourbon in Paris, Buckingham Palace in London, and Sans-Souci at Berlin, are little grander than this residence of a simple citizen of our republican city, a steamboat builder and proprietor; but a mighty good fellow, and most hospitable host, as all who know him will testify. Twenty ladies and gentlemen, besides the host and hostess, were seated, a few minutes before seven o'clock, around a round table of sufficient capacity to accommodate them pleasantly and conveniently; the ornaments of the table were magnificent, and in excellent taste. The dinner consisted of all the delicacies of a French *cuisine;* the honours of the feast were performed with the utmost good-breeding and unobtrusive hospitality; and the company, judging by the constantly spirited conversation which prevailed, exceedingly well pleased with their entertainment. The party consisted of Mr. and Mrs. James G. King, Mrs. Clinton, Mr. and Mrs. William S. Miller, Mrs. Ledyard, Mr. and Mrs. Mortimer Livingston, Mrs. Douglass Cruger, Mr. and Mrs. Henry A. Coit, Mr. John A. King, Mr. and Mrs. James B. Murray, Mr. Anson Livingston, President Moore, Mr. Edwin Stevens, Mr. and Mrs. William Kemble, and myself.

FEBRUARY 5. — The tone of writing and speaking in Europe on the subject of the United States is greatly altered of late. Even in England the public press, as well as the popular orators, not only speak of us with a certain degree of respect, but hold us up as an example to their government and people. They may occasionally abuse us as an arrogant people, grasping at extended territory, disregarding the rights of our neighbours, invading peaceful countries, fighting like lions, and negotiating like foxes. But the language of contempt is heard no more; the little foibles of Brother Jonathan are forgotten in the contemplation of his indomitable courage, his never-dying perseverance. The thought of manhood begins to be blended with the ardour and activity of youth. He is growing to be a "big boy," and must be treated with a little more respect. The "hasty plate of soup" may do to laugh at, but the conquering sword of the hero of La Vera Cruz and Mexico, who penned the unfortunate expression, has effaced its recollection. The Yankees may be ignorant of the most approved method of using the knife and fork; but it cannot be denied that they are competent to make a good use of the sword and musket. They eat fast, but they go ahead wonderfully; they use some queer expressions, but in defence of their rights are apt to talk much to the purpose.

MARCH 13.—The fashionable world is agog again
upon a new impulse. Mrs. Butler, the veritable " Fanny
Kemble," has taken the city by storm. She reads
Shakespeare's plays three evenings in the week, and at noon on
Mondays, at the Stuyvesant Institution, in Broadway, a room which
will hold six or seven hundred persons, and which is filled when
she reads by the *élite* of the world of fashion: delicate women,
grave gentlemen, belles, beaux, and critics, flock to the doors of
entrance, and rush into such places as they can find, two or three
hours before the time of the lady's appearance. They are compensated for this tedious sitting on hard seats, squeezed by the
crowd, by an hour's reading — very fine, certainly, for Fanny
Kemble knows how to do it — of the favourite plays of the immortal bard. She makes $2,000 or $3,000 a week, and never was
money so easily earned. There is no expense except the room
and the lights, and the performance is a " labour of love." Shakespeare was never paid for writing his plays as Mrs. Butler is
for reading them.

MARCH 16.—This gentleman's influence with the
new administration seems to be gaining strength. He
has not been thought very friendly to the present ruling
powers; but he likes them better than he does the Clay men, and
Mr. Clayton, the Secretary of State, knowing his importance in the
Senate, would like, no doubt, to have him on his side. The evidence of this revival of the influence of the great Massachusetts
senator is indicated by the appointment of his son, Fletcher Webster, as district attorney for Massachusetts, and that of his brother-
in-law, William Le Roy, as navy agent in New York. This last
appointment sends adrift the brothers Wetmore, whose politics have
been made subservient to the very natural desire of retaining in the
family the emoluments of this lucrative office. One of these
gentlemen is a Whig, and the other a Loco-foco; so that, like
the buckets in the well, when one went down, the other came
up.

General
Scott.

MARCH 17.—This accomplished soldier and gallant commander made his first appearance since his return from Mexico, on Wednesday, in Washington, when he paid his respects to the President. And I rejoice to hear that the meeting between those "dogs of war" was friendly and affectionate, especially as there have been some "foregone conclusions" which made me doubt, knowing Scott's disposition, whether this desirable result could be attained. I went to see General Scott the evening before his departure, and had a long talk with him on this subject. I begged him to let "by-gones be by-gones," and to remember that General Taylor is President of the United States, and his superior officer. He gave me a long account of his grievances, making himself, as usual, the hero of his tale; but he knows my attachment to him, and that I love him, even with his little faults, and I should not be surprised to learn that his good heart and sound judgment approved my advice.

Mr. Hone as
Naval Officer.

APRIL 17.—My new office, that of naval officer, brings me care, trouble, and vexation, especially in relation to applications for office, which have showered down upon me in torrents. It is distressing to see how many worthy persons look to these small offices for the support of large families, and to me it is a source of pain that so many are doomed to disappointment. The official patronage of the naval officer is confined to the clerks who are employed about his person; the collector makes all the appointments of officers who are engaged in the collection of the revenue; my office is advisory and adjunct to the collector. But, to counterbalance these drawbacks, I am pleased with the office; and the warm congratulations I receive, from all quarters, all conditions of men, and all sorts of politicians, leave me no room to doubt the popularity of my appointment. Friends rise up all around me; I am infinitely richer than I ever supposed in these precious treasures of the heart. If I open one of the numerous letters I receive, petitioning for office which I cannot bestow, I am consoled by finding alongside of it another filled with the kindest expressions of personal regard.

APRIL 20.—Mr. Charles H. Russell gave a dinner to-day in compliment to me on my appointment. The party consisted of the following gentlemen, principally members of the Hone Club, and all my devoted friends, who rejoice greatly: Francis Granger, M. H. Grinnell, George Curtis, Edward Curtis, Simeon Draper, Daniel B. Fearing, J. Watson Webb, J. Prescott Hall, R. M. Blatchford, R. L. Colt, Thomas Tileston, Hugh Maxwell, D. S. Kennedy.

My Commission.

APRIL 23.—Yesterday's mail brought my commission as "Naval Officer for the District of New York," with the broad seal of the Treasury Department, signed by Zachary Taylor, President, and countersigned by William M. Meredith, Secretary of the Treasury; with an order to Mr. Bogardus to march out of the office, and another to me to march in, both of which will be accomplished this morning, on or about the hour of ten o'clock. I hope, by the blessing of God, to be enabled to perform my duty with fidelity, ability, and integrity.

APRIL 25.—The painful part of the duties of my office, the removal of the officers and clerks, has commenced. I have removed the three deputies, Messrs. Spinner, Sandford, and Lee, and appointed my nephew, Isaac S. Hone, my son Robert, and Mr. Franklin; and the worst is yet to come.

Theatrical Riot.

MAY 8.—Mr. McCready commenced an engagement last evening at the Opera-House, Astor place, and was to have performed the part of "Macbeth," whilst his rival, Mr. Forrest, appeared in the same part at the Broadway theatre. A violent animosity has existed on the part of the latter theatrical hero against his rival, growing out of some differences in England; but with no cause, that I can discover, except that one is a gentleman, and the other is a vulgar, arrogant loafer, with a pack of kindred rowdies at his heels. Of these retainers a regularly organized force was employed to raise a riot at the Opera-House and drive Mr. McCready off the stage, in which, to the disgrace of the city, the ruffians succeeded. On the appearance of the "Thane of Cawdor," he was saluted with a shower of missiles, rotten eggs, and other unsavoury objects, with shouts and yells of the most abusive epithets. In the midst of this disgraceful riot the performance was suspended, the respectable part of the audience dispersed, and the vile band of *Forresters* were left in possession of the house. This cannot end here; the respectable part of our citizens will never consent to be put down by a mob raised to serve the purpose of such a fellow as Forrest. Recriminations will be resorted to, and a series of riots will have possession of the theatres of the opposing parties.

MAY 10.—The riot at the Opera-House on Monday night was children's play compared with the disgraceful scenes which were enacted in our part of this devoted city this evening, and the melancholy loss of life to which the outrageous proceedings of the mob naturally led.

The Riots.

An appeal to Mr. McCready had been made by many highly respectable citizens, and published in the papers, inviting him to finish his engagement at the Opera-House, with an implied pledge that they would stand by him against the ferocious mob of Mr. Forrest's friends, who had determined that McCready should not be allowed to play, whilst at the same time their oracle was strutting, unmolested, his "hour upon the stage" of the Broadway theatre. This announcement served as a firebrand in the mass of combustibles left smouldering from the riot of the former occasion. The *Forresters* perceived that their previous triumph was incomplete, and a new conspiracy was formed to accomplish effectually their nefarious designs. Inflammatory notices were posted in the upper ward, meetings were regularly organized, and bands of ruffians, gratuitously supplied with tickets by richer rascals, were sent to take possession of the theatre. The police, however, were beforehand with them, and a large body of their force was posted in different parts of the house.

When Mr. McCready appeared he was assailed in the same manner as on the former occasion; but he continued on the stage and performed his part with firmness, amidst the yells and hisses of the mob. The strength of the police, and their good conduct, as well as that of the Mayor, Recorder, and other public functionaries, succeeded in preventing any serious injury to the property within doors, and many arrests were made; but the war raged with frightful violence in the adjacent streets. The mob — a dreadful one in numbers and ferocity — assailed the extension of the building, broke in the windows, and demolished some of the doors. I walked up to the corner of Astor place, but was glad to make my escape. On my way down, opposite the New York Hotel, I met a detachment of troops, consisting of about sixty cavalry and three hundred infantry, fine-looking fellows, well armed, who marched steadily to the field of action. Another detachment went by the way of Lafayette place. On their arrival they were assailed by the mob, pelted with stones and brickbats, and several were carried off severely wounded.

Under this provocation, with the sanction of the civil authorities, orders were given to fire. Three or four volleys were discharged; about twenty persons were killed and a large number wounded. It is to be lamented that in the number were several innocent persons, as is always the case in such affairs. A large proportion of the mob being lookers-on, who, putting no faith in the declaration of the magistrates that the fatal order was about to be given, refused to retire, and shared the fate of the rioters. What is to be the issue of this unhappy affair cannot be surmised; the end is not yet.

MAY 11. — I walked up this morning to the field of battle, in Astor place. The Opera-House presents a shocking spectacle, and the adjacent buildings are smashed with bullet-holes. Mrs. Langdon's house looks as if it had withstood a siege. Groups of people were standing around, some justifying the interference of the military, but a large proportion were savage as tigers with the smell of blood.

Dinner at
Mr. Vail's. I was one of a large party who dined to-day with Mr. Vail, at his splendid mansion, Fifth avenue. The dinner was sumptuous, the table superb, the guests numerous, and we dined at seven o'clock. The party consisted of General Scott, Mr. Fearing, Robert Ray; Mr. Vail, of Troy; Washington Irving, Daniel Fearing, James J. Jones, Charles H. Russell, Colonel Thorn, Mr. Bates, General Tallmadge; Stephens, the traveller; West, the artist; Hulseman, Austrian *chargé*; John Van Buren, Mr. Mildmay; Mr. Corcoran, of Washington; James G. King, Charles A. Davis, Lispenard Stewart, and myself.

MAY 12. — Last night passed off tolerably quietly, owing to the measures taken by the magistrates and police. But it is consolatory to know that law and order have thus far prevailed. The city authorities have acted nobly. The whole military force was under arms all night, and a detachment of United States troops was also held in reserve. All the approaches to the Opera-House were strictly guarded, and no transit permitted. The police force, with the addition of a thousand special constables, were employed in every post of danger; and although the lesson has been dearly bought, it is of great value, inasmuch as the fact has been established that law and order can be maintained under a Republican form of government.

The Cholera. JUNE 1. — The cholera increases, the weather is foggy, murky, and damp,—just such weather as produces and propagates this dreadful disease. A panic is created; vegetables and fish, oysters and clams, generous wine and nourishing porter, are repudiated; foolish people run from one extreme to another; let them live well and temperately, wear flannel, and think less of cholera, and defy the foul fiend.

JUNE 30. — Died this morning, Cornelius Low, aged fifty-four years. Dr. Francis says it was a regular case of "blue cholera."

This dreadful disease increases fearfully; there are eighty-eight new cases to-day, and twenty-six deaths. Our visitation is severe, but thus far it falls much short of other places. St. Louis, on the Mississippi, is likely to be depopulated, and Cincinnati, on the Ohio, is awfully scourged. These two flourishing cities are the resort of emigrants from Europe; Irish and Germans coming by Canada, New York, and New Orleans, filthy, intemperate, unused to the comforts of life and regardless of its proprieties. They flock to the populous towns of the great West, with disease contracted on shipboard, and increased by bad habits on shore. They inoculate the inhabitants of those beautiful cities, and every paper we open is only a record of premature mortality. The air seems to be corrupted, and indulgence in things heretofore innocent is frequently fatal now in these "cholera times."

AUGUST 13. — This man of many generations, this politician of many parties, this philosopher of many theories, has finished his long and eventful career. He died yesterday, at the house of his son-in-law, Mr. Stevens, at Astoria, aged eighty-eight years.

Albert Gallatin.

Mr. Gallatin was a native of Geneva, in Switzerland. He came to this country, and landed at Boston, on the 14th of July, 1780. He served as a volunteer, under Col. John Allen, at Machias and elsewhere. In 1782 he was Professor of French in Harvard. He went to Virginia in 1784, and thence to Pennsylvania, where he settled on a farm on the banks of the Monongahela. He was a member of the convention to amend the Constitution, in 1789. In 1790 he was a member of the Legislature, and in 1793 a senator in Congress for that State. The latter office he did not enjoy, being ineligible from not having been long enough in the country to entitle him to a seat. At this period Mr. Gallatin was a violent Democrat, and affixed a stain to his political character by participating in the whiskey insurrection of Pennsylvania, in opposition to General Washington. I have no doubt that the latter half of his life gave him frequent occasion to wish that the page in the record of the former part, on which this event was inscribed, could be expunged. In Congress he was the great leader of the Jeffersonian Democratic party; on the accession of Mr. Jefferson he was appointed Secretary of the Treasury, and sent to Russia on a diplomatic mission. Thence he joined the illustrious board of commissioners who negotiated the treaty of Ghent.

He has written a great deal, and his works will form a valuable legacy to the nation. Industrious, ardent, persevering, he must have collected, like his contemporary, John Q. Adams, a mass of interesting and instructive matter connected with the history of his adopted country. Amongst his other stations of useful-ness he was the venerated president of the Historical Society, the duties of which his age and infirmities compelled him to relinquish to Mr. Luther Bradish, the able and accomplished vice-president. Mrs. Gallatin was the daughter of Commodore Nicholson. She died a few months since, at about the same age as her husband.

Death of Christopher Hughes. SEPTEMBER 19.—Another of my friends and contem-poraries gone. Poor Christopher Hughes died yester-day, in Baltimore, aged sixty-four years.

One by one these companions of my former pleasant days are dropping off, and I begin to feel like the solitary, leafless, weather-beaten tree, on the sandy beach of Rockaway, which, for half a century, has "bided the pelting of the pitiless storm," stretch-ing out its sapless arms to the ocean blast; its age, infirmities, and insignificance forming its best claim to the forbearance of the elements.

Visit to Paterson. SEPTEMBER 22.—I wrote, the other day, to Mr. R. L. Colt, at Paterson, that, knowing the value he set upon his baskets, I would not trust the one we had (which he had kindly sent to us filled with delicious grapes) to a hireling hand, but be myself the bearer of the important envelope of the grapes, and should expect a good dinner for my pains. So he sent more grapes, and bade me to a dinner on Thursday,

Friday, or Saturday, with an injunction that I should bring with me two or three good fellows.   On this provocation, Blatchford, Fearing, John Ward, and I went to Paterson yesterday, in the train, at half-past twelve o'clock, and arrived in less than an hour.   We admired the swans, wild-geese, and muscovy-ducks; envied the pigs, measured the pumpkins, munched the grapes, gathered the flowers; had a capital dinner, fine wine, and a farmer's tea; and at twenty-two minutes past seven o'clock (the precise time prescribed in the railroad programme) came away from this delightful place, every man with a basket of grapes, the return of which may form an excuse for future dinners.   Colt's hospitality is of the right sort.

OCTOBER 1. — Mr. Alexander Duncan, who arrived
Mr. Duncan.   this morning from Liverpool, is one of the most extraordinary instances of good fortune, so far as money is concerned, that has occurred in this country.   In the winter of 1821–22 he was a fellow-passenger of mine on a voyage from Liverpool, in the ship "Amity," Captain Maxwell.   He was then seventeen years of age; a rough, awkward, shaggy-headed Scotch boy, on a voyage to see his relation, the respected John Grieg, of Canandaigua, and to try his fortune in the new "land of cakes." There were only three of us in the cabin, Mrs. Pritchard, an English lady, being the third.   We had a long, stormy passage, and I, of course, became intimate with the young Scotchman; and, unpolished as he was, I took a great liking to him.   He was bright, intelligent, and of good principles, and a friendship was formed which continues until the present time.

Young Duncan, after a few weeks with his uncle at Canandaigua, went to Providence, Rhode Island, to finish his education; entered as a sophomore in the college, and improved his time so well, that by the time he graduated he had engaged the affections of a young lady, whom he married, relinquishing one baccalaureate as he assumed another.   Mrs. Duncan had two rich uncles, named Butler, immensely rich, and increasing in wealth every day; for they laid up prodigiously and spent nothing, — a method which, they say, accumulates amazingly. One of these worthies died a few years after the niece's marriage, and made her heiress to all his property. This induced Duncan and his wife to remove to Providence, where they have resided ever since. My fellow-passenger in the " Amity " bids fair to become one of the richest men in tangible productive property in the United States. And the best of all is, that he is a liberal, generous man, who will make a good use of his money ; unless, like many others, his immense riches shall make him penurious, as was the case with the person from whom he inherits this mountain of wealth.

NOVEMBER 23. — Mr. Clay remains in town, though
Mr. Clay.   people will not indulge him in his desire to enjoy quiet
              and seclusion at the house of his friend Benson. They pester him to death, haunt him by day, serenade him at night, follow him in his walks, shouting, hurrahing, Harry Claying him wherever he goes. Denying him the liberty he has contributed in so great a degree to secure for them, they insist upon a speech in return for every hurrah which proceeds from their vulgar throats, and compel him to return the unmerciful squeeze of every dirty hand.

DECEMBER 3. — The good, orderly town of Boston is
Murder of   in a state of fermentation ; the people look aghast and
Dr. Parkman.
               wonder-stricken at one of the most horrid murders ever heard of or read about. Thistlewood's case in England, and Colt's here, do not equal it in atrocity ; indeed, it resembles the latter in some shocking particulars. Dr. Parkman, a respectable physician, son of old Samuel Parkman, and brother of Mrs. Robert G. Shaw, left his house on Friday, 23d ult., and has not been heard of since. His strange disappearance, of course, occasioned alarm and consternation. The police were sent in all directions ; rivers were dragged, and woods searched. Mrs. Shaw offered a reward of $5,000 for information to lead to a conviction of the assassins, if murder had been committed, and $1,000 for the recovery of the body. All these measures were unsuccessful until the last of the

week, when circumstances were brought to light so awful as to be thought incredible; but sufficient, in my judgment, to prove unquestionably the guilt of the accused.

The horrible facts which have come to light have fastened suspicion, amounting almost to certainty, upon Dr. John W. Webster, Professor of Chemistry for the last twenty years in the Medical College connected with Harvard University, — a person connected with some of the best families in Boston, who has a wife and several children; himself a man of talents, amiable, urbane, and hospitable in his intercourse with society. This frightful case is similar, as I before remarked, but even more atrocious, than that of Colt in this city. Dr. Webster was indebted to Dr. Parkman $480, secured by a mortgage. The latter was very rich, a penurious man, and a hard creditor; and his debtor in this case extravagant (as scientific persons frequently are), and a bad manager of pecuniary matters, consequently embarrassed in his finances. Urged by his creditor, he called at his house on the morning of Friday, the 23d, and left word that if Dr. Parkman would call upon him at one o'clock he would pay his demand. Dr. Parkman called, was seen to enter, and was never seen afterward. Things went on without any discoveries until Friday last, when suspicions were aroused that Dr. Webster was the murderer. A search was made in his apartments, and there the mutilated remains were found, partly consumed by fire, and disclosing a scene too horrible for description, but proving, strong as circumstances ever can prove, that murder had been perpetrated; and, to my mind, equally conclusive that this Dr. Webster, so clear in all his former relations to society, was the perpetrator of the dreadful crime. He is in prison on the charge, whilst further investigations are going on. The effects of this wonderful catastrophe are dreadful. Two estimable families, with " troops of friends," are plunged into unmitigated grief; the whole community is in a state of the greatest excitement, and men stand aghast at this new development of the infirmity of human nature. Poor, erring, human nature, — the victim of violent passions and uncontrollable propensities by nature, and selfish desires and unreasonable prejudices by education ! To religion alone, and its benign influence upon human actions, can we look for that wholesome restraint which is competent to establish " peace on earth and good-will to men."

1850.

JANUARY 1. — With the commencement of the new year is that of the twenty-eighth volume of my journal. The records of the last are marked with public and private manifestations of the goodness and tender mercy of the Maker and Ruler of the Universe, and the Father and Friend of his people. It has been a year of national prosperity, under the wise counsels of an honest and enlightened administration, which, with all its claims upon the gratitude of the people, has failed to receive their support ; and the force of prejudice and the perversity of faction have produced in the general and State legislatures majorities opposed to the Executive and his cabinet. The Senate of the United States is decidedly in the opposition ; and the new Speaker of the House of Representatives, who was elected by a plurality of one vote, has evinced his determination to carry out the views of his party by rejecting all the leading Whigs from the important committees, and by not appointing a single chairman from among their number. This man owes his election to the Speaker's chair to the magnanimity of the Whigs, who might have prevented it, if they had preferred party to peace and union.

With the exception of a dreadful visitation, during the summer and part of the autumn, of the cholera, that fell destroyer of the human race, general health has prevailed in a good degree, commerce has flourished, peace prevailed, and plenty abounded ; and if the people will vote wrong — why, let them. They are the masters, and have the right to do wrong.

As to myself and my concerns, I have much to be thankful for. My health has improved; the disease which for so long a time subdued my strength and wasted my flesh is greatly mitigated. I am stronger, but my flesh and good looks have not returned.

However, I eat my allowance, drink as much as is good for me, and sleep with a good conscience; and so the Lord be thanked.

Congress.

JANUARY 7.—The spirit of party faction and disorganization prevails in the House of Representatives.

Their constituents sent them to Washington on public business, for which they were to receive eight dollars a day. They have received it without as yet having done anything to earn it. The same difficulty which for so long a time prevented the election of Speaker now exists in relation to the clerk. The Loco-focos and the Whigs proper are so nearly divided, that the Free-Soilers—the Ishmaelites whose hand is against everybody, the fire-brands who are ready to tear down the edifice of government to erect altars for the worship of their own idols—have the power to prevent a choice of clerk, and thus obstruct the people's legislation,—a power which they exert with a recklessness without parallel. Whilst this disgraceful state of affairs continues, national legislation stands still.

JANUARY 21.—The noble mansion on the Fifth avenue and Ninth street, belonging to the family of the late Henry Brevoort, with ninety-two feet of ground on the avenue and one hundred and twenty-six feet in depth, has been purchased by Mr. Henry C. de Rham, for $57,000.

JANUARY 22.—We had a pleasant dinner-party. The following were the guests: General Scott, Dr. Wainwright, Mr. George Bancroft, Mr. August Belmont, Mr. R. M. Blatchford, Mr. C. H. Russell, Commander Perry, Mr. Luther Bradish, Mr. Vail, Mr. Pendleton, Mr. Fearing, Mr. George Curtis.

Municipal Honours.

JANUARY 24.—By the polite invitation of the Mayor, I attended this day the presentation of a gold box and the freedom of the city to Captain Cook, commander of the barque "Sarah," of Yarmouth, Nova Scotia,—the noble fellow who saved the lives of three hundred and ninety-nine passengers and crew of the packet-ship "Caleb Grimshaw," Captain Hoxie, burned at sea in November last. This was a well-deserved compliment; the glorious achievement was performed at a fearful risk of life and property. Eight days were spent in this " labour of love; " during a greater part of the time in a severe gale, which made the communication with the burning ship a severe and dangerous service; but, by the unequalled good conduct of Captain Cook, all were saved, with the exception of those who lost their lives by their reckless insubordination and self-abandonment in the moments of despair.

JANUARY 25. — Died yesterday, in the seventy-first year of his age, Nicholas Saltus, another of my contemporaries, — a queer, priggish-looking little fellow, a very Dr. Syntax in appearance, with more imagination than knowledge, and a dealer in fancy more than in fact.

JANUARY 26. — My daughter and I went to a dinner-party given by Mr. and Mrs. Vail, at their superb mansion at the corner of Fifth avenue and Fifteenth street. The party was given in honour of Mrs. Scott, late Miss Cornelia Scott, daughter of my friend, the gallant General; she was recently married to the General's aide. It consisted of the following (and for fine women, and lovely women, and handsome women I should like to find any dinner-party in this city presumptuous enough to enter into comparison with Mrs. Vail's) : Mrs. Clinton, Bishop Hughes, Colonel and Mrs. Scott (*la belle mariée*), Mr. and Mrs. Philip Van Rensselaer, Mr. and Mrs. Sydney Brooks, Mr. and Mrs. Boreel, Mr. and Mrs. Frederick de Peyster, Mr. and Mrs. Lispenard Stewart, Mr. Robert Ray and his daughter Cornelia, and Captain Hamilton, her *fiancé*, Miss Dehon, Mr. and Mrs. Hone.

JANUARY 28. — I witnessed this morning, at nine o'clock, a novel, exciting, and glorious exhibition.

New Steamers.

Three steam-vessels, of the aggregate cost of more than $1,000,000, were launched in succession from the ship-yard of William H. Brown, at the foot of Twelfth street, East river. I walked over at an early hour, and saw the several launches in the following order: The " New World," intended for the navigation of the rivers of California. Her dimensions are as follows: length, 216 feet; breadth of beam, 27 feet; depth of hold, 10½ feet; burden, 650 tons. The interest of the transit of this vessel from the land to her destined element consisted in her being launched with all her machinery on board, which, as soon as she touched the water, was set in motion; the wheels revolving, the smoke ascending, and the steam whizzing with its usual vivacity, she went to see the launch on the other side of the Point. A rush now took place of the countless multitude to the yard of the Novelty Works, where anxious faces were seen from every dock, vessel, storehouse, and roof, looking towards the great object of attraction. I was so fortunate as to get a place on board the "Atlantic," where a large company of the best sort of men and women to be found in New York was assembled, by invitation, and admitted by ticket, issued by Mr. Collins, the representative of the enterprising owners of the new line. I had not these credentials, but my reception was cordial and complimentary.

Whilst we were waiting for the crowning glory of the occasion, a noble steamer, of eight hundred tons, called the "Boston," took her departure from the land alongside of the leviathan of the ocean. She is intended to run between Boston and Bangor; and, in addition to her fine model and tasteful decorations, she has the strength required for that service, frequently so tempestuous and dangerous.

Soon after the "Boston" left her ways, the "Arctic" began to move slowly and gracefully, heralded by the shouts of the immense multitude, who had been anxiously looking for this event. The first movement of the largest vessel ever built in the United States, several hundred tons larger than a first-rate man-of-war, she sat so easily that her bows did not displace four feet of water. This great specimen of American enterprise and skill in naval architecture and mechanical science belongs to Collins's line of New York and Liverpool, which carries the mail between the two ports. She is to be connected with the " Atlantic," " Pacific," " Antarctic " and " Adriatic." They cost nearly $600,000 each. There is nothing like it in the world. The dimensions of the " Arctic," are as follows: Length on deck, 295 feet; width of beam, 46 feet; depth of hold, 32 feet; burden, 3,500 tons. She has 95-inch cylinders, with 9-feet stroke; wheels, 35 feet diameter; 12-feet buckets, four decks, excellent sleeping accommodations, and cabins decorated with all the splendour and extravagance for which our Yankee marine palaces are famous the world over.

After the launch I squeezed myself into the cabin of the " Atlantic," to witness, with hundreds of ladies and gentlemen, the manner in which more than half a million can be expended. If John Bull can beat this, let him; but, if not, " Britannia " must no longer pretend to " rule the seas." The vessels of Collins's line are so constructed as to be convertible into vessels of war.

FEBRUARY 13.—When we read the accounts of the loss of human life by steam and its machinery, boilers bursting, flues collapsing, running into each other at sea, and running off the track on the land, besides the dreadful shipwrecks, the accounts of which occupy the principal column of every newspaper, there would seem to be some reason to apprehend a diminution of the human family. But in a walk up the Bowery, in the slums of Corlear's Hook, or through the classic region of the Five-Points, the swarms of ragged, barefooted, unbreeched little tatterdemalions, *free-born Americans* (free enough, in all conscience), will afford abundant proof that suitable means are taken to keep up the supply.

FEBRUARY 18.—The dreadful question of slavery,
The Union. which has cast an inextinguishable brand of discord between the North and the South of this hitherto happy land, has taken a tangible and definite shape on the question of the admission of the new State of California into the Union with the

Constitution of her own framing and adoption. The flame is no longer smothered; the fanatics of the North and the disunionists of the South have made a gulf so deep that no friendly foot can pass it; enmity so fierce that reason cannot allay it; unconquerable, sectional jealousy, and the most bitter personal hostility. A dissolution of the Union, which until now it was treason to think of, much more to utter, is the subject of the daily harangues of the factionists in both Houses of Congress. Compromise is at an end. Mr. Clay, the great mediator in time of trouble, has been making a conciliatory speech, which is applauded by all parties, and flying in pamphlet form the length and breadth of the land. But in vain: the charm of his eloquence is dissolved, the fever of party-spirit is beyond the reach of palliatives, the flame of faction has arisen to a height beyond the control of the stream of reason. Passion rules the deliberations of the people's representatives to a degree which, from present appearances, will prevent the despatch of public business of any kind. When will all this end? I see no remedy! If California is admitted with the prohibition of slavery which themselves have adopted, or if the national district is freed by the action of Congress from the traffic in human flesh, the South stands ready to retire from the Union, and bloody wars will be the fatal consequence. White men will cut each other's throats, and servile insurrections will render the fertile fields of the South a deserted monument of the madness of man. On the other hand, the abolitionists of the North will listen to no terms of compromise. Equally regardless of the blessings of union, they profess to hold it of no value unless the power is conceded to them of restraining the extension of the great moral evil which overshadows the land.

FEBRUARY 22. — The birthday of Washington was observed with some demonstration of respect, — a military parade and a procession of the Odd Fellows. What would the " Father of his Country " say, if he were still amongst us, a witness of the factions which prevail in the councils of the nation, of the dangers which threaten the existence of that

Union for the preservation of which his prayers were directed to heaven to the very close of his illustrious life! Have this people forgotten so soon the precious injunctions of their warrior, statesman, oracle, father? They give large sums for his paternal legacy, but they disregard the solemn truths which it inculcates.

FEBRUARY 26. — There was a great meeting last evening, at Castle Garden, of men of all political parties, to express a determination to stand by the "Union, the whole Union, and nothing but the Union," at all hazards, and to support the principles of Mr. Clay's compromise resolutions. General Scott was there. His appearance on the stage was hailed with the most rapturous applause, and every allusion to him brought forth similar manifestations of delight and admiration.

MARCH 5. — The South Carolina senator, the leader of the Southern disunionists, the slave-holders' oracle, the daring repudiator, has made his speech. The gaping gossipers have "supped deep" on oratorical horrors; the quidnuncs have something to chew upon. Mr. Calhoun has been ill during the whole session, so ill as not to be able to deliver his speech, a written copy of which was read, at his request, by Mr. Mason. This is probably his last kick; and, if he is to be judged by the sentiments of this effort, the sooner he is done kicking the better. If this manifesto is to be taken as the text-book of the South, all attempts at conciliation will be fruitless. It is a calm, dispassionate avowal that nothing short of absolute submission to the slave-holding States will be accepted; there is no compromise proposed, no conciliation offered. The prosperity of the North — the natural fruit of industry, perseverance and skill — is a mortal offence to South Carolina. New York is more populous than Charleston. Boston notions sell better than Southern productions, and New Bedford oil and candles shine brighter than slavery manifestoes.

Mr. Webster is to speak on Thursday. His position is extremely delicate and embarrassing, even to a man like him, of iron nerves.

I apprehend some disappointment amongst the anti-slavery spirits of the North and his own State of Massachusetts. Union is his paramount motive, the Constitution the star by which he steers; to preserve these he will probably concede more to the South than the fiery politicians (Whigs even) of the North may think expedient. Much, however, may be effected by a conciliating temper and discreet measures. Webster, Clay, and Calhoun,—these three "old men eloquent,"—how they labour with "harness on their back"! and Bissell, too, who made an admirable speech; and fiery Stanley, and steady Winthrop, and a host of worthies,—all praise to the defenders of the Union!

MARCH 6.—There was a great Union meeting on Monday, in Baltimore, similar to ours at Castle Garden. The Mayor, Mr. Stansbury, presided, with a long string of *vices*, among whom I recognize the names of Meredith, Kennedy, Carroll, Barney, McLane, Frick, Morris, Birkhead, Monroe, and Stewart. If his Worship has no more *vices* than these, he has less to answer for than most men. The resolutions are very good; the orators required to be warmed by their subject, as the meeting was held in Monument square,—the coldest, bleakest spot in America, except the corner of Broadway and Wall street, in our own city of New York.

Governor Seward's Speech.   MARCH 12.—Governor Seward made his great speech yesterday, in the Senate, on the California question. It was able, of course, but wild on the subject which agitates the country; opposed to Calhoun, dissenting from Webster, making battle against the South; uncompromising, right in some things, wrong in more, eloquent rather than argumentative; honey to the Northern abolitionists, wormwood to the Southern factionists; and so we go. I go with Webster.

Mr. Webster's Speech.   MARCH 14.—Mr. Webster's late speech seems to be "buying golden opinions." Some opposition is made by the violent anti-slavery men in his own section of the country (the very men who brought this trouble upon us, by voting for the annexation of Texas), on the ground of his having conceded too much to the South; but a large proportion (and there is reason to hope a majority) of the discreet, reflecting men of all parts of the Union approve the principles and sentiments of this great speech, are willing to make it their text, and augur the most auspicious results from its dissemination far and wide. The exordium of this speech is in every man's mouth; the effect must have been prodigious. The position which the speaker occupied in the discussion of the momentous question, and the appearance of the man (I can imagine how he looked), were things to be remembered, with a sort of awful admiration, by the closely packed audience who had the good luck to hear him. He began thus: "I rise to speak to-day, not as a Massachusetts man, not as a Northern man; but as an American, and a member of the Senate of the United States."

MARCH 22.— This Senator *Foote* seems to be tripping up everybody who comes in his way. He is a pestiferous demagogue, bent upon kicking up a dust whenever he gets a chance. This is the same man who had a fight in the street, the other day, with Borland, a brother Locofoco; and now a most disgraceful scene has been enacted on the floor of the Senate between this loafer and Benton, the " Father of the Senate," in which epithets were applied to each other in the most approved style of Five-Points eloquence. The most vulgar language was made the vehicle of personal vituperation; the capacious stern of the Missouri senator was a spot in which the belligerent *Foot* might have been placed to some advantage; but it did not get so far. How can such men as Webster, Clay, Calhoun, Berrien, Davis, etc., sit and listen to such ribaldry !

MARCH 23.— An English newspaper has the following astounding and veracious article of intelligence: "The Honourable Daniel Webster, the great American statesman, is to be tried for his life for the murder of *Dr. Parker*." This is worthy of the "New York Herald" or "Washington Union."

APRIL 2. — The great South Carolina senator died in Washington, on Sunday morning, March 31, of a disease of the heart. Overworked, terribly excited, the frail body was insufficient to sustain the burning, restless, ardent mind. One of the great lights of the Western world is extinguished; the compeer of Webster and Clay is removed from the brilliant trio; the South has lost her champion; slavery, its defender; and nullification and (we are compelled to say) disunion, their apologists.

Death of Mr. Calhoun.

Possessing talents of the highest order, irreproachable integrity, and amiable deportment, he wanted the expanded patriotism, the disinterested political morality, of his great rival, — Webster. The latter goes for the country, the whole country, first, and Massachusetts after; the Union, the Constitution, the principles of the Revolution, are the stars by which he steers his political course. The other great man would sacrifice all these for the interest, the aggrandizement, of South Carolina. The first is a *statesman* in the broadest sense; the last was the *man of a State*.

What effect his lamented decease will have upon the questions which agitate, in so fearful a degree, the minds of men and the councils of the nation, it is difficult to foresee. Will the withdrawal of the leader have the effect of disbanding the forces of Southern opposition? Or will they rally under some leader equally ardent and uncompromising, but of motives less pure and action more unscrupulous? God save the Republic! should be the prayer of all good Americans in this crisis, pronounced at one extremity of the Union and echoed at the other.

APRIL 8. — I dined on Saturday with Mr. August Belmont, the agent of the great house of Rothschilds, at his splendid mansion in the Fifth avenue. The guests were Washington Irving, Commodore Perry, Edward Jones, Rev. Dr. Wainwright, Daniel B. Fearing, Bache McEvers, William Kemble, and myself.

APRIL 13. — I went, last evening, to the opening of the exhibition of the National Academy of Design, at their new rooms in Broadway, opposite Bond street. There was a collation, with a large party of artists, literati, men of science, and men of taste to partake of it. The Academy has made an admirable arrangement; the stables of Brown have been converted into a temple of the Muses. The Academy has now a local habitation and a name. They have five rooms filled, for the approaching exhibition, with an unusually fine collection of pictures. The Academicians have made a successful effort to do some work worthy of their good name, and to give *éclat* to their new quarters.

APRIL 18. — A personal conflict, disgraceful to the parties, and humiliating to every good American who has been taught to revere the exalted body in which it occurred, was enacted yesterday on the floor of the Senate, by Colonel Benton, who likes to be called the father of the Senate, — but, as it appears in this matter, does not always act up to the dignity and decorum of the character, — and that pestiferous fellow, Foote, who disgraces himself, his State, and the body of which he is an unworthy member. Benton appears to have been the aggressor; for it requires more patience than the Missouri senator is thought to possess, to bear the attack of so filthy an animal. The other drew a pistol, which, if it had not been for the interference of the gentlemen near by, would probably have left Missouri unrepresented, and the Senate, fatherless. Pistols in the Senate! This Foote should be amputated from the body, of which it is a disgraced member.

Senatorial Fracas.

APRIL 19. — I dined with my friend Giraud on Wednesday, on capital clam soup, and a fore-quarter of lamb and mint sauce. Nobody understands the science of good living, the whole arcana of gastronomy, better than my old bachelor friend Giraud.

APRIL 22. — My wife and I came from home this morning to make a visit to Mr. and Mrs. Alexander Duncan, and to bring with us my daughter and Miss Adèle Granger. We left New York at eight o'clock, on the New Haven railroad, came by Hartford, Springfield, and Worcester,

Visit to Providence.

and arrived at Providence at six o'clock P.M., — a ride of two hundred and forty miles in ten hours.   Mr. Duncan and the girls came out to meet us at Blackstone, and brought us to our pleasant quarters, the honoured guests of our hospitable and kind friends, where every comfort was prepared for us, and a good night's rest followed the fatigue of our railroad journey.

APRIL 23. — The unpretending elegance, good taste, and admirable house-keeping of Mrs. Duncan's establishment leave us nothing to wish for.   Mr. Duncan's immense wealth is judiciously used for the enjoyment of his family, the gratification of his friends, and the good of the community, of which he is an active and beneficent member.   After walking with my host, and visiting the interesting objects of this pleasant town, I went to a dinner given to me by Samuel G. Arnold.   The party consisted of Mr. Moses B. Ives, Mr. Whipple, Dr. Parsons and his son, Mr. Charles Potter, Mr. Birkhead, Mr. Duncan, Mr. Robeson, Colonel Halsey, Dr. Mauran, and myself.

APRIL 24. — Went with Mr. Duncan to return the Governor's call; visited the College Library, which has been richly endowed by Mr. Brown, the Athenæum, etc.   Mr. Duncan has contributed largely to the support of these and other similar scientific and benevolent institutions, and his literary taste has been evinced by a tasteful and well-arranged private library.   Mr. Duncan gave us a handsome dinner; the guests, besides our party, consisting of Governor Anthony, Mr. Zachariah Allen, Mr. Philip Allen, Moses B. Ives, Dr. Mauran, Professor Gammell, Mr. Birkhead, and Mr. Brown.

APRIL 25. — After another day spent pleasantly at home and abroad, and a sociable, comfortable dinner, we terminated our agreeable visit, and left Providence at six o'clock P.M., on the Stonington railroad, to return by the steamer on the Sound.   Mrs. Daniel B. Fearing joined our party, with her children.

There is a new carpet on the library floor, and my

At home.   books have undergone a dusting, under Margaret's judicious superintendence.

I dined with Mr. Tileston, on an invitation received before I left home ; it was pretty much of a club dinner. We had Blatchford, George Curtis, Spofford, Prescott Hall, Jaudon, Governor Fish, Matthew Morgan, Henry A. Colt, two Messrs. Brice, sons-in-law of Mr. Tileston.

APRIL 27. — The great steamer "Atlantic" went to sea to-day. She went off in fine style ; but the fog compelled her to stop three or four hours at Staten Island. She will create a sensation in England. If John Bull does not open his eyes in wonder, and scratch his head in jealousy, he will have lost his usual characteristics. Let him beat her if he can ; if he does, we will try again.

APRIL 29. — Died on the 19th, at his residence, New Bedford, Cornelius Grinnell, father of Moses, Joseph, and Henry. He was in the ninety-third year of his age, a hale, hearty, cheerful old gentleman, — a fine example of green old age. I was at his house when at New Bedford. His son Moses arrived in New Bedford a few minutes before he expired. On the morning of the day on which his long account with this world was closed, he told his family that Moses was expected on that day, and ordered some champagne to be iced for him, on his arrival. Mr. Roach, another native of New Bedford, of about the same age as Mr. Grinnell, died within a few hours of his decease.

APRIL 30. — I saw Mr. Webster on Sunday. He is on a short visit to his favourite Marshfield. He went to Boston yesterday, where he was received by his friends with distinguished honours, and replied, — in front of his hotel, the Revere House, — in his usual style of eloquence, to the complimentary speeches which were made to him. If he does not "buy golden opinions" now, it must prove that the article is scarce in the market. He is no longer at a loss to find his position, and seems determined to maintain it.

MAY 2. — Another, and another, and another. The Disasters.   steamer "Belle of the West" was blown up a few days since on the Ohio, below Cincinnati, and many lives lost. These are melancholy events ; but "it's of no consequence," as Foote says ; "there were more born on that day to supply their places." Steam has come into the world to do the work of war, — equally certain, and, in the aggregate, equally extensive in its operations; but it wants the prestige of present glory and future renown; boilers burst, and so do bomb-shells. Men are blown up as well by steam as gunpowder. Death's doings, all.

MAY 4. — Congress has passed the bill, and the President's signature has made it a law, to receive the two vessels to be fitted out by Henry Grinnell to proceed to the North pole in search of Sir John Franklin. The little squadron about to be engaged in this work of beneficence is placed under the rules and regulations of the United States Navy, which is also to furnish the officers and men for the expedition. Success attend them; but I have no faith in the enterprise. Captain Franklin and his companions will never, I fear, be seen again. They lie " five fathoms deep " in their icy shrouds. It is to be hoped that those who go out on this " labour of love " may not meet with any fate worse than frozen toes and red noses, and return in good time to relate their adventures in the great ice-house of the universe.

Grinnell Expedition.

MAY 23. — I continue very ill and suffer excruciating pains from the sores in several parts of my body, the effects of the severe treatment for the dangerous disease with which I have been afflicted. The erysipelas is removed, but I am exceedingly weak and emaciated, and require all the unwearied care and tender nursing which are bestowed upon me. But I have sorrow, deep and alarming, beyond the apprehensions of my own case. My beloved wife lies in her chamber above me, in what I consider a hopeless case. Nature is sinking; her strength has departed, and a cough, with which she has been long afflicted, seems to be insurmountable. Which of us will be first called I dare not presume to imagine. The Lord's will be done !

Illness.

MAY 24. — My worst apprehensions are realized. The crowning blessing of my long life, the enjoyment of which the Lord has permitted to me for a period of

Death of Mrs. Hone.

nearly half a century of uninterrupted love, affection, and confidence, He has seen fit to resume. The most excellent partner of my fondest associations, the best of wives, the mother of my children, my comforter in affliction, the participant of my joys, the promoter of my happiness, my friend and example, died this morning at fifteen minutes past four o'clock, — died as angels live, — peaceful, serene, sensible to the last moment, free from pain, and perfectly resigned to the will of God. And there she lies, with a benignant expression which seems to impart sweetness to the flowers with which her beloved frame is decorated. Teach me, blessed Lord, to receive this chastisement with suitable resignation and submission to Thy will. Thou hast permitted me to enjoy for a long period the blessing of which Thou hast now deprived me, and I have no right to complain. Thy will be done in this as in all other dispensations of Thy Providence !

MAY 27. — The last act of our melancholy tragedy was performed yesterday afternoon. The mortal remains of my dearly beloved wife were consigned to the vault in the cemetery of Saint Mark's Church. The following were the pall-bearers : President William A. Duer, President Charles King, General Scott, Luther Bradish, Gardiner G. Howland, Richard M. Blatchford, Benjamin L. Swan, Jacob P. Giraud.

The Old Hull afloat. MAY 30. — This was the first day of my leaving the house. The weather is very bad. A long, easterly storm, the end of which we have not seen, has retarded my recovery. I am better, but my sufferings are extremely distressing. I went to the Naval office, where I found my faithful troops rejoiced to see me. I signed some papers, and remained about an hour.

Broadway. If they do not pull down the houses in the annual renovation of Broadway, they fall of their own accord.

The large, three-story house, corner of Broadway and Fourth street, occupied for several years by Mrs. Seton as a boarding-house, fell to-day at two o'clock, with a crash so astounding that the girls, with whom I was sitting in the library, imagined for a moment that it was caused by an earthquake. Fortunately, the workmen had notice to make their escape. No lives were lost, and no personal injury was sustained. The mania for converting Broadway into a street of shops is greater than ever. There is scarcely a block in the whole extent of this fine street of which some part is not in a state of transmutation. The City Hotel has given place to a row of splendid stores; Stewart is extending his stores to take in the whole front from Chambers to Reade street; this is already the most magnificent dry-goods establishment in the world. I certainly do not remember anything to equal it in London or Paris; with the addition now in progress this edifice will be one of the "wonders" of the Western world. Three or four good brick houses on the corner of Broadway and Spring street have been levelled, I know not for what purpose, — shops, no doubt. The houses — fine, costly edifices, opposite to me, extending from Driggs's corner down to a point opposite to Bond street — are to make way for a grand concert and exhibition establishment. All this is very well; men have a right to improve their property as they please; but it really would be well if more precautions were used in pulling down and underpropping. Lives enough have been sacrificed; but the inquisitive people require something to gratify their curiosity, and some went away from the ruins to-day a little disappointed that no lives were lost. It was nothing to the accident in Hague street.

JUNE 1. — This has been a week of festivity among the members of the old club; it arose out of a reciprocation of the hospitality of some of the Baltimore gentlemen, who were the hosts on the occasion of the canvas-back party last fall at Maxwell's Point. Invitations were given and accepted, and a round of dinners was the consequence. George Curtis, Prescott Hall, Moses H. Grinnell, and Samuel Jaudon saturated these Baltimore sponges with the finest old wine in the country; and how it went! I was not at Maxwell's Point, and, of course, not at the result here. I have no interest in such matters. These things will never again delight me.

But there is one circumstance about these pleasant reunions which gives me a gratification far above the festivities which my friends enjoyed, — a banquet of the heart, an overflow of grateful acknowledgment, a tribute, never to be forgotten, of love and affection, and this is it : Jonathan Meredith refused to come on with the party, out of tenderness and consideration for my affliction and that of my family, and I have reason to believe that John P. Kennedy was restrained by the same generous feelings. The Lord reward them for this manifestation of friendship, and teach me not to forget it !

JUNE 14. — I received an invitation from the citizens of Burlington, Vermont, to attend the grand railroad jubilee intended to celebrate, with appropriate festivities, the establishment of railroad communication between the State of Vermont and the Atlantic seaboard. I declined this invitation. Broken down in health, and sorely afflicted in mind, I am no longer the man for such enjoyments. There was a time when I should have responded cheerfully to such a summons.

JUNE 17. — As a proof of my convalescence, I record the fact that I went yesterday forenoon to Trinity Church ; not walking all the distance (I availed myself of the Bowery railroad), but I could have accomplished even that feat. I am weak, very, and thin as a pair of tongs ; but my sufferings have subsided. Who knows that I may not be a man again?

JUNE 28. —There seems to be no hope of a settle-
Congress.   ment of the exciting questions which agitate the minds
of men at Washington. Faction, violence, intemperance, and ungentlemanly deportment prevail in both Houses of Congress. They have been in session six months, and no public business has been accomplished. Parties are so divided, that either may prevent the action of all the rest. Good men begin to despair of the Republic. The excellent Chief Magistrate, striving as he does to get things to rights, is assailed by a gang of desperadoes, who hate him as the infernal spirits do the angels of light,

for the virtue and purity of his character, the contrast of which renders apparent their own deformity.

JULY 10. — The American people are suddenly called upon to mourn the loss of another Chief Magistrate of the Union. The face of the land is clad in the habiliments of woe ; the hand of death has stricken down the good old man, the brave soldier, the able and successful commander, the patriotic citizen, the wise and discreet ruler, whom the people, by their unsolicited choice, placed in the highest office in their gift.

Death of General Taylor.

JULY 11. — Mr. Fillmore, Vice-President, having resigned the presidency of the Senate, was sworn into the office of President of the United States, yesterday, at twelve o'clock, in the Chamber of the House of Representatives, in the presence of both Houses. *Le roi est mort,* — *Vive* Fillmore ! The speeches of Messrs. Berrien, Downs, and Webster in the Senate, after the inauguration, were marked by ability, eloquence, and the most touching sensibility of the nation's loss in the sudden death of the excellent man who has so admirably succeeded in his " endeavours " (to use his own words) " to do his duty."

JULY 22. — The steamer " Atlantic," the great favourite of the Knickerbockers, in whose successful competition with the navigation of the whole globe our citizens of all parties and professions take so lively an interest, arrived yesterday at her berth, in this her native city, making her voyage in ten days and fifteen hours, thereby justifying the predictions of her constructors and owners in making the quickest passage yet known.

JULY 24. — The funeral obsequies, ordered by the city authorities in honour of the lamented President, took place yesterday, commencing at three o'clock. The grandest and most numerous military and civil procession ever witnessed in this city took place. It was five miles in length, and was three hours passing my house. The concourse of people on the whole route was prodigious ; 250,000 men, women, and children witnessed the solemnities ; orderly, decorous, no resistance

Funeral Obsequies.

to authority exercised gently, no drunkenness. All seemed to be impressed with the solemnity of the melancholy event which was the object of this display.

AUGUST 5. — Good old Commodore Jacob Jones died in Philadelphia, on Saturday morning, in the eighty-third year of his age, — the eldest captain in the navy, with the exception of Barron and Stewart. The sting of his "*Wasp*," in one of the first naval engagements with the maritime forces of Great Britain, stung their "*Frolic*" past recovery, and obtained for the gallant commander the command of the "Macedonian."

AUGUST 6. — Mr. Clay arrived yesterday in Philadelphia on his way to Newport, where he wishes to enjoy peace and quietness, which, notwithstanding his earnest remonstrances, are denied him. In this he is perfectly sincere ; he hates humbug, the prevailing evil of the day, and is satiated with popular applause. But the Philadelphians shouted him, hurrahed him, and made him address the multitude, sorely against his inclination. Mr. Clay will be here to-morrow, to the gratification of the politicians and sight-loving mob, who, like the famous giant in "Jack and the Bean-stalk," vow that, "dead or alive, they will have some."

Two new houses in the process of erection fell down yesterday, — one in Mercer street, and the other in Spruce street, near Gold street. Both these disasters have been attended with loss of life, and dreadful mutilations of the workmen. The shameful manner of constructing houses intended for renting demands a remedy. Laws should be passed, and inspectors of buildings appointed with arbitrary power, to prevent the erection of these man-traps. I have noticed, especially in the eastern section of the city, blocks of new buildings so slightly built that they could not stand alone, and, like drunken men, require the support of each other to keep them from falling.

AUGUST 8. — The value of my friend Scott's services
General Scott. begin to be appreciated at home and abroad, now the veil is removed with which jealousy, cabal, and

intrigue sought to cover his well-earned fame. He now conducts the affairs of the War Department until the arrival of the new Secretary. "Now, General," said President Fillmore, on the General's arrival in Washington, taking his hand, "your persecutions are at an end." A motion has been made in the House of Representatives to confer upon him the brevet rank of Lieutenant-General, which has never been held by any but Washington.

AUGUST 15. — North Carolina, a Whig State, has gone Loco-foco by reason of the slavery question; and Missouri, — Loco-foco, — Whig, in consequence of an unappeasable difference between the supporters and opponents of Colonel Benton. Old party lines are broken up. In this State the Democrats are all at swords' points; the Old-Hunkers say, Whigs rather than Barnburners, and the Barnburners profess to prefer Whigs to Old-Hunkers. So it is at present. We shall see if the never-failing cement of party *drill* does not unite these discordant political materials before the fall elections. In the mean time the Whigs are in no better condition. Between the friends of Seward and Nullification in the western counties, and the hatred of the people in this part of the State to the man and his principles, it is impossible to say what is trumps, or how the game is to be played.

Political Changes.

AUGUST 30. — The bill from the Senate to admit New Mexico and settle the boundaries of Texas has been set afloat in the troubled sea of congressional violence and opposing currents in the House of Representatives, where it is assailed by the furious tempests of party malignity, driven upon the rocks of sectional jealousy, and made the prey of a set of political wreckers, who care not for vessel, cargo, or crew, if their own unrighteous objects can be attained. Hopes have been entertained of late that this dreadful controversy would be settled by the passage of the bill; that there would be found, among the friends of Union in Congress, strength enough to rescue the ark of the Constitution from the hands of the despoilers, and preserve the sacred tables of the law from pollution and desecration. But prospects are more gloomy within the last day or two ; the two extremes of reckless opposition have met together in numbers sufficient to prevent (it is feared) the passage of any measures to restore harmony and union upon the basis of compromise and concession. These men have been employed more than eight months, like noisome excrescences obstructing the current of wholesome legislation. The best thing they can do is to break up their unprofitable session and go home to their constituents for fresh instructions, and if the people approve these doings, in God's name, be it so !

> "The people's wayward voice
> Must be the Nation's choice."

SEPTEMBER 3. — "Sing a song of sixpence," at the rate of a thousand dollars a night. Our good city is in a new excitement. So much has been said, and the trumpet of fame has sounded so loud, in honour of this new importation from the shores of Europe, that nothing else is heard in our streets, nothing seen in the papers, but the advent of the "Swedish Nightingale." Jenny Lind arrived on Sunday, in the "Atlantic." This noble steamer was a most fitting fiddle-case, a suitable cage for such a bird. The wharf was thronged with anxious expectants of her landing.

Jenny Lind.

SEPTEMBER 5. — The committee appointed by Mr. Barnum to award the prize of $200 for the best song to be sung by Jenny Lind, at her first concert here, have adjudged it to Bayard Taylor, for his song entitled "Welcome to America." The committee state, in their report, that the number of competitors for this prize amounted to seven hundred; a large proportion of the productions were "not fit to feed the pigs." The committee to make the selection were George Ripley, Jules Benedict, L. Gaylord Clark, J. S. Redfield, George P. Putnam.

SEPTEMBER 9. — There is rejoicing over the land ; the bone of contention is removed ; disunion, fanaticism, violence, insurrection, are defeated. These horrible

Beginning of the End.

slavery questions, which have suspended the public business for more than eight months, are settled; but how? The lovers of peace, the friends of the Union, good men, conservatives, have sacrificed sectional prejudices, given up personal predilections, given up everything, for Union and peace; and for this sacrifice the Lord be good to them! But, although all good men rejoice that the affair is settled, none are satisfied. It all comes of that crowning curse of national legislation, the annexation of Texas; and did not Daniel Webster warn the Loco-focos of all this? Did not Henry Clay sound his admonishing trumpet? Did not every Whig orator previous to General Harrison's election prophesy what would be the effects of this unnatural connection? and did not I, even I, in my harangues, portray the evils to result from this idle assumption of gratuitous trouble and vexation?

But the question is settled: we have made war upon Mexico, gaining glory by the gallantry of our warriors; conquered them all, and then, as in the case of Dr. Franklin's Frenchman, agreed to pay for heating the poker. But all is well. The House of Representatives on Saturday got rid of all the vexation in a bunch. The Texas boundary bill was passed, California was admitted as a State, Utah and New Mexico came in as Territories; all obstructions were removed, all amendments rejected. They came into the House, determined to cast all political differences, all sectional jealousy, all party violence, upon the altar of Union, harmony, and the Constitution; and I presume the rest of the nation's business will be hurried through head over heels, and the people's representatives will go forthwith to their wives and children, their farms and merchandise.

SEPTEMBER 12. — The Jenny Lind excitement in

Jenny Lind.   New York seems to have increased to fever heat. Her second rehearsal was given with renewed spirit and effect, and received with new enthusiasm. Tickets have been sold to the amount of $55,000. The good people of New York are anxious to part with their money *for a song*, and the "nightingale" will make a profitable exchange of her *notes* for specie.

SEPTEMBER 17.—Another of those dreadful railroad disasters which every mail brings us, and the news-packets transmit on their paper wings to every corner of the country, occurred one day last week on the Western railroad between Albany and Boston. The train ran off the track, the cars were demolished, several persons were injured, and three passengers killed, of whom one was a young lady, daughter of the proprietor of the Delavan House, Albany; another, Col. S. Jones Mumford, of this city. So much for railroad travelling. Give me the post-coach and seven miles to an hour. I enjoyed it lately, and travelled for once again like a gentleman and man of sense.

The Nightin-
gale.

Jenny Lind's second concert took place on Tuesday, and was attended as numerously and enthusiastically as the first; crowds follow her wherever she goes. She has been compelled to leave the Irving House, in my neighbourhood, to escape from the persecution. This Siren, the tenth Muse; the *Angel*, as Barnum calls her; the *nightingale*, by which she is designated by the would-be *dilettanti*,—has secured the affection as well as the admiration of the mass of the people by an act of munificence, as well as good policy. Her contract with Mr. Barnum has been changed. Instead of $1,000 a night, she gets one-half of the net profits; her share of which for the first night, after deducting the large expenses of a first performance, amounting to the enormous sum of $12,600, all of which, with unprecedented liberality, she distributed among the charitable and benevolent institutions of the city. The list is headed by the fire department fund, to which she gives $3,000, to the musical fund $2,000, and the balance is divided in sums of $500 each to all the other charities. The noble gratuity to the firemen is a great stroke of policy. It binds to her the support and affection of the red-shirt gentlemen, who will go to hear her sing as long as they can raise the money to pay for a ticket, and will worship the *nightingale* and fight for her to the death, if occasion should require. New York is conquered; a hostile army or fleet could not effect a conquest so complete.

SEPTEMBER 20. — The Union Club has removed to the large house belonging to Mr. Kernochan, opposite to me. The club has never before been so well and pleasantly accommodated; it will be convenient for me, also; perhaps too much so, — it may cause me to visit it too frequently.

SEPTEMBER 24. — The Knickerbockers are crowing like the lusty chanticleer at the great voyage of the " Pacific," one of the famous steamers of Collins's line. She has beaten the Cunarders this voyage, which has been made in ten days and four hours from dock to dock, — the shortest yet; she went to and returned from England in less than thirty days. What wondrous changes have occurred in our day and generation! The summer after I married I was nine days going in a sloop from New York to Albany, — this voyage which is now made in as many hours; then it occupied one day less than is now required to make a European passage. We fly through the air, glide over the bosom of the ocean, and dive beneath its waters with the speed of lightning; speed is the ruling principle of mankind; the wind is a laggard, and the shooting-star comparatively slow in its movements.

William H.
Prescott.

SEPTEMBER 27. — The Niagara steamer arrived this morning from Liverpool. In her came passenger William H. Prescott, our eminent historian, and excellent good fellow. I had a visit from him this morning at my office. He returns in good health and excellent spirits, after an absence of five months, during which time the greatest respect and attention were paid to him by the distinguished people of England, from the Queen down; as an evidence of which he told me (but without any vainglorious boasting) that he had, during his sojourn in London, twelve dinner invitations for one day. These highly merited compliments reflect equal honour on both parties.

OCTOBER 16. —, The Loco-focos have nominated Fernando Wood for mayor. There was a time when it was thought of some consequence that the incumbent of this office should be at least an honest man. Fernando Wood! Let the books of the Mechanic's Bank tell his story. There is no amount of degradation too great for the party who expects to "rule the roost," and probably will. Fernando Wood, instead of occupying the mayor's seat, ought to be on the rolls of the State Prison. But our blessed universal suffrage will raise a flame with this *Wood* to drive away Whigism, Conservatism, and good, honest Democracy as we formerly knew it. Fernando Wood, Mayor!!

OCTOBER 19. — I was at a pleasant dinner to-day at Mr. Daniel B. Fearing's. The party consisted of Francis Granger, William S. Miller, Mr. Haight, Thomas Tileston, Charles H. Russell, James W. Otis, George Dorr, and myself.

OCTOBER 25. — My birthday, — I am seventy years old; a mere wreck of what I was. I have lost my bodily strength, and dwindled away into the "lean and slippered pantaloon." But, thanks to the God of Mercy, the Physician of soul and body, to whom I should bow with submission and resignation, I am still in the enjoyment of many blessings; my heart is good and my mind sound, and my home is the abode of happiness and tranquillity.

OCTOBER 26. — The Whigs have nearly completed their nominations. Ambrose C. Kingsland is nominated for mayor by a strong vote, and greatly to his satisfaction.

OCTOBER 31. — I left the Bank for Savings at six o'clock, putting my friend Conover at the desk as my *locum tenens*, and went to make one of·a pleasant dinner-party at Mr. Fearing's. The party consisted of Mr. George Bancroft, T. Butler King, John P. Kennedy, John C. Hamilton, Mr. Vail, Mr. Henry Cary, Mr. S. S. Howland, and myself.

Union
Meeting.

Castle Garden was filled last night with thousands, as it was when Jenny Lind commenced there her round of enchantments. But this occasion was widely different; no nightingale warbled to steal away the hearts and bewilder the senses of the admiring multitudes; but stalwart men, commercial magnates, comfortable millionaires, Whigs and Loco-focos, assembled to stand by the Union and to support the Constitution; to applaud Clay and Cass, Webster and Dickinson, and to condemn Seward and Weed, Greeley and Hunt, by a tempest of vituperation, and all the Whigs by a side-wind of innuendo. George Wood was the president, with *forty vices;* enough, one would think, to *screw* the multitude up to the proper pitch. Speeches were made by the president, sensible enough, doubtless, but didactic and forensic, savouring of the bar, and redolent of the Court of Errors, and long and dull, like the galleries of " Lord Hoppergollop's country house." Other addresses were made by Nicholas Dean, Robert C. Wetmore, James W. Gerard, Charles O'Conner, William M. Evarts, Edward Sanford, and Ogden Hoffman ; and it is reported about town that there was not so large an assembly at the close as at the commencement of this great demonstration.

NOVEMBER 4. — There never was such a set of silly politicians as the Whigs of this city. Some of them, who call themselves Whigs, — men of wealth and character, merchants who have prospered in the general prosperity, in which they have participated without having contributed to it (I have met some of such lately), — declare that they will not vote for Washington Hunt. " Who, then, will you support, — his Loco-foco opponent?" — " Yes." — " Why? " — " Because Hunt is an Abolitionist and an Anti-Renter." — " That may be a reason sufficient ; but where is the evidence of it? There is nothing in his public life, in his actions, speeches, or writings, to justify such a suspicion." — " But he suffers the Abolitionists to vote for him." And this is the " head and front of his offending." If the Devil, or Bennett of the " Herald," were to vote for me, if I were a candidate, I would thank them ; the vote of either of those worthies is just as good as that of the best man in the land ; but the truth is, — it has ever been so, — these wise politicians take their cue from the infamous " Herald," which abuses the can-

didate for Governor, because, I presume, the other party has paid
him for his support.   These men have grown fat upon the general
prosperity, and make a show of independence by opposing the
party to which they owe their modicum of consequence.

NOVEMBER 5. — This is the general election. Parties
The Election. are so broken up, mixed up, and scattered, that
nobody knows what the result may be. The dregs
have risen to the top of the pot. The Loco-focos support Fernando Wood — a fellow who stands branded as a swindler — for
mayor, and Captain Rhynders — a notorious bandit — for the
Legislature ; and both will probably be elected. The want of union
among the Whigs will deprive them of the success which they might
have achieved. James Bowen, in the third congressional district, runs
against the Whig candidate ; by which means Emanuel B. Hart, the
Loco-foco, will be elected.   In our district, George W. Blunt, from
personal motives, in the plenitude of vanity which belongs to his
family, sets himself up against Brooks, the present member, who
has done his duty well in Congress, and is the regularly nominated
candidate.   I voted, of course, the whole regular Whig ticket,
wherever I could find it.

NOVEMBER 6. — The election throughout the State was held yesterday.   The result in the city has been highly favourable to the
Whigs, who have succeeded in all their tickets except where they
have been defeated by their own perverseness and suicidal policy.
We have elected thirteen out of the sixteen members of Assembly,
by which means there is very little doubt that we shall have majorities in both Houses, and thereby secure the election of a Whig
senator in Congress in the place of Mr. Dickinson, unless the
devil and the slavery question should put it into the heads of our
men to split upon this choice. Ambrose C. Kingsland, Whig, is
elected mayor.

NOVEMBER 11. — Bennett, the editor of the " Herald," was attacked and cow-skinned on Saturday, in Broadway, by a Mr.
Graham, the unsuccessful Loco-foco candidate for district attorney,

against Nathaniel B. Blunt. I should be well pleased to hear of this fellow being punished in this way, and once a week for the remainder of his life, so that new wounds might be inflicted before the old ones were healed, or until he left off lying; but I fear the editorial miscreant in this case will be more benefited than injured by this attack. The public sympathy will be on Bennett's side; the provocation was not sufficient, the motive was a bad one, and the character of the assailant not much better than that of the defendant.

NOVEMBER 13.—The steamer "Atlantic" arrived yesterday in twelve days and twenty-two hours from Liverpool. Among her passengers, of persons known and distinguished, are Mrs. DeWitt Clinton; A. G. Stout, wife and daughter; Mr. John Kane, A. Bowden and wife, Rev. Dr. Bethune, and a young son of my friend Daniel B. Fearing.

NOVEMBER 14.—Margaret and I went this morning to visit the new steamer, the "Baltic," of the Collins line, at the wharf, foot of Canal street, where are to be seen at this time the three finest vessels in the world. The word *world* is in great use with us Americans, when we would assert our superiority and discourage competition. The best in the world, the handsomest in the world, the fastest in the world, unmatchable; there is no use in the world, for the world to try to equal us.

NOVEMBER 20. — Mr. Webster is here on his way to Washington. He was last evening at Jenny Lind's concert, where he was cheered with great enthusiasm; and the ladies joined by waving of handkerchiefs with the huzzas of the men, in honour of the advocate of the Union and supporter of the Constitution. Washington Hunt, Governor-elect of the State, by the closest squeeze ever known, is also in town.

NOVEMBER 26. —N. P. Willis gives an account of Mr. Webster's appearance and deportment at one of Jenny Lind's concerts, at which he was present with his wife, and Mr. and Mrs. Hunt, the Governor-elect and his wife. It is very flowery and Willis-like, but graphic and amusing. He described the Secretary's appearance in the following inflated terms: "We raised our opera-glass, with no very definite expectation, and with the eye thus brought nearer to the object, lo! the dome over the temple of Webster, the forehead of the great *Daniel*, with the two lambent stars set in the dark shadow of its architrave." At this concert Mr. Webster was accidentally heard to say, "Why doesn't she sing one of her beautiful national airs?" This wish was immediately conveyed to the charming songstress, who substituted a Swedish melody for the air set down in the programme; and her acknowledgment of the applause of the audience finished by a graceful courtesy to the recipient of the compliment, who arose and received it with a bow of recognition.

DECEMBER 12. — The annual time-honoured Thanks-
Thanksgiving. giving-day throughout the State. No nation, ancient or modern, ever had more causes for thanksgiving, and reasons to praise the Author of all good, than the people of the United States. Yet there are many, at the present time, ignorant and unworthy of the blessings they enjoy, who would throw all things into confusion, break up the blessed union which binds the States, and should bind the individuals forming their population; who would destroy the harmony, and condemn the obligations, of Constitution and law. Factionists, traitors, madmen, — the Lord preserve us from the unholy influence of such principles!

DECEMBER 31. — The last day of this eventful year, — a year in which the bad passions of men have been employed to counteract the beneficent designs of Providence; when the prosperity of the country and the happiness of the people have been in danger of sinking beneath the violence of sectional jealousy and the rude attacks of factious demagogues, who would rend asunder the bonds of union which have hitherto raised us to an unprecedented state of prosperity, and set at naught the Constitution and laws on which our fathers laid the foundations of the Republic.

1851.

ANOTHER year is passed, and its successor is ushered in pleasantly, and with every inducement (so far as the weather is concerned) for pedestrians and those who "ride in chaises" to please themselves and gratify their friends, by paying in person the cheerful compliments of a "Happy New Year." In the midst of these festivities and the friendly greetings of the season my house is closed, for the first time in many years. It is still "the house of mourning;" "the light of other days" has been withdrawn; but we have still a happy family, united in the bonds of domestic affection, with much reason to thank the Lord for the blessings they enjoy. I have reason, in an especial degree, to express my thankfulness; though it has been a year of bodily infirmity, and the extreme illness which I suffered in the spring has left me weak in my limbs and wasted in flesh, it would be sinful ingratitude to fail in grateful acknowledgment of the goodness of God in preserving my faculties, and enabling me to rejoice in their exercise. My health has improved; I am weak in body, but I sleep well, eat well, and drink well, — for all which blessings the Lord be praised!

JANUARY 3. — I broke into my stay-at-home-temperance-system to-day by dining with Mr. Blatchford, at his elegant new house, in Fourteenth street. It was a handsome dinner, and an agreeable, but somewhat mixed, company; and the best of it is, that I feel well after this indulgence. The party consisted of Mr. George Bancroft, Mr. Wetmore, Benjamin F. Butler, R. L. Colt, John J. Palmer, Stephen Whitney, William S. Miller, Robert B. Minturn, George Curtis, William B. Astor, M. Morgan, George Schuyler, Dr. Stevens, and myself.

January 28. — My old friend, Benjamin Strong,
Another gone. died last night, in the eighty-first year of his age.   He
was a most worthy, upright gentleman of the *old school*,
devoted to works of benevolence and usefulness, and the promotion
of public prosperity and individual happiness.

February 17. — A negro riot took place on Saturday in Boston ;
a fugitive slave was rescued by the mob, and conveyed away by a
seditious process in *black and white*. All the better. It will
bring matters to a head, in the headquarters of abolitionists.

February 19. — In consequence of the late riotous
President's Proclamation. proceedings of a mob in Boston, composed principally
of blacks, in which the marshal and other officers of
the law were assaulted, and a negro fugitive rescued and carried
away, President Fillmore issued yesterday his proclamation, calling upon the authorities of Boston to execute the laws against the
offenders, and declares his determination, and that of the other
officers of the general government, to apply the power of the administration to punish the offenders, and protect the local authorities in the discharge of their duties.

This measure accords with the character of our firm, energetic
Chief Magistrate ; he knows his duty, and will not shrink from its
performance.   How different is the course of this successor of a
deceased President from that of the man who was placed by a
similar dispensation of Providence in the executive chair ! Millard
Fillmore and John Tyler, — how different will be the pages of American history in which the actions of those two men shall be written !

February 21. — I was at a pleasant little dinner-party at Mr.
Daniel B. Fearing's, which I enjoyed much.   The guests were Dr.
Wainwright, Mr. Bancroft, James W. Otis, Frederick Prime, J. G.
Pierson, James Brown, and his brother, John A. Brown, of Philadel-
phia, and myself.

March 1. — I have been reading a book, in one vol-
Ik Marvel. ume, called "Reveries of a Bachelor," by a very clever,
ingenious writer, under the assumed name of Ik Mar-

vel. I am much pleased with it. It represents imaginary scenes in life; written in an easy, unpretending style, of deep pathos, causing tears to flow, and alternately bright with the radiant sunshine of life. Mr. Ik Marvel (they say his true name is Mitchell) has furnished three hundred pages of as pretty amusement as can be found in any of the numerous publications of the present overflow of the press.

MARCH 17.—I perceive with pleasure, in the account of the Queen's drawing-room, the presentation, by Mr. Abbott Lawrence, our Minister, of two very nice Yankee boys,—William Butler Duncan, son of my friend, Alexander Duncan, of Providence, and young Gerard, son of another friend, James W. Gerard, of New York.

MARCH 19.—The exciting subject of the election by Senator Fish. our Legislature of a senator in Congress was settled in joint ballot this morning at two, by the choice of Hamilton Fish, the Whig candidate, to fill the place of D. S. Dickinson, for six years from the fourth of the present month, by every Whig vote, with the exception of Mr. Beekman, who voted with the Loco-focos, and whose opposition to the Whig nominee has succeeded, during the session, in preventing the joint ballot.

Governor Fish was opposed by Mr. Beekman and two or three other Whigs, because he would not declare his sentiments in opposition to Governor Seward and the Free-Soilers; but I have no apprehension that he will fail in his support of the administration. He is a safe man, a true Whig, comes of good blood, the son of a patriot of the Revolution, who was himself every inch a gentleman, and (what ought, in these times, to have influence) a man of independent fortune.

APRIL 10.—Dr. Francis will not let me go to the office, and my migrations are confined to the sofa and the large easy-chair. My appetite has failed me. I eat no breakfast and very little dinner, which is forced down against my inclination,—a state of things which the best medical authorities inform us is not the best plan to promote a restoration of strength.   The doctor plies me with brandy-toddy, milk-punch, and other buttresses to my feeble frame-work.

APRIL 11. — No better; I am constrained to neglect my office business, and pass another day in the library.   Francis is unremitting in his attentions, and my nurses — my daughters — watch me with the utmost fidelity and anticipate all my desires.

APRIL 19. — A week of distress and misery.   I crept down to the office for a short time, but the weather is very bad; my feebleness continues.   I have not eaten a morsel of nourishing food during the week, and am incapable of labour, physical or mental.   Several circumstances have occurred during the week entitled to a place in this journal, and for which I have prepared suitable reflections.   All I can do is to bring them in edgeways.

Mr. Webster at home.   The Corporation of Boston refuses the use of Faneuil Hall to a company of gentlemen of different political parties for the purpose of doing honour to Mr. Webster, and having an address from him on the state of affairs.   The "cradle of the Revolution" refused to its favourite child !   "Where am I to go?" asked the Secretary, on a recent occasion.   His townsmen have told him where he shall *not* go.   Webster ostracized in Boston !

APRIL 30. — This volume of my journal, which has only four vacant leaves to be completed, has been suspended during nearly the whole month by continued unmitigated illness and incapacity to perform any act of mental or physical ability.   Feeble beyond description, utterly destitute of appetite, with no strength in my limbs, and no flesh upon my bones, shall this journal be resumed?   During this illness I have gone occasionally to my office for a short time, and performed a little *pro forma* business; but it could have been performed by deputy.   To-morrow will be the first of May.   Volume 29 lies ready on my desk.   Shall it go on?

Epitaph.   A few years ago, during a visit I made with my dear wife to the Greenwood Cemetery, I was so struck with the beauty and simplicity of the inscription on one of the monuments, — "There is rest in Heaven," — that I was induced on my return home to extend the idea, in order, perhaps, that it might be appropriated to my own use. It was copied in the journal at the time.

Has the time come?

PRAYER.

Prayer is the soul's supreme desire,
   Uttered or unexpressed,
The motion of a hidden fire,
   That trembles in the breast.

Prayer is the simplest form of speech
   The infant lips can try;
Prayer the sublimest strains that reach
   The Majesty on high.

Prayer is the Christian's vital breath,
   The Christian's native air,
His passport at the gates of death —
   He enters heaven with prayer.

Prayer is the contrite sinner's voice
   Returning from his ways;
Whilst angels in their songs rejoice,
   And cry, " Behold he prays! "

Prayer is the burden of a sigh,
   The falling of a tear,
The upward glancing of an eye,
   When none but Heaven is near.

By prayer on earth the saints are one,
   They're one in form and mind;
Whilst with the Father and the Son
   Sweet fellowship they find.

O Thou, by whom we come to God, —
   The Truth, the Light, the Way;
The paths of prayer Thyself hast trod;
   Lord, teach us how to pray!

As o'er the past my memory strays,
  Why heaves the rising sigh?
'Tis that I mourn departed days,
  Still unprepared to die.

This world and worldly things beloved
  My anxious thoughts employed,
And time unhallowed, unimproved,
  Presents a fearful void.

But, Heavenly Father, wild despair
  Chase from my labouring breast;
Thy grace it is that prompts the prayer,
  That grace can do the rest.

This life's brief remnant all is Thine;
  And when Thy firm decree
Bids me this fleeting breath resign,
  Lord, speed my soul to Thee!

---

* The first seven stanzas are from James Montgomery's hymn, " What is Prayer?"
The last four were added by Mr. Hone.

END OF VOL. II.